IRRESISTIBLY DANGEROUS

J. SAMAN

Chapter One

Lenox

"FULL HOUSE, aces over kings. Read 'em and weep, boys." Aurelia fans her cards across the felt table, a triumphant gleam and Cheshire grin spreading clear across her face. A collective groan emanates from everyone here. Everyone except for me. I'm too busy focusing on my phone that's blowing up like a series of grenades.

It's likely a glitch—no one can get into my Boston place that I don't want in—but it's weird that my alarms are sounding all the same.

"Reils, you could let us win one hand," Asher bemoans, but for real, considering Aurelia has been playing poker with us—and beating us—for more than a year at this point, I don't know why we bother complaining when we still willingly play each month. "How come you never let us win *one* hand?"

Aurelia stands up and does a little victory dance, twirling past her fiancé, Zax, and giving him a quick peck on the lips. "Because Goonies never say die."

My lips twitch at her *Goonies* reference while I squint at my

1

phone and quickly scroll through camera after camera without finding what triggered the alarm.

"Lenox?" Greyson calls out, snapping me away from my screen. He's shuffling the cards, his expectant gaze on me, clearly having been trying to get my attention a few times already. "You in, man?"

I stare around the table at my lifelong best friends and then over at Aurelia, who has now become a part of our family, and debate if I should say anything. Instead, all I do is shake my head and move to stand when Ash throws out...

"You know, now that you're the only single one of us, we really should try and set you up."

Fuck. Not this shit again. Not them too.

"It's time," he persists when I don't respond. "Even Thor falls in love in the movies, silent warrior. You too can follow in your doppelganger's footsteps. Every Thor deserves a Jane."

"Jane dies, bro," Callan informs him as he bites into a buffalo wing. "Come up with a better analogy."

I stare blankly at them, not even bothering to entertain the notion when Aurelia jumps in with, "Oh, yeah. Definitely. I mean, not with a Jane, because that was tragic, but we should totally set you up. It'll be great."

Only not so much.

"But with whom?" she continues, glancing around at the guys and puffing out an annoyed breath. "Ugh. I need Layla, Wynter, and Fallon in here for this. They'd have ideas."

Yes, I'm sure my best friends' women would have lots of ideas, so it's perfect that they're down the hall watching a movie and not in here with us.

"It can't be someone in the fashion world," Greyson picks up, looking at Zax and Aurelia who own fashion houses. "Could be a musician like me. He plays piano like a god, and women swoon for that. Especially musically inclined women. Could be a tattoo artist like him, but that feels cliché and I'm not sure there are any other people who do that who live close enough to him in Maine to make that work."

"True," Asher agrees, pointing at Grey. "That's a good call, and he does know the industry since we were Central Square once upon a time. I'm not much help. My teammates are all dudes, and there are very few women who work for the Rebels. Not a doctor."

"No," Callan states contemplatively. "Unless maybe she works in the ER like Layla and I do, but I can't think of anyone off the top of my head. Especially since Lenox lives in fucking Maine. Besides, she needs to be—"

"Fiery," Grey finishes for him as if I'm not sitting here, privy to their conversation and plans to set me up. I want no part of either. I have more important things on my mind currently, like my alarm going off. "And she has to be able to deal with the fact that he rarely speaks unless he has to."

"Enough," I shoot out, proving his point. "No one is setting me up." It's like they're taking a page from the town yentas as my assistant Brooklynn calls them. Every woman in my small town in Maine is actively trying to do the same. They all have a cousin or an aunt or a niece or a daughter who is so absolutely perfect for me I just have to meet them.

Never. Going. To. Happen.

"Oh, I've got it!" Aurelia exclaims, snapping her fingers in an "ah-ha" way, giving me a coy smirk I don't like. "What about Georgia?"

"No!" Grey and Zax immediately shout, and ice fills my veins even as my chest clenches at the mere mention of her. I get it. I even deserve it. She's their cousin, more like a little sister to them with how close they are, and I tested every friendship limit they had. Just thinking about that knocks me with a pang of old guilt. "Definitely not her," Zax finishes gruffly. "But someone else."

"Or not." And just like that, I get up under the pretense of going to the bathroom. No one questions me. Sometimes being mostly mute has its advantages.

I walk down the hall of Zax's massive penthouse, catching sight of my friends' women and their kids, and immediately keep going.

My heart picks up a few extra beats as I enter the nearest bathroom and shut and lock the door. I scroll back through the outside cameras, and now that I'm able to give it my full attention, I see it.

Movement. A shadowy figure punches in a code only me and the people in the poker room have and enters my house.

What in the absolute fuck?

Did I get doxxed? Did someone I've hacked and brought down find me? I shake my head. There really is no way. But that doesn't change the fact that someone is most definitely in my house. I tap from camera to camera until I find them… sitting on the sofa in my family room without turning on any lights.

Huh?

That's… weird.

I zoom in on them, and my breath catches in my lungs. The glow of their phone illuminates their face, cast in warped shadows, their green eyes colorless and dark, and their red hair looks inky black.

But it doesn't change the fact that I'd know those eyes, that face, and that hair anywhere.

What the fuck is Georgia Monroe doing in my house?

Is this some sort of joke? Did Aurelia mention her name because she knew she was going to my house? No. That can't be.

Speak of the devil, and she shall appear.

I close the toilet seat and sit down on the lid, wiping my mouth and jaw with my hand as I watch her. I haven't seen Georgia in years, and that has been entirely by design. She comes up to Boston with some frequency to visit Zax and Greyson, but I always—freaking always—make sure I'm at my house in Maine when that happens.

I can't see her. It's not good for either of us, but it's part of the promise I made all those years ago.

And now there she is, sitting on my couch in the dark, doing something on her phone instead of coming here to Zax's, which would make far more sense. What purpose could she have for seeking me out and not her cousins? Especially after all this time.

My heart gives a painful thud against my ribs. Fuck. This isn't going to be good.

Rising off the toilet, I exit the bathroom and follow the sound of shouting back into the poker room. Callan is picking at the pile of bar food on his plate, and Grey is sipping on his bourbon, a smirk on both of their lips as they watch Asher and Zax go back and forth with Aurelia over their current hand.

"All I'm saying is if you're too pussy to bet, then fold."

Asher narrows his eyes at Aurelia. "Doll, I am never too pussy for anything. You can't throw shit like that out at a football player, especially a quarterback, and not expect us to play for the win. But when you drop three grand on one hand, unless you have a royal fucking flush, I'd like to know what sort of game you're trying to play with me."

"You can't ask that," Zax cuts in. "You know the rules. You either play or you fold. You either think she's bluffing or not. It's poker."

"Yeah, fucking Vegas, street-style poker," Asher grumbles. Sighs. Stares at his cards. "Fuck it, I'm in."

Fool.

He slides his chips to the center of the table and flips his cards over. And in fairness, he has three aces. But then Aurelia reveals a straight, and everyone breaks out into laughter. Except Asher, who looks like he swallowed a bug.

His arms fly out, hands waving wildly in the air as he shoots to his feet. "Oh, come on. It's not even possible! You totally cheat."

Aurelia grins devilishly, dragging the healthy pile of chips her way. "Maybe you just don't know how to poker the way I do."

"Honey, I may not know how to do a lot of things, but I know exactly how to poker. Every place she wants it."

And that's my cue. "I'm leaving."

Five sets of blinky eyes turn my way. "But it's early," Callan exclaims.

"Yeah!" Grey stands. "Can't you stay a bit longer? Whatever you're hacking can wait, no?"

I shrug. It's what I do, and no one challenges it. I don't speak a lot, hardly ever, and I don't sleep much because I spend my night-time hours hacking and my daytime hours tattooing in my shop. I live alone and mostly off the grid in Maine, and that's exactly how I like it.

But Georgia at my house waiting for me is stirring things, and I need to get to the bottom of it now.

"Are you staying in town tonight or going home to Maine?" Ash questions.

"Staying."

"Good stuff." He stands and walks over to me, his three grand loss already forgotten, and gives me a fist pound. "You're welcome to come over for brunch tomorrow, and if you want to stay through for Sunday Night Football, we're home against Detroit."

I think about that. I would actually like brunch tomorrow and to stay and watch him play on Sunday, especially since the shop is closed on Mondays, so I don't have to race home after. But now everything has changed, and I'm not sure what the weekend holds for me.

"I'll text you."

He smacks my shoulder and goes back and sits down at the table, stealing the cards from Grey so he can shuffle. One by one, the other guys and Aurelia come over to say goodnight, and when I fist-pound Zax and Grey, part of me wonders if I should tell them that Georgia broke into my house. That she's even in Boston because I don't think they know that either, but I don't.

Telling them she's at my place would draw questions. Questions like *how does she still know how to get into your house* and *why would she seek you out and not us?* Questions like *are you secretly going behind our backs with her again?*

I need to figure out why she came to me first when I already know I'm the last person she'd ever want to see.

I throw my friend's women and their kids a wave and head out the door into the cold Boston night, hop in my car, and drive to my house in Cambridge—the house I grew up in. The house surrounded by neighbors who know me and don't question how I come or go or even what I do.

They know what I've been through, first with losing my twin sister, Suzie, and then my parents.

I pull into my driveway and straight back into my garage, where I turn off the car, already dreading going inside. Dreading having to face her and learn why she's here and why she came to me specifically. I enter through the backdoor and flip on lights as I go, walking straight for her, not even bothering to pretend I don't know she's here.

She knows me. She knows I have cameras everywhere. She knows I don't fuck around with security.

A point she proves when she says, "I was wondering how long it would take you to leave Zax's."

Her sweet, melodic voice and the faint hint of her fragrance in my house are an immediate sucker punch. I hold my breath as she stands and turns to face me, and I force myself not to think about how fucking beautiful she is when I finally get a good look at her. Her emerald-green eyes immediately lock on mine and narrow into slits, as if she too has to mentally prepare herself for seeing me for the first time after six years. Still, her visible hatred of me is more than apparent, and that's what I cling to.

For a moment, we're both silent, simply staring at each other, unable to stop. My blood thrums, and my breath quickens. The sight of her still manages to knock me sideways, even after all this time.

"What are you doing here, Georgia?"

She steps around the sofa she was sitting on and approaches me with a familiarity that has my pulse spiking. The last time I saw her, she had tears in her eyes and her broken heart all over her face. She called me a thousand awful names, all of them I more than deserved. Still, I don't regret walking away.

It's everything before that I regret.

"You never changed my code." She points over my shoulder toward the door I came in. The door she came in.

"An oversight. I never thought you'd use it again."

"I hadn't planned to. Not ever."

And yet here she is. I raise an eyebrow at her, wanting her to cut to the chase and go. But then sadness takes over her face, her expression crumpling before me, and I feel like an asshole. She's been through a hell of a lot in the last six months. She was set to get married—to a total douchebag, I might add—and three days before the wedding, her father's plane blew up over the Atlantic Ocean. Not just went down.

Fucking blew up.

Foul play was most definitely considered, but without a black box and most of the plane unable to be recovered since a hurricane came barreling through the waters the next day, no one knows for sure. She postponed her wedding, and then the media started relentlessly crawling all over her. Everything from tabloids to news networks.

The celebrity heiress of Monroe Securities and a former child star, who happened to inherit fifty-four percent of her father's company. I watched it all from the sidelines. I didn't go to her father's funeral, though I was insanely tempted to.

She sniffles and wipes at an errant tear. "Sorry. I didn't expect to cry. Certainly not in front of you. It's just…"

I nod. I know. It's been impossible for her. She's a midwife now after having walked away from acting, not a businesswoman, but she's also smart enough to hold onto her father's company with both hands. Especially since she still doesn't know why her father's plane blew up. Her mother is an actress and was the reigning queen of Hollywood. Georgia wasn't too far off, starring in movies until she decided to go to college and step away from it all.

She sucks in a shaky breath. "Anyhoo, I need your help. That's why I'm here."

I sigh, shake my head, and leave her standing there, walking into my kitchen for a glass of water. She follows me. I expected that from her, but I still need a second after the way her words hit me. After the way seeing her and watching her cry hits me.

I take a sip of my water, keeping my back to her. "Why didn't you go to Grey or Zax? They'd help you. They'd help you with anything."

"What? And ruin poker night? And no thanks, I didn't want any water, but your offer is appreciated."

I turn back to her, unamused.

She sets her hands down on the island counter, palms flat, fingers splayed as she levels me with an unrelenting determination I

8

hate on her. Fun, flirty, sexy, sweet, playful—Georgia was all of those things. This is a different woman before me.

"They can't help me with this. Only you can."

Fuck.

"You want me to look into your father's plane?" I had made the same offer to Zax and Grey when it happened, but with all the agencies, both public and private, looking into it at the time, they told me to hold off.

To my complete surprise, she shakes her head.

"If you're not here for that, and I already know you're not here for me to ink your skin, then I have nothing else to offer you. You should go. Go to Zax's or home to your fiancé."

She laughs, but there is no humor in it. "My fiancé isn't my fiancé anymore."

Double fuck. That I didn't know.

"And actually, he's part of why I need the favor."

"You said help."

She tosses her hands up. "Favor. Help. What's the difference? I need it all the same, and you are the only person who can do this, Lenox. You have to know, I wouldn't be here otherwise. I was honestly quite content going the rest of my life without ever seeing you again."

I grunt.

She makes a strained, nervous giggle. "Before I tell you, you're not allowed to say no. I mean, you just can't. You owe me."

Another grunt because I do sort of owe her in a way.

I used her for two years. I came home after my sister's death in utter ruins. I was shattered. Broken every which way a person can be. Suzie wasn't just my twin. She was the better half of me. My best friend. And when she dropped dead from a stroke in the shower, I died too.

It was my fault. I knew about the headaches. I knew she was pregnant, though she hadn't come straight out and told me. I could have prevented her death, but I didn't. We were traveling the world with Zax, Grey, Callan, and Asher as the band Central Square. We were huge. Unstoppable, especially with Suzie as our manager.

Then it all fell apart when she died, and I came home to another nightmare that threw me into an absolute tailspin. I was unrecognizable, even to myself. So close to the edge, I was toying with throwing myself over it.

And then one night Georgia, who was eighteen to my twenty-two and studying nursing at Boston College, called to check in on me. I had never thought of Georgia as anything more than my friends' little cousin. But when she called me, something inside me stirred. Maybe it was her voice—her sweet, melodic voice—or the way she somehow got me to smile. I still can't say why I did it. Why I went to her dorm like a goddamn fool who knew better. Perhaps it's because I didn't have any fucks left to give.

Whatever the reason, I lost myself in her body.

Unleashed myself because she was willing to take it and kept coming back for more.

For two years, I did this. All the while knowing it was wrong. I kept it a secret from my best friends, her cousins, who would have rightfully killed me for touching her. She was my drug. My addiction. The only thing that kept me breathing.

Until I learned she was in love with me, and I finally forced myself to do the right thing and not only come clean to Zax and Grey but walk away.

"Just tell me what you need from me, Georgia."

She crosses the kitchen and stands before me, staring up at me with wide, resolute eyes. "I need you to marry me."

Chapter Two

Georgia

"I CAN'T TELL if you're kidding or not."

I snort, rolling my eyes in derision, my tone wrought with sarcasm. "Do I look like I'm kidding? Do you think I woke up this morning and was like, you know, I haven't seen Lenox in like six years. Why don't I fly to Boston from LA—getting on a fucking plane, which you can imagine is not something super fun for me right now—and play a prank on him by asking him to marry me?"

He's not amused, but frankly, neither am I.

He falls back into his silent man routine, but I'm not very good at waiting. My patience is already thin, and being here is about as fun, desirable, and painful as having a tooth pulled.

"How long do you plan to stare at me like that without speaking?"

Lenox doesn't even so much as blink, but that doesn't surprise me. It's funny, it's not his silence that's throwing me—hell, I'm used to that from him—it's the way he's looking at me with this bold, unrelenting eye contact.

That's what's making me nervous. That's what's new for him.

And the way he's looking at me with those bright blue eyes—such a contradiction to the cold, broody man he is—has my body inadvertently humming. Undivided attention is not something he hands out idly, and when you're on the receiving end of it, he makes you feel like you can fly.

Only flying is the last thing I want to do, especially with this man.

I'll admit, I was scared to see him. Scared of how it would feel after all this time.

I've been avoiding Lenox Moore since I watched him walk out of my apartment at the start of my junior year and felt my heart shatter from within my chest. I had been in love with him my entire life. Before I knew what love or attraction even was. It's why I used to beg my parents to let Suzie babysit me, even when I was getting a little old to have a babysitter. Even after we moved from Boston to LA, I still carried a torch for him. A torch that only burned brighter when I returned to Boston for nursing school, and we started our affair.

But now that torch is long since snuffed out, never to be relit, and I hate that this is where my life has taken me. To his doorstep, needing help only he can provide.

Lenox has been staring at me so long that not only am I starting to sweat, but I can actually feel my blood pressure climbing. He's annoyingly stoic, as he always is, and I can't tell if he's genuinely considering my proposal of sorts or if it's simply been too long since someone has demanded this much of his attention.

Still, I'm already over being this close to him—especially since he still smells the freaking same, like sandalwood, cedar, and musk with hints of leather and badassery, and his intense gaze is locked on me. I forgot how big he is. Tall enough that I have to lift my chin to see his face and broad enough that I feel eclipsed in his shadow.

It used to be one of my favorite things about him.

The way he could swallow my small body up with his while taking up eighty percent of my dorm mattress, and how occasionally, if I was feeling particularly playful, I'd jump up into his arms and make him catch me, marveling at how that would drag a rare smile from him.

I take a few steps back, needing distance as those memories sweep over me, and I hoist myself up onto his island, protectively crossing my legs at the knee and folding my arms over my chest as I wait him out.

I'll be honest with you. I would have much preferred to ask Asher or Callan, but then they both went and fell in love. Good for them, but it totally sucks for me, and it's not like I can just go out and ask anyone to be my fake husband. It has to be someone I trust, especially considering what's going on in my life that brought me to this point. I may not trust Lenox after what he did to me, but Grey and Zax do and their level of trust in him is not one that I question.

Part of me also knows how unfortunately perfect Lenox is for this.

He lives in the middle of nowhere. The press leaves him alone. He never speaks. He's genius-level brilliant with savantish hacking skills. He's tall and forbidding and gives fuck-off vibes like no one else. As loathsome as I am to admit it, I'd feel safe in his presence.

And I know there is no chance of either of us catching feelings because I already know Lenox isn't capable—at least with me—and I'm a fool me once but never twice gal. So here I am, standing in front of my quasi-ex, asking him to marry me. My lips bounce at the movie reference and he catches it, lifting an eyebrow as he folds his arms, matching my pose.

I puff out an annoyed breath that makes my auburn bangs fly up my forehead. "Just ask me already." My hands shoot out, only to land with a *smack* on my thighs, far too agitated to play it cool for another second.

"Why?"

I glare at him, and it isn't a kind glare either. "It straight up took you five minutes of staring at me like I'm Medusa and I turned you to stone to ask me *why*?"

"I've been trying to figure it out, but I can't seem to make the *I need to marry a man I hate* thing fly in my head."

That's fair. "I'm going to need a drink or fifteen for this."

Without skipping a beat, he turns, grabs a freaking martini shaker from one of his upper cabinets, and goes about making me a Manhattan. I can't help but scowl. Six years, and the man still remembers what I drink. Only I already know that's simply a matter of his massive brain and photographic memory, not based on anything resembling affection or caring.

God, I was so stupid. So young and naïve and so freaking blindly in love.

If I could crawl back in time and smack some sense into that girl, I would.

For two years, I gave him my body, my heart, and every piece of my soul. All the while, he never reciprocated a thing. It was one hundred percent sex to him, and yet I had convinced myself that I was going to be the woman to turn the bad boy good. To make him fall as helplessly in love with me as I was with him.

Even thinking about that now, I mentally roll my eyes at the idiocy of that. I knew it was toxic. I didn't even require my friends to validate that for me, though the few who knew about it did and did so regularly. I didn't care. I wanted him. And I believed he wanted me too, though, in the end, he proved me wrong.

Thank God he walked away. I never would have had the strength.

Lessons learned and pretty scars formed and here I am, stronger because he once made me so weak.

He sets the amber drink next to my thigh. "What? No cherry?"

He grunts and I smile. Still a bit easy to ruffle, I see.

Fuck it. I pick it up and down half of it. These last six months… my mom said it right. I was a little miss sunshine, and now all I see are overcast skies and nothing but rain. If Lenox agrees to this, she won't be happy with me—for several reasons. But marrying Lenox will especially infuriate her. I cried to her on the phone for months after he ended it with me.

He retakes his position, a glass of bourbon now dangling idly from his long fingers as he waits me out.

I exhale a weary sigh, ready to tell him everything if it means he'll do this for me. "As you know, when my father died, he left everything to me. What people don't know is that my father's will was very specific. I am to inherit fifty-four percent of Monroe Securities. But with one caveat. I have to be married in order to inherit the shares."

He stares at me, a stone statue, and then finally he shoves one hand in his pocket and takes a slow, lazy sip of his bourbon. "Isn't that what Ezra is for?"

I shift uncomfortably on the counter and slowly drag my gaze back to him. This is where it starts to get complicated and desperate. "Yes. Only I can't marry him."

He gives me a bored, almost impatient look. "Seems like he's your easy choice and I'm not, so explain to me why you're here asking me to marry you when you could easily marry your fiancé."

"I'm going to start at the beginning because it's a lot and you need the back story. No one, not even Zax or Grey, knows what I'm about to tell you."

Lenox's eyebrows bounce in surprise.

"I couldn't marry Ezra. I've known him my entire life. His father and my father were best friends and business associates. From the moment I moved back out to LA, our families had been pushing us together. I wouldn't say our marriage was arranged, but it pretty much was. Us being together and eventually getting married was a foregone conclusion and was spoken of as when and not if. About two years ago, Ezra asked me out, and I naturally said yes. At first, when we started dating, everything was amazing. He was this dream guy who treated me like a queen. He came in and swept me off my feet and swore to me that he wanted me regardless of our parents' expectations. After about six months together, I moved in with him."

I swallow, thinking about that time, blinking through the haze of memories.

"The second I moved my things into his place, everything changed. He changed. He became paranoid, aggressive, and hostile. Not physically abusive or anything. He never laid a hand on me in anger," I tell him hastily when Lenox pushes away from the counter, his jaw and fist locked with a dangerous look in his eyes. "But I'd go out with friends, and when I'd come home, he'd interrogate me on where I'd been and who I'd been with. He'd make comments on the things I'd wear or how I did my hair and makeup. He demanded I dress a certain way, wear specific clothes, and behave a certain way, especially in public.

"I'd challenge him on this, we'd fight, and then he'd apologize and blame stress from work or a hundred other things. He'd buy me expensive gifts and act like that perfect guy again until the cycle repeated itself. After he proposed and I stupidly said yes, things got a lot worse. He began isolating me from my friends, from the life I had, and started demanding that I quit my job. It became too much, too stressful. I was always on edge, waiting for the next event to drop on me, and I knew what was happening. Being a nurse and a midwife, I knew where situations like that could eventually lead, and I wasn't blinded by love enough to overlook it. I had to get out, and about two months before the wedding, I told my parents I was leaving him."

Lenox tilts his head, appraising me with quiet observation, though the hard glint in his eyes and the firm grip on his glass tell me he's hanging on my every word with the serious intent of a man ready to snap.

"That's when my father stepped in. He told me under no circumstances was I allowed to leave Ezra. That our union was imperative for the future of Monroe Securities. I didn't love Ezra, but that didn't matter. My father told me that if love and a happy marriage were important to me in this life, then I'd learn to love Ezra and make myself happy with him."

I sigh, staring down at my hands in my lap.

"Did Ezra know you wanted to leave him?"

I nod. "I had told him I wasn't happy and that I wasn't sure I could go through with the wedding. In response, Ezra apologized again and told me he loved me. He vowed to make me happy and promised he'd change."

"But he didn't."

"No," I quietly mumble. "He didn't. It was the same pattern, and I didn't know what to do. I was having panic attacks for weeks leading up to the wedding. I wasn't sleeping. I was hardly eating. I was in the middle of my final fitting, literally wearing my wedding gown, and passed out from a panic attack. My father was in Paris working a deal with a French software company, and I called him and told him I couldn't go through with the wedding. He was furious. He flew home a day early and…" I trail off.

"His plane never made it home."

"No." I lift the glass and down the rest of it because clearly I need it, and he used smooth fucking bourbon, so it's goddamn delicious. I set my glass down, running my finger along the thin rim of the glass. "Originally, all they said was that my father's plane had gone missing on radar. That was it. That was all they knew for days because of the storm that blew through where his plane was last recorded. Then they found small pieces of his plane, and that's when everything started spiraling out of control. My father was gone. His plane had exploded. My mother and I were inconsolable. I blamed myself. *Hated* myself actually." I swallow and look away, blowing out a breath as grief slams through me, making the backs of my eyes burn with unshed tears.

"And then?" he prompts when I fall silent, but I don't want to talk about that. Not anymore. So I cut it down to the basics.

"And then I called off my wedding, told Ezra I was done, and I moved out. It was the only good thing to come out of this," I continue when I'm back in control. "Until my father's will was read."

"Why would there be a stipulation in your father's will about you having to be married?"

I shake my head, my hand flying out and knocking the martini glass in the process. It goes careening off the counter and smashes into a million pieces on the floor. "Shit. I'm so sorry." Clearly, I'm a hot mess of nerves right now. I move to jump off the counter, but he puts a hand up, stopping me.

"Don't move."

"I need to clean it up."

"You need to stay where you are before you somehow manage to hurt yourself. I'll clean it up. You keep talking." He grabs a broom and dustbin from a nearby closet and starts sweeping up the pieces of glass that are littered across his floor. I fall back on the counter, staring up at the ceiling, my legs dangling over the edge.

"I don't know why my father did that," I admit. "It doesn't make sense, and the only thing I can come up with is that my father wanted Monroe to stay in family hands, and he knew I was a midwife, not a businesswoman equipped to run a multibillion-dollar organization, and I was set to marry Ezra anyway. In the meantime, my father's best friend was named CEO, Ezra his COO, and they made me chairperson of the board."

"Because you will have a controlling interest in the company?"

I twist my head toward him, watching as he dumps the glass in the trash bin in the cabinet beside the sink. "Only if I'm married." I rest my hands on my thighs and sit back up. He returns the broom and dustbin, the mess forgotten, as he moves back to his previous spot against the counter. "So now you can imagine how Ezra and his father, Alfie, are frantic that I ended it with Ezra before the will was read. And I use the term frantic lightly. They're both relentlessly —in their own ways—trying to get me to marry Ezra because I have to marry in order to inherit, and Ezra is the man my father wanted me to marry."

"What do you mean by relentlessly and in their own ways?"

"Alfie is like my second father. He's doing this from a place of love and concern for Monroe Securities and for me. Ezra... not so much. Ezra, well, he's... tell me you have a stalker without telling me you have a stalker."

"What?"

I roll my eyes and pull out my phone, showing him the texts from Ezra. The desperate ones, the obsessive ones, the threatening ones.

Lenox's face grows hard, his jaw visibly clenching, but that's his only reaction.

"And with the press and Ezra all over me, the clinic I was working for kindly asked me to leave as it was too distracting for them and their patients. It broke my heart, but I understood their position. No one wants press hanging outside a women's health clinic."

"So now you're jobless, dealing with a company you don't feel comfortable dealing with, managing two men who want you married to their family so they can take over Monroe on your behalf, and you have the press hounding you about all of this and your father's plane and guilt over that."

I point at him. "In a nutshell. Wow, you just took a long story and paraphrased it into like two sentences. I need to learn that trick. I also need to be married, but I can't marry the man I'm supposed to marry, which is why I'm here."

"How about you lay it out for me without paraphrasing."

I swing my legs back and forth. "It's simple. If I'm married to you, I don't have to marry Ezra. If I'm married to you, I'll inherit Monroe and though I don't care about the money from it, I don't want my father's company falling into other hands. It needs to stay in my family. My father's will never stipulated who I had to be married to, just that I had to be married in order to inherit. It doesn't even say I have to stay married, though my attorney advised I remain so for at least a year after so it can't be contested."

"And if you don't marry? What happens then?"

"I can't claim the shares and neither can my mother, so they will escheat to the state, which means the state will become the owner of the stock and then sell it. Monroe will no longer be owned by my family, and the state, with controlling interest, will be able to do basically whatever it wants."

"I see."

Looking up at him, I try to keep my breathing steady. "I'm so glad you do because I can't let that happen, and I *can't* marry Ezra. I just can't. I'll never get out of it. He'll never let me go. I just know it. I love my father with my whole heart. He was a great dad and did everything for me, but I can't sacrifice my life like that even in his name. I want to marry you—well, that's a lie—I *need* to marry you so I can get them off my back for good. And I need you to come to Vegas with me, marry me, and after that, attend the Monroe Securities conference with me and tell me what I'm missing with all the tech lingo."

"Vegas?"

I smirk at his surprised tone since I did quickly tack that on the end. "Yes. Las Vegas, Nevada. Party capital of the world. I need you to come to Las Vegas with me tomorrow for a Monroe conference meeting thing, but I figured it was perfect since it's super easy to get married there. Two birds, one stone."

Now he starts blinking. "Tomorrow?"

"You're fixated on that of all things?" I hop off the counter and cut our distance, getting right up in his face. "Yes, tomorrow. Las Vegas. Monroe Securities is hosting a huge company conference, and I'm about ninety-nine point six percent positive you could be an invaluable asset there. Tell me I'm wrong."

He shakes his head. "I'm not following."

"Bullshit, you're not." I poke his chest and then do it again for good measure. "You might not want anything to do with me, and you might enjoy playing dumb to the people who don't know any better, but don't forget who I am. I know you, Lenox Moore, though I seriously wish I didn't. I know all about your skills with a computer and I am desperate. My life is all kinds of fucked up, and not only will my ex-fiancé be there but also his father, and since both are actively trying to hitch me to the altar like I'm some piece of cattle they can prod with their brand, I cannot show up alone."

His head dips, his stare hard. "Do I look like someone's plus-one? I'm not a bodyguard."

"Funny, since you're the size of an NFL tight end and Asher calls you Thor."

"You have cousins."

I shake my head, immediately cutting him off. "They can't help me with this. I need to be married, but I also need someone who speaks the language and can help me navigate through it while keeping his mouth closed. This isn't my world, Lenox. I deliver babies and help women with their reproductive health. Medicine is my practice. But since my father died, I've been a mess, and this marriage stuff… it's not a joke. I need your help."

That's when he falls silent. And it lasts a thousand years until he grits out, "They'll never agree to this."

I laugh bitterly at that. I don't even know why. He's talking about Grey and Zax because they're what matters to him. Not me. Never me.

"They will because I need this. Because you're the only one. Plus, they've always hated Ezra, and they know you'll never touch me again." It's true. He won't. He regrets that he ever did, and it's just another reason why I hate him.

"I can't marry you, Georgia."

I stare at him for a long, hard minute, ready to tear him apart for dismissing me so flippantly. My insides boil as frenzy claws at my skin.

"For real? Just like that?" I hiss out a harsh breath, running my hands through my hair and clasping them at the back of my head, glaring indignantly at him. "You do realize I'm not looking for love in all the wrong places, right? This is a business arrangement."

"You have nothing I want."

Ouch. I mean, sorta. If I allow it to ouch. "I'll have fifty-four percent of Monroe Securities, and I know about our latest tech. It's part of what this conference is about. You'll get that info, even if I shouldn't share it with a hacker."

He stares without budging.

"I'll give you three percent of Monroe," I offer.

"Your money is the least appealing thing about you."

I snort. "Don't I know it? I just wish everyone else did too. But you do want my insider info on my tech and all the pretty ways it manages to keep dickwad hackers like yourself out of the systems you're trying to gain entry into, right?"

"Nope. No challenge in that."

My feelings explode like an atomic bomb, wreaking havoc and destruction with my emotions and thrusting me right into unglued territory. My eyes burn, and I can feel my face turning redder by the second. I pace away from him, barely able to catch my breath. I hate being like this. It's not who I am. I am all take charge. I am the master of my ship. But spool by spool, I've been unraveling, and this is the only thing I can think of to stop that and regain control.

"Do you hate me that much, Lenox? Did I mean so little to you that you can't even help me when I am so fucking desperate that I show up at your house?" I turn back to him, my arms falling heavy at my sides. "I know I'm asking a lot. I know I'm asking you to marry me and all that comes with that craziness."

I stop here, about to break down again. I just want him to marry me to give me some breathing room to figure out my life and my situation. I hardly trust anyone right now, but I trust him because he doesn't give two shits about me. He never did, and he doesn't care about Monroe or my money—he has tons of his own, likely billions, and is the definition of a loner.

I wipe angrily at my face, slashing at the tears as they fall on my cheeks, only it's futile as more keep coming.

"I know this is a one-sided arrangement, and the last thing you want is to be around me. I don't exactly want to be around you either. I'm not going to move in with you or anything. I'll stay in LA or possibly move back to Boston to be near Zax and Grey. You won't have to deal with me other than these few days and possibly on rare occasions if something comes up. Please, Lenox. Just… fuck." My hands rake through my hair, feeling so exhausted and defeated I can hardly stand it. "Please. I let you use my body for two years. I'm not even talking about what you did to my heart. I was the stupid one in that, and I know it. But you owe me, and if you won't do it for that reason, then do it for Zax and Grey. I know you feel guilty about lying to them and hate how it eventually all came out. Please."

Maybe that was wrong to throw at him—he already has so much guilt sitting on his soul that if he stepped into the ocean, he'd immediately drown under its weight—but I don't care. I need this too badly. All's fair in true hate and marriage.

He makes a displeased noise in the back of his throat as he sets his glass down on the counter. "How long are we talking?"

"A year," I tell him, and I can see he doesn't care for that answer as he rubs his hand across his mouth and jaw and stares at me with tense eyes. "As much as you hate the idea of being married to me, I hate it equally as much. But you're the only one who can do this. Please don't say no."

Chapter Three

Lenox

EVERYTHING inside of me is telling me I need to say no to this. That it's dangerous on a hundred different levels, but the most dangerous of all is the woman standing before me. Guilt trip aside, I can't stand to see her like this. I can't stand what this has done to her. And if her ex and even his father are taking things too far and not letting her go…

But fuck, I can't marry Georgia.

I mean, fucking *marry* her?! Even if it's fake and I rarely have to see her, I'll have to touch her in Vegas. I'll have to come across like a man in love with his woman, and I can't go down that road with her again. It'll risk everything. It'll break promises.

I can't marry her.

But how can I not help her either? Just the thought of her ex stalking her, making her feel uncomfortable or unsafe makes me want to burn his world down. And I will. In my own way. Until then, how do I leave her out there alone? Or worse, stuck in a situation where she ends up marrying the bastard?

"Do Zax and Grey know about what Ezra is doing? Do they know he and his father are trying to coerce you into a marriage you don't want?" One that will hold you captive and fill your days with misery.

She wipes more of her tears away and sighs plaintively, her hands going to her hips as she shakes her head. "I haven't told them about that. They've already been worried enough about me. They do know I have to get married, but I think they believe I'll just turn around and marry Ezra. Only my mother knows about them and isn't much help because she wants the shares to stay with us, and Ezra seems like the only way for that to happen."

"You know that won't stand, right? I'll have to tell them. I don't keep things like that from them. Not anymore, and I promised never again. They need to know what he was doing to you." I rub the back of my neck. "You don't feel like they can help with this?"

She gives me an unhappy look but doesn't ask me not to tell them. "No. I don't. I think men are possessive and territorial, and my cousins telling them to fuck off won't do a goddamn thing. It certainly hasn't done anything when I've told him to back off and leave me alone."

"And a restraining order…" I trail off, already knowing her answer.

"Will be a public record. I already have the press all over me. Not to mention Ezra and his dad work with me at Monroe, and that won't look good for the company or for shareholders. I have to see them and be around them. Besides, Ezra's not dangerous, just… not willing to let me go."

Hmm. I mentally store that away for later and plan to do a little—or more like a lot—of digging into Ezra. I looked into him when they got together—Zax had asked me to, much to my surprise—but that was a couple of years ago, and a lot has clearly changed.

Speaking of. "I'd have to ask Zax and Grey if they're okay with this."

She hiccups out a laugh, but there is no humor to it. "I figured as much."

"They don't want me near you, Georgia. Not after what I did to you before. They made that damn clear at the time."

She walks toward me, her big green eyes glassy and her cheeks flushed, but my body still stirs at the sight of her and how she smells —sweet and spicy like Christmas, like vanilla and cinnamon. If possible, she's even more beautiful now than she was then, and I haven't been able to stop looking at her. Not once since I first set eyes on her. I feel her on me like a wool sweater, warm and itchy on my skin yet somehow cozy and not uncomfortable enough that I want to take it off.

She affects me, and I hate that about her. I always have. All the ways she's irresistibly dangerous to me are all the reasons I need to say no to marrying her.

"You realize the hypocrisy in what you're saying considering Zax was with Suzie for a hundred years, not to mention I'm a grown-ass woman and can be with whomever I want. That notwithstanding, you won't be near me. Not like that anyway. I think we both know those days are over and better left in the past." Her head tilts as she reaches me, studying me. "Are you considering saying yes?"

Am I? Who am I kidding? I was never going to say no. "Yes. But I'll have rules."

She smiles, and it's like the first breath of dawn after a stormy night, and something inside me twists in the worst and most painful of ways. This is going to cost me.

"Oh, trust me, Lenox, I have plenty of my own." She pats my shoulder, and I immediately pull back, making her frown. "You're going to have to get over that for a few days. Married people are generally in love and touch each other as such, and we're going to have to sell it even if we're not."

The thought of touching her, of pretending to be in love with her makes my pulse quicken and my fingertips tingle. I remember every line of her body. How her hair feels and smells when my face is buried in it. The sounds she makes and the way she looks when my hands are on her body, giving her pleasure or simply holding her.

It'll be a fucking nightmare even if the touch is innocuous and purely for show.

I quickly change the subject, needing to clear that from my thoughts. "And you feel Ezra will believe this? That we're in love and married when you only ended it with him four months ago."

She flushes and shrugs. "I once told him that I had been in love with you when I was younger. I believe I had referred to it as a stupid teenage infatuation. But frankly, there is nothing to argue if I'm married. That's the point of this. They have no recourse or ability to force my hand or guilt me into it."

Only I doubt he'll take that lying down if he's grown obsessed with getting her to marry him and then she ups and marries someone else. Things like that make men dangerous and unpredictable, especially when he already perceives her as his.

"We'll have a prenup," she explains. "It's already been drafted since I had one with Ezra. It says you keep your stuff and I keep mine, and any assets we acquire in our marriage are divided in half, though I don't think that last part will be an issue for us. And, if you agree to do this, I will have another contract drafted that gives you three percent of Monroe Securities."

"Keep your company, Georgia, I'm not interested. If I say yes, I'm doing this for other reasons." *Like keeping you safe. Like not wanting you to ask this favor of anyone else, or worse, end up marrying Ezra.* "You should go now. I'll give you my answer by seven tomorrow morning."

She swallows, takes a step back, and without another word, turns and leaves.

The moment I hear the door shut, I spin around, drink down my bourbon, and then chuck the glass across the room until it shatters against the wall. This time I don't bother going to clean it up.

Fuck! What the fuck am I going to do? I scrub my hands up and down my face as I try to think.

But all I see are her broken eyes and the way she begged. And then hearing all that she had to say? Yeah, I understand why she feels this is her only option. But I can't imagine these men are going down so easily. Monroe Securities is a very pretty commodity with a stunning woman running its show. A stunning woman they want to own as much as they want to own her company.

I need to call Zax and Grey. I need to tell them Georgia was here and all about her proposal. My stomach twists into knots, the bourbon churning like acid, eating away at me. With a wasted breath, my mind wanders back to that night.

My body dropped onto Georgia's, heavy and boneless, as I panted for my life. Sweat coated our bodies, and my tongue swiped out, tasting it on her neck. A sweet, little contented hum emanated from the back of her throat, and I found myself smiling—a rare fucking phenomenon that only happened with her—as I rolled us over until she was on top of me, my half-hard cock still inside her.

I needed to leave, but with every time that thought hit my brain, I found myself bargaining against it. Just five more minutes. Just a little while longer. Letting go of Georgia required herculean strength, and in moments like these, I had none to spare. Especially when she snuggled into me, her head on my chest, listening to my heart beat as if only she could hear it.

My fingers trickled through the soft waves of her hair when her head popped up, her cheeks flushed, and her eyes bright, as she killed me with a smile and then killed me all over again when she said, "I love you." Just like that. Like she couldn't hold the words in a second longer. Like they had been eating at her and setting them free unburdened a weight from her soul, when all they did was send a rush of heady warmth and burgeoning panic through mine.

I froze. I didn't ask her what she said because I was terrified she'd repeat it. My heart raced, thumping painfully against my ribs, and I found myself pushing her off me and sitting up, unable to catch my breath with her on top of me, looking at me like that.

In a scramble, I snatched my boxer briefs from the floor and tugged them hastily on and then stood up and did the same with my jeans, all the while knowing she was watching me. "Well, that's not the response I was hoping for," she teased, but I could hear the hurt in her voice. And fuck. How did I do this to her? How did I allow this to go so far? It was my fault. All of it. I told her from the start it would only be this, only sex, but… it'd been two years.

Two years because I didn't know how to let go of her.

Only I was the last man on earth Georgia Monroe should ever love. I was nothing. I was empty. Fragmented. Nowhere near worthy of her or her love. My inability to act was why my sister and father were dead, and my inability to act was why Georgia loved me. Georgia loved me. A fresh wave of sweat broke out on my forehead, this one as cold as ice. What had I done?

"Lenox?" she clipped out, breaking through my panic, and I turned to her as I slipped my shirt over my head. She had her sheet pulled up over her naked body, her eyes questioning and angry. "What are you doing?"

Do the right thing. Walk away from her. Save her from yourself. You'll only hurt her more later if you don't. She deserves better than you. She deserves everything you're not.

It was true. I knew it. Deep in the farthest reaches of my soul, I knew it. I didn't want her love. Her love was pure and good—like she was—and I wasn't that. I was as fucked in the head as a man can get, sinking deeper and deeper into the darkness instead of drifting toward the light. I hadn't done a thing right by her since I first came to her bed two years ago, and it was fucking time I did. I used her. I drank from her like a vampire, needing her to sustain life.

"Leaving," I said, my voice flat despite the riot in my body and mind. It was getting harder to breathe, harder to put one foot in front of the other.

"Just like that? I tell you I love you, and you leave?"

Pain swam in her eyes, and the urge to hold her, to kiss it all away overwhelmed me. I didn't want to hurt Georgia. I fucking loved her. But loving her was finally doing right by her.

"Yes." Fuck. "I... I shouldn't have let this get so far. I should have stopped this sooner."

Her eyes flared, and she sat up, wrapping the sheet tighter around her chest and tucking it in so it wouldn't slip. "Are you kidding? You're ending this because I told you I love you?"

"You shouldn't love me, Georgia."

She crossed the room to me and stood boldly before me. "That's for me to decide. I'll be the one to judge who I should love and who I shouldn't. The question is, do you love me back?"

Yes. *"No." The word rang out between us, harsh, cruel, irreversible.*

She reared back as if I'd hit her, and I forced myself to look at her, to witness the damage I'd inflicted, all the while keeping my features even, detached. A tear hit her cheek, and it felt like a saw was severing to my limbs.

"Are you fucking kidding me? Two years we've been doing this. For two years you've been coming to me. What did you expect? That I'd let you fuck me forever without developing feelings?"

29

Shame, hot and miserable, rushed through me. "I should have ended it a long time ago."

She shook her head, her features twisted in fury. "No. Fuck that and fuck you." *She shoved my chest. Hard.* "Why are you doing this?" *Her voice cracked with desperation and emotion.* "You feel something for me. I know you do. I see it in your eyes, and I feel it in the way you touch me. Don't lie to me and tell me you feel nothing." *She crumbled before my eyes, her body caving in on itself as she openly began to cry.* "Please. I love you, and I don't want to lose you."

My body vibrated, shaking uncontrollably. I was barely hanging on. I took a step back toward the door. "I don't feel anything for you, Georgia." *I do. I feel everything.* "I don't love you." *It's a lie.* "And I never will." *I took another step back and then one final one, reaching the door. I turned away, my eyes closing and my breathing ragged.* "You'll never see me again."

"You're a bastard. You're a miserable, cowardly bastard," *she yelled.* "I hate you. I hate you so goddamn much."

I nodded, my hand on the door. "Good. You should."

I made it out to the parking lot and veered to my right before I came to a tree and started punching it. Over and over until my bones cracked and my skin was pulp. I sagged against it and stared up at her apartment building. Was this who I was? Was this the man I had allowed myself to become? Suzie would have been ashamed. I was ashamed.

I'd been lying, keeping secrets from my best friends for two years, all the while I was fucking their beautiful, perfect cousin, and now I broke her heart. I was a monster. And I was tired of being a monster. I was tired of being so hateful to myself. Tired of drowning in an endless sea of guilt that had become so familiar to me, like a second skin, that not only did I not know how to shake it, I reveled in how I hurt myself because of it.

Only I didn't just hurt myself this time.

I hurt Georgia.

A surge of something I couldn't name swarmed up through me and had me running to my car. My hand burned, swollen and bleeding, but I reveled in that too. The pain made me sharp. It solidified my resolve. I drove across town, deep into Boston, and rang the buzzer on Zax's front door. Grey wasn't in town. He was on tour. His first solo album after Central Square was released a few months ago, and it caught like wildfire.

"Yeah?" *Zax's growly voice came through the buzzer.*

"It's me."

He buzzed me up, and I ran up the steps instead of taking the elevator, blood dripping from my hand, leaving a trail of my crimes behind me. I pounded on his door, and when he swung it open, terror and relief hit me.

"What the fuck, Lenox? Are you okay? What happened?" he asked as he took in my bleeding hand and harried disposition.

I was about to lose my best friend, but it was no less than I deserved. But I couldn't fix myself until I wasn't hiding this from him anymore. "I fucked Georgia."

He stared at me, unsure what to make of that before his features visibly hardened and his jaw locked. "When?"

"For two years. I've been fucking her behind yours and Grey's back for two years."

His fist launched, knocking me straight in the cheek, just below my eye. I flew back, slamming hard against the door as searing, white-hot pain shot through my face. I forced myself upright. Forced myself to face him, as I'd forced myself to face Georgia.

"Fuck!" he yelled, backing away, his hands in his hair as he started to pace. "Georgia?! You've been fucking Georgia like that behind my back? Why?"

I didn't have answers for him. None that mattered. What was I going to say? Because I needed her. Because I couldn't breathe without her. They were useless things to say, and they didn't make anything better. I had no excuse for what I had done with Georgia.

"You should know, she told me she loves me tonight," I said quietly.

He was about to rip me apart. Knock me out where I stood. He'd just barely been holding himself back. "I suppose I don't have to ask what you said in return. I can see it all over you." His gaze hit my shifty body and fucked-up hand. "Two years, huh? I hope it hurts, you stupid motherfucker. Giving up a girl like her. I hope it hurts like hell."

I lowered my head and stared at the floor, and Zax fell silent.

If anyone understood the misery and pain of guilt and loss and self-loathing along with it, it was him. He was like my brother and Suzie's death had destroyed both of us. He hadn't dated since her. Two years alone and as fucked in the head as I was about her death. He also turned into a miserable, angry prick, hating on the world as much as I did, only he was less self-destructive than me. He hadn't lost all that I lost and not the way I did.

"Why are you here? Why tonight? Why now?"

I backed up into the door, my hands on my head. "I want…" I trailed off, but I found it surmised everything I wanted. It was the first time in two years, but I wanted. I wanted things. A life. Potential. I wanted to not hate the skin I was wearing. I wanted to feel worthy of Georgia's love, even if I never had her again.

He looked at me, really looked at me, and said, "I see."

My hands met my hips, and I started shaking.

"I won't forgive you for hurting her. I don't want you to forgive yourself either, if that's what it'll take for you to crawl your way out of this. Still, I'm fucking furious with you, and Grey will be too. Possibly worse. I want to kick the shit out of you and hug you at the same time. Do you know what that's like for me? Do better. Be better. I love you. Go. But stay the fuck away from Georgia. You will never touch her again. And you will never lie like that to me again."

Scrubbing my hand up my face, I slip my phone out of my pocket and dial up Zax. "Hey," he answers quickly, as Zax always does. "Everything okay?" Because I text and rarely ever call unless it's something that shouldn't be texted.

"I'm merging in Grey." Without waiting for him to say anything, I hit the merge button on my screen and then dial up Grey, who also picks up quickly.

"Lenox?"

"I'm patching Zax in." And when we're all on the line, I start to pace my kitchen. "Georgia was just here," I start without any preamble, and then I proceed to tell them everything. By the time I'm done, I'm sitting on my couch with my elbows digging into my knees and my head in my hand.

"You're doing it then," Zax states, and I chuckle humorlessly at his surefire tone. "You wouldn't have called us otherwise. You would have simply told her no, and that would have been that."

"How do I say no?" I ask, genuinely curious about their thoughts.

"You don't," Grey shoots out because he is the emotional brother, whereas Zax is the methodical, pragmatic one. "If that's what she needs right now and you're willing to do it, then what is there to question?"

Everything.

"If anything, she's right," Grey continues, building steam. "You fucking owe her."

My eyes pinch shut, and I exhale a silent breath.

"*Are* you willing to do it?" Zax presses. "Because what she needs right now is someone who can help her and look out for her." While keeping their hands to themselves, he doesn't say, but it's spelled out in his tone. I've known Zax since I was five. He dated my sister for eight years. I know him better than any other person on the planet. Still, I don't plan to touch her this time, so it won't be a problem.

Am I doing this? Am I going to marry Georgia? I'm not sure I ever had a choice.

I was a piece of shit who lied to them and used their cousin and subsequently broke her heart.

Because of that, because I do owe everyone involved, I say, "Yes. I'm willing to do it." My voice is even, masking the raging inferno inside me. Unlike my ability to read Zax, no one can read me unless I allow them to. There is no place for feelings in this. No desire for them either. They'll do nothing but complicate an already complicated situation.

"Okay," Zax finally says with a resigned breath. "But remember the promises you made to us."

"I do." And I'll abide by them.

I'll keep my hands to myself. My eyes where they belong. My thoughts on lockdown.

And everything I ever felt for Georgia Monroe will stay where it is… buried six feet under.

Chapter Four

Lenox

I DIDN'T BOTHER TRYING to sleep. Sleep isn't something I'm known for anyway, but I didn't sit in front of my monitors playing with the system I've been trying to penetrate either. I was edgy, uncomfortable, turbulent. I went for a run in the middle of the night, and then I lifted weights until my muscles screamed and threatened to give out. That wasn't new for me either. It's how my brain works things out.

It's always going. Never quiet unless I push it to the point of exhaustion.

But by the time dawn rolls around and I'm showered and dressed and sipping on coffee, I'm no longer agitated. If anything, I'm resigned. It's a few days of bullshit with Georgia, and then I'm back to Maine, and she'll be somewhere else. I'll keep my promise to Zax. I'll stay the fuck away from Georgia after this.

I text Brooklynn and tell her she's going to have to rebook everyone and hold onto my dog, Alice, for a bit longer. I don't tell her I'm getting married. This is Georgia Monroe we're talking about, and it'll be on the news soon enough. The only good thing to come out of this might be getting the town matchmakers off my back.

Then I text Georgia.

Me: I'll see you on the plane at nine.

She replies immediately, and I drag my thumb along my bottom lip, watching the bubble and the three dots dance.

Georgia: Ah! Thank you. Thank you! I could kiss you, but I won't. Incidentally, how did you know what time we're taking off?

I don't bother responding to that as I slide my phone into my pocket and head upstairs to pack, only by the time I reach the top step, my phone vibrates.

Georgia: Zax came by my hotel room late last night. He told me he spoke with you and is glad you're going to do this for me. He was worried about me, but I told him I hated you, so he didn't have to worry about any of that. Also, he gave me something that might upset you. I thought you should know I have Suzie's ring, and I'm not sure what to do with it.

Fuck. Why did he go and do that?

The engagement ring Zax was never able to give Suzie because she died right before he could has made the rounds recently. Callan gave it to Layla when he needed her to be his fake fiancée so he could secure guardianship of his niece Katy. But once that ruse was over—and now that they're actually engaged—Callan gave it back to Zax.

I know what Zax is doing. I know what he's thinking. A woman like Georgia Monroe, with her money and social presence, doesn't get engaged or married without a rock on her hand, and he wants this to appear as authentic as it possibly can for Georgia's sake.

But fuck.

Suzie's ring on Georgia's hand.

I wipe my hand across my brow and enter my bedroom, where I pull out a suitcase and shift through the things I have here. I don't go out in Maine, so any events or things I'm dragged to all happen in Boston, which is why my closet here is full of expensive items—most with the Monroe label since Zax owns Monroe Fashions, a designer brand.

Finally, I manage a reply.

Me: You should wear it.

Because it would give Suzie the biggest fucking kick to know I was getting fake married to Georgia and that she was wearing her ring. She would have laughed and teased me relentlessly—as only she could. She would have said something along the lines of "Don't fall in love the way they do in my romance books." And I wouldn't have said anything in rebuttal because it wouldn't have been necessary.

Falling in love isn't a natural part of who I am.

Except the only woman to ever challenge that is the woman I'm about to marry.

Two hours later, I'm through security at Logan Airport and walking toward the terminal when I spot her red hair. The plane is just about to board, people are standing all around, but Georgia is sitting, her face cast down toward the industrial carpet, two black suitcases upright beside her.

I take the seat next to her, but she doesn't move or speak. She's simply breathing hard, her eyes pinched shut.

"We'd now like to welcome our first-class passengers," chimes out through the PA system, but Georgia is still unmoved despite us now being able to board. On her hand is Suzie's ring, a big fucking diamond sparkling almost mockingly at me. There isn't a moment of any day that I don't miss my sister. That I don't wish she were still alive.

I'd give *anything* for that.

I tap Georgia's finger with the rock on it. "You can't ever tell Zax this, but Suzie would have hated that ring."

Her head slowly rises, her face pale and clammy, even as her eyebrows pinch together, confused by my statement. I stand, take the handles of her suitcases, and start to head for the boarding area. She quickly scurries to her feet, clutches her mammoth purse to her chest, and starts to follow me.

"What do you mean she would have hated it?" she asks, only to indignantly squawk, "Hey. What are you doing?" at me as I grab her phone from her hand, use her face to unlock it, and swipe her boarding pass to get her on the plane. She starts to resist, but I push her in front of me, forcing her along as I drag our suitcases behind me, giving her no room to escape.

"Suzie didn't like flashy or ostentatious."

Georgia takes exception to this, turning her head over her shoulder to give me a scathing look. "It's not flashy or ostentatious. It's beautiful." She holds up her hand, admiring the ring.

"It's a mafia bride ring."

She laughs, but it's shaky. "Is that what I am then? Because I would have loved a ring like this." It is a beautiful ring. I helped Zax pick it out, and Suzie would have loved it.

She falters at the edge where the walkway meets the plane, and I shove her on, practically making her stumble onboard.

"Good morning, Miss Monroe," the flight attendant greets her, but Georgia is a hot beat from losing her shit, so I thrust her down into the window seat and then block the aisle as I toss her heavy fucking bags up into the overhead bin.

I take the aisle seat, watching as passengers board, eyeing Georgia as they walk past us because everyone in the country knows her face and not just from what she's been through in the last six months. She's been a celebrity her entire life. The girl was in a dozen films between the ages of fourteen and eighteen and before that, she was a fixture at award shows with her mother.

I turn to her, noticing how she's wringing her hands and how her knees are bouncing. "You didn't like what Ezra picked out for you?"

"Huh? Oh." She stares down at the ring and shakes her head. "It was pretty, but if you think this ring is ostentatious, you should have seen that one. It's single-handedly what sank the Titanic but had a ring of large yellow diamonds around it."

"You don't like yellow diamonds?" I couldn't care less. I just want her to keep talking as the plane fills up and the flight attendants start going through their safety checks.

"Not really. I mean, on their own, they're beautiful, but didn't look good surrounding a large diamond. Or more like getting engaged to him never felt right, and the ring was a constant reminder of that. I honestly don't know anymore."

"Good thing you're marrying me then," I quip mockingly.

She blinks at me, but right at that moment, the door to the airplane shuts and locks into place, and she immediately starts trembling. I reach across her body and buckle her seat belt for her.

"Can I get you anything to drink before takeoff?" the same flight attendant asks politely.

Georgia shakes her head, her breathing ragged, and the woman goes on to the people behind us, giving me a sympathetic look.

"Where are we getting married? Walk me through this."

She's still shaking her head as the plane starts to pull away from the gate. "I didn't take my Ativan."

"Why?"

"It made me too groggy on the flight here because I have to take so much of it to calm down, and I… I can't do this. I need to get off the plane."

She starts to move to get up, fumbling with her seat belt, and I cup her face in my hand and force her terrified eyes to mine. "Where are we getting married, Georgia?"

Her hand grips my forearm, and her nails dig into my skin as her eyes scrunch closed, making a tear leak out. "No Elvis," she utters, and I can't stop my bemused chuckle.

"Elvis isn't a location?" I deadpan.

"My dad won't be there. I don't want anyone to walk me down the aisle."

Oh.

Her grip tightens, and I wouldn't be shocked if she was drawing blood as the plane picks up speed.

"Lenox…" A gasp. "Please. I can't…"

"Breathe, Georgia. I've got you." Only she's not breathing. She's rocking in her seat and practically hyperventilating.

"This isn't who I am."

"I know, but there is no shame in this."

She shakes her head again, her red hair flying about. Sweat coats her brow, her face is growing pale, and she's trembling like a leaf. "I can't... I don't know how to make it stop. I can't... I can't breathe. I need to go. Please, I need to go. I need to get out of here."

Fuck. She's losing it and all of my distraction attempts aren't doing anything to stop her panic attack. I don't know how to make it stop either. How do you make a panic attack stop? I can't smack her or shake her, and they no longer have vomit bags for her to breathe into. Feeling helpless, I stare at her face in my hand, at her teeth sawing at her bottom lip, and I already know I'm going to regret this, but I genuinely can't think of anything else.

I don't want to kiss her—I mean, I fucking do, but I'm not going to—so instead I lean forward and bite her bottom lip, making our teeth tap painfully and jolting her back an inch. Her eyes flash open, wide and startled, but I hold her face close and bite down harder before sucking her lip into my mouth and forcing myself not to groan at the taste of her.

I chew on it before dragging it out, scraping the soft, plump tissue with my teeth, and then doing the same with her top lip. She tastes like the vanilla ChapStick she loves and peppermint mouth-wash, and my hand on her cheek slides back until it's cupping the side of her head. She whimpers into me, her eyes staring directly into mine from centimeters away, giving me full access to their beautiful shadenes of green, but she's not thinking about anything other than the fact that I'm biting her.

Her breathing slows into choppy bursts but then gradually becomes more even as color returns to her cheeks. I keep my tongue in my mouth, and I don't dare close my eyes or press against her. I nibble and chew, and occasionally sink my teeth deeper until I see a flash of pain through her eyes.

But that's all this is.

Pain. Distraction. Anger at her for forcing me into this. Frustration with myself because just being this close to her and biting her lip has my cock straining against the zipper of my jeans.

I never knew how to deny myself when it came to her, but I'm going to have to learn, and learn fast. With that, I bite a little harder, making her whimper and her hand slide down my forearm.

And when the plane is high in the air and that dinging noise sounds, I pull back, releasing her and wiping my mouth with the back of my hand. Only it does nothing to dispel the taste of her or the way my cock loved every second of that.

She's still staring at me with those wide emerald eyes, visibly unsure what to think about what I just did or how to react. Good. Let her mind get spun up in that the way mine is instead of all her panic. I give myself a second to get my shit back together and remember my mission and why I'm here. .

"You bit me."

"Are you still panicking?"

She thinks about that for a minute. "No. But you *bit* me."

"You're welcome," I say, my voice cold and unaffected. "Now, tell me about this wedding you're forcing me into."

Chapter Five

Georgia

EXCUSE ME, flight attendant? I believe the cabin has lost air pressure, and I now require an oxygen mask. And I thought I was short of breath before. Jesus Harold Christ… Lenox just *chewed* on my lips. Never has a man done that to me, and it's not something I would have thought I'd find as erotic as I did, but wow, it was hot.

I'm fully aware of why he did it, and that's not helping my mindset either.

He's here with me on the plane, flying to Las Vegas to marry me at no personal gain, and then he just spent the last twenty minutes talking to me—something he hates doing—about nonsense like diamond rings and where we're getting married in Vegas, when I doubt he gives two shits about either. And when I was still losing my mind, he bit me to snap me out of it.

It was a move only he would do, but boy was it everything I needed at that moment. It short-circuited my brain. Turned it from rapid fire to stun. It's funny, or maybe not so much, but I never gave flying a second thought until my father's plane went missing. I don't know what happened to my father's plane, but the special investigators couldn't say either way.

Foul play has neither been confirmed nor eliminated as a possibility. All they know is that it exploded, and not enough of the plane was recovered to know what caused it.

But after what Lenox just did, how on earth am I supposed to get through the rest of this week when all I can think about now is Lenox nibbling on my mouth? And would that feel as good if he tried it on a different set of lips?

The flight attendants come around, delivering warm nuts and a dish of marinated olives, and Lenox takes it upon himself to order me a whiskey and Diet Coke. I don't argue it. I can use it, frankly.

Especially as I say, "Do you think we should draw up a contract?"

Now that my panic has abated, Lenox has all but zoned me out, doing God only knows what on his laptop. He's wearing glasses and typing about a thousand words a minute, and whenever I try to coyly look at his screen, none of it makes sense. For one, it's not like any laptop or home screen I've ever seen before.

For another, everything he's typing immediately encrypts on the screen into binary code.

"What is that?"

His head twists in my direction, and his blue eyes pierce straight into mine. His only response is to raise a *do you actually expect me to answer that* eyebrow.

I shrug, taking a sip of my drink. "It doesn't look like any computer I've ever seen before is all."

"That's because it's not. I built it."

I shouldn't have asked. His genius brain always turned me on, and after the lip-biting, I need to remember all the ways I hate him and not all the ways he can still get me hot with a simple look.

"And the glasses?" Because I hate to admit how sexy he looks in them. Damn sexy nerd.

"Blue light."

Makes sense. I clear my throat, speaking in a low tone since we're on the plane—with many ears close by—but I want this settled before we reach the hotel and our suite because shortly after that, it's wedding time.

"I sent you the prenup this morning. We're allowed to e-sign it per my attorney if you're comfortable with all the language in it and don't require any amendments."

"I don't. I already signed it and sent it back to your attorney."

"Oh."

He sighs, not happy at all to be here, and that's what worries me. There is nothing in this for him. He could pull out at any second. "What sort of contract are you looking for beyond that?"

"I don't even know," I tell him honestly. "Last night you said you have rules, and I feel like we should discuss those. Hash them out. I definitely have boundaries we both have to stick to."

He types for another few minutes, and just when I don't think he'll answer me, he hits one last key, shuts the screen of his laptop, and turns to me, giving me his full and undivided attention, which is nothing short of unsettling from a man like him.

I set my drink down on the small tray at the end of our armrests and reach down for my bag, coming up with a red lip liner and not a pen, but whatever, it'll work. I rip the cap off with my teeth and then set myself in a position to start writing on the white cocktail napkin.

He chuckles, a rare chuckle, and waves a hand, indicating I should go first, but stops me by tugging the liner from my grasp and recapping it. "We're not writing them down, Georgia."

"Why ever not?"

"Because something like that can be lost and very easily found."

Fine. I yank the liner from his hand, toss it back into my Louis, and then take a sip of my drink, giving him the floor. "Age before beauty. You go first."

He smirks. "Whatever we discuss, whatever you see stays private and entirely between us. You can't tell your mom or your girlfriends anything about me. You know what I do." His gaze pointedly slides to his closed laptop before returning to me. "But the world does not. I am a tattoo artist and nothing else. Understand?"

"Absolutely. I think you know I never would and that I never have. It sorta already goes without saying." I hold out my pinkie, and he stares at it like he's not sure what to do with it. "Would you rather we do a spit shake or I slice open my hand and make this a blood oath?"

"I've already tasted your spit today, but let's get through the rest of this first before we decide on how to make it binding. What are your rules?"

I lick my lips, inching in closer to him, looking around at the other people in first class, but everyone has on their noise-canceling headphones and isn't paying us any attention. "Whenever we're in public, we hold hands or touch like we're in love. This may not be real, but I want it to *look* real. That illusion is paramount for me."

He bobs his head, which I take for his agreement and muster on.

"I haven't said anything about this, and I haven't asked because I'm already asking a lot, but…" I blow out a breath. "But do you think—"

"I'm already looking into it, and you don't have to worry. I'll make sure you're safe."

I crack a smile. "How do you know what I'm asking?"

"You're easy to read," he says simply, and I frown. I don't like that idea. Not with him. Not with anyone. "Georgia, aside from the fact that you will be my wife, and that makes you my responsibility, you are also my best friends' cousin. I will keep you safe, and part of that task is ensuring there are no threats to your safety."

"You're going to make me wet with talk like that."

He chokes on nothing, glaring at me, and then steals my drink to wash it down.

"Hey! That's mine."

He finishes his sip and hands it back to me, and I take a sip of my own.

"For the record, I can keep myself safe. I am a blackbelt in jujitsu and karate, and while you might be twice my size and have more muscles than is street legal, I can handle my own. It was more that I wanted to know if there are any skeletons in my ex's closet I should be aware of. I don't need his nitty-gritty, and frankly, I don't care, but I want to know if he's doing anything that will hurt or impact me."

He looks at me as if he can crush me like a tin can, but I do have a few cool tricks up my sleeve and don't mind being underestimated because that's always an advantage.

But then I sober and ask something I'm not sure I want the answer to since he got me thinking about it. "Do you think Ezra took down my father's plane?" Other than me, Ezra is the one who stood to benefit the most.

"No clue right now. But I promise to tell you if I ever find out."

I can live with that. "Okay. Your turn. Hit me with your next rule. I'll call them the laws of Lenox."

He plows past that as he shifts in his seat, but his gaze never wavers. "This is nonnegotiable for me as well."

"Alright." *Gulp.* "Spill it." I curl my legs up on my seat, hanging over the large armrest that separates our seats.

"I'm possessive. It may not be real between us, but the marriage will be legal as well as real to the world. If you're married to me, you're not fucking anyone else."

But…

"We're not fucking."

"That's my condition. My law, as you put it."

My heart pulses out an extra beat. "Does that go for you too?"

"Yes."

I stare skeptically at him. "You're going to go a year without any other women?"

"We're not fucking," he says, throwing my words back at me. "But yes. No one else as long as you're my wife."

Hard to argue. Especially when men aren't part of my recovery and rebuilding my life era.

I clear my throat—I swear this man is giving me hot flashes with his I'm possessive and I'll keep you safe stuff. "Deal. No one else—

or each other—for that matter—since that didn't work out well for me in the past. Anything else?"

A head shake.

"I'm not sure I have anything else either. Can we agree that if we have to add more, we do?"

A nod.

"So blood, spit, pinkie swear, or something else? I'd get a tattoo, but I don't want your signature inked on my skin."

He smirks at me. "Your word will do fine. You're trusting me, so I'll trust you."

Fair enough. "I need to go shopping," I tell him, and I don't even know why other than talking seems to help. "I need a wedding dress, or at least a dress I can wear to my wedding."

He frowns but doesn't look my way again as he resumes whatever it is he's doing on his computer.

"We're staying at Caesars. That's where the conference is." I swallow, feeling an annoying flush creep up my cheeks—sometimes being a fair-skinned redhead sucks like that. "We have a suite, but—"

"It's shared," he cuts in, and I nod warily, chewing on my lip because I do that when I'm nervous, but I immediately stop because… well, yeah. I don't know why I'm so nervous. Maybe because I expect him to change his mind at any second and turn around and go home. Maybe it's because I haven't seen him in six years, and the last time I did, it was awful, and since then I've grown hateful and resentful toward him. Or maybe it's because I'm fucking *marrying* him, and that feels nothing short of wrong despite my knowing I'm doing it for all the right reasons.

If this had been Asher or Callan, we'd be laughing, drinking champagne, and teasing each other about the wedding night that was never going to happen. But I don't have a history with Asher the way I do with Lenox, and everything about this is a minefield waiting to explode.

"It's a suite though, so there's a couch, I believe."

"A couch in a Vegas suite. I'm sure it's the hallmark of cleanliness and sanitation."

I choke on the sip of my drink, half of it spraying out of my mouth in a brown shower that covers the back of the seat in front of me while the other half goes down the wrong pipe, causing me to hack up a lung as the bubbles from the soda shoot up my nose and tickle the back of my throat, making my eyes immediately water. He reaches over and smacks my back without removing his eyes from his screen.

When I can finally manage to drag air back into my lungs, I go for my purse, pulling out some tissues to wipe my face and the back of the seat.

And when that's done, I gawk at him and wheeze out, "You made a joke."

His lips twitch. "If that's how you respond to them, I'll be sure not to make another. I'd hate to end up like that seat."

I laugh and smack his shoulder. "That's another one. Quit it."

He's done talking to me as he continues to type gibberish into his weird-ass laptop.

I shake my head at this conundrum of a man. Talk about an onion, but the last time I tried to peel back his layers he left me in tears, so no thanks on that.

I let it all end there, slipping in my AirPods, turning them to noise-canceling, and watching the least romantic movie I can find on the airline's streaming. I end up falling asleep only to be jostled awake when the plane hits the tarmac with a bumpy landing, the Las Vegas Strip just beyond my window.

We've arrived, and by tonight, I'll be married to Lenox Moore.

And just like that, those nerves are back and firing through me like bullets.

The plane pulls into the gate, and the door opens and then Lenox stands and pulls down our suitcases. I stand and follow after him while wishing my mom were here. I should have brought her along for emotional support. She would have gone dress shopping with me. She would have held my hand through all of this. Even if she would have told me to marry Ezra instead of Lenox.

Tonight is the first event for the conference—a cocktail hour—and Ezra will be there. He already messaged me asking what plane

I'm on and what time I'm checking in and if we can meet for a drink before the cocktail hour to talk. I haven't responded to him because any time I have, he's more all over me than he was before. If I give him an inch—even a benign inch—he wants a mile and seriously dislikes the word no. It's been unsettling with him to say the least.

I've had boyfriends. I've ended it with them, sometimes when they didn't want that, but it's never been the way it is with Ezra. Pounding drunk on my door at midnight. Telling me he'll never let me go. Demanding that I marry him. It's weird, and something about it isn't right. His desperation doesn't make a ton of sense to me other than he wants my money and Monroe.

We make our way through the airport and down to baggage, where I find our driver holding a sign with my name on it. Lenox and I haven't said another word to each other since the choking incident, and it's just as well. I haven't wanted to be overtly cruel or bitchy to him because, well, it's honestly not who I am, but he's doing me the favor of the century, and being that way won't help my cause.

The Las Vegas air is mild, cool, but not too cold, aided by the blinding sunshine and desert air. I slip into the backseat of the car with Lenox beside me. The driver finishes loading our bags and we're off, headed toward the hotel. My knee is bouncing, and my hands are knotting.

He turns to look at me finally. "Relax, Georgia. I'm not going to back out."

Wow, when he said he could read me, he wasn't kidding. Relief shoots like a geyser through me, but I still don't understand why he said yes. "May I ask why you're doing this when there is nothing in it for you? I don't mean to sound ungrateful, because I'm extremely grateful, but as you said, I have nothing you want."

His eyes dance about my face in the dim light of the car in such a way that it makes my face flush ever so slightly, if for no other reason than he's much better at this than I am. His gaze isn't heated or even kind. It's cold and detached. Hell, he stared at his computer screen with more warmth and interest than at me.

And I decide I don't care anymore why he's doing this.

Does it matter? I need him to help me wade through the maelstrom of the situation I've found myself in, but that's where this thing between us ends. He signed the prenup and says he isn't going to back out. We created rules and laws—both of us. He's silently telling me it's business and his reasons are his own. Though in all likelihood, he's doing this for Zax and Grey and the guilt trip I threw at him where they're concerned.

I don't need or want more from him than this. I don't want his time, attention, or interest.

I go to turn away from him when he catches my jaw and turns my face back to his. His blue eyes darken, his pupils expand, and with that, a chill sweeps over my body. "You are to tell me about any and all texts, calls, or conversations you have with Ezra."

My tongue thickens in my mouth at the way he says that—so unrelenting, so unnegotiable—but I somehow manage to maintain my easy disposition even as my nerves are scraped raw. Sarcastically, I bite out, "Sure thing, hero."

I turn away, jerking my jaw free of his touch and breaking eye contact first when my phone pings in my purse between us. Inadvertently, I scowl, somehow already knowing it's Ezra. For a moment, I don't move, even when I can feel Lenox's expectant gaze on me. I'm salty after his demand and debating if I want to give him access to my private messages when a second ping comes through. I sigh and pull out my phone.

Ezra: I had our suites moved next to each other with a connecting door between them.

Ezra: After you get settled, come to my room, and we'll have a drink and talk. Can't wait to see you. XO.

I go to toss my phone back into my purse when Lenox catches my wrist, stopping me. He twists my arm, moving my phone so he can see the screen, and taps the glass twice, his hard eyes on me before taking the phone from my hand.

"Hey!" I bark, trying to snatch it from him, only to have him plant his hand on my shoulder and hold me back. "What are you doing?"

"Sending Ezra a coded link to a bullshit website that will give me backdoor access to everything on his phone. And telling him to fuck off."

"What? Why are you doing that?"

He glares furiously at me after he hits send, his jaw tense and tight as he grits out, "Because I want to see his emails, texts, apps, spending habits, and search history. I want access to his banking and credit cards. *And* I want him to know that you're with me now."

"That was not for you to do," I say with an indignant, sharp lift of my chin.

He tilts his head as if to say *too late* and then hands me my phone back. I take a look at the screen, at what he wrote.

Me: Did you send me this?

There's a link following it and another message from me.

Me: I won't be coming to your room for a drink or a talk or anything else. I told you it's over. Please respect that. I'm married to Lenox Moore now.

Oh shit.

"I was going to tell him in person," I snap, resentful of his high-handed approach. "You had no right. I was with him for two years, and though I may not love him or want much to do with him, that's not the way this needs to go. I still have to deal with him."

He gets right up in my face, his impassioned blue eyes scorching a path straight into mine. "I am here about to *marry* you because you told me he's not taking no for an answer. You told me he's been stalking you, which judging by him moving your suite without your consent, he is. He needs to know you're going to be *my wife,* and you'll never be his. You asked me why I'm here. *That's* why I'm here, Georgia. To get these guys to finally leave you alone so you can have the life you fucking deserve. Isn't that what you begged me to do?"

Fire blazes between us, a thick red haze I can almost taste. I'm at war with myself. On the one hand, he's right. It is what I asked him to do. It is why he's here about to marry me. I certainly wasn't looking forward to that particular conversation with Ezra, and in truth, I was afraid of how he'd react.

But still, I don't like Lenox fighting my battles for me or

handling something that should fall squarely on my own shoulders. I was going to tell Ezra tonight, once Lenox and I are officially married, and by doing so, I'd eliminate Ezra's options. I'd be removing him from my life simply because I am married to another man. He can't beg me to come back or try to return my ring to me or even show up at my house or place of business.

I'm not a woman who does things halfway. I'm simply a woman stuck in the worst possible position who needs a bit more leverage than I had to ensure my freedom from my ex and ensure that the future of Monroe Securities stays in safe hands.

I try to push my fear and ire back down, but the bitches won't relent.

"Marrying me doesn't mean I want you to speak for me. It doesn't mean I'm some damsel in distress who doesn't know how to handle her business. I'm learning. I'm adapting. I'm a fucking midwife thrust into the tech world. I went from vaginas to computers. I went from having two parents who love me to one. I went from having a guy who I thought I'd spend my life with to needing to marry someone else, so I *don't* have to spend my life with him. I'm questioning everything and everyone right now. So excuse me if I need a bit of a learning curve. That doesn't make me weak. That doesn't mean I'm not strong. And that doesn't mean I wasn't going to tell him I'm married when I'm *actually* married."

His hand dives into my hair, and before I know how it happens, his forehead is practically pressed against mine, his wild eyes ensnaring me. "You believe I think you're weak?" he snarls. "Georgia, you're a ruby in a world of simple diamonds. They're clear, colorless, and boring. That's never been you. You are durable, surprising, and fucking radiant. You are impossible to let go of. Which is why he won't do it unless forced to, and I know you. You're sweet and kind and don't relish being intentionally cruel or hurtful. It's not a flaw, but there is no room for that kind of devotion to gentility, as he will not return the favor. You need to remember that you are not the sort of woman to be held down by the weight of men and their schemes. Do you hear me? Because he will not take this easily or lying down and you have to be ruthless with this."

I swallow, my throat working, but I manage a nod.

His eyes vacillate back and forth between mine before they bounce down to my lips and hold. All at once I'm hyperaware of our proximity, along with his heat, the firm press of his hand in my hair, and the scent of his skin since Lenox is never one to wear cologne. Suddenly the notion of his weight over mine doesn't feel so caging or awful. It feels almost freeing. Like his is the weight I've been missing all these years, all the while trying on others that never quite fit right.

Only I know that's not the case.

Nothing about Lenox ever fit right on me.

I just tried to make it so, and in doing that lost sight of the woman I am at my core. Or more importantly, the woman I wanted to be. I sacrificed everything for him. My head and my heart were a price I was willing to pay for whatever I could get from him. I told him I was fine with what we had, all the while silently believing he'd come around.

The sad truth is, I was willing to do anything to keep him.

It wasn't his fault. It was mine. He told me from the start and never swayed. Just sex. Just our bodies. Nothing more.

Mistakes are meant to be learned from and not repeated. So while his words about my strength and how I'm a ruby in a sea full of ordinary diamonds might hit the vulnerable part of me that recently lost her father and lived with a man who treated her like a trophy or an expensive watch—something to be kept in a case, looked at and admired, but never allowed out—longer than she should have, I know better than to allow them to linger in my mind.

He used to say things like that to me. During quiet moments when our lust had been sated, and our breathing was once again calm, and our bodies were sleepy. His hands would roam my skin, his eyes all over the motion, and he'd tell me things like that. Things that made my heart swell and swell, practically to the point of bursting.

Until finally he jammed a knife in me, and not only did I burst, I bled out.

Thankfully the car pulls to a slow stop in front of the hotel, and my phone pings simultaneously.

Ezra: No, I don't even know what that is. I never sent you that. And what the fuck do you mean you're married?!

Lenox reads the text and smirks, his eyes darker than they've been all day. "Looks like he got the message, and I'm in."

Chapter Six

Georgia

"MISS MONROE, welcome to Caesars, Las Vegas. We're delighted you're staying with us and hope your trip was as pleasant as it could be."

I shake the hostess's hand, offering her the warm, inviting smile I'm known for. "Yes, thank you."

"I have your suite all ready for you. Right this way."

Before she can lead me to my suite, I start to ask her if she can move my room—away from freaking Ezra—when Lenox takes my hand, squeezing it tightly in warning. My eyes flash up to his, and he shakes his head ever so subtly.

"Didn't you want to do a bit of shopping before it got too late, Georgie?"

Georgie?

My eyebrows bounce and not in pleasure.

The hostess turns back to us, her eyes snagging on our joined hands before climbing expectantly back up to my face. "I can arrange to have your things brought up for you if you'd rather set out and explore."

"Um. Yes. Thank you. That would be great."

"Of course. Enjoy yourselves."

Lenox starts to walk, giving me a firm tug as our bags are handled by a valet and our hostess. "What in the name of Jiminy Crickets was that?"

"You said you needed to buy a wedding dress."

"No, no. Not that. Georgie."

His lips quirk up, but that's the only response I get. *Jerk.*

"And why didn't we move our suite? I don't want to be next to Ezra."

"I can keep a better, closer eye on him if he's in the next room. I like having access should I need it. My guess is that despite the fact that he works for a cyber security company, he'll use the open access network of the hotel. Therefore, I can get his laptop or any other device in addition to his phone, and sometimes proximity helps with that."

Fine. Whatever. I don't argue it.

My phone has been vibrating like it's trying to make my purse orgasm, but for now, I'm ignoring it and Ezra. I'll have to deal with him soon enough.

Lenox and I head toward the Forum shopping area of Caesars all the while he's holding my hand, fiddling with the ring on my finger. He's strolling casually, his chin high, eyes scanning, completely unaffected. As if this is the most natural thing in the world, and this is how we always are with each other when I haven't actually seen him in six years before last night.

People stare at him as we pass, doing double takes and watching him with unabashed interest. And not because he's Lenox Moore, former Central Square bandmate. I doubt most people recognize him as that since he always went out of his way to avoid the limelight. I think it's him, the man. His size and gorgeous face and the visible tattoos on his forearms beneath his rolled-up sleeves, and the way he radiates complete control and dominance over everything, every space he enters, even here in Las Vegas.

He must sense me staring because he quirks his head down, lingers for a beat, and then continues straight ahead, leading me deeper into the shopping area that is cool and dark, meant to look like Rome at night on a piazza.

We stop in the middle of an open area, a circle of designer shops surrounding us on the periphery, and he pans his hand around us as if asking where I want to go first.

"You're not coming with me," I tell him, and his chin dips down, his eyebrow raised questioningly. "It's bad luck."

A bemused sort of chuckle hits his full lips.

I roll up on the balls of my feet, bouncing twice, and then go digging for my ChapStick, smearing the vanilla-flavored wax on my lips. "Whether it's real or not, I no longer like to tempt the devil unless I have to. Don't let my red hair deceive you."

He shrugs, leans down, plants a chaste kiss on my cheek, and walks off, leaving me here staring after him. Fucker plays the part of fake fiancé way better than I do. I shake that off and head into Valentino, already knowing I'll find something perfect in there, and I'm not wrong.

"May I help you?" the sales associate asks.

"I'm marrying the man who broke my heart six years ago in a little over two hours, and I need to look and feel amazing for it."

He smiles eagerly at me. "Oh girl, I've got just the thing for you. And for him."

He leads me directly to a stunning white crepe couture dress with cute little bow accents and a high neckline that make it appear demure and even a little playful, but the way it hugs my frame and cuts off just around mid-thigh adds a sexier, more adult element.

Ricardo also wisely insists I pair it with baby blue satin pumps— for my something blue—lined with gold studs that add some edginess. Then he takes me by the hand down the hall to a small shop I would have missed entirely and tells Fabrizio to give me the works, because it's my wedding day.

The works turns out to be having my hair twisted into an elaborate braided updo that still manages to softly frame my face and makeup that makes me look like a shimmery angel, with the exception of my vamp-red lips—my calling card and armor. I decline the waxing, informing him that I've had so many lasers on my vagina nothing will ever grow down there again, and then Fabi—as he insists I call him—walks me down to Agent Provocateur.

Now I know I'm in trouble.

My new bestie, Cathy, hands me a much-needed glass of champagne, and by the time I leave the store I'm wearing the sexiest thong and bra I've ever worn, along with a white lace garter she insisted I get. It doesn't matter that my groom will never see them. Somehow, they feel like sexy weapons. Like a confidence boost I didn't realize I needed.

Finding my way back to where we started, I text Lenox, wondering if he'll be pissed that I took so long. Time sort of got away from me. My phone immediately vibrates in my hand.

Lenox: Turn around.

For unknown reasons, my stomach lifts and nerves skitter under my skin as I slowly turn. I tell myself that it doesn't matter what he thinks about my hair, makeup, or dress. I bought them for me. Because *I* wanted to feel and look beautiful. Because after the wedding, we're immediately going to the cocktail hour, and that will be trial by fire, and I wanted to feel equipped to handle and dominate any situation.

That's what the right clothes and makeup do for me. I don't even care if that makes me shallow because show me a woman who doesn't feel more confident when she feels beautiful and sexy, even if all women are always beautiful and sexy. Something about dressing up changes the game.

But when my gaze slowly drags up his body, starting at his new black boots, trailing along his black slacks, up to his black button-down dress shirt and no tie, I realize I hadn't expected him to go shopping or dress up for the occasion. Speaking of tempting the devil, the sight of him like this—looking so fucking hot and sinister and sexy—slams into me with more force than I was prepared for.

His longer on top blonde hair is brushed back from his face, showing off the vibrant color of his sky-blue eyes and the strong line of his stubbled jaw and dimpled chin. His clothes fit to perfection, expensive fabrics hinting at the taut lines and ridges of muscle beneath. For a moment, all we do is stare at each other from about ten feet away, hordes of people coming and going all around, but it's as if the world around us is paused, muted, nonexistent.

My skin prickles at his slow, sweeping drags of me. At the way he takes in every line and inch I'm comprised of as if he refuses to be rushed or miss discovering even the smallest piece of me. He snags on the bows at the bottom of the skirt and gives the barest hint of a smile as if he likes the flirty challenge of unwrapping me.

His thumb meets his mouth, dragging along his bottom lip, and I catch sight of a silver cufflink with a pearl accent—white—the only thing on him that could mildly suggest he's ready for a wedding.

My heels tap on the hard surface of the floor as I cut our distance until I'm standing right before him. "You look very hand-some, Mr. Moore," I tell him, wanting to adjust his shirt simply so I can touch him but refraining. "Are you ready to get married?"

He gives me a firm nod, takes the shopping bag holding my old clothes and undergarments from me, and retakes my hand. I'm positive he can feel my pulse thrashing against him, but thankfully he doesn't comment. I haven't told him where we're getting married yet. He tried asking on the plane, but I was mid-panic attack, so it never happened.

I picked the least romantic or special wedding chapel in the hotel.

This isn't about love, and there is no romance between us. It's business, and the last thing I wanted was a beautiful location to haunt me in the future for when I do actually get married to someone I love and want to be with.

Making our way through the casino floor, we stop in front of two double doors, and after sucking in a deep breath, I pull one open. The wedding organizer, who is acting as our witness, along with the officiant, are already here, talking up by the front of the room, standing in front of a gaudy painting of a Romanesque building.

"You have your license on you, I take it," I murmur to Lenox, my heart rioting in my chest, pumping blood noisily through my ears.

A nod. That's it. Oh, Lenox, how I wish this was the moment you'd bestow me with soothing words.

We make our way up to the front of the chapel, and the moment the organizer sees us, she immediately goes after Lenox, hugging him like they're ancient friends. Lenox is not a hugger, nor is he a people person. He throws me a what do I do mixed with a what the fuck is going on look.

"I'm sorry," the woman exclaims, still hugging him fiercely even though he's trying to pull away as gently as he can. "I just love you so much. Central Square is my all-time favorite band, and you were my favorite member. I love the piano." She pulls back, her cheeks flushed as she bats her eyes up at him. "I play the piano too. I could play for you now if you'd like, or even better, we could play a duet."

I choke on a laugh and cover it as a cough. It's almost fun watching Lenox suffer. Still, as the man marrying me, I feel the need to save him. Just a bit.

"Um. I'd rather there not be any music," I state, and she rolls her head over her shoulder and throws me a scathing look like I'm keeping her from showing off for the love of her life.

She turns back to him. "I can't believe you're getting married. And to a Monroe! That's just so perfect. And wow, to do it like this… on the fly." She fans her face. "It's so romantic. I wish the other members were here. I'd love to meet Greyson, especially. Zax is a bit intimidating." She emits a girlish giggle. "But oh, Asher and Callan are dreamy too." She gives me a brief side-eye, hating me on sight, and then it's all about him once more. "You know, I haven't heard anything about the two of you even being together. Last I knew, she was engaged to someone else. Are you sure this is the right thing for you to do?"

Is she for real?! "Uh, yeah, he is. You know, since he's my *fiancé* and we're about to get *married* here. That is what I'm paying you for, isn't it?"

"Right. Of course." Her eyelashes flutter up at him like a hummingbird's wings. "You must have kept it a secret then."

"We did," I say, my tone short. "But our love was the stuff of Shakespeare for years." Unrequited and tragic. Lenox throws me an amused look, and I shrug at him. "Anyway, can we get this going? Young love is impatient, as I'm sure you constantly witness."

More rapid blinking at Lenox, and if she keeps this up, I think she'll use her lashes as wings and fly out of here like a goddamn fairy. Finally, she reluctantly peels herself away and takes our bags, promising to have them delivered to our room. I wouldn't be shocked if she slips her digits and maybe her underwear in his bag.

After that, we get down to business as she and the officiant proceed to go over everything with us, asking us a few last-minute questions about music—I decline again—us saying our own vows—again, I decline—or if there is anything special or meaningful we want to incorporate in our wedding—that's a hard no.

We sign our marriage license, which feels so strange to do, and it's already been requested that it remain private so the press doesn't get their hands on it before I want them to know about it.

Once all the business is concluded, the planner asks, "Ready?"

No. That's the first word that comes to my mind. No, I'm not ready to marry Lenox. Because when I was a little girl and I'd imagine this moment, I imagined it with my father walking me down the aisle, and me in a large Cinderella-style gown, and Lenox smiling at me like he loved me instead of glaring warily at me as if I'm the bane of his existence and he's suddenly doubting himself.

It wasn't supposed to be like this.

Even what I was planning with Ezra, though not quite my dream wedding, it sure as hell wasn't going to be me standing in an orange room with awful carpet and a gauche painting of a random building with two strangers marrying me.

I start to tremble. Maybe I don't need to do this. Maybe I don't need to actually marry him. I mean, if I keep telling Alfie and Ezra no, eventually they'll give up and the press will give up and I'll be fine. I'll figure out my father's company and—

"Yes," Lenox finally says in a low voice. "We're ready." He gives my hand a small jerk, snapping me back and my eyes up to his.

"We're ready," he repeats, this time for me, and I swallow hard and force myself to nod.

It's a year at most. I'll hardly ever have to see him. Everything will be fine.

"Fantastic," the woman exclaims, all fucking jubilant like this is the best day of my life, and I'm so tempted to tell her, *Honey, this ain't it.* "Do you have rings?"

Rings? I bark out a humorless laugh. How could I have forgotten to purchase rings? I meant to. When we were shopping, that was part of my plan, but between all the hair and makeup and lingerie, that somehow got lost.

Lenox reaches into his pocket and pulls out two boxes, and my eyes narrow in on them. He opens one of the boxes to reveal a thick, black band—so very Lenox—and slips it out, then hands it to the wedding planner to hold for me since I'm supposed to put it on his finger. He doesn't open the second box. Instead, he slides it back into his pocket and bows his head toward the officiant, indicating that we should begin.

There is no walking down the aisle to my groom. There is no music.

It's just the four of us in this room as Lenox retakes my hands, holding them between us with his eyes locked on mine. The officiant begins saying the standard words of love and commitment, and I can't stop the tears as they start to fall.

I'm so fucking heartbroken I can hardly breathe.

Lenox reaches our locked hands up and wipes at them, stepping closer to me, and something about his tenderness breaks me even more. I do much better when we're adversarial or distant. I just don't know how I got here. How my life spun so far and so fast from what it was to this point.

I'm trying to reclaim it. I'm trying to steal it back from those desperate to take it from me. I just have to remember this is step one in that process.

"Do you, Lenox Moore, take Georgia Monroe to be your lawful wedded wife, to have and to hold from this day forward, for better, for worse, for richer, for poorer, in sickness and in health, to love and cherish, till death do you part?"

"I do," he says, no hesitation in his voice. Releasing my hands, he takes out the box with my ring in it. And when he opens it up, I gasp and proceed to absolutely fall apart.

He bought me a ruby wedding band.

Why did he have to call me that and then buy this for me? Why? His hands recapture mine, trembling ever so slightly as he slips the ring on my left hand, right above Suzie's diamond ring.

The officiant asks me the same question, though I hardly hear the words. I hardly register myself say, "I do." His ring is placed in my hand, and I slide it onto his finger.

"By the power vested in me by the state of Nevada, I now pronounce you husband and wife. You may kiss your bride."

Oh, hell. The kiss.

I blink away the tears and slowly look up to find his eyes already on me, filled with something I can't decipher. His ringed hand comes up to cup the side of my face, slips back into my hair, and then his mouth is on mine.

His lips are firm and warm, powerful as they press rigidly to mine. My hands meet his biceps, ready to push him back but instead, I end up holding onto him because it's been six years since I've really felt his lips on mine, and the sensation is electric. He sucks in a breath through his nose, feeling this too, and he inches in, pressing against me as his other hand comes up, cupping my face.

His mouth softens, and he licks the seam of my lips. Automatically I open for him, and he doesn't hesitate. His tongue plunges straight into my mouth, stroking, seeking, and the moment our tongues meet, his control snaps.

In a flash, he walks me backward until my back slams into the wall. He groans, and then he's all over me, using the wall as leverage to press into me tighter. His thumb strokes my jaw as he tilts my head and deepens the kiss, suddenly unable to get close enough, deep enough. There is nothing gentle or sweet about this, though there never has been where Lenox is concerned. It's wicked and sensual, passionate and desperate.

My hands grab fistfuls of his shirt, yanking on him while our tongues thrash, our lips mash, and I hold on as my knees feel like they're about to buckle beneath me. He pulls my hair the slightest bit, shifting one of the pins, and the quick zap of pain has me moaning into his mouth.

And just as quickly as it began, it ends.

Hands fall from my face, and he takes a step back, his chest heaving as rapidly as I'm positive mine is. His lips are wet, stained ever so slightly with the red smear of my lipstick. The hungry look in his eyes tells me that kiss surprised him—and not in a good way. Without a word, he turns and storms straight out of the chapel, the door flying open only to slam shut with a loud, resonating bang behind him.

For a moment, I stare after him, at the now-closed door, debating what I should do. My lips still tingle from that kiss, and I'm not entirely sure what to make of it other than I don't plan to give it room to breathe or grow in my thoughts. It was a strange and emotional moment, but for me, the hardest part of it is done, and we can move on to the next phase of this.

I shift my weight. Do I go after him? That seems weird. This is Lenox we're talking about. He has the emotional aptitude of a cobra, and I already know any comfort or reassurance I could offer would be unwanted and likely unnecessary.

It isn't until I hear the sound of a throat clearing uncomfortably across the room that I remember I'm not alone.

Well, this is awkward.

I shrug, willing my heart to slow and my features to even out. "That was his first kiss," I say. "He's a virgin." I don't even know where the words come from. Even if you don't know who Lenox Moore is, one look at that man, and you know he's no virgin. Still, it manages to make me laugh and relax all at the same time. "Thank you!" I throw out over my shoulder as I run from the chapel to go and find my new husband.

We have a cocktail party to attend.

Chapter Seven

Lenox

THE INCESSANT NOISE and clatter and flashing lights of the casino surround me as I tear through it, weaving without purpose, until finally, far enough away from that fucking chapel, I drop down onto a random slot machine seat. The old woman in the seat beside me scowls, giving me a venomous look that I can't figure out.

"That was my machine," she clips out in the raspiest voice I've ever heard before she takes a drag of her ten-foot-long cigarette.

I stare at the machine that shows it was cashed out and then back to her, still confused.

"If you're going to steal someone's machine, you can't just sit there. You have to play."

Fucking Vegas.

I slip out my wallet and shove a hundred-dollar bill into the machine, raising an eyebrow at her that asks, "Happy now?" She grumbles under her breath but thankfully turns away and I spin on my chair, giving her my back. I hit a button or two on the machine, and the wheels start spinning, sevens and diamonds and bars and who cares?

I ignore it.

Because I just did the one thing I swore I wouldn't do in all of this.

I lost my head in Georgia.

I watched her walk into Valentino, and then I went off, finding a bench in an unobserved corner and diving straight into my phone. It didn't take long to find what I was searching for. It took even less time to find all of Ezra's secrets.

I told her I wasn't going to back out, but it wasn't until that moment that I was fully solidified in her scheme. Her ex is a real piece of work, and Georgia needs protection from things she doesn't even know about. After that, it was too late.

I was even more invested than I was after my call with Grey and Zax last night.

I went and bought an outfit and the rings, seeing that ruby band and knowing that was the one I wanted on her hand, even if I didn't allow myself to linger on why. And when I saw her turn—so fucking beautiful it physically hurt to look at her—part of me knew I was screwed. That feeling only multiplied when I was standing across from her, holding her hand, staring into her teary eyes, and saying I do.

That kiss…

It was meant to be chaste. It was meant to be nothing. But the moment my lips pressed to hers and I tasted the salt of her tears and felt her body trembling against mine, it was like a match to gasoline. It was like I was right back to where I was all those years ago with her.

Every time with her, I'd tell myself it was the last time. I'd promise myself that. And then, like the addict I was for her, I'd need another hit. Every time I went to her, I told myself I was simply going to see her to tell her it was over. Then she'd do something like smile or laugh or touch my arm or say something witty or just fucking look up into my eyes like she could see inside my head and wasn't bothered by what she found there, and I was powerless to stop myself.

One more time. One more taste. Then I'll stop.

And here I am, testing that addiction all over again. An alcoholic living in a bar or a junkie in a crack house. Only now, the temptation is stronger than ever having gone so long without her. I'm here to look out for her. I'm here to protect her.

But the one thing I can't do is fuck or fall in love with my wife.

My wife…

I take in the black band on my left hand, twirling it around and around my finger with my other hand. The weight of it doesn't feel as odd or misplaced as I was hoping it would. I'm married to Georgia and none of it is real, so I focus on the reason behind it. The reason I said yes in the first place.

I pull out my phone and bring up my text stream with my guys.

Me: It's done. Georgia and I are officially married.

Asher: Mazel Tov. *Pops champagne*

I roll my eyes but smirk all the same. Thank God for fucking Asher and his inability to be serious. That was exactly what I needed.

The woman lighting a new cigarette from her old one glares at me from her chair and clears her throat loudly, and I groan. For fuck's sake. I hit the buttons again and return to my phone.

Zax: How'd it go? Georgia okay?

I honestly don't know because I kissed her like her mouth was the incarnation of the Holy Spirit and I'd just found God and enlightenment all at the same time, and I'm not even a religious man.

Me: She cried, but she's tough.

Grey: I still can't believe this. You're fucking married to my cousin.

Me: It's not real.

It's not. Even if I can't stop thinking about her as my wife.

Callan: Sorry I wasn't there to be your best man, but it sounds like you did fine without me.

Asher: Dickwad, if anyone was going to be the best

man, it was me. I am the best best man ever. I'm just sad I didn't get to plan your bachelor party. Vegas would have been perfect for it.

Callan: Thank God you didn't, or we'd all end up arrested and needing Lenox to wipe our records. Again!

Asher: That wasn't all my fault! Suzie aided and abetted.

Zax: Suuuuure, blame Suzie for you getting wasted and stripping down in public.

Asher: Twat, she dared me!

Grey: What are you? Five. Oh, she dared you. *eye roll emoji*

Callan: I wouldn't talk, brother. If I recall, you got yourself arrested one drunken night with Suzie.

Grey: *Middle finger emoji*

Asher: Enough with that BS. Thor, how does it feel to be the first one of us to get married? Give us the insider tips. The dos and don'ts of saying I do to an irresistible woman.

Me: You're an asshole. Do I look like a magazine?

Asher: Tatted and Pierced Hackers Weekly. 100%

I choke out a laugh, rubbing my hand over my mouth and across my forehead. I have no fucking clue what I'd do without these guys other than be more of a recluse than I already am. Their friendship has been the mainstay in my life. The saving grace when I was a hairsbreadth from letting it all go.

And how did I repay their loyalty, friendship, and brotherhood? By fucking Georgia, keeping it a secret for two goddamn years, and then hurting her. So this is it. Another round of penance. I'm doing this for her, but I'm also doing it for them. Because they would do it for me without ever thinking twice. Because they didn't let me go, even when I deserved for them to.

I hit the buttons on the machine again, so I don't get clubbed with the woman's cane, and type…

Me: I found stuff. I'll need a call later. It's nothing urgent, and I'm handling it. Just… a bit fucked.

Zax: Just tell me what time. You're three hours back from us, but that doesn't matter.

Grey: Do you need us to fly out there?

I hit the buttons again, watching the wheels on the machine spin and ping into place, showing me I just won five dollars. Evidently, it's my lucky day.

Me: No. I've got it. We fly back to Boston on Tuesday. If I don't call you tonight, I will first thing tomorrow.

I tuck my phone into my pocket and lean back against the seat, my eyes scanning the casino, my thoughts scattered, when a flash of white moves in beside me. "I've been looking for you."

I glance up at Georgia, who you would never know was crying or had my hands in her hair not even fifteen minutes ago. There's not a streak of mascara beneath her eyes, not a hair out of place. She even has her red lipstick reaffixed. As always, she is the vision of perfection.

I turn back to the game, hitting the buttons again. Georgia watches as the machine rolls and then nudges me over a bit on my chair so she can sit on the edge of it, practically right up against me.

"A bit too late for second thoughts."

I grunt. I'm not having second thoughts. I'm having other thoughts, and those are far more dangerous. She doesn't know that if love had been enough, I never would have left her, and if broken pieces could ever be made whole again, she would have always been mine.

"Are we okay?" she asks softly, her voice tinted with worry.

"We're married. How could we not be okay?"

"I suppose we weren't okay before all of this, but hating you doesn't sit well with me anymore. You know, since we're married now." I get an arched eyebrow and a wry grin. "But we have to go upstairs and pretend to be newlyweds. We have to pretend to be in love. Do you think we can do that with each other?"

"You're the actress, Georgia. I'm only here because I was the last single man standing, and I know how to keep quiet."

Her mouth twists in annoyance at my petulant tone. "Were you always this sarcastic before, or was I too blinded by my childish infatuation to notice?"

"I didn't speak before."

She twists and fully meets my eyes. "You did to me."

I blink at her, at the assurance in her tone and countenance. It has my heart racing in my chest. I have no memory of talking to her or anyone at that time in my life. I was barely existing, and where words were never comfortable for me before, they were impossible then. I remember being captivated. I remember being obsessed. I remember not knowing how I'd ever be able to stop.

But talking? Nope.

"We have a cocktail party to attend if you're done throwing money away on this machine."

I look around, taking in all the people around us, the cacophony of the machines and boisterous chatter of people, and lean in so only she can hear me. "I need to speak to you about something."

"Can it wait?"

"Do you want it to?"

She sighs and leans back against me in a way that feels so natural my insides hurt. She's over hating me, but I wish she still did. I wish it weren't so familiar with her. I wish it didn't feel so good having her this close. I'm hoping she's simply too indifferent toward me to hate me any longer so I can match that, but that's not how Georgia works.

She's never indifferent. She wears her heart and her emotions proudly and without apology.

"No," she says quietly after a contemplative beat. "That said, not knowing might help me get through the cocktail hour without committing first-degree murder."

"Even if it's about him?"

"Did he kill my father?" she whispers in my ear.

I shake my head. At least not as far as I can tell from his phone.

"If you're going to tell me that he's been using me for the last two years—"

"Would you rather I lie?"

She stares down at her hands on her lap, at the rings on her finger, and starts to fiddle with them. "It doesn't matter. I already told you I didn't love him and that our marriage was all but arranged." She laughs bitterly, but then lowers her voice once more. "I suppose he's a better actor than I am. So what was he after? Money, my father's company, all of it?"

"All of it," I parrot. "Especially the money. He has quite the lavish lifestyle and the credit card debt to prove it. Not to mention he has a serious gambling habit and a penchant for losing."

"His daddy has money."

"I haven't gotten into his father's phone or information yet, so I can't speak to any of that. He likes to text his father about you, though his father doesn't offer up much that way. Despite that, they're both are furious that you ended it with him and are trying to find a meaningful way to change your mind, which is an aristocratic way of saying coerce you. He also asked his attorney if once you were married if he'd have access to your money with the prenup in place. But in fairness, I think there is love there too. Or more like a sick obsession and an unwillingness to let you go."

She sucks in a shaky breath, the side of her head curving perfectly into the space between my neck and shoulder. I can smell her shampoo and a hint of her perfume, something expensive and exotic but intoxicating all the same, and I refrain from burying my nose in her hair so I can feel it on my face and breathe her in deeper.

"Ironically, you are the last person I should be leaning on for support after hearing that. You mastered the art of using me long before he came along."

"Only I never cared about your money." Just your body. While pretending I didn't also want your heart as a map that only led to me.

She hiccups out a laugh. "Right. Maybe that's why this hurts less than that did."

"Georgia—"

She shakes her head, immediately cutting me off. Fine. I let it go. Probably better if I don't tell her.

"It's more than that, and while he is after your money and

company, he's also having you followed around LA, though it doesn't seem they knew you left for Boston until you were already in the air. He was pissed."

Her breath hitches high in her throat, and her hand claps over her mouth. "Oh my god. I don't even know what to say. When did that start?"

I band my arm protectively around her.

"Four months ago."

She hisses out a curse. "When I ended it with him." Then she snorts out a sardonic laugh. "If he was looking for blackmail material, he couldn't have picked a more boring woman. The raciest thing about me is my reading collection and the fact that my hands have been in more vaginas than his have. Is he in my phone or computer or anything like that?"

"Not as far as I can see on his phone."

She's silent for so long I'm about to turn her face so I can see her eyes, when she finally says, "That's seriously troubling. For him and for me. Good thing I broke up with him, and good thing we're in Las Vegas, the gambling capital of the world."

I smile dryly, chuckling lightly.

"Thank you for marrying me. Ironically, your reasons for doing so have been far more honest and altruistic than his." A sigh. "He's really been having me watched?"

"Yes."

"That filthy, slimy motherfucker. I can't tell you how invaded I feel right now. Does his father know?"

"About that? I'm not sure, but it doesn't seem that way."

"What do I do other than sever his balls from his body before shoving them down his throat until he chokes to death on them?"

"Actually, I don't want you to do anything of the sort."

"What?" she gasps in outrage, sitting up straight and twisting on me.

"He knows you're married now, and he'll turn more desperate than he already was and potentially try to come after you. Whether he's able to find blackmail material on you or not, that likely won't stop him from creating something to try and use against you or come after the validity of our marriage. Will you trust me enough to allow me to handle it, knowing I will never let him get away with any of that and that I intend to punish him greatly?"

"Punish him greatly. Do I want to know what that entails?"

I shake my head. No one wants to see the ruthless side of me. No one wants to know what happens to them if they hurt one of my people, and Georgia is one of my people. Whether that's because she's an extension of Zax and Grey or because she's now mine, it doesn't matter.

"So I'm supposed to go up there and see him and not break every bone in his body until he cries like a little bitch?"

I smirk. "Yes."

"Christ, Lenox. That's a lot of trust I'm putting in you, and a lot of trust you're putting in me."

"You can handle it."

She turns, her eyes grazing over mine momentarily. "You may look like Thor, but I'm thinking you're more like Batman. Dual identity, growly disposition, and all."

"Hit the button, Georgie."

A jab from her elbow to my flank makes me oomph. "You need to stop with the Georgie stuff. It's a new rule in the State of Georgia. That nickname is forbidden. But what button are we speaking of?"

"This one." I tap the white rectangle that's been flashing for the last few minutes since she sat down.

"Max bet?"

"Is there any other way?"

She smacks the button, making the wheels spin, and we lose. "Well, that sucks. I was expecting megabucks."

A grin tickles my lips, and I pound my fist down one last time on the button. The wheels spin once more, and then the first one stops on the bright gold Megabucks symbol. Then the second one. Then the third.

"HOLY FUCK! You just won!" Georgia leaps off the chair as the machine goes absolutely berserk. Bells and sirens and flashing lights. We've immediately drawn a crowd, but then Georgia grips my hand and points to the digital winnings tally at the top and how it's climbing, climbing from hundreds to thousands to hundreds of thousands all the way up to millions. "LENOX, YOU JUST WON TEN MILLION DOLLARS!"

Shit. For real?

How unfortunately ironic.

How very public this is.

I sigh and stand. People are taking pictures of us and of the machine. Georgia is holding my arm, shaking it like the thing is not attached to my body. The old lady who snapped at me that this was her machine is about to steal the oxygen tank belonging to the man beside her and bludgeon me to death with it.

Security, as well as a man in a suit with a red tie come flying over to us, pushing the crowd back and making a makeshift perimeter around us. "Congratulations on hitting the megabucks." The suited man shakes my hand, and then Georgia's. "I am Gerald, the casino manager. We have alerted our in-house technician of the winning spin, and they will come and perform a check on the machine to make sure this is a legitimate win. Would you like to come with me in the meantime? Have a drink or something to eat. On us, of course."

No. Not even a little.

We'll make the news over this. I just know it. People will recognize Georgia, and though I'm not so recognizable now, I do still have a name people know thanks to my days in Central Square and then Suzie's and my father's deaths.

Privacy. Anonymity. Simply being left the fuck alone. All that's gone now.

Or maybe it was the second I said I do to Georgia Monroe.

Georgia takes in my expression, the way I draw back from the crowd of observers, and turns to the casino manager. "Actually, we're expected upstairs at a work event, but we're staying in this hotel," Georgia tells him.

"Excellent," he exclaims. "I just need a bit of information, and when everything is sorted out, we'll be in touch with you. There will be paperwork to fill out and things of that nature."

Georgia mercifully takes care of handing over my information, and then we manage to escape, heading toward the elevators. Georgia offers people who congratulate us small smiles and soft thank yous and keeps her face averted from people blatantly taking photos or videos. It feels like I don't take a breath until we step into the elevator, shooting up to whatever space Monroe Securities rented out for their cocktail hour.

"You don't like crowds."

I stare straight ahead at the elevator doors. "No."

"Is that because of Suzie?"

"She loved them, and I was mostly indifferent when we were on tour. Suzie couldn't play an instrument to save her life but got a thrill out of managing five teenage boys. Most of the time the press never bothered with me—not when we had Greyson as our lead singer—until she died. Until my dad…" I trail off, unable to finish that. I clear my throat. "Then they were relentless. Everywhere. All the time."

She bobs her head. "I remember that. I remember how you'd have to sneak out to come see me."

"Yes." The only place I found peace was in Georgia's bed, even if all I was doing was watching her sleep or listening to her talk about her classes.

She hums and turns to me, a smile lighting up her face in a way that tells me she's changing the subject for me. "What do you plan to do with all that money you just won?"

"Is this an interview?"

She snickers, rolling her eyes.

I grin but immediately rub it away with my fingers. "Donate it."

She likes that answer. "Where?"

I turn to her just as the car slows and take her hand, staring down at her rings. At how they look side by side on our hands. "Where do you want it to go?"

She shakes her head as we step out of the car into the mostly empty hallway that will lead us to the event room holding the cocktail hour.

"No," she says adamantly. "You won that money. Where do *you* want it to go?"

"I couldn't care less."

"I take it you don't need the money?"

"Georgia, I have more money than the Catholic Church, the Royal Family of England, or pretty much anyone else on this planet combined. Yet no one knows about it because no one knows me or what I do or how I hide it."

"How is it you have all that? I know you have a lot of family money, but…" She trails off, her eyebrows raised expectantly.

I grunt. "I've been playing the stock market since I was a young kid and figured out how it works, then I made a ton with Central Square, and over the years I've invested in things that have been very lucrative. So I don't give a fuck what you do with that ten million. Donate it to a worthy charity, something that speaks to your heart, and we'll leave it at that."

"Don't you have a charity that speaks to your heart?"

"You're implying I have one."

"Don't you?" she questions, and though I think it's meant to be teasing, it's not. The serious set of her eyes as they scroll all over me tells me my answer is everything to her, and it shouldn't be. The more emotionless she thinks I am, the more of an emotional divide I place between us, the better.

There's no other way we'll survive this arrangement.

I grin smugly, poisonously. "What do you think? I used your body and left when you tried to give me your heart."

You need to hate me, Georgia. I can't handle anything else. Not right now.

A flush rises swiftly up her cheeks, her eyes dark and narrowed, shocked and hurt. "Christ, you're an ass, aren't you? If you want me to hate you again, I will. Is that your game with me?"

"I don't play games. The money is yours to donate. Consider it my wedding present to you."

She squints at me, and I watch as sharp points reforge from places within her that had grown dull and complacent. I watch as they stab at her skin. I hurt her and I hate myself for it, but once again, I find myself dangling precariously on the edge of wanting to be everything to her while not being nearly enough. I'm not the man she needs. I live in the middle of nowhere, own a town with not much of a name, and avoid the limelight—and fucking people —every chance I get.

Georgia Monroe could never find happiness in that. Or with me.

Chapter Eight

Lenox

THE MOMENT we step foot over the threshold of the room, my eyes are everywhere. Georgia's hand is held firmly in mine, and she pushes out a bright smile, but when she gives me a fleeting glance, I can see it doesn't reach her eyes. If anything, I just made this more fake than it was an hour ago. But I also know she's worried about Ezra and any confrontation coming there.

She swoops a pink concoction in a martini glass off one of the passing trays and brings it to her lips, taking a large sip. Her lips smack, and her cheeks brighten. It's a look on her I can't resist, and I find myself staring at her lips, wanting to know what that drink tastes like from its direct source.

"Yums."

I steal the glass from her hand and finish it off, much to her objection. But it's the closest I'll get to her lips again, and why not taste what they taste like when I know exactly how it looks to anyone watching? Especially when I give her a wink and a playful kiss to her temple.

"Get yourself another one, but I'm going to find you something to eat," I murmur in her ear.

Her hand trails up until it's locked in my hair. She gives it a firm rip that makes me smirk. "I don't need you to take care of me. Nor do I want you to."

Except I know she hasn't eaten in hours, and now she's drinking because she's mad and feels betrayed and is nervous—and she's not wrong about any of that.

"You're my wife now, Georgia. That means it's my job to take care of you. Whether you like it or not." I rub my nose along hers, our eyes locked in a fierce standoff, but her focus is quickly intercepted by a group of people vying for her attention, and I use that as my excuse to part from her, going about the duties of making her a plate of food.

But that's not all I'm doing.

I'm waiting, and I don't have to wait long. Within seconds, he's beside me, casually making a plate at the massive buffet as if he doesn't know who I am, nor does he care. Only he cares. He cares a lot. I can see the sweat already lining his brow despite the chill in the room, and the rim of red lining his eyes, indicating he's already several drinks in.

I continue filling the plate, popping a piece of cheese into my mouth for show and making sure I turn in his direction as if entirely aloof. When I stand upright, his focus is all over my ring, his jaw locked, his dark eyes wild, and his pupils totally blown out.

Hmm. Interesting. That coupled with the sweat, makes me think he's on something.

He's tall, thin, good-looking in that rich, preppy asshole way with a too-expensive haircut and a flashy gold watch. For a man I know to be in his early thirties, the stress of losing his fiancée and her company is aging him greatly.

"Are you here with Georgia Monroe? I saw you walk in with her."

I give him a nod.

"Ezra Earnheart." He extends his hand for me to shake. "I'm her ex-fiancé."

I shake his hand, almost smiling at his lame attempt at trying to crush mine. "Eric?"

"E-z-r-a," he repeats, enunciating the letters of his name. Douche. Who falls for that?

"Lenox Moore. I'm her husband. But you already knew that." I wink at him, which makes his eyes bead up.

"The former boy bander," he says tightly, taking a hasty sip of his scotch, his plate all but forgotten. "That's right. I think I heard her mention you once. I just don't remember it being all that favorable." He sniffs, wiping his nose with the back of his hand.

I don't take the bait, and it irritates him to no end.

"When did you and Georgia reconnect? As far as I know, this week is the first time she's left LA since her father's death."

I tilt my head. "And how would you know that?"

He grits his teeth only to blow out a scotch-soaked breath, trying to maintain his calm presence and failing terribly. "I don't know what game she's playing, but she's using you in her scheme. She doesn't love you."

I give him a version of a pitying smile and continue to add a few things to Georgia's plate. I drop a piece of shrimp cocktail on the white porcelain and give him an arrogant look. "It's her favorite."

His face pinches, and his eyes flash. "How much is she paying you? I'll pay you—"

"We both know you can't."

"How can you even—"

"Make basic assumptions without an education and tattooing people's skin for a living? No clue. Perhaps it's a wild guess based on your desperation."

"If you think you're going to get Georgia's money—"

"As I told Georgia, her money is the least appealing thing about her." I shrug nonchalantly, keeping my tone light.

He shakes his head, growing ruddier, more frazzled, a man visibly coming unglued at the seams. "This can't be real. There's no way." He pans his hand across the room as if he knows exactly where she is, which I'm positive he does since I do as well.

As a man who was obsessed with the same woman, I suppose we

share that commonality. Only I never stalked her or made her feel trapped or wanted to control her while taking her for all she's worth. And that thought turns me mean. The desire to hurt him—to actually destroy every piece of him—compels me.

I hold up my left hand, flashing my black band at him. "It's as real as it gets, Ethan."

"You motherfucker. You think you know what you're getting into. You're just a tattoo artist. A simple, uneducated lowlife, just like you said. Your best friends and your sister's death are your only claim to fame." He pauses here, watching to see my reaction to his mentioning Suzie, but again, I don't take the bait, and he slams his glass down on the buffet table, rattling a dish and drawing attention to himself. "She hasn't gone to see you, and I know you haven't gone to see her. It's bullshit! All of it."

"You might want to keep your voice down, Elliott. You are at a corporate event."

I glance over and see Georgia talking with two other people, but her eyes are on us, worry creasing her forehead when a third person —Alfie Earnheart—joins her. He smiles warmly at her, resting a hand on her shoulder and then drawing her in for a hug she returns.

I turn back to his son. "Nice talking to you, Earl. If you'll excuse me, I need to make sure my wife eats something." While I go meet your father and see if he's just as big of a weasel as you are.

Ezra is a hot head. But I'm not sure how smart he is. From what I've read online about Alfie Earnheart, without even getting into his real stuff yet, he's the complete opposite.

With slow, even strides, I make my way over to Georgia, who is now alone with Alfie, a middle-aged man with salt-and-pepper hair, dark eyes like his son's, and a suit that is all power. I haven't had a chance to send him the link yet, but I will. And when he opens it, I'll have a lot of fun digging through all his secrets to see if his mild-mannered exterior is fake or not.

Georgia is telling him something I can't hear, and I watch as he squints at her, steps into her personal space, and I swoop in, wrapping my arm around her waist and moving her body so that I'm between them and he can no longer touch her. She starts, but quickly recovers when she sees it's me and snatches the plate from my other hand.

"Oh, Lenox. Perfect timing. I'm starving." She turns back to him. "Alfie, this is who I was telling you about. I'd like to introduce you to my new husband, Lenox Moore. Lenox, this is Alfie Earnheart, the current CEO of Monroe Securities and my father's closest friend."

He reaches out and shakes my hand, though he doesn't try to crush it the way his son did. He's assertive and calculating, his eyes assessing, almost sizing me up, though he's visibly unhappy about hearing I'm Georgia's husband. "Her husband?"

I lift her left hand and kiss her knuckle just beneath her rings. "I'm a lucky man, wouldn't you say?"

He glowers at me, realizing I'm likely taunting him despite my even tone, and he gives me a disdainful once-over. I refrain from grinning. "Did she pick you up off the street?"

"No, my tattoo parlor, actually. I see your son hasn't told you anything about me yet. I've known Georgia her whole life."

"Funny, so have I, and I can't remember ever hearing about you as a person in her life."

"Yes," Georgia chimes in as she takes a bite of the shrimp. "He's best friends with my cousins Zax and Greyson."

His eyes round, but then he quickly dismisses me as anything of substance, putting his full weight on her. "Georgia, what on earth have you done? What could you have been thinking making a decision like that?"

"I'm very happy, Alfie."

He shakes his head as if that's inconsequential. "Honey, this is not the time for that sort of thing. You have a company depending on you. Your father would be so disappointed."

My jaw tics and I take a step forward before I can stop myself, using my height and size to my advantage as I glare down at him since he's a solid four inches shorter than me. "Do you make it a habit to be condescending and disrespectful to your company owner and chairwoman?"

Alfie is nonplussed, and I'm assuming no one has ever challenged him before. Not even his sniveling little worm of a son. "As she stated, I was her father's best friend and I've known her for her entire life. I'd say as both someone who cares about her and the current CEO of the company she is to inherit, I have every right to challenge her on this. She was supposed to marry my son," he snarls. "That was the agreement. She was not supposed to marry some bottom feeder looking to strike it rich through an advantageous marriage."

"An advantageous marriage? Who are you? Jane Austen?"

Georgia spits out a spray of pink alcohol straight into the air and then glares at me as she wipes at her lips and chin. "That's twice today, funny man."

I lean in and kiss the corner of her lips. Just to fuck with him and his sniveling son, who I know is watching us.

"You're not even part of this," Alfie continues, growing a head of steam. "You're simply some scum she picked off the bottom of her heel. Georgia, please come with me. We need to discuss this immediately."

"Alfie, while I appreciate your concern, I am a grown woman capable of making my own decisions. I was not going to marry Ezra. I've told you both that repeatedly. There is nothing more to discuss. It's done."

"My darling girl, you have to know how dangerous what you've done is for yourself and Monroe. He is using you. How can you not see that? Look at him." He waves a hand up and down in front of me. "It is incumbent upon me to act on this. Your father wouldn't have it any other way."

His overestimation of his own self-worth and his underestimation of mine will ultimately lead to his downfall. It always does. Hubris is the ultimate deadly sin. "We'll be sure to worry about that between now and never."

"My son is twice what you are."

Really? Does he even know his son? "I just had the pleasure of meeting Edwin," I say. "I agree, he seems like quite the guy. A bit of a drunk, sloppy with his secrets, and definitely uncouth if you ask me, but what would I know?"

Alfie shifts his weight, not liking the comment about secrets, and edges in toward Georgia as if he's about to grab her and run. I give him a dangerous look he does not mistake.

He shakes his head in dismay. "Georgia, please be rational with this. I can help you. It's not too late to make your father proud."

Georgia bristles, and I can see the hurt that flashes through her eyes. "I like to think my father would want me to be happy. Hence why he didn't stipulate who I had to be married to in his will."

"Regardless," I continue deliberately. "I'd watch the way you speak to my wife, if you have any sense at all."

Alfie tries to be the tough guy, but he doesn't intimidate me, and he knows it. "Are you threatening me?"

"*Threatening* you? No. Telling you? Yes. I won't allow you to intentionally manipulate her by pulling on her big heartstrings."

I stole his little ruby for myself, and men don't like it when other men steal their treasure. He thought he was entitled to something he wasn't, and Georgia officially flipped the tables on him and Ezra, and they're not happy about it.

I get it. We fucked with their schemes.

Maybe Alfie's motives come from a place of concern for her and the company. But maybe not. Nevertheless, that doesn't mean I'll let him speak to her like she's a five-year-old in need of a time-out and make her feel guilty about her father when she already feels guilty enough.

Georgia clears her throat. "Well, as I was saying before, I can't have dinner with you tonight because Lenox and I are dining together. Tomorrow morning is still fine though, if you'd like to meet briefly before breakfast. Have a good evening."

I place my hand on the small of her back and proceed to follow her as she strolls off. After we're about twenty feet from them, she turns and places a piece of cheese in my mouth. She smirks at me as I chew. "That was the most words I've ever heard you string together."

"I'll need tea with honey for sure."

She laughs, her head flying back. "Stop! Your sarcasm is killing me."

"Aw, Georgie, but you're so cute when you regurgitate your alcohol."

She smacks my shoulder, but there is no hiding her smile. "Thank you. For all of that. I've never seen him that upset with me before, but I suppose I'm not shocked given the circumstances."

"It's what I'm here for."

She sobers. "Right. I have more people to meet with if you're okay with that."

I nod and pan my hand for her to lead the way, and then I spend the rest of the evening following her around like a besotted puppy, quiet and loyally by her side. She charms easily, everyone she meets and talks to is eating out of the palm of her hand. I listen to small comments here and there, discussions of products and software that will revolutionize information security and keep hackers out.

I don't smirk, but the urge is there.

Nothing keeps hackers out because we're persistent and patient and rarely sleep. Not to mention, no system is foolproof, or in this case, hacker-proof. Where there's a will, there's a way. For myself, I'm not a black-hat hacker. I don't penetrate systems to bring them down or hold them for ransom. I do it for a challenge, and occasionally, depending on the company, I anonymously send them the details of how I broke in so they can patch the software or fix the vulnerability.

It's almost ironic that Georgia and I married.

She's the queen, and I'm her antihero.

Not evil enough to be considered a villain, but morally gray enough that I have my own notions of right versus wrong and am dangerous enough that you don't want to cross me. I don't fight fair. Especially when people I care about are involved.

I don't look, and neither does Georgia, but I can feel both Alfie and Ezra watching us, their hard gazes fixated on us the entire evening, and I already know this is only the beginning with them.

Chapter Nine

Lenox

WHEN THE COCKTAIL party comes to an end, I send a delighted Georgia down to deal with the winnings from earlier—she is my wife now and was sitting there when I won—and I go to the suite, anxious to get started and dive into both Ezra's and Alfie's secrets.

The room is nicely appointed in variations of gray with gold and brick red accents and a view of the Bellagio fountains and the Paris hotel across the way. The couch is laughable, designed for beauty instead of comfort—not long enough that I'll fit on it without pulling it out though, and there is no fucking way I'm pulling out a couch in a Las Vegas suite. I don't care how nice or clean the room looks.

I grab my computer and sit at the dining table, immediately getting to work.

My father taught me how to write code before I started speaking. I was late to that ballgame, having no interest in it, which naturally worried my mother and had doctors throwing out all sorts of diagnoses at me. But my father—a hacker himself—sat me down and taught me code. A language I instantly took to. A language I enjoyed communicating in.

Just thinking about him now hits me in the worst ways.

I came home from Switzerland, Suzie's body in a fucking coffin beneath the plane, and the first things my mother and father did were slap me and blame me for her death in that order. When Central Square hit it big, they sent me off with Suzie—a wild child if ever there was one—with one mission: keep her safe and bring her home alive.

I remember my mother saying that to me, almost in jest, but when I returned home with their daughter dead, they were suddenly oh-so-serious about my charge and how I had failed. I failed Suzie. I failed my parents. And our family of four that had been impossibly tight—thick as thieves, as my father called us—was broken.

My father drank and drank and drank until he couldn't see or think straight, and then he got angry and fought. Fought me, fought my mother, fought anyone who looked twice in his direction.

One night I got called down to his local bar to come and tend to him. He wasn't yet ready to leave, and the bartender said fine, so I sat and nursed a beer at the bar, watching bullshit on television when a man was dumb enough to make a joke about Suzie. That was it for my father. He smashed a bottle over his head and then plunged the broken remains into the man's throat. He killed the man before I could act. Before I could reach them. And after, with his eyes right on mine, he told me it was my fault she was dead and that I had done this to us.

Then he stabbed himself the same way he had stabbed that man.

I stood there and watched it happen. In all fairness, I didn't know he was going to kill himself. He was brandishing the bloody, broken end of the bottle like he was going to come after me next, and I didn't move because I hadn't decided if I was going to stop him or not. Plus, the police had already been called and were on their way, and I wasn't the only one frozen from what had just transpired.

But I didn't act when he stabbed himself. And I didn't force him to leave the bar when I knew I should have. I didn't want the resulting fight it would have caused, and because of it, a man lost his life along with my father.

It became a media cyclone.

My mother was long done by that point, and after my father's death and with the way the press relentlessly hounded us, she up and left Boston. Left the country. Last I bothered to check, she was living in Australia and teaching English.

Clearing away those thoughts, I'm just about finished when I hear the click and swish of the mechanical lock on our suite door, and in walks my wife followed by a man in a livery uniform carrying bags of what appear to be food and alcohol behind her.

She treats me to a dazzling, happy smile, and my heart thuds painfully against my ribs.

"Where would you like it, ma'am?"

Isn't that my question for her?

"Right over there by my husband is perfect," she tells him, indicating the table I'm sitting at with my computer, an amused laugh tickling her lips at the way she calls me her husband.

The man gives me an apologetic look but then sets down three large bags right beside me, the scent of garlic, onions, tomatoes, and something spicy immediately hitting me.

"Thank you so much." Georgia hands him a large bill, and he gives her a bow like she truly is a queen, then he leaves the suite.

"What's this?"

"Dinner," she explains as if it's obvious. "I was in the mood for Italian. Ten million dollars minus a large chunk that went to the casino and another large chunk that went to taxes is now being sent to my favorite women's health charity."

Her cheeky, playful tone has my lips twitching. She's in a good mood, the brightest I've seen her since she showed up at my house in Cambridge last night. I'd marry her every day just to see that smile on her red lips, and it's thoughts like this that I need to eradicate immediately.

She prances over to me, still in her wedding dress with her hair up and her heels on, and begins unloading dinner from the bags along with a bottle of red wine, a bottle of tequila, and a bottle of expensive bourbon.

I raise an eyebrow and she winks at me. "We're quasi-celebrating, right? I mean, that's how I'm trying to spin it in my mind. I didn't have to marry Ezra, and come Monday, Monroe will be mine. Besides, I didn't know what you were going to be in the mood for tonight."

You instantly slingshots through my mind, but I rapidly pull it back and ram it into the locked place in my head, where I seem to be collecting a lot of thoughts about her tonight.

I clear my throat. "I need your phone."

Without questioning me, Georgia hands me her phone, already unlocked. I text Alfie my link, and when I hand it back to her, she examines it.

"Another one of your phishing schemes."

"Social engineering is one of the easiest ways to penetrate. And you claim to know nothing about information security or hacking."

She snorts. "I *don't*. But everyone knows what phishing is, though I didn't know it was a form of social engineering, so there you go, I just learned something new." She reads what I wrote aloud. "Is this where you want me to meet you tomorrow?" Her eyebrows rise, and her green eyes find mine. "Where exactly am I supposed to meet him?"

"The lobby. But I don't want you to meet him, so it wouldn't have mattered if I had picked a random lab in China. Don't click the link, or it'll fuck up things I don't want fucked up."

"Alfie isn't a bad man," she tells me as she takes a seat at the table diagonally from me, a mountain of food between us. "He's nothing like Ezra, and I understand why he's upset. He's worried about me, and he's worried about Monroe."

"We'll see once I start digging into his secrets."

"Unethical. Beautiful. Dangerous."

"What's that?" I ask absently, returning to my laptop and entering the commands I need.

"You." The tone of her voice has me glancing up to find her studying me. "That's exactly what you are. A vigilante. A dark knight."

I feel my throat moving as I swallow.

She clears her throat and looks away, a small flush on her cheeks. "Anyway, Ezra has been blowing up my phone. He doesn't think we're the real deal or that you're serious about me. Can you imagine?" Her eyes widen in mock horror, and she puts a hand to her chest.

I smirk, shutting the screen of my laptop, removing my glasses, and opening up one of the containers of food.

"I'll get the wine then?" she mocks.

"If that's what you want."

"I got married today. I want wine, but I also *need* tequila."

I wipe at the smile on my lips. "Don't you need to not be hungover tomorrow?"

"I don't think a glass of wine and a shot of tequila will leave me hungover."

I can't argue with that, so I get up and go over to the bar inside the TV cabinet and pull a few glasses out—two wine, and two regular glasses—since, shockingly enough, there are no shot glasses here. Setting them down on the table, I twist off the top of the wine, pour us each a full glass, and then a shot and a half of tequila, because it seems I could use some as well.

Georgia raises her tequila glass to me. "Here's to lying, cheating, stealing, and drinking…If you're going to lie, lie for a friend. If you're going to cheat, cheat death. If you're going to steal, steal a heart. If you're going to drink, drink with me."

"Who said that?" I ask as I drink down my shot, watching as she does the same. She winces and blows out a heavy breath, but then licks her lips and does a little shudder that tells me she liked it.

She shrugs. "No clue, but we didn't make it up. It's what we used to say in nursing school when we'd all go out. That and please, God, don't let us kill anyone."

"Have you?"

"Not yet, but the night is young."

"And you are so lovely." I sit back down. "Do you love what you do?"

She pops the lid on her container and digs into her shrimp fra diavolo. It's been six years, but if you had blindfolded me and asked me what Georgia had ordered for herself, I would have told you that.

"I love what I do," she exclaims, her face lighting up in a way that has nothing to do with the food. "It's the absolute best. I miss it, and hopefully I'll be back to it now that this is taken care of. Do you love what you do? You weren't tattooing when I knew you. I mean, at least not professionally."

"I wasn't doing anything when you knew me other than killing time." While trying not to kill myself. I sip my wine before setting my glass down. "I love what I do. All of it."

"If I were brave enough, I'd want you to ink my skin."

My cock jumps in my slacks at the idea of inking her smooth, creamy skin. I dig into the creamy chicken pasta and salad she ordered for me because, clearly, she still remembers what I like too. The food is fucking fantastic and so is the wine, and I have a nice warmth running through my veins from the tequila and the view. The one I can't seem to remove my eyes from. The one with hair nearly the same color as the wine.

"What would you have me ink?" I ask after a quiet beat, no longer able to hold my curiosity back.

She shrugs, twirling spaghetti around on her fork and shoveling the bite into her mouth. "I have no clue. It's why I've never had anything done."

Her phone pings, and I don't have to look to know it's Alfie. I will have a full night of research and digging ahead of me. She frowns, sipping her wine. "Do I need to check that?"

"Not unless you want to."

"I don't. And I don't want to go back to my townhouse in LA," she whispers, spinning her glass between her hands and staring sightlessly out the large windows. "Ezra will be able to watch me there, and that makes me sick. Plus, even though my mom is there, I feel isolated. More vulnerable to him."

"We can have people pack it up for you or remove them from the scene. Whichever you prefer."

Absently, she shakes her head and returns to her food, going for a piece of shrimp. "That part of my life might be done, even though I love LA and California. I grew up in Boston and then returned for school. It feels as much like home to me as LA does, and I haven't had the chance to move back there until now."

I squint at her, finishing up the pasta and closing the lid on the to-go container. "Why?"

She shrugs, taking the last sip of her glass of wine. "My family wanted me to stay in LA, but now that doesn't seem like the best place for me."

"If it were your choice, where would you go?" I can't help but ask.

"I don't know." She pours herself more wine and leans back in her chair, bringing her glass with her. "That's part of my problem. It's difficult to figure out your life when so many people want a piece of it."

I swirl my glass and then finish it off, declining when she motions to pour me more. I don't drink a lot, and I think my reasons for that are fairly obvious. "If you go back to Boston, will you stay with Zax or Grey?"

"I doubt it. They're both about to get married, and I'd be a third wheel. Plus, I like my space and privacy. I'll likely buy a place or rent. If Ezra is having me followed though..." She gives an exaggerated shudder.

"You're safe, Georgie," I promise. "I won't let him hurt you."

Her eyes gleam with challenge. "Can you extend the same promise to yourself?"

My breath quickens, even as I say, "I have no intention of crossing lines with you."

"Hmm." She stands and walks over to the window. Her head rolls over her shoulder, and her eyes catch mine for a moment before she returns to the view. Mine haven't left her. "And yet, that's exactly what I want you to do. It's my wedding night. Who will believe a marriage that isn't consummated?"

"Georgia—"

My breath tumbles from my lungs as she reaches up into her hair and starts removing one pin at a time, setting each down on the table beside her. Thick, auburn locks fall in heavy, silky waves one by one until a full mane of red splashes down her back, a stark juxtaposition against her white dress.

And speaking of…

Her arms stretch and her hands search until they find the zipper high up on the back of her neck. My hands grip the table in front of me as she slowly starts to unzip her dress, her body framed perfectly against the window.

"What are you doing?" I grit out.

"Enticing my husband," she explains without so much as a glance. "You see, your law on the plane got me thinking, and I realized I haven't had sex in months. Well before my father died, actually. I couldn't stand Ezra touching me, so I rarely let him. Anyway, I'm in Vegas, and I got married today. Even though it's not real"—her head rolls again and she meets my eyes—"I think I want to pretend it is. Just for tonight. Just for now. And then tomorrow, it'll all go back to whatever it's supposed to be with us. Hate or simple antagonism or bland amicability. But I don't want to go the next year without having had sex in so long I'll forget what it feels like to have a man touch me."

My throat is dry and raw—likely from overuse since I don't recall ever talking as much in my thirty-one years as I did today—or more likely it's from the woman standing in the silhouette of the window. The glow of the Strip and flash of the fountain lights cascade over her skin as she lets her dress fall to reveal her white lingerie like a delicious invitation.

I need to say no.

I made promises. Serious promises. Promises I cannot go back on.

Does she have any clue how dangerous this is? How it's so much more than a thrill or a simple fuck? We're married now, and that immediately complicates this.

I can't have sex with her. My addiction is barely hanging on—a thin, fraying thread—and it's been one day. One fucking day. I promised I wouldn't do this. I swore I wouldn't cross this line. I need to be honorable. Worthy.

And I cannot betray my best friends—not again.

The dress is pooled at her feet, and she steps out of it and bends forward, treating me to a stunningly unholy view of her perfect ass in her tiny thong, the barest hint of her pussy peeking through beneath the lace. And speaking of lace, she's wearing a goddamn garter on her upper thigh. Something I want to snag with my teeth and pull roughly from her.

Her body... motherfuck. Her body is my living fantasy. Long lines and gorgeous curves in all the right places have my hands and mouth desperate to feel and taste them.

She sets the dress over a chair, and then, still in her heels, with her red hair flowing all around her and her green eyes deadly and locked on me, she saunters in my direction. Her full breasts overflow the confines of her minimal white lace bra, bouncing and enticing, fucking mouthwatering as she reaches the space between my legs.

Using her heeled foot, she kicks them wider and inserts herself between them.

"Help me out of these?" she whispers, hiking up one foot and planting it on the bench seat beside me, her knee spread wide, putting her pussy right fucking here in front of me.

Fucking temptress.

I take her foot in my hand, and with my eyes on hers, I unhook the clasp on her shoe, removing the heel and setting it aside. She switches feet, and I repeat the motion. And once she's barefoot, so small and delicate, my hands run up the backs of her legs, and I watch as goosebumps erupt across her skin.

"You can keep going. You can go all the way."

Was she ever this bold before? Yes, she was. Just in a different way. A more timid way. A way that was asking instead of taking but offering all the same.

I shake my head at her, and she smiles, her fingers running through my hair, her nails scraping my scalp, and I hum from the pleasure of it. She's not the only one who hasn't had sex in a while. When you don't talk a lot or trust people, or hell, even *like* people all that much, and live on the fringes of right versus wrong, sex is dangerous.

I think the last time I fucked someone was in the club Zax is still a member of because Aurelia likes to go there and play with him sometimes. But it was masked and anonymous, and this is not that. This is Georgia, and I need to say no.

But I want her too fucking badly. Even if it's just for tonight.

"No." I shake my head. "No, Georgia, we can't."

"Are you hard for me, Lenox?" she asks as she slips herself onto my lap and sets her pussy in her sheer thong straight over my throbbing cock. "Mmmm. Feels like you are." She rocks forward, pressing against me, and I die right here with her in my lap. Her body shifts around on me until her tits are right up against my chin, her head angled playfully, and her cherry lips smiling, because I'm not just hard for her, I'm fucking stone, and she likes it.

I reach up and cup her tits, lifting their swell and dipping my mouth down to them. "Was this your plan all along?"

She emits a breathy laugh as I sink my teeth into her lace-covered nipples, my hands sliding to her hips, holding her steady so she can't grind on my cock the way she's trying to.

"Not even close. Tell me you don't want it though."

I can't. I've wanted her every minute of every day for the last eight years. Even after I walked away from her, I wanted her. But that doesn't make it right, and it certainly doesn't mean I'm entitled to it after what I did to her.

"We shouldn't."

"It's just this one time," she whispers breathily, her head falling back and her hands going to my shoulders as I nip and lick and eat at her tits still partially kept from me in her bra. "Just to make the marriage official."

God. I can't say no. Not with her like this.

I grasp her wrists and yank them behind her back, thrusting her tits toward my face. "Did you forget how I do this?"

She shakes her head, her red tresses falling over her shoulders and framing her face, making her look like an angel ready to sin. "It's exactly what I want. Can you give me this, Lenox? Can you fuck me like a bride and a whore all at once?"

Christ. I'm so fucked now.

Chapter Ten

Georgia

IT'S BEEN the most ridiculous day. A day that started out with a long-ass flight and a panic attack and now has me sitting astride my fake husband's lap asking him to fuck me. After I took care of the winnings—also freaking crazy—and was waiting on dinner, I called my mother and told her about Lenox.

She wasn't happy I married him, but after I told her what Ezra had been up to, she relented. Some. I told her it was fake. I told her being married to him meant nothing because he doesn't have a heart, and I won't ever give him a shot at mine again. I won't say that being married to Lenox doesn't present its numerous challenges, but the relief coursing through me is too sweet to deny.

I know better than to believe Ezra and Alfie are done after the first round of strikes.

Only while I was speaking to her, I was struck with the *anger* of it all. With the manipulation of men. With them believing I'm some weak being here for their pilfering. My father was included in that.

Who puts a stipulation in a will that their daughter has to be married in order to inherit?

Fuck. That.

So I flipped the tables on them. I took matters into my own hands, and now I control the narrative of my life and choices. And that's what led me here.

I hadn't planned on seducing Lenox. I intended to go through our marriage like a nun, and I knew he was going to be the same.

He's not here to take advantage of me. He's here because he loves my cousins like brothers and has enough guilt about the past that he couldn't say no. He doesn't want my money. He doesn't want my company. In fact, he doesn't want to be anywhere near me.

And that gave me power. A power I hadn't realized I needed until I saw him sitting there drinking and eating dinner with me, wearing a wedding band he purchased on his left hand. For the first time since my father's plane went down, I feel light as a feather. Untethered and fucking free. I'm high on it, and I don't want this high to end.

Not yet.

Not when I'm craving more of it—almost as much as I'm craving the brutal way Lenox likes to dominate and fuck. He'll make it good for me. Of that, I have no doubt. Lenox is nothing if not generous in bed, but more than that, he likes watching me come whether it's on his mouth, fingers, or cock.

It was as much of a release for him as it was for me, and I think right now that's something we could both use.

Even if it's just tonight and means nothing more than that.

His blue eyes are darker than midnight, but I can see in them what's about to come next, and when he says my name, I know I'm not wrong. "Georgia—"

"Don't try to get rational with me, Lenox," I tell him, pushing against the resistance of his hands on my wrists and hip to rub myself up and down his pants over his straining cock. "I'm not some eighteen-year-old girl who is going to fall in love with you. We're both adults and can make this decision for ourselves. It's just us, and we agreed it's just tonight. I need you to fuck me, and I know you want to."

"Wanting to fuck you is more natural to me than breathing. It's you who has me——"

Abruptly, he cuts himself off there, as if he was about to say more than he wanted, and stares into my eyes, as if that shocked him. I don't push it because I don't want to know. It'll only poke at the scars he made if I do. I'd rather be able to move back to antagonistic or business-like after this.

Like at our wedding, like he can't help or stop himself, his lips spear down against mine, punctuated by a growl of frustration. His hand abandons my wrists in favor of diving into my hair while mine grip the black fabric of his shirt. He licks once, twice at the seam of my lips and forces me open when I resist. He grins against me because, even though I seduced him, I still want him to take from me, to force me just enough that I feel as though I'm not giving him anything he hasn't earned and I haven't fought to keep.

The velvet slide of his mouth is so familiar and yet entirely new as he splits my lips and delves in, his tongue immediately seeking mine out. I groan at the taste of him. At the way his hands fist my hair and run through the silky ends, giving them a firm tug that has me grinding down on him a bit harder.

He grunts into me, twisting my head the other way and switching his position, diving in deeper as he explores every inch of my mouth as if he can't get enough. Unlike our wedding kiss, there is no urgency, no frenzy, or how did this happen. The warm wetness of his tongue slides over mine as he inhales my every breath, tasting the wine, tequila, and spicy sauce on my lips. He finds the straps of my bra, running his fingers back and forth under them before letting them slip off my shoulders. The cups drop an inch, revealing the top part of my nipples, and he breaks the kiss so he can look for himself.

"You bought this today." It's not a question, but I nod, panting out air through my overused lungs. His gaze slides up to mine. "And you didn't plan for me to fuck you?"

I smirk and bite my lip, shaking my head. I'm not even being coquettish, more amused than anything at his expression. "No. It was my armor."

"Sexy fucking armor."

I fight my smile because I forgot this about him. I forgot he likes to talk and sort of narrate, and I remember realizing he only speaks when he's worked up about something, but since he rarely allows himself the emotional merit, he rarely talks. On nights he'd show up particularly out of sorts or broken, those were the nights he'd talk to me the most. He'd tell me things, things that floated in and out of his brain, and I took them in like a sponge, like a needy cat desperate for more of him in the form of his words.

This isn't emotional for him, but the endorphin rush is similar enough.

"And this?" He reaches down and snaps the garter on my thigh, making me jolt up and whimper at the zap of the elastic on my overheated skin.

"They talked me into it."

He makes a sarcastic noise, but I can tell he likes it. "Unhook this for me." He gives my bra strap a tug.

Without hesitation, I reach behind my back and unclasp my bra, allowing it to slip from my chest and arms and setting it down on the bench seat beside him. For a long moment, he's silent, staring at my chest.

"God, you're so beautiful you make it impossible to breathe." An incredulous head shake, and then his hands slide down my back and around my backside until they're almost cupping my pussy from behind. Without warning, he stands, taking me with him and forcing me to wrap my legs around his waist and my arms around his neck, though I know he won't drop me.

He walks us into the bedroom and sets me down on the bed, pressing his hand into my shoulder and forcing me down onto my back. He's standing in the valley of my thighs, still with his eyes roving every inch of me. In my next breath, he's back on me, eating at my mouth and sucking on my chin and throat. His body presses me down into the mattress, heavy and warm and so fucking good a wave of satisfaction rolls through me.

His hands are all over me, playing with my breasts, lifting them, touching them, toying with them, pinching my nipples. All the while, he devours my mouth like an animal. Lips and teeth and tongue. Like a man no longer in control when I doubt that's the case.

I reach for his shirt, starting at the top button and trying to work the rest, anxious to get to his skin, to be able to touch him the way he's touching me. I shudder out a pleased breath when I manage the last button and shuck it from his shoulders, dragging it down only to whimper in frustration. Biting my lip, he growls in protest as I force him back to free his stuck wrists caught on the cufflinks. He pries himself away, unhooking the cufflinks as he goes, dropping each heavy piece of metal on the nightstand with a thud before he slips off his shirt and tosses it on the floor.

His knee hits the mattress, one and then the other, his eyes locked on my lips—his wet and puffy from his kisses—and my breasts—swollen and heavy with hard pink peaks.

He positions himself at the head of the bed, sitting up against the headboard, his tattoos and nipple piercings a buffet for my eyes.

He runs a lazy finger along his bottom lip and says, "Roll over and crawl to me. Show me what a good, obedient girl my wife can be."

My panties flood so fast that not even Noah's Ark can save them.

I roll over onto my stomach, but when he motions toward my thong, I rise onto my knees and slide it down and off. I start on the garter next when he shakes his head.

I arch a brow. "Oh really? My husband wants me in nothing but a lacy garter?"

"It's your wedding night, Georgie. My bride deserves to feel like one."

I flip him off for, well, for all of that, and he grins, crooking his finger at me.

I lower my hands to the bed and start to crawl to him. More like prowl. An alley cat all attitude and tenacity until I get within striking distance, and he grabs my hips faster than I can anticipate and rolls us until I somehow end up straddling his face. My chin drops, and my eyes meet his, such a deep blue, they're nearly black.

He can't keep the smile from curling up his lips.

With his eyes still on mine, his tongue comes out and circles my clit before it slips lower and plunges straight up into me as deep as he can go.

"Ah!" I cry out, my head flying back, my back arching, and my eyes closing. My ass gets a solid smack, and then he's taking my hips and dragging me down onto his face. He buries his nose in me, inhaling deeply and making a noise that I don't think can be called human. His fingers dig brusingly into my hips as his tongue and lips make out with my clit. Deep kisses and hard licks that have me breathless in seconds.

He slides me back and forth, grinding me against his rough chin, feasting on me like a man possessed, and growling like an animal as he does. Swirls and deep fucks and noises that make my clit vibrate and my pussy leak.

Holy Christmas in Toledo, his mouth. His wicked, diabolical, *sinful* mouth. I can't remember the last time someone went down on—

Oh shit.

"Lenox," I moan, even as I try to regain control because he's sucking my clit into his mouth and using his tongue like a delicious weapon. "Do you think Ezra can hear us?"

In a flash, Lenox flips me over and gets right up in my face with a look that robs me of my breath. One hand meets my neck in a possessive clasp, and his other plunges two fingers straight inside me, all the way to his knuckles, until I'm moaning and whimpering at how deep his long, thick fingers can take me.

"You are not to have another man's name on your lips while I am inside of you." He starts pumping fast, furious, and without mercy. "Whether that's my tongue, my fingers, or my cock."

I can't even respond because I don't think I've ever been this turned on in my life, and I don't trust my words or my voice. They'll betray the maelstrom of all that just did to me, and I can't have that. Not when we're this and not anything else.

"Then fuck me so hard, yours is the only name I know," I challenge instead, quirking an eyebrow even as he rails me so hard and so good with his fingers that I'm a beat away from coming all over them. It's noisy and mind-twisting and I'm so wet, and then he's gone, sliding down my body and flicking the tip of his tongue all over my center. "Fuck!" I yell, grabbing his hair and ripping at it.

He blows cool air on my throbbing clit and uses his other hand to smack it, once, twice, three times, all the while he continues to thrust and thrust his fingers in and out of me, curling them, quirking them, blowing my absolute mind.

My back arches and my grip on his hair tightens as spasms start to build from within my core, intensifying until I'm a shaking, quivering mess of a woman. Until I'm screaming and ripping more of his hair and holding his mouth on my clit, *pleading* with him to never ever stop. My climax crawls up my spine and splinters me from the tips of my toes to the ends of my hair.

I don't know how loud or quiet I am. I might in fact be singing, but I'm also moaning, and words spill from my lips. Needy words. Begging words. Words along the lines of fuck me and give it to me now and I need you inside me and I want, I want, I want.

His tongue swirls one last lingering lick, making me whimper at how sensitive I am, only to whimper again when his fingers slide out of me. I manage to quirk open my eyes even as I lie here boneless in the center of the king-sized bed. He licks his fingers clean and then crawls up my body and kisses me again, holding the sides of my head. He kisses me for a few minutes as if he can't make himself stop while I catch my ragged breath.

"Don't move," he quips with an amused twist of his lips.

"Ha. Funny."

His body slips from mine, and he takes off his pants and boxer briefs—thank God.

"You're a midwife."

I choke on a deranged laugh. "Um. You don't have the right anatomy for that question."

He climbs back over me and bites my shoulder. "You were on the pill. Are you still?"

Oh. Right. That stuff. "No," I tell him. "But I do have an IUD, and yes, obviously I've been tested since I last had sex."

"Me too." He smacks my breast, watching it jiggle like it's the most fascinating thing in the world. "I need to show you something though."

Um. "Please tell me it's not medical."

He bites down hard on my nipple, making me yelp, and sits me up, giving me a firm tug and another smack to my other tit. Immediately when I sit up, I see what he's talking about. My jaw drops, and my mouth goes dry.

I count... one, two, three, four. Fuck. He has three barbells going through the underside of his cock and a ring through his tip. Four piercings. In his dick. In his large, thick, veiny, angry-looking dick. He definitely did not have those the last time he was inside me.

I blink and look up into his hooded eyes. "I'm assuming they feel better than they don't. For me, I mean, as I don't really care about your pleasure." I reach out and touch them, dragging my finger up through the thin skin covering the metal and even pushing on the side of a barbell to slide it.

His lips part, and he leans in to kiss me deep and ravenous as I continue to touch him. To play with his piercings because fuck, I don't want to stop. I drag my thumb up over the barbells and pull gently on the hoop, and a groan rips past his lungs and into my mouth. Suddenly, he's everywhere, pushing me down, flipping me over until I'm on my stomach, and then hoisting me up, forcing me on all fours.

His chest covers my back and his mouth hovers by my ear as he growls, "You tell me."

And then he plunges straight into me, all the way to the hilt. I cry out, because, yes, he is thick and long, but I can *feel* the metal. I can feel the barbells roll along my G-spot since he's taking me from behind, and I know that's no accident. The walls of my pussy contract and somehow manage to grow more sensitive than ever before, clenching and unclenching as they grip him.

"Fuck," he curses, his forehead falling between my shoulder blades. "Fuck, baby. How could I have forgotten how goddamn good your cunt feels?" He sighs a shaky breath. "Or maybe this is why I forced myself to forget."

His whole weight is on me as he slides almost all the way out and then thrusts all the way back in. My breath scrambles from my lungs as he starts to piston into me over and over, creating a grueling, punishing, almost cruel rhythm. With his body over mine like this, he controls my movements, how I take him, how deep he goes.

The friction is like nothing else, rooted deep from within me, awakening every nerve ending I'm comprised of both inside and out. I grind against him, my hands clawing at the bed linens, and all I can do is gasp and moan. I quake with how good this feels, my head bowing and my eyes closed as I absorb him pounding into me.

Rough teeth scrape along my spine, the flash of pain quickly followed by his soothing tongue as he licks up my back. His hand wraps around my neck, not cutting off my air but holding me, using it as leverage, as his possessive way to control how this goes. His other hand is on my hip, gripping the hell out of me.

My pussy feels swollen and tight around his thick, hard cock, but it's his piercings—the way they edge and simultaneously play with pain and pleasure—that are twisting up my mind, splintering my thoughts, and yet have me seeking more. Craving it so bad I can hardly stand it. I want him to fuck me until he's torn me apart. Until I experience a new kind of pleasure I never knew existed.

I arch against him and drop to my elbows, reaching back to rub my clit, needing the extra friction when he reaches down and snags my wrist, bending it behind me and stopping me. On my next breath, he's jerking me upright, grabbing my other hand, and pinning both of my wrists behind my back, trapping them between us in the manacle of his large hand.

"Mine," he grunts, tugging me back until I'm leaning against his chest and he can lock my arms between us. He releases me, and the hand that was on my hip slithers up to my breast, holding it firmly while his other hand goes to my clit.

He hasn't stopped fucking me. He hasn't even slowed to take a breath or change up the pace. But now the angle is different, less direct, and he's forced to pump up into me.

And hell… the way he does that rubs my front wall while his fingers work furiously on my clit.

"My kryptonite. You're so fucking sexy, Georgia." He licks a trail up my neck, but if I thought I was at his mercy before, that has nothing on me now. I'm his plaything. His toy. All I can do is shift my knees a little wider to give him better access to my clit, to let him slide into me a little deeper, go a little harder.

It's everything, and in a matter of seconds, I'm coming so hard my orgasm splinters through me, shredding me completely. I grind down on him, against his fingers, as my head falls back against his chest. A feral groan, low and rough tears from his lips as he slams into me, fucking me to the very brink of what I can take, and then he's coming too, his release filling me up and already leaking down onto my upper thighs.

His arms wrap around me, and we tumble down onto the bed, both of us panting for our lives as he holds me and tucks me against him, my back to his chest. "Don't move," he commands after a quiet moment and then he's up, going to the bathroom only to return with a cloth to clean me up. And when that's done, he pulls back the blankets and drags me under the covers, holding me in a way that naturally makes my traitorous heart thump in my chest.

His fingers glide along the curve of my hip, lulling me into an exhausted stupor. One where I don't allow any thoughts about what we just did to linger.

That is until I feel him stir behind me, his cock getting hard once more, and he whispers in my ear, "This time I'll make you feel like a bride."

And I wonder if once again, I'll live to regret him.

Chapter Eleven

Georgia

DAWN COMES LONG before I'm ready for it. Lenox and I had sex again in the bed and then moved to the shower for a third round before I passed out. I have no idea what he did after that. I didn't allow myself to do much more than climb into bed after brushing my teeth and fall asleep—something I know he doesn't do much of.

But when I wake up, I discover he's fast asleep beside me. On his side, with his eyelashes fluttering as if he's dreaming, his full, soft lips parted ever so slightly, he breathes in and out so quietly, you'd never know he was breathing if you didn't see the rise and fall of his chest.

I can't stay in this bed. I can't wait for him to wake up and still be here. We didn't talk about where he'd sleep, but I can't have him in the bed beside me for the rest of the trip.

Distance is paramount—especially after how epic last night was —so I slip out of bed, climb into gym clothes, and then sneak out of our suite, heading to the gym to take an early morning yoga class. The room is packed, and I take a spot in the corner, keeping my head down and my face averted.

No one gives a shit in LA. Everyone there is a celebrity, but here it's different, and the covert looks and hushed whispers I'm getting only add to my agitation. I only wish they had a punching bag or something I could take it out on. Despite the rough start, an hour later, I'm starting to feel like myself again. Like Georgia of old. Like I can manage all the things being thrown at me, and with that, I can turn a new page and start a new chapter of my life.

After the class, I head into the lobby, covered in sweat, and get in line at Starbucks so I can order myself a Venti Americano and Lenox… fuck. I have no clue what Lenox drinks because we so rarely did the morning-after thing. I order him the same thing as me, along with a double shot of espresso, thinking that must be the drink of hackers everywhere.

While I wait, I stand off to the side, aimlessly scrolling through my Instagram, only to groan when I come across a video of Lenox winning the ten million dollars. Thankfully there is a comment about how we donated the money to charity, but it's definitely showing me, and it's definitely showing Lenox. By some mercy, it doesn't mention anything about a wedding or us being together as a couple.

I want to put that off as long as possible.

I'm just about to like the video when a shadowy figure looms tall over me. Turning, I find Alfie wearing his standard power suit—dark pinstripe, white shirt, navy tie—and an impatient expression. Alfie is giving the welcome speech this morning before the departmental heads take their turns. Spouses aren't supposed to attend the all-hands meetings today, but since I owe Lenox, if he wants, I'm going to let him listen in.

"This is not where we agreed to meet. I've been waiting for you for over half an hour."

Oh. I completely forgot about his texts after Lenox sent him that link, and well, all the sex after.

"I'm sorry. It slipped my mind, and yoga ran longer than I thought. Do you want a coffee?"

"Georgia!" the guy behind the counter shouts, and I go over and grab the cardboard tray, lifting mine out and taking a sip. I'm going to need this more than I thought.

"I've already had mine," he hisses in displeasure. "Can we go somewhere and talk privately?"

"Of course."

He starts walking along the corridor, glancing around, and then heads over to the high-stakes slot room that is empty at this early hour.

"Georgia, what on earth is going on?" he starts without any preamble. "Please tell me you didn't actually marry the Neanderthal, and if you did, tell me you have a prenup bigger than Texas."

I set the tray of coffee down on the floor beside my feet, still holding mine in my hands. "Yes, I actually married Lenox. He's not a Neanderthal. He's someone I've loved for a very long time." Not a total lie per se, just a bit of a stretch of the truth. "And yes, we have a prenup. He signed it without hesitation and made no amendments. He gets nothing out of this other than me."

Alfie sighs, his rigid posture slacking. "I don't like it, Georgia. Your father would like it even less."

I stare down at the plastic lid of my coffee. "I couldn't marry Ezra. I told you this. I told him this. But none of you would listen."

"Marrying Ezra is how this company stays together. It's how it grows. It's how we ensure it's a family company without any outside interference because your children would one day be the largest owners with my ten percent and your fifty-four. Don't you see that? Don't you see the power of that? The necessity for Monroe?"

When he puts it like that, it makes me feel selfish and self-centered, but then I think about Ezra. About what our relationship was like and how he was treating me. About the fact that he's having me followed and was blatantly using me. Who's to say Alfie isn't doing the same thing under the guise of fatherly love and concern?

I lift my chin. "It will stay in the family. My fifty-four percent aren't going anywhere, and I will continue as chairwoman of the board."

"We had an arrangement, Georgia. You signed the contract.

You marry Ezra and inherit the fifty-four percent and our families tie together, securing ownership of Monroe Securities for future generations. Everyone gets what they want."

"Except for me," I state clearly. "What was I getting out of this other than being used as a pawn by all of you?"

"How about your wealth, security, and comfort? How about the security of your father's company? Is that not good enough for you?" He curses under his breath and runs a hand through his slicked-back hair, trying to rein himself in. "Christ, Georgia. Couldn't you at least have tried with Ezra? I get it, sometimes marriages don't work out, but you could have tried."

"I did try. I tried a lot."

"I told you I'd talk to him for you. That I'd get him to be less..."

"Controlling, manipulative, stalkerish," I finish for him, and he sighs again, this time harder. I wonder if this is how he was with his wife. She was a quiet, sweet woman who ended up losing control of her car and going off the side of a cliff into the Pacific about ten years ago. He never remarried or dated after her, as far as I know.

"He just loves you and felt you slipping through his fingers. Please, divorce this Lenox person and marry Ezra. For us. For Monroe."

"The irony is, I never wanted the money. All I've ever wanted is a normal life. Something all of you have tried to take away from me time and time again. Marrying Ezra meant giving up my career and my freedom. It meant dealing with his controlling ways. No thanks. The only contract I ever signed was a prenup. My father's will never stipulated who I marry, just that in order to inherit the shares, I have to be married." I shrug nonchalantly. "So I got married. Problem solved."

He takes a deep breath, but his composure is slipping. "You will get an annulment or a divorce. Whichever is fastest. Then you will marry Ezra as your father wanted."

It's interesting... he's the CEO of the company now, earning plenty of money, not to mention the ten percent of Monroe he already owns. Is this just about money or power or even controlling

Monroe? Or is this about something else? Something deeper? Something more dangerous than what meets the eye?

"No. I'm sorry, Alfie, because you've always been like a second father to me, but I won't be doing that. I will never marry Ezra. I don't know why my father was so adamant that I marry him, but it doesn't matter now. I'm married to Lenox. And there is nothing you can do now to change that."

"Don't be a fool, Georgia. Your wall of dumb muscle might have been smart enough to sign the prenup, but that doesn't mean he isn't only with you for the money and is easily swayed by greedy things."

I smirk. "Don't be a fool, Alfie. Lenox Moore is a hell of a lot more than dumb muscle and doesn't give a shit about my money. You might want to do your homework and learn how he's connected to me before you start speaking about things you know nothing about." I pick up the coffee from the floor and walk off, so very done with him and this conversation. "You know what we women hate most about you men? How you think you have the right to be high-handed and judgmental over our choices. News-flash: You don't. I'm married to Lenox, and that's final."

There isn't anything he can do now.

After I speak to the attorney and my father's financial company, I'll own fifty-four percent of Monroe Securities. And while I have no intention of actually running the company, I also have no intention of letting it go either. Certainly not to Alfie and Ezra and their greedy things. It's funny or not so much, all I've ever wanted was a simple, quiet life. And the only time I've ever had anything remotely close was in college and graduate school.

Before that, my mother thrust me into Hollywood, making me a child star, and now all of this.

I knew I was going to have to face their ire. But truly, it's done now, and they'll simply have to learn to live with it. That thought floats me up the elevator and down the long hall toward the suite as a smile quirks up my lips. I go to take a sip of my now-tepid coffee, just as a strong hand snatches my arm and slams me up against the door of the room next to mine. The coffee goes tumbling from my hand, spilling most of it down the front of my yoga shirt before landing on the carpet and splattering everywhere. And while I was annoyed it wasn't hot before, I'm beyond grateful it's not now.

"What the fuck, Ezra?!" I shove him back, using the cardboard carrier and coffee that's still in my other hand to create some distance between us, hoping some of it spills on him in the process. "This is getting way out of hand."

"Out of hand?" he snaps, grabbing the coffees and setting them down on the floor. "I haven't seen you or spoken to you in over a week, Georgia, and I was looking forward to seeing you here so we could work this out between us, and then not only do you show up fucking married, but I have to listen to you fucking him all night?"

That last part is a bit of an oops, and it wasn't intentional. And now that I get a better look at him, he does appear as though he didn't get a lot of sleep. Still, he always liked making me look like the crazy, irrational one. Like, he wasn't being overbearing or controlling, but rather attentive and concerned for my safety. Like, he wasn't being isolating, he just wanted me all to himself. Like, he didn't want me financially dependent on him, he just didn't want me to work so he could take care of me.

If our relationship hadn't all but been arranged and I had been blinded by love, I might not have seen the warning signs. Possibly not until it was too late.

"I don't know what you want me to say. We broke up months ago, and I've repeatedly told you we have nothing left to discuss with that."

His hands fly around him. "Bullshit. We have everything to talk about. Goddammit, Georgia. How could you marry him?"

Because I don't want him to be able to state marriage fraud or try and contest it, I say, "Lenox and I reconnected shortly after I ended it with you and have been talking since. I love him. I always have." If I was still the Georgia of six years ago, that wouldn't even be a lie.

He grips my shoulders and gets right up in my face. "You know he doesn't love you, right? That he's using you."

"There is this saying about stones and glass houses and also black pots and kettles. Are you familiar with them? Maybe you can remind me exactly how they go."

His hand slides up along my cheek, and he stares into my eyes. "That's not how it was for me. I *wanted* to marry you."

My hands plant into his chest and I push him off me. "You wanted to own me. You wanted to suffocate the life out of me until all I knew was you. But more than that, you wanted my money, and you wanted Monroe."

He growls, running a hand through his hair and making it stick up all over the place from all the product he has in it. "And all he wants to do is fuck you and take your money!" he shouts. "Jesus, Georgia, use your brain and see what's right in front of you. At least I'm trying to grow our empire. Marrying me makes sense. There is no sense in marrying him."

Except for the freedom it gives me from you and this life.

"I love him, and it's done. There is nothing you can do about it now."

Something about that, as if he just finally realized it's done and he won't win this battle, sets him off. He starts to charge at me, mania dancing in his brown eyes, and I react the same way I would to a predator coming to attack me in a dark alley. Years of martial arts tell me to take him down, and I do so the fastest way possible. The second he reaches me with his hands outstretched like he's going to pin me, I strike. My knee flies up, and I nail him straight in the balls, my fists at the ready should I need to punch him.

His face puffs up like a red blowfish, and he grunts as he falls to the carpet in a heap just as the door to my suite flies open and there is Lenox wearing nothing but a towel around his waist, his hair wet and unbrushed like he just got out of the shower and heard the commotion.

"Morning, darling," I drawl, trying to ignore how freaking hot he looks like that. Hello, wet skin, tattoos, and nipple rings. "Glad to see you're finally awake." I smile brightly at him, and his gaze drops to the man on the floor, still groaning and holding his junk as he snarls out expletives. "I'm starving, and since most of my coffee ended up on my shirt instead of in my stomach, I'd love to—"

Lenox cuts off my words as he grabs me by my upper arm and swings me inside the suite, slamming the door shut on Ezra. He drags me into the living room and releases me, doing a long, sweeping once-over of me as if he's checking for injuries.

"Did he hurt you?"

I shake my head.

"Did he touch you?"

"He got handsy but not aggressive so much until the end. I wasn't sure what he was going to do, so I took a proactive approach."

He nods, pleased with this, but then, before I know what the hell he's doing, he spins around and storms back for the door. I scramble after him, grabbing his arm.

"What are you doing?"

"You didn't kill him, Georgia. I'm going to kill him."

"What?!" I laugh the word. "No. Stop." I jump in front of him and press my hands into the giant wall of muscle that is his chest. I push against him, but he keeps walking, and even though I'm leaning all my body weight into him, digging into the floor with the balls of my feet for extra leverage, he keeps going, pushing me along as if I'm barely a hindrance. "Oh my God, Thor, stop! You can't kill him!" My feet slide back along the carpet. "He's not worth the jail time."

And since Ezra *is* the sort of man who would press charges, I take matters into my own hands. Twisting my body, I plant my left foot into the carpet and drop into a crouch, sweeping my right leg in a fan motion as fast and as hard as I can—because, let's face it, Lenox is a big guy—straight into the backs of his legs. His legs swoosh out from beneath him—the leg sweep far more effective than I thought it would be on him—and he goes crashing down to the floor, landing with a hard thud on his back.

"Holy hell! That's two I brought down today." I climb on top of him, straddling his chest so he doesn't get any ideas to try and go for Ezra again. "Are you okay? Can you breathe?" I'm worried I knocked the wind out of him.

He's staring up toward the ceiling, stunned.

"Blink if you can hear me."

He blinks.

I sag. "Oh good. Sorry, I didn't think that would work as well as it did. Twenty years of martial arts has officially paid off today." I high-five the air but can't help but start to crack up.

His chin drops, and his bewildered blue eyes meet mine. "How did you do that?"

I shrug. "Legit, no clue. You're like twice the size of me. But how cool is it that it worked? Anyway, as I was saying before you decided you wanted to kill my ex, I'm already done with all things Monroe Securities for the day after dealing with two of their finest. And since the coffee didn't make it anywhere other than my shirt, we should go out for breakfast." I pull my coffee-soaked shirt away from my chest for emphasis. "The conference starts in like an hour, but whatever, I can be late or play hooky. I own the company now. It's not like they can ground me or put me in a time-out for ditching."

"You okay?"

"Dandy as a peach tree in the rain."

He raises his eyebrows at me but gives me a look that tells me he wants a real answer.

"I don't know what I am. I'm a lot, I think."

"That's for sure."

In a flash, he rolls us until he has me pinned beneath him, his forearms on either side of my head and his body pushes down on mine without putting the full force of his weight on me. With him like this, so close and only wearing a towel with his body heat surrounding me, and smelling like the shower and like Lenox, it's nearly impossible not to squirm.

Or wrap my thighs around his waist and grind myself to an orgasm for that matter.

My heart races at the idea and I wonder if he can feel it through my thin sports bra and soaked shirt. My nipples are certainly hard, but I can blame that on the coffee perking them up.

"I don't like him touching you."

"He won't again."

He licks his lips, and my eyes naturally track the motion. "I would have ripped him apart. No one puts their hands on my wife."

Swoon! Bastard. I frown. Because yeah, he made me swoon. Even in jest, which I'm positive that's what that was. "Unnecessary. Clearly. I took him by the balls. Literally."

His lips bounce. "Are we okay?"

I force my gaze back to up his because, I realize a fraction too late, I've still been staring at his mouth longer than I should be. "You mean because I physically took you down to the ground or because last night you fucked me six ways to Jesus?" And once again, I have a nervous mouth that doesn't know the meaning of limits.

His blue eyes smolder, and his mouth twists to the side in a hint of a smirk without actually smiling. "Is that what I did?"

I'm having palpitations. "It's what I did too."

"Then I guess I'm wondering about both."

"If you're asking if I still don't like you, the answer is yes. Does that help?"

"That was the answer I was hoping for."

He grinds into me, and I gasp at the feel of his hard cock, only covered by a measly white towel. He winks devilishly and pops up off me—thank God, right?—and extends his hand to help me up.

"Give me fifteen to shower, and then I want a Vegas-style buffet. One not in this hotel," I say as I pull off my coffee-soaked sports shirt and toss it toward the corner of the room where my suitcases are sitting. I shut the bathroom door behind me and start the shower, ready to wash off a night of sex followed by a morning of yoga, coffee, and assholes.

After I do all that, I change into late-fall in Vegas attire—with an elastic waist because I do want that buffet—and then find Lenox dressed in a blue T-shirt that makes his eyes more vivid than the summer sky and low-slung dark jeans working on his laptop from the couch.

"He hires gatekeepers," he tells me, and my brows furrow. Lenox rises off the sofa and puts his laptop thing in the safe, punches in a code, and then immediately heads for the door, holding it open for me to pass through. Ezra is long gone, but I expected him to be by this point.

"Who are you talking about, and what is a gatekeeper?"

He points to the floor, where Ezra's body was last seen. "I was right about his open source, and with him next door, I went into his laptop. Gatekeepers are people who protect personal systems."

I shrug as we step onto the elevator. "Is that unordinary? He is the COO of a cybersecurity company."

"Do you do that? As the owner and the daughter of one?"

My head bounces to the side. "No."

"No. Only people with something to hide protect their assets, and there is nothing more valuable than information."

"So he's protecting himself. Does that mean you can't hack it?"

Lenox takes my hand, playing the part of my husband as we step into the lobby. "I can hack anything. I just don't want him or his cronies to know someone is doing it. *That's* what will take a bit more time. I have a feeling Alfie will be even more fun to sort through. He's smarter than his son."

"Have fun and all that. If only you allowed me to pay you for your hacking or husband services, this arrangement wouldn't be so one-sided."

He twists until his eyes meet mine, the outside Las Vegas sun hitting his back through the glass doors, creating a halo around him. An angel with the devil's intent.

"I'm paying off a debt I owe to you and your cousins. Think of it that way."

"I don't care what you think you owe them. It's me you have to deal with."

His eyes search my face. "Dealing with you is only half the battle."

I smile up at him, batting my eyelashes playfully. "I never said I'd make it easy for you."

"You're too beautiful, Georgia. I'm not supposed to think that way about you. This is a fake marriage, but when you smile up at me like that and the sun hits you just right, I start to think about last night and all the ways I want you, and that can't happen again."

Oh. I flush. And then obviously want to keep looking exactly like this forever, but that's not going to be helpful for anyone. He's not alone in that. A woman could easily grow addicted to the way he looks at them and how his hands and tongue can't seem to get enough of their body.

"It won't, so you don't have to worry. What happens in Vegas…" I trail off, and he's utterly unamused. "Will always stay here and never travel."

"I can't go down that road with you again."

I look away, hurt flashing like a flood through me. He means the road where I fell head over heels for him and he felt nothing for me. The road where he betrayed his best friends because he liked the sex and wasn't in the best of mental places.

I turn back to him, all traces of my smile now washed away. "Agreed. Never again," I tell him with an assurance I feel down to the marrow of my bones. "So stop worrying all hell is about to break loose."

Except the moment we step outside, all hell does break loose.

Chapter Twelve

Lenox

YOU KNOW that scene in *Christmas Vacation* when all the cops come swarming in, breaking through windows and doors, and taking down that giant Christmas tree only to leave Mrs. Griswold holding poor Clark's nuts? Yeah, that feels like me right now.

Only it's not the cops swarming us, it's the press. And Georgia unfortunately is not holding my dick, just my nipple. To the point where I'm tempted to groan and need to smack her hand away because she's pinching it and my nipple ring.

But what in the almighty fuck is going on?

"Georgia! Lenox! Over here!" *Click, click, click.* "How long have you secretly been together? Do Zaxton and Greyson know you're married? Why didn't they attend the wedding?"

Questions fire at us one after the other, cameras and phones shoved in our faces. We're completely surrounded, unable to see anything past the mass of bodies. On instinct, I wrap my arm protectively around her—clearly, I lied when I told her I wasn't a bodyguard—tucking her into my side and crisply walking us forward. To where I have no clue, but I don't care. Just as long as I get us out of here.

"Georgia, what does this mean for Ezra? Were you having an affair with Lenox behind his back? Lenox, were you really a virgin when you married Georgia?"

Virgin? I trip on that last one but don't stop moving, familiar enough with the whole paparazzi routine to keep my features neutral and void of reaction. Security comes flying out of the hotel, and somehow I'm being directed to a limo like we're living out some cliché Hollywood movie.

Which I suppose we are since I'm married to Hollywood's former sweetheart.

The door opens, and I shove Georgia in first, climbing in beside her and slamming the door shut behind us. The car slowly inches out of the driveway, pushing past the throngs of press and somehow hitting the light just right and taking a quick left.

"Where would you like me to take you, sir? Ma'am?" the driver asks quietly from the front.

"Anywhere private where we can be alone would be great," Georgia states breathlessly, and the driver gives her a thumbs-up before raising the partition. She pivots to me, her face twisted in fury. "Freaking vultures," she hisses. "I'm so sorry. I had no idea this would happen this soon. I assumed once the press learned of our marriage, they'd go a bit nuts, but I figured that would be on me and happen in LA or even if I moved to Boston." She places a palm over her racing heart.

I lean over and whisper in her ear, "Virgin?"

She coughs out a laugh. "It was the wedding planner," she murmurs contritely. "The one who was fangirling all over you. After you ran out of the chapel, I was… flustered and, well, not thinking all that clearly obviously because somehow it just slipped out that you were a virgin, though it didn't make any sense, but it did make me laugh, and that was exactly what I needed in that moment. I can't believe that woman sold you out like that," she mocks in feigned horror. "She's your biggest fan."

I stare balefully at her.

"If it's any consolation, you were great for your first time." She pats my shoulder and then falls forward, covering her face with her hands and pressing them into her knees. "Just when I thought I was out, they pull me back in."

"Is this a *Godfather III* moment?"

"The press hasn't bothered me much over the last few weeks. Not since the investigation for my father's plane concluded. I was hoping it was finally starting to die down, and now *they're baaack.* Ugh. Now I'm quoting *Poltergeist II.* I guess it's all about the sequels with us, isn't it?"

I laugh at that. I can't help it. She's right.

Her head pops up, her red hair wild and all over the place. "It's been a day, and it's not even ten. Between Alfie and Ezra and now this, I've had enough."

"You verbally sparred with one man and dropped two others to the ground, and *now* you're going to give up? Where did all that cute Georgie tenacity go?"

She jabs my flank as she does every time I call her that, but I have to imagine it was also because I tauntingly called her tenacity cute.

Still, she doesn't skip a beat. "You're right. I'm tenacious as fuck. I have a vagina of steel."

I cough out a laugh. "Vagina of steel?"

She rolls her eyes. "Um. Yeah. You felt her last night. My girl is strong and doesn't mess around. Men aren't the only ones entitled to genitalia of steel. That's sexist and simply wrong."

If it wouldn't get me in trouble, I'd kiss the hell out of her right now. Because even though I was teasing her, she's irresistibly cute.

The car stops drawing my attention out the window. We're in a parking lot, but before I can ask where we are or what we're doing, the driver says, "Give me a few minutes. I'll be right back."

He steps out, and then it's just me and Georgia in the back of a dark, quiet car. After the anxiety and adrenaline of the morning with Ezra, her tackling me to the floor like a fucking ninja, and the press after that, the quiet is too much. Everything is amplified. Like the smell of her still-damp hair and the sweetness of her skin. The sound of her breathing, still slightly accelerated from the press—or perhaps from something else.

I shouldn't have fucked her last night. I knew it then, but it's worse now because all I can think about is doing it again.

I can't. And I won't. But hell, why does everything about her have to be so alluring?

Like magnets, her lips demand my attention, and the moment I focus on them, images of last night flicker through my head. She passed out somewhere near two, and instead of going to my computer to work the way I told myself I would, I found myself crawling in bed behind her, running my fingers through her hair, and watching her sleep like a goddamn creeper.

I assuaged myself by saying this would be my last shot ever to do that. It had been one of my favorite things to do with her—a soothing balm to my ravaged thoughts—and I couldn't pass it up. But with it came… familiar thoughts. Familiar thoughts about her.

Familiar thoughts I cannot be having about my wife.

But then I did the unthinkable. I fell asleep beside her and slept better than I have in I don't even know how long. I woke alone—grateful for that—showered, and then everything else happened. I'm in this to protect her from those assholes, and yet I haven't sorted through Alfie's information. I haven't started my attack strategy though I'm positive they're already working on theirs.

I'm failing her—again—and it's more than I can take.

Thankfully she's still too worked up to notice where my mind is. "You must be regretting this," she says softly, dejectedly. "I pretty much turned your life upside down. I've brought a man, possibly two, into your life who won't hesitate with threats or bribery. The press knows about the wedding, and…" she trails off, once again feeling too many feelings.

"Asked if I was a virgin," I finish for her.

She winces, even if she can't stop the resulting giggle. "Yes."

Her eyes flicker to mine—the most gorgeous fucking eyes I've ever seen—and the fact that I'd do anything, even speak, and inten-tionally be sarcastic to get her to laugh is troubling.

"I feel like I'm underwater, and no matter how hard I swim or how visible the surface is, I can never reach it to take a breath. There is always something dragging me back down."

Without thinking, I take her hand, intertwining our fingers, and bring the back of her hand to my chest. Our rings flash in the muted sunlight shining through the tinted windows. A man knows he's fucked when he can't stop watching or thinking about a woman, and I can't stop watching or thinking about my wife. The woman who hates me because all I've done is disappoint and hurt her.

"Isn't that why I'm here? To help you reach the surface and finally be able to take that breath?"

I stare at our joined hands, pressed against my chest, right over my heart, and slowly my gaze rolls up to hers. She's watching me, caution in her brow yet with a look that makes my lungs feel like they're burning. My problem is—and has always been—I find her inexorably perfect. In all the things she does. Even her pain and sorrow make me hard, because all I want to do is fix them. But what kind of man gets off on something like that?

I'm not the hero of her story. It's not a title I'm deserving of. I'm not sure I'm even worthy of being her dark knight. But God, does she make me want to change that. Everything about Georgia Monroe makes me want to strive to be a better version of myself for her, and for the last six years, that's all I've done.

I stop short, cutting my useless thoughts off with a goddamn butcher's knife, my breath suddenly coming out in harsh pants.

It's not until the back door opens, letting in a stream of blinding light and cool air, that I realize how close I am to her. My face is right up in hers, our lips inches apart, and I jerk back.

A spike of restlessness flares through me. I need to get a grip on myself.

Thankfully Georgia steps out of the car, her curiosity about where we are taking over, and I hear her squeal as I step out.

She points up. "Look!"

I don't have to look. I know exactly where we are, and it automatically makes me suspicious.

"I've always wanted to go on this."

She treats me to an enthusiastically bright smile, and considering the morning she's had, that's saying something.

"Thank you! This is perfect!" She throws her arms around the driver who immediately blushes.

"Of course, ma'am. Here, sir." The driver hands me two tickets. "Just tell them that you belong to Paulo. I'll be here waiting for you after."

I nod at him, reaching out and shaking his hand.

My fingers thread with Georgia's, and I take us on the escalator and up to the entrance of High Roller, always keeping her behind me even as we approach the line and the woman up front, where I relay the message about belonging to Paulo.

"This way, please." She unclips a chain and brings us up to the front, holding the line back. I tug Georgia in front of me, keeping my back to the crowd waiting behind us, and when the next car stops, she waves us on. "All for you."

I push Georgia over to one of the benches until she's seated, and the doors start to slide closed. I continue to stand, obscuring any view of her through the glass.

"It feels crazy having this whole booth to ourselves." Georgia's hands pan around the vast pod. "It looks like it could accommodate a few more dozen people."

"You asked for privacy. In Las Vegas, this is probably the closest you'll get." Even if it's far from private.

"Truth."

The car starts to move, slowly carrying us up and over Las Vegas. The sun shines brightly through the glass as the screens overhead flash with ads for various Vegas attractions, and a voice comes through a loudspeaker telling us about the rules, including that we're not allowed to smoke.

"Dammit, I guess I can't light my blunt in here."

I smirk and take the bench seat opposite her. "Have you ever smoked weed?"

"Once," she tells me. "I was sixteen at a Hollywood party, and people were passing joints around. I took a few hits, hacked out a lung, and that was that."

"Such a naughty thing for such a good girl to do."

She rolls her eyes at me.

"They have other things now. Edibles."

Her eyebrows bounce. "Do you do them often?"

I shrug. "No. But if it's been too long since I've slept, sometimes I'll eat one to get myself over the hurdle."

"Such a pristine thing for such a bad boy to do," she mocks. "You slept last night."

I don't bother responding.

"Are we going to talk about this morning?" she asks.

I wait her out, curious if she'll mention my reaction. I don't normally physically react to situations. I don't have to. My size intimidates, and my quietness makes people uneasy and uncertain. But when she said he got handsy with her and she wasn't sure if he was going to hurt her or not, I snapped. And if she hadn't brought me to the ground and climbed on top of me, I would have found him and showed him exactly what happens when people touch things that don't belong to them.

"Not here."

She plows past my warning and gives me a warning of her own. "They're not done with us. For everything you're doing, they're trying to do it back."

I fold my arms and extend my legs out into the open space between us. She has no real semblance of who I am or what I'm capable of. She views me as a hacker, someone who can break into a system or a phone and play around. Her notions of that are anecdotal—as in what she's read in books or magazines or seen in Hollywood films and television. I didn't get into computers or even hacking when I was a teenager or going to college the way most do. I also don't need to live in an empty apartment, wear all black with a permanent hoodie over my head, cover my face with a mask, or walk around with either no ID or six fake ones.

There's a reason behind that.

But this isn't the place for that reassurance.

"I'm sorry," she says again, her gaze scrolling over me. "You're dragged into the middle of this."

She's tried to warn me about this a few times, but that's simply because Georgia worries I'm going to run the first chance I get or fire at her that I had no clue what I was getting into with this. But the truth is, she's distrustful of me with good reason. I walked away from her in the past and have no perceptible skin in this game other than my guilt over being a shitty friend and breaking her heart six years ago. She doesn't need to know the other reason why I'm here. It won't help either of us.

I simply stare at her. "We're married, baby. It's all going to be fine."

She shakes her head at my partially mocking tone, her teeth working her bottom lip in a way that makes me jealous of her teeth. "I don't know what comes next," she states, an air of defeat and uncertainty in her voice. "I was hoping this would be the end, but it somehow feels like I'm back at the beginning again."

Vegas and the mountains in the distance bloom around us, and she rises from her seat, walks over to the glass, and peers out at the obscurity and contradiction that is Las Vegas. Flashing lights against sprawling nature. I don't answer her. Not only is she not interested in a response, but my phone rings, cutting off any need for one.

I slip my phone out and glance up and around the booth. Then I answer. "We're stealing a moment together on the High Roller."

Zax clears his throat. "You're with Georgia? I tried calling her, and she didn't answer."

"I am. I'll put you on speaker, but remember what I said." Meaning there are cameras and possibly audio that could be accessed by anyone, and it's far from secure.

I set the phone down on the seat beside me, and Zax's aggravated growl comes through. "Your phone is off, Georgia."

Her eyes snap wide and she digs through her purse. "Right. Sorry. I shut it off after the press bombarded us." She holds the button on her phone. "Back on now. Happy?"

"Georgia!" Aurelia's screech comes through the phone, making Georgia laugh. "Zax was worried, but I'm planning. When do you both come to Boston next?"

Georgia crosses the pod and takes the seat on the other side of my phone. "I don't know," she says, her voice changing its tone. "It was supposed to be Tuesday, but... I don't want to stay here anymore, and I don't see why I need to."

"Fabulous. Zax is sending the Monroe plane to bring you both home." I watch as Georgia tenses at the word plane. "We don't want you flying commercial after this morning. Your pretty faces are all over the internet."

Georgia shakes her head in annoyed aggravation but doesn't say anything about the plane. "I'm supposed to stay here for the rest of the conference. I'm already ditching out this morning."

"I think this is more important, and while I know Monroe Securities is very important to you, what are you actually missing there? I think it's better if you're back here with us right now, given everything we're starting to learn."

She sighs. She knows Zax has a point. One I'm inclined to agree with. Georgia isn't a quitter. She is loyal beyond words, but right now, it's just not safe for her to be around Ezra, or likely even Alfie, with how he's coming down on her.

"Fine," she relents. "We'll fly home."

"Excellent!" Aurelia chirps. "Then we're planning your wedding party."

I groan but release an indulgent smirk all the same. I should have anticipated this. It is Aurelia, after all.

"Our wedding party?" Georgia parrots, her attention drawing up to me.

"It'll just be family, as in *our* family, but I think it's important to celebrate this together. Don't you?"

Oh, Aurelia. So clever. I trust four people in this world without question, but their women are next tier on that scale.

"Yes. I agree," I say. "I think there's a lot to *celebrate* right now. When does the plane arrive?"

"Three hours. It's already en route," Zax answers, and I can tell by his tone, he's not happy. I mean, he's rarely happy—that's just Zax—but he's overwrought with this situation. He's the protective big brother, but right now he's forced to take a back seat and let me lead. Which hits me with a fresh wave of guilt over last night.

I broke my promise to him. And I'm breaking another by keeping it a secret.

Georgia is blinking at me, her brow furrowed ever so slightly as she starts to pick up on the tone and sub-context of the conversation. I shoot my gaze up toward the cameras in the corner, and when she realizes her blunder, her eyes close and her breath stalls. When she reopens her eyes, they're bright and dazzling—a happy princess, a perfect actress.

"Great!" she exalts, leaning forward and kissing my cheek. "I know we did this on a whim, but the idea of actually celebrating with you is just everything."

"Fabulous," Aurelia exclaims. "I'm on it. I have the perfect dress for you. I can't wait. We'll see you soon."

"See you soon."

I disconnect the call, and without thinking, drag Georgia onto my lap, holding her body firmly against me. My intent is to whisper in her ear while appearing as a couple in love to the cameras. Only my body doesn't catch up fast enough that this is meant to be fake. It's in full-on Georgia is in our lap mode.

I shove it down and whisper, "Wrap your arms around me."

She does immediately.

"I am going to dig into all things Earnhart," I whisper. "I will take care of them. I promise. You are not to worry about them anymore, but if or when they reach out to you, remember, you have to tell me or show me everything."

She nods against me. Even gives a small shudder as my breath fans against her ear and neck. Again, I shove that down or I'll be hard beneath her sweet ass in a second, and I can't do that. Last night is over and will stay in Vegas, where it belongs.

"I will have trouble not worrying about this," she says quietly.

"Do you trust me, Georgie?"

She nods even as I get a pinch to the flank for the Georgie comment. I smirk against her, breathing her in because I have to breathe her in. "Then trust me that I'll take care of this and them for you."

She twists her head and drops a kiss on my neck. "Okay. I'll trust that you've got this for me. Thank you. I'm not good at relying on others, but I will rely on you now."

"What do you need me to do to get you on that plane? Because I agree, we're done here in Vegas."

I want her back in Boston. I want to go through everything on Alfie and Ezra. I want her away from them, especially while I do it, and I want her back in the safety of her cousins, where I can't fucking touch her like this. I'm not sure I could make it through another night in the suite with her.

"I'm not sure."

"Medication, meditation, biting…" I trail off on that last one, making her laugh, which merely feeds my addiction.

She breathes out a long, hot exhale and pulls away, meeting my eyes from inches away. And with her sitting sideways on my lap like this, with the whole of Las Vegas and the beautiful sprawl of mountains beyond, I realize I'm a man in great danger. In danger of not just falling for good—but of losing my heart along with it.

I'm going to fall in love with Georgia Monroe.

And it will be for forever. I'll never learn how to fully exist without her again. And I have no idea how to stop it or what to do about it. I've spent the last six years of my life rebuilding myself to be a man who deserves her, all the while knowing I'd never have her. But with her in my arms, I'm starting to feel that *want* again.

And it's stronger than it ever was.

"Honestly?" she asks, her long, dark lashes fanning over her cheeks as she blinks.

"Anything," I find myself saying.

"I will likely take something in there, but…" She bites nervously into her lip.

"Just say it. It's yours."

"It sounds so dumb in my head."

I grasp her chin and force her gaze, compelling her to tell me.

"I might want you to hold my hand."

I cough out a laugh. "Easy. Done."

"And if I require you to bite me?" she challenges, and I can feel my gaze growing dark, volcanic, dangerous.

"Then you know I won't bite you gently. I'll make it hurt until all you can think about are my teeth on you."

She pushes me back, her hands on my shoulders as she adjusts herself until she's straddling my waist. Her warm pussy is directly over my aching cock that didn't get the message about not getting hard. Four brutal layers are all that separate us. That's it.

She leans in, pressing her tits against my chest and bringing her mouth by my ear, forcing her neck by my nose, so I have no choice but to breathe her fragrance in again.

"Do you know what I used to love most about your pain?"

Fuck. I can't speak. Like, this time, I actually *can't* speak.

"The way you'd save it all for me," she continues without waiting on me. "The look in your eyes as you finally succumbed and let me have every piece of you—something I knew you gave no one else. You don't scare me, Lenox. You never did. I loved nothing more than turning your pain into our pleasure and watching your demons evaporate in my bed. So bite me, husband. Make me feel it. Distract me from my panic. But this time, I promise not to fall in love with you in the process."

If only I could make the same promise for myself.

Chapter Thirteen

Georgia

LENOX WAS, of course, right about the High Roller. Video footage of us appearing to cuddle and me straddling his lap hit Interntainment first and then went viral. I have no idea how much they paid for that video, but I'm assuming it was a lot.

Security brought us into the hotel through a back way, and I made my apologies to other members of the board about my early departure, but they didn't care. I'm married. The shares of Monroe Securities are mine now. They're thrilled.

And honestly, it's not like I was adding anything extra beyond a face and a smile to this conference. I didn't even know what an event actor was—I almost thought it was a barb at me when I first entered the conference room and heard the term. I frowned, and Lenox snickered before whispering in my ear, "That's what you cybersecurity people call a hacker who infiltrates a system with the purpose of disruption or theft."

Oops.

I didn't see Alfie or Ezra before I left, nor did they text me

again. Lenox ordered room service—since I hadn't gotten to eat—
and then we packed and went to the airport. By the time we
boarded the plane two hours later, that's when Lenox showed me
the alert on his phone. Twenty minutes later, our High Roller video
was everywhere.

"You didn't try to stop it," I note as I sink down onto the
buttery-soft leather. I always liked this plane. It's pretty.

Lenox picks me up and moves me over to the bench seat beside
him, his fingers on my wrist, and it takes me a moment to realize
he's checking my pulse.

I snort. "It's one milligram of Ativan. It just makes me a bit...
loopy, I guess it's the word you'd use. I'm not going to die."

"It's the only way I'll inherit—section four, clause b, line eight."

I cough out a loud bark, or at least it feels loud in my head. Who
barks?

"You do," he tells me holding me against him, and I might be
musing aloud. "And no, I didn't try to stop it," he says, answering
my question from like five minutes ago. "Right now, we appear like
a newlywed couple in love. No one can contest that. Not even Alfie
and Ezra. It's why I put you in my lap in the first place."

Oh. Smart. Wicked Smaht. Lenox doesn't have much of a
Boston accent, but every now and then certain words catch a hint of
it, and I like it. It's cute. Not that Lenox could ever be construed as
cute.

"Then I straddled you because you've got a man piercing.
Which, incidentally, I enjoyed a lot, though I am a bit disappointed I
didn't get to play with them using my tongue."

He makes a strangled noise and brushes the hair back from my
face, his other hand still on my wrist, and when did my face end up
on his lap? Speaking of his man piercing... I squeeze his dick
beneath my head, and he hisses out a breath, forcing my hand away.

"Jesus, Lenox, are you ever not hard? Did you take a certain
blue pill while I took mine?"

He doesn't answer, but I don't really care because the plane
starts to pick up speed, and despite the Ativan and my proximity to
Lenox's pierced monster, I stiffen and grip his thigh.

His hand strokes my hair, his fingers gliding through the tresses, and he brushes his fingers over my eyes, forcing them closed. "Just breathe. You're fine."

"Don't be so nice to me," I murmur.

"Would you rather I bite you?"

I smile, though it's heavy, weighed down. "Depends on where? My nipples are very sensitive."

"Go to sleep, Georgia. I'll wake you when we get there."

"Why won't you tell me now? Now is later, and you told me you'd tell me later."

After Lenox took five minutes to pack, he worked for the remaining two hours we were in the suite before we left for the airport. He's been quiet—*quieter*—since. Or maybe just more stoic, keeping his cards close to his vest.

I know he found something in that time. I know it.

"Because you're drugged."

"It'll distract me." My eyes clench tight as the plane lifts off the ground. "Then you can tell me again when I'm more alert. You said there was stuff to figure out. What else is there to figure out?"

"Plenty," he tells me, shifting in his seat and tapping his fingers on the armrest. "Alfie's phone is very precise."

"I don't know what that means. Stop using three words when I need you to use at least fifty."

He sighs. "It means everything on there is very deliberate and closed off. He has no banking apps, the only email account is his work email, all of his apps are very specific, things like airlines and such, but there are no saved passwords on his phone. Any laptop, iPad, or other electronic devices he owns are not linked. He has only a few text message streams, one with Ezra, one with you, a few members of the board, and your father. That's it. Nothing is personal, not even with Ezra. Everything is business. I saw some of this on Ezra's phone, but he's sloppy and arrogant, has a strong weakness for money and a vice for expensive things, and that was his downfall. It made him careless, unlike his father."

"Okay..." I draw out the word. "I appreciate that you used a lot of words, but I still don't get it. What are you saying?"

"I'm saying it's not simply Alfie's business phone, Georgia. I'm saying he runs it the way a hacker would. The way a man who doesn't ever want it to be used against him in a court of law or infiltrated by an enemy does. He has other devices, I'm positive of it, but this is a closed circuit with no access because he's made sure it is. It makes sense why Ezra has a gatekeeper. His father is a hacker."

Suddenly I'm dizzy and loopy all over again, and it has nothing to do with the Ativan or the ascending plane that dips and shudders, making me gasp.

"Is he evil or someone who uses his powers to fight evil?"

"Fight evil?" He raises an eyebrow at me.

"Like Batman, though you're my Batman already. More like you have to be one to properly fight one."

"I don't know how he uses his skillset or how in-depth his skillset actually is yet. Does that answer your question?"

"Yes, but that was not nearly as fun as I was hoping for. I was hoping you'd give me some Jedi to Anakin Skywalker reference."

"Now you're mixing comic books and Star Wars."

I yawn, twisting on his lap so he can get more of my hair because what he's doing feels soooo good. "I don't care. I like both. So what now?"

He smirks, a sparkle of challenge lighting his eyes. "Now I start to play, and you sleep, and if you don't remember this conversation when you wake up, I'll remind you."

I let out a heavy breath, succumbing to the ministrations of his hand in my hair, allowing it to lull me into a half-awake, half-asleep stupor, and mumble, "Thank you."

———

MY COUSIN ZAX doesn't fuck around. When we land and deboard the plane, his driver, Ashley, is waiting for us. I make a beeline for him and throw my arms around his large shoulders.

"Ashley! Oh, Ashley."

He laughs at my *Gone with the Wind* reference and squeezes me back. "The great state of Georgia. How are you, honey?"

"Better now that I'm off the plane and seeing you."

"Glad to hear it. Come with me. We're not going to Zax's."

"Oh." That surprises me, and I turn to Lenox, who is his normal, stoic self, his face back on the screen of his phone after he gave Ashley a what's up head nod. I slip inside the car, anxious to get out of the frigid November air. Lenox follows me in, typing on his phone. "Do you know where we're going?"

"Rebels Field."

My eyebrows pinch together. "Rebels Field?"

"Asher is playing on Sunday Night Football."

I shake my head, still not understanding.

"Sunday Night Football is a nationally televised game."

"Lenox, once again, I'm asking if you can just spit it all out at once instead of spoon-feeding it to me in pieces."

He drags his gaze away from his phone, finally giving me his attention as we start to pull away from Logan Airport. "It means we're going to be in the luxury booth together as a couple, along with your cousins and their significant others. Cameras will train in on us, and we'll be on national television looking happy and in love."

"Didn't we already do that this morning on the High Roller?"

"Yes, but this is with my best friends and former bandmates, as well as your cousins. It's showing family approval and us at a public event together—not some stolen surveillance camera. And since Ezra and Alfie have hired an attorney and investigator to look into the validity of our marriage as well as into my person, this will go a long way."

I groan, my head falling back against the leather seat. "They hired a freaking lawyer and a PI?"

"Yes."

"That's so lame. Why are they doing this? It's not like they're getting the shares or that I'm going to marry Ezra after and give them the shares if they disprove the validity of our marriage. Like... grow up and get over it already."

"I don't think that's their plan."

"Fabulous." I turn to him. "What about you? They're investigating you?"

He's not the least bit ruffled. "They won't get anything on me other than I own a tattoo shop, a house in Cambridge, and an apartment in Maine, which is already public knowledge."

"I didn't know you had an apartment in Maine."

"It's my technical residence, though it's used for little more than storage. Neither my house nor the land and properties I own are searchable."

I'd question that, but why bother? This is Lenox we're talking about.

"I ruined your privacy."

He smirks at me. "Did you think I wasn't aware that was going to happen when I said yes to this?"

"It doesn't seem right. I'm asking so much of you, and you get nothing out of this."

Because truth? This marriage will only work if I continue to hate him. If I remember all the ways he hurt me and how if I let myself go even just a little, he'd do it again. Likely worse this time. But what Lenox did for me—what he's *doing* for me—feels like a life raft, giving me back my safety and freedom.

And he wouldn't take anything in return. Who does that?

I should have insisted on something. Made it transactional.

His eyes hold mine for a long beat before returning to his phone. "I already told you; you have nothing I want."

"Is it just for Zax and Grey?"

He's silent for a moment and then quietly says, "There isn't anything I wouldn't do for them."

But that doesn't feel like the whole truth, or at least not the entire answer. It feels like there's more he's not saying, but my still slightly foggy brain can't keep up with it, and dissecting Lenox's layers takes a lot of brain power. He's a computer with an impenetrable firewall, and I'm still a midwife with no discernible computer knowledge beyond sending emails and navigating the internet.

Hacking Lenox is beyond my skill set and knowledge base.

I decide it's better if I don't know and just take what he's doing for me and simply be grateful that there isn't anything he wouldn't do for Zax and Grey because there isn't anything Zax and Grey wouldn't do for me. I need to stop quasi-apologizing and feeling bad. It's a chronic problem of mine, but he just said he knew what he was getting into when he said yes, and he did it anyway. He's a grown-ass man, capable of making his own decisions.

"When this is all done, can I buy you a new motorcycle because I'm assuming you don't need one of my kidneys?"

His lips twitch. "A new motorcycle?"

"Something cool and vintage or new and super fast. Whatever you like. Or if you don't want another bike, something else then. Anything really."

"How did you know I ride?"

I roll my eyes. "You mean other than the times you took me out on your bikes?" I roll my eyes again, just to let him know I'm annoyed. "Yeah, we fucked for two years, Lenox. Even though ninety percent of the time I don't know what you're thinking unless you directly tell me, I do know you to a certain extent. Despite your penchant for wearing all black, your favorite color is green. You love to draw and are insanely talented at it, which is why you got into tattooing, but you did it because it just fit, and you don't have to talk while doing it. Speaking of being insanely talented, you never sing, but you love to play the piano and write songs with words to them, even though you don't ever plan to have anyone sing them. You love spicy food but prefer your own cooking over takeout, and I suspect a lot of that is because that's pretty much all you ate for four years when you toured with Central Square. You love dogs, big, quiet, non-hyper dogs, and are allergic to cats. My hair, especially when it catches the sunlight, is your favorite thing about me. You'd stare and touch it constantly, even when you weren't aware you were doing it."

He leans forward, moving right up into my face as we inch along in Boston traffic. His blue eyes dance about my face, and he snatches a lock of my hair, twists it around his finger and gives it a harsh tug. "You're wrong about your hair."

"Am I?" I challenge.

"Yes," he clips out, his sweet breath fanning across my lips.

"Your *green* eyes are my favorite physical feature of yours. Your hair is second. But they're not my favorite thing about you, Georgia. Just my favorite things to look at on you."

I ignore the swoosh in my stomach and the jump in my pulse. The ones that make me desperate to know if my eyes are why green is his favorite color. If that's why he emphasized the word when he said it. But if he says yes, I'll mount him and ride him like a bike right here, and if he says no, I'm not sure if I'll believe him, and again, I'll be tempted to mount and ride him.

So in order to stop myself from doing just that, I ask, "What about everything else? I was right about that stuff, wasn't I? I can keep going if you want. I enjoy unnerving you with my crazy personal knowledge and brilliance." I bat my eyelashes prettily at him.

"You don't want to know my favorite thing about you?"

"I was sorta dodging that one."

His stubbled cheek grazes my soft one as he dips toward my ear. "Your crazy personal knowledge and brilliance don't unnerve me. But let me try out my own on you. Your favorite color is pink, though you rarely wear it because you believe it clashes with your hair. Your favorite food is shrimp, and you'll eat it any way you can get it, but if you had to eat one meal for the rest of your life, it would be jambalaya. You feel brave and more confident in high heels and red lipstick—and apparently sexy lingerie—and wearing scrubs is your least favorite part of your job. Your favorite is your patients and seeing their faces the first moment you hand them their baby. You hate having your hair up because it makes your scalp ache, and you take it down the first chance you get. You hated acting but did it to make your mother happy—a chronic problem of yours since you're a people-pleaser and it pisses you off, but you don't know how to change it either. Unlike me, you love to sing and do it *very* well. Sorta like Grey, but you had no desire to be a rock star like him. And, apparently, you can take a man twice your size down with a single leg sweep."

The heat in the car intensifies, my pulse along with it, as adrenaline snakes like a heady cocktail through my veins while we play this game with each other.

I pull back until our noses are practically touching and then I graze mine against his. "You are fastidiously tidy and hate it when things are disorganized."

He tilts his head, inching in closer, his lips hovering over mine, making my breath shallow and choppy. "You are not, nor do you care. You're a throw things wherever and clean them up later person. Every time your watch shows all the same numbers, like 11:11, you make a wish, and you check your watch frequently when the numbers get close so you don't miss it."

My eyes bounce down to his lips and then back up. "You love the rain, but snow is your favorite to walk in. You hate chocolate, which is frankly one of your biggest turn-offs for me."

He smiles, his lips skimming ever so subtly over mine to the point where it could be construed as unintentional, though I know it wasn't. "You love being around people, but sometimes prefer the quiet solitude of reading tucked under a blanket. You prefer sweet over salty, which is pretty much your personality."

"You prefer salty over sweet and back atcha."

The car comes to a stop, but neither of us moves, not wanting to be the first to back down. Only I'm forced to break the spell first when Ashley opens the back door on my side. Before I can climb out—or take a breath that doesn't taste or smell like him—Lenox's hand dives into my hair, and he drags my ear back to his mouth.

"You. You're my favorite thing about you. What I know and what I don't. And that is also what I hate most about you."

My breath hitches, but then Ashley is reaching his hand out for me, thinking I need help to climb out of the SUV. He's not wrong. Not after Lenox makes a statement like that. And now I have to pretend to be happily married and in love with him in front of my cousins and the world. And I have no idea how I'll make it through when everything between us is hate, fuck, or foreplay.

Chapter Fourteen

Lenox

I USED TO AVOID ZAX. Him more than Grey. Zax's pain after losing Suzie was as acute as mine, and not only was it crippling to witness his grief, it exacerbated mine. His suffering was different, but no less tragic. If anything, his was more tragic than mine. I lost my sister, but he lost the love of his life—well, the love of his life until Aurelia came along.

For a while, he avoided me too, for the same reasons I was avoiding him.

Or at least, that was the reason I told myself I was avoiding him.

The reality was that I couldn't look him in the eye. I was positive he'd see through me. See how I felt about his cousin, what I was doing with her and to her. I didn't want him to call me out on it because then I'd have to stop, and I didn't want to stop, or worse, I'd be talked into being her man when I was in no shape to be him.

It wasn't until I came clean to him after I walked away from Georgia that I could finally face him. Somehow then it became easier to be around him. Less strangling, even though I still felt like shit about it all. Or maybe because that was when I forced myself to crawl out of the gutter of my mind and become something better.

For Suzie, for myself, and… well… mainly for Georgia.

I let her go with no intention of returning, but that didn't mean part of me wasn't anxious to become a man worthy of her. It was a notion in my head. A guiding force. I will always regret not acting and saving Suzie, and I will always regret that I stood still and allowed my father to spiral so far out of control with his grief over losing Suzie and venom toward me that it cost him and someone else their life.

But Georgia telling me she loved me turned that self-loathing into a wake-up call. A motivational fuel. I realized what a gift I had been given in Georgia's love, and though I couldn't keep it for myself, I couldn't squander it either. It was time I used my guilt for good.

Except now I'm holding Georgia's hand, entering the luxury suite we all co-own as her husband, and I don't want to be here. The rational part of me knows I shouldn't feel guilty. I stepped in when Georgia needed me. I married her, and now I'm not only thrust into a media circus as a headlining performer—something I hate being—but I'm also about to embark on a dangerous hacking game.

I will protect her. I will keep her safe.

So I shouldn't feel guilty. Not at all.

But after spending the night inside Georgia's body, and the day touching and teasing and tormenting each other, I'm once again realizing I don't want to stare into Zax's eyes and have him see beneath my facade of emotional indifference.

Fallon had the brilliant idea of letting the world see us out in the open in public. Fallon is an heiress herself and dodged her own arranged marriage before running off with Grey, so this isn't unfamiliar territory to her. And while I agree with it on principle, how the fuck am I supposed to kiss her and hold her and touch her for the cameras under the guise of it all being one hundred percent fake, and not have Zax see right through me?

"Well, if it isn't Mr. and Mrs. Georgia Monroe." Asher, wearing his game gear including pads and cleats, grabs me and hauls me in for a big hug, and then does the same with Georgia.

Fucking Asher.

"Aren't you supposed to be on the field?" The game is set to start in about thirty minutes.

He gives me an incredulous look. "And miss the chance to be the first to congratulate you and officially welcome you to the Our Women Own Our Balls Club? Pfshaw. Never. But now that I got my moment, I do have to go." He smacks my shoulder. "You know, I didn't think you'd take my trying to set you up to the next level so fast, but I suppose it's fate that you became a Monroe."

I roll my eyes, but I'll never be able to stop myself from smiling. "I hope you get sacked on your first play."

"Thanks, Thor. You know we could use an offensive lineman since Bruno got hurt, but now that I know you'd let the defensive end through to tackle me, I won't present the offer."

I extend my fist for him to pound. "Kill Miami."

He grins at me, his gray eyes sparkling as he pounds my fist. "I plan to. See you after, brother."

He grabs his girlfriend Wynter's hand, and they walk out of the suite since she's the team orthopedic surgeon. It's actually how they reconnected after a bad one-night stand nearly two years prior that left Wynter with their son, Mason, and no clue who Asher was or how to contact him.

Zax steps right in front of me and pulls me in for a bro hug, and the sinking weight of I'm an asshole hits me. When he first wanted to start dating Suzie, he asked my permission and promised to never hurt her. He kept that promise as well as being respectful as fuck to our friendship.

I, in turn, did not extend the same courtesy or promise when I fucked his cousin behind his back and then broke her heart. The night this all began, Aurelia mentioned Georgia's name when everyone was teasing me about setting me up with someone. Both of them said no, and I don't have to guess why. I promised to stay away from her. Hell, I promised I'd never see her again, and now here I am.

Both before her and after her, I haven't had relationships. I never sleep with a woman more than once. The hacker in me doesn't trust anyone. I do heavy, hard, illegal shit and live a mostly isolated life. And frankly, I've had no desire to open myself or my life up to anyone.

She's the only one who has ever managed to break through, and she didn't just crack my shell, she shattered it. Georgia is sunshine, and I am the darkness that creeps in before the storm.

Georgia launches herself at Zax, jumping up into his arms and giving him a death squeeze that makes him laugh. "You're heavy," he lies teasingly, and she leans back and smacks his shoulders.

"Or more like old age is finally starting to creep in and you're weak," she counters, planting a ruby-red kiss on his cheek before hopping down and doing the same thing to Greyson and then hugging Callan, Aurelia, Fallon, and Layla. Fallon is Grey's woman, and Layla is Callan's.

"When do you go home?" Grey questions once we're all seated watching the game. Georgia is sitting beside me, my hand on her knee, simply resting there. She's busy chatting with the rest of the women.

By home, Grey means Maine, and we can't get into too many specifics here in the booth. There are cameras sporadically trained on us, not to mention the suite attendants who come and go with regular frequency.

"Tomorrow or the next day," I answer, sipping a beer and watching the field as the Rebels defense tries to keep Miami out of the red zone.

He's smiling. Grey hasn't stopped smiling once. "You know you're officially something like my brother now."

"Like he hasn't always been?" Callan quips, devouring a huge plate of dip and chips, mini lobster rolls, buffalo wings, and pretzel bites. "Like when Zax was with Suzie, that didn't seal the deal?"

"I know, but... he's actually married to Georgia. Fake or not, that does make us family beyond us already being family. It's next level."

Zax makes a noise, and Grey shrugs at him. "What? Don't give me that look. I know what you're thinking, but tell me any other situation you would have been happy with."

Zax takes a sip of his bourbon and looks directly at me. "None. I wouldn't have been happy with anyone else doing this."

"But?" I challenge, and he angles his head as if to say, *do I need to go there?* He doesn't. I got the message loud and clear when I first told him what was going on, and he has every right to call me out on it now. I would if I were him. If it had been Suzie, you better fucking believe I'd call him out on it.

"What am I missing?" Callan asks.

"Nothing," Zax answers, still looking at me. "I'm being an asshole, over-protective big brother type."

"Shocker," Callan deadpans.

"What about you, Georgia? What's your deal? Are you staying in Boston or going back to LA?" Grey asks, changing the subject.

She turns to him and then searches around the box, making sure the attendant isn't here to overhear. He's not. Asher already told them we'd handle everything tonight and wanted privacy.

"I'm thinking I'll stay here for a while," she says, making sure her face is away from the wall of glass where cameras could possibly read her words. "I honestly have no pressing need to return to LA right now, and with all that's going on with a certain someone, I'd rather not be there."

"What?" Aurelia squawks, cutting herself off midsentence from whatever she's saying to Fallon.

Georgia gives her a bemused look. "What? What's wrong?"

Aurelia climbs up on her seat, her expression serious, even as she twists her face so she too is shielded from potential cameras. "You can't stay here in Boston *or* go back to LA. You just told me your ex and his father are looking into having your marriage invalidated or at the very least questioned, and that your ex has been having you followed."

The back of my neck starts to prickle at where I'm afraid she's going with this.

"Yeah..." Georgia trails off as if she's not following.

"So you have to live with Lenox," Fallon finishes, picking up where Aurelia left off, her hand covering the side of her face. "You can't give them any avenue to challenge you, and not living with your new husband would do just that."

"Right. Exactly." Aurelia points at Fallon.

"No," Zax and Grey say in unison, and it's like fucking déjà vu.

"Yes," Layla presses, pushing her long blonde hair back behind her ears as she stands and turns her back toward the field so she's not seen talking either. "Not only will her ex be all over that if she doesn't, but so will the press. We're here tonight to prove you're a couple. Living separately, especially when you have their watchful eyes on you, will show the opposite."

Georgia's face turns red, and she throws me a quick, uneasy glance before returning to the women, who are all staring at us as if they're ready to take up this charge. "What are you suggesting? That I move to *Maine?*"

"One hundred percent that's what we're saying," Aurelia states adamantly.

"It might not be ideal or your first choice, but it's the smart one." Fallon takes a sip of her drink and stares Georgia down.

"No. I can't do it," Georgia says softly, folding her arms defiantly and staring straight ahead out the glass only to remember herself and soften her position in case anyone is watching.

"Then why bother marrying him?" Callan asks. "Listen, I hate to side on this since I can tell none of you want that, but I agree with the women. They're right. It's why I had Layla move in with me as my fake fiancée when I was trying to win guardianship of Katy. You need to appear legit."

Georgia chews on her lip. He has a point. They all do. But having Georgia in Maine in my house for who knows how long is a seriously bad idea. For both of us.

"I'm sure we can figure something else out," she mumbles. Only I can tell in her voice that she isn't so sure. "Shit," she hisses, and then twists until she's leaning over the armrest of the chair, practically crawling in my lap. I stiffen, but she presses her lips to mine. "Smile like you love me, put your hand in my hair or on my face, and kiss me like you mean it. The cameras are right on us. I see us on the television in the corner."

The national broadcast for the game is playing, and sure enough, she's right. My hand lightly touches her face before I gently press my lips to hers, so very mindful of our audience. Still, the feel of her lips never fails to steal my breath, even with her cousins sitting right beside me.

Aurelia whistles a catcall, and Georgia covertly flips her off, much to Aurelia's delight.

"Done. They've moved on." Georgia retakes her seat in a harrumph. She's not happy.

"Yeah, but that image will be all over social media and the internet within seconds," Grey says, giving me a wan smile. "I'm sorry. I mean, I'm grateful as fuck for all that you're doing, but I'm also sorry."

"I'll survive," I mutter.

"You do realize it's not just social media and the internet. The paps will be all over you. Both of you," Layla asserts from the other side of Georgia, her head angled toward us. "It won't just be Vegas or even Boston." Layla comes from a family of billionaires. Famous billionaires at that. She, like Fallon, is no stranger to this sort of thing either.

"What about in Maine?" Fallon asks.

Zax makes a noise in the back of his throat. "I'd love to see them try. They won't be able to get within five hundred yards of Lenox's house, and the town doesn't take kindly to outsiders digging for information. Especially on him."

"What does that mean? Especially on him?" Georgia asks and I shake my head, refusing to answer, so no one else does. Not that anyone else knows beyond the guys.

"Whatever. That's exactly my point. It's why she needs to move there with him." Aurelia's words ring out through the suite, and we all fall silent, the only sounds are the muted fans and the game outside the thick glass wall of the suite.

"Absolutely not. I'm not doing it." Georgia is furious, whether it's about moving to Maine or living with me or the impact that has on her life, I'm not sure.

"There has to be an alternative to this," Grey says with a note of desperation, except we all know there isn't one. I throw Grey and Zax a quick glance, and neither is visibly happy, but the truth is, as much as I don't want that, it's what needs to happen. And we all know it.

Done with all of this, I stand and extend my hand to Georgia. "Enough. I need a moment alone with my wife."

Chapter Fifteen

Lenox

"LENOX," Zax growls urgently, clearly not liking the fact that I just called Georgia my wife. Judging by her expression, she doesn't either. It was meant to drive home a point, not stake a claim. This is what they wanted me to do. All three of them. So here we are.

I look at him and then Grey. "Give me a different way."

Grey's mouth twists, and he turns to Zax, whose displeasure is all over his face. It doesn't matter, though. He can't, and he knows it.

I drag a fuming Georgia through the suite and shove her into the bathroom, shutting and locking the door behind us. "Oh, really?" she glares, folding her arms defiantly and leaning against the sink. "This is going to be a door-locking situation?"

"Depends on how reasonable you are," I retort. "We're going to move you into my house in Maine."

"What?!" she shrieks, her hands flying about. "You're on their side with this? Come on, Lenox. No. We can't live together, and you freaking know it." She pokes the center of my chest.

"Keep your voice down. We don't need everyone to hear us fight.

Your ex and his father plan to contest the marriage. That much is clear. They're going to say all sorts of things, like how you're not mentally stable after your father's loss and that I'm taking advantage of you."

Her eyes narrow.

"You'll be safe there," I continue in a low voice. "No one can touch you, not even the press—at least at my house—and it'll give me time to figure everything else out."

"I can't work in Maine," she grits out between clenched teeth.

"You can get your license in Maine, Georgia. That's a bullshit excuse, and you know it."

"Zax and Grey don't think I need to live with you."

I give her an unamused look.

Her hands hit the top of her head. "Lenox, I don't want to live with you!"

I chuckle, but there is no humor in it. I press her back into the sink, my hands going on either side of her body, caging her in as my anger builds. "You think I want that? You think bringing you into my house is a good time for me?"

She shakes her head, aggravation crawling through her features. She shoves me back, but I don't go far. I don't want outside ears to hear us. "Then why be so adamant about it?"

"I fucking married you, Georgia. Our agreement is for a year. That means for the next year, you're mine to take care of whether I like it or not."

"You can't want that."

"I just told you I don't."

"Then why are you doing this?" Her voice climbs, and I give her a warning look. Only Zax and Grey know how things are between us, and I'd like to keep it that way. She tempers herself. "Beyond saying I'm your responsibility because you fake married me, because that's not adding up all the way."

"Except it does. You're my wife. That's how this goes." I hold up my left hand, showing her my band, getting right up in her face. "It's like Callan said. Why bother marrying me if you're just going to give them an in to disprove it? You told me yourself that the appearance of this being real is paramount. It was one of your goddamn rules for us. Fight me all you want, but your ass is coming home with me to Maine tomorrow."

She grips my shirt, giving me a rough yank until we're practically nose-to-nose. "Fuck you, Lenox. Husband or not, you don't get to tell me where I'm going or what I'm doing. In fact, I'd never let my real husband get away with that shit."

"Good for you and your imaginary real husband. If you wanted that, you should have married Ezra. But here, now, this is it. Stop being a stubborn pain in the ass and get over it."

Panting rushes of air cleave from both of us, mixing in the minuscule space between us. She wants to fight this, and I get it because it's a bad situation in the making, but what other choice do we genuinely have?

The problem is, we can't seem to get our bearings with each other. We're boiling hot and ice cold and occasionally flirt between both lines. And with that, I don't know how to navigate her, and I think it's the same for her with me.

We're scarred love and bleeding hatred with a sutured-up form of gratitude and guilt connecting both sides. I want her. I'm crazed with want for her. Moving in with me will only make that worse and harder to fight, but the more I think about it, the more I want it. Fuck how irresistibly dangerous it is.

I've had this time with her, and I don't want it to end. I don't want it to be over. Even if she's just there. Except when she sees my house... Fuck. That could be—

"I can't move in with you," she reiterates, cutting off my thoughts.

I growl a frustrated breath. "For fuck's sake. Why not?"

"Because of this," she snaps and then grabs my shirt in two fists and slams my lips to hers before shoving me back just as fast. "That's why."

My hands dive into her hair, and I grab her head, bringing her back to me and kissing her urgently. "You're afraid you won't be able to keep your pretty manicured hands to yourself?"

"Stop kissing me," she hisses against my mouth, biting my lip. "I fucking hate you."

Only her hands are in my hair and she's holding me close, tilting her head, and kissing me back. Taking her by the hips, I lift her up and then drop her down onto the edge of the sink so I can step between her spread thighs.

"And yet I bet if I reached into your jeans, I'd find you soaked for me."

She shoves angrily against me, breaking the kiss, but no fucking way am I letting her go anywhere without proving my point. I yank her back down off the counter and flip her around so I can undo the button and fly on her jeans. I'm fully aware we're in a suite bathroom with our friends, her fucking cousins, who don't want me touching her, just outside.

I should stop. But first…

I slide my hand down the front of her jeans, straight into her thong. She sucks in a rush of air, but instead of ripping my hands from her jeans, she puts hers on the counter, palms flat, fingers splayed.

I smirk, sucking on her earlobe as I find her bare pussy just as wet as I knew it would be.

"Still want me to stop?" I start to play with her clit, watching as her flushed face and hazy eyes grow hungrier in the reflection of the mirror.

She gasps, and I cover her mouth with my other hand.

"Hush. This is between us, and I don't want them to hear," I murmur in her ear, licking, nipping, biting, tasting. "We have something. There is no denying that." I continue to play with her clit for another minute, watching her fucking stunning face in the mirror as I do before I slide lower and slip two fingers straight inside of her. She moans against my hand, and I rub my hard cock against her ass. "But you asked me to marry you for a reason. And with that reason, comes certain things we're just going to have to live with."

Her head falls back against my chest even as she can't stop watching the motion of my hand as it moves in her jeans. I'd give anything to yank down her pants and slam inside her, but all that will do is pit her against me further. But making my girl come? That I can do and still get her to move in with me.

I shift my wrist and dive deeper into her, hitting her spot while giving my thumb access to her clit. I want to watch her fly because her face when she comes for me is like nothing else. I'd slay any dragon she has just for that chance. I press my hand tighter against her mouth, and a rush of wet heat coats my fingers. She likes this. Me stifling her moans. Us risking getting caught.

I should feel bad about this, and I know I will, but that time will come later.

"Georgia, you're moving in with me." I continue to fuck her with my fingers, picking up speed because we're on borrowed time. "Tomorrow, you're coming with me to Maine. And I'm fucking done arguing with you about it."

She shakes her head against me.

"Yes," I tell her. "Now come for me. I want to watch my beautiful wife come all over my fingers. I want your scent on them all night. I want to be able to lick them and taste you. And after that, I'll stop. I won't fuck you, and this will be it. But there is no way this isn't happening."

"Fuck," she mumbles into my hand, grinding against me, seeking more, unable to stop.

"After this, it's over," I promise, wondering if it's a promise I'll actually be able to keep this time.

Her reflected gaze slinks up to mine, and then she's coming all over my fingers, watching me watch her, knowing she's just given in and yet also knowing she will always hold the upper hand with me. There will never be a time when I'm not hers. Whether she can see it in my eyes or feel it in my touch, I don't know.

I'm risking my everything, and I need to get a grip before it all slips away from me.

The moment she comes down from her high, I slip my fingers out and lick them clean. "They'll still smell like you. And I'll keep them buried under my nose later as I jerk myself to the image of your face in that mirror."

I pull away from her and go for the door, leaving her here to figure out the rest of her mind. Only the moment I open the door, I'm greeted by Aurelia. I quickly slam the door shut behind me, blocking it with my body.

"Relax." She laughs lightly. "Lucky for you, I don't have to pee, though I told them I did." I scan to my left, but the suite is empty. "I sent everyone else downstairs, telling them I'd stay up here and wait for you to finish fighting."

I squint at her, and she laughs harder.

"The game ended five minutes ago. Asher scored the winning touchdown on a quarterback sneak up the middle."

"I…" I don't know what to say.

"Do you know why I said her name that night at poker when everyone was teasing about setting you up?"

I don't answer.

"You never came to town when she did. You'd always grimace or look away whenever her name was mentioned, but I'd see the ancient hurt in your eyes. Asher wonders why I'm so good at poker. It's because I can read people. And I can read you. You love her."

I startle back a step, relieved the door is closed and the water is running in the bathroom. Hopefully, Georgia didn't hear that.

"You love her," she repeats, and I grab her arm and walk us out of the suite and into the empty hallway, all the while she keeps talking. "But your guilt over the past and your love for your friends isn't something you know how to overcome."

I stop us a few doors down from our suite. "How do you know about my past with her?"

"Zax mentioned it without going into full details, but like I said, I can read you and I can put pieces together easily enough."

I look down at the carpet between us, not willing to speak.

"When I first met you, I was terrified you'd hate me," she says, and my head slingshots up until our eyes lock. "I was the woman doing stuff with Zax, falling in love with him as he fell for me, and I was worried you'd hate me for it because of Suzie."

I shake my head, losing my words, but still managing, "I didn't."

She smiles softly at me, her blue eyes sparkling. "I know."

I shake my head again. "She would have hated what he turned

into and loved you for everything you've given him. I loved you for what you were doing for him."

Her hand reaches my shoulder. "I know. Because you have a big, beautiful heart, Lenox. You don't see it. I know you don't. But only someone with a heart capable of that sort of love and under-standing would want it for others. Suzie may have been like that, but you are too."

"I hurt Georgia. Terribly. Unforgivably. I hurt my best friends too and did not deserve their mercy. Not after what I did. Georgia hates me, and with good reason."

"If she were indifferent to you, then I'd believe she hates you. Her sort of hate is self-preservation and protection. Sometimes the right person comes along at the wrong time. That doesn't make them wrong for us, it makes us wrong for them. Maybe you didn't do things the right way back then, but you walked away and changed your life. You didn't blame anyone else for your mistakes. You owned them, faced them, and came out stronger because of them. You do so much for others, but what do you do for yourself?"

It's as if she's ripping out my insides and feeding them through a meat grinder. Helping Georgia is supposed to be a salvation. A way out of this omnipresent guilt, at least where she, Zax, and Grey are concerned. But this… I don't know how to breathe through this.

Her warm hand finds my face, and though she doesn't look like Suzie, their features are somewhat similar. Blonde hair and blue eyes and such fire and strength, you can't help but love them.

"You are deserving, Lenox Moore. Every bit as much as Zax was, if not more. If you love Georgia, which I suspect you do since you look at her like she's your universe, then don't let that go simply because you didn't do right by her once. Don't stand in your own way when you can have everything."

Aurelia turns and walks away, leaving me here for a moment, feeling like I just had the wind punched out of me. She called me deserving. And being deserving of Georgia is all I've ever wanted to be.

GEORGIA IS SINGING at the top of her lungs, as she has been for the last two hours since we left my house. She woke up like a chirpy bird, twirling around my house this morning in what she mockingly referred to as pajamas—a thin tank top and tiny boy shorts—drinking coffee and asking me about the most painful places on the body to get tattoos. It's a total one-eighty from how we left things last night, and when I raised a questioning brow at her, she simply shrugged and said, "What else can I do?"

I left it at that with no desire to argue with her further, and now she's commandeered my car's sound system, her phone connected to it, playing all kinds of music from Taylor Swift to eighties pop to fucking Central Square to Cian O'Connor and even Dex Chapman.

But it's a fucking Central Square song she has on now that has her leaning over the console of my car, using her fist as a microphone, and serenading me in a virtual duet with Grey all the while I grumble and pretend to be annoyed just so she'll keep singing to me. Georgia's voice gives me chills, it's so good.

The song comes to an end, and she turns it down now that I've taken an exit off the highway for Lavender Lake.

"What? No Whitney Houston?" I quip.

She sighs dramatically. "Oh, if only I could belt it like Whitney."

I won't tell her she sings better.

"So, does this mean we're here?"

I thump my thumb on the top of the steering wheel. "There are some things you need to know."

She curls up in her seat and places her elbows on the console and her chin on her fists. "Enlighten me. You know I've been waiting for this."

I rub at the threatening grin on my lips. "We're going to drive to my shop first. We need to switch cars before we pick up Alice at the shop where Brooklynn is meeting me with her."

She blinks at me. "Alice? Brooklynn?"

"Alice is my dog, and she has been staying with Brooklynn, who is my shop assistant and piercer. The shop is closed on Mondays, but she's waiting for us there."

"Your dog is named Alice?"

"I didn't name her that. She was abandoned, her tracking chip cut out of her leg, but she still had a tag on her neck that said Alice. I found her digging through the dumpster near the shop."

A slow, easy, sexy-as-all-sin smile spreads across her face making her green eyes sparkle against the sunlight filtering in through the windshield. "You really have a thing for helping bitches in distress."

I let out a soft chuckle, yanking on a piece of her crimson hair. *You are deserving, Lenox Moore. Every bit as much as Zax was, if not more. If you love Georgia, which I suspect you do since you look at her like she's your universe, then don't let that go simply because you didn't do right by her once. Don't stand in your own way when you can have everything.*

The way Aurelia's words are drilling holes through me and filling up the emptiness with hope and possibility is killing me.

"I can't tell you how excited I am to see your world and you in it, Lenox. It's like getting unfettered access to Batman's cave. A perfect example is I didn't know you had a dog or an assistant named Brooklynn. I still can't wrap my head around how you're a mild-mannered business owner by day and a dangerous vigilante by night."

"You're mixing comic book heroes."

She shakes her head. "It's all part of your mystique, and I get a front-row view. Has any woman other than Suzie ever had this privilege?" Her hand quickly shoots up. "Wait. Never mind. Don't answer that. I definitely don't want to know."

"No," I answer anyway. "There hasn't been."

"Phew!" She wipes the nonexistent sweat from her forehead. "Thank God, right? I may still want to run your balls through the food processor, but I don't want to hate on a woman I've never met before. It's bad form."

"And what about for me? I've had to hear about your past lovers and am dealing with your most recent ex."

"Yes, but you don't possess the weird jealous streak I clearly do."

If only she knew.

"Go on. Tell me more."

"Take out your phone and Google Lavender Lake Town Forest."

She arches a graceful brow at me but immediately picks up her phone and Googles it. "It says it's a state preserve, swamp, and wetlands and that hiking, camping, fishing, swimming, or boating aren't permitted in that area."

"That's my house."

"Huh?"

"I own roughly fifteen hundred acres, including seventy percent of Lavender Lake. There is a small public beach with access from closer to town, but there is a divider in the lake and the part I own isn't accessible. Considering how close we are to the ocean, no one really cares."

"I'm... confused."

"The town of Lavender Lake sits between the mountains and the ocean. When I bought the land and built my house, I removed any information about myself from any searchable database. I pay taxes, but the government has no real record of my home or my owning the land."

"That's why the paparazzi, Alfie, and Ezra won't be able to find us there."

I nod. "Now you've got a better understanding of why we pressed for this." Though there is more I haven't discussed with her yet. A lot more. "The townspeople more or less know that I live somewhere in there, but none of them bother me and never cross over the divider line in the lake, which would be the only accessible way to get to my house."

She tilts her head, studying me, curiosity dancing across her features. "Why? I mean, most people seem anxious to exploit in the name of a buck."

I don't answer her. Instead, I take a left and drive down Main Street toward the shop. "We're here. Welcome to Lavender Lake."

Chapter Sixteen

Georgia

LENOX NEVER ANSWERS MY QUESTIONS, but the second he takes the turn and we slowly drive down Maine Street, I no longer care. This town... now I see what Aurelia was talking about last night when she told me it was the cutest small town she'd ever seen. This. Town. Is. Fucking. Everything.

Adorable storefronts with sweet awnings, perfect signage, tons of New England fall charm, cute sidewalk displays, and people walking by, chatting and saying hello as they pass. Autumn leaves fly through the air, catching the breeze and glinting off the random shards of sunshine that break through the clouds. It's like something out of a Norman Rockwell painting. A diner, a hardware store, a bank, a flower shop, a bakery, a grocery store, a coffee shop, a yoga studio, a post office, a library, a swanky restaurant, and lastly, a tattoo parlor with no signage to indicate anything about the shop other than it's a business.

So very Lenox.

Only... "How do you live here? It's so picturesque, I can hardly

stand it without wanting to pinch its cheeks and make it my own."
Seriously, I'm struggling to imagine this surly, tatted, reclusive, and
pierced man walking these sidewalks. I feel like the cement would
crack beneath his black boots. "What on earth made you pick this
town, or are you about to show me where all the bodies of the stray
kittens you've murdered are kept?"

Lenox takes a right and then another right, and then pulls into a
mostly empty parking lot behind his building.

He puts the car in park and shuts off the rumbling engine. "The
town didn't look like this when I bought it," is all he says before
getting out and leaving me here to try and figure out if I heard him
correctly.

When he bought it? As in the whole town? Is that even possible?
Can a person purchase a town like a handbag or a piece of art?

The more I know of this man, the less I understand.

Or maybe the more I learn, the more my perception of him
changes.

He's like a weed in my flowerbed. I can rip him out and spray
him with poison, but his roots are so embedded in my soil, there is
no way to fully eradicate him.

I climb out of the car, wrapping my arms around my chest and
quickly snatching my coat from the backseat and putting it on.
Right now, it's sunny and eighty in LA, and here it's overcast and
maybe forty degrees.

Maine. Who moves to Maine at the beginning of winter?

And we haven't even discussed how long this prison sentence
with him will be.

Lenox is unlocking the back door of his shop, and I quickly
scramble after him, anxious to get inside where it's hopefully
heated. He holds the door open for me. The lights in the back of
the shop, which is used for storage, and where the bathrooms are
located, are already on. A scratching noise calls my attention away
from surveying the neatly organized equipment, and before I can
brace myself, a giant black dog that looks like a lab mix comes
barreling at me and jumps up, slamming two large paws onto my
chest.

"Alice, down," Lenox commands from behind me at the same time a woman in front of me says, "I'm so sorry!"

"It's fine," I exclaim, laughing as I rub Alice's face and ears. "She's so sweet. You are, aren't you? You're a total love bug. How is he your daddy?" I motion to Lenox as I continue to nuzzle, pet, and receive wet kisses. "You're such a good girl."

Lenox groans. "I should have known. Is there a creature alive who doesn't instantly love you?"

"Only you," I quip, only to catch myself when Brooklynn comes into view. Lenox and I are married and supposed to be in love, only he doesn't seem to care or notice, and neither does Brooklynn, who greets me with an enthusiastic smile. I'm guessing Lenox doesn't bring his women to his shop a lot.

"Come here, Alice." Lenox lets out a sharp whistle, and the dog lowers herself to the ground before she goes straight for Lenox, then nuzzles and licks at him like the attention whore she is.

"Sure, I see how it is. You're a love the one you're with gal." I turn back to Brooklyn and squeal in delight. "Hi, I'm Georgia. You must be Brooklynn. And you're pregnant!" I extend my hand, and she plows right past that, giving me a giant hug, her awesome round belly giving me the equivalent of a baby fist bump.

"You're real. I can't believe you're real. I was positive you were a blow-up doll version of Georgia Monroe. Why else would you marry him?"

"Ha," Lenox bites out.

"Oh my God! I love you!" I hug her back. "Anyone who gives him shit is my new best friend. Plus, you're pregnant, and pregnant women are my absolute favorite. I hope you don't mind. I know no one here, and I'm a clinger. Just ask Lenox."

"I would but he never talks."

I bark out a laugh and roll my head over my shoulder to find Lenox. I point at her and mouth, "I love her." He simply rolls his eyes at me, but there is no hiding the slight curl of his lips as he continues to pet his dog.

"Come inside," she says, waving me forward. "You must be curious. Lenox's casa es su casa now, right?"

I snort at Lenox's less-than-amused expression. "Absolutely."

I follow after Brooklynn, whom I was sort of picturing looking like Rosie the Riveter. You know, tall, muscular, blazing red hair that she wears up in a cool bandana. But no. Brooklynn is short—my guess is not even five feet—with ink-black hair down to her ass, almost equally dark round eyes with mega lashes, gauges in her ears, a nose ring, a lip ring, and arms as colorful as Lenox's. Her belly takes up half her size since she appears to be about eight months pregnant.

But mostly, I can't stop looking around at everything I see. Wide plank distressed hardwood floors run throughout the space. There are three private rooms in the back where I assume they do the inking and piercing, each with exposed brick and clean white walls. The ceilings are tin tiles in an oil-rubbed bronze, and in the reception area, the walls that aren't exposed brick are black.

There are no images of tattoos on the walls the way I expected there to be. Just some cool, very simple black-and-white photographs of various places or things—hands playing a piano, a street in what I think is Paris, the back of someone's head who I immediately recognize as Zax standing on a balcony in Rome, and my breath catches.

I spin around, searching the room, and find Lenox casually observing me while leaning against the wall that separates the front part of the shop from the back. "These are Suzie's photographs." It's not a question, but he nods all the same. For some reason, that immediately makes me choke up, and I turn back to the one of Zax, twisting her engagement ring around my finger.

I wish I could hug her one last time. Suzie gave the best hugs. She hugged you the way a grandmother hugs—unapologetically and free of any embarrassment. I wonder if the passage of time makes it easier for Lenox to take a breath or if he misses her more because he's gone longer without her. She'd laugh at this. At me being married to him. She knew all about my girlish crush on him.

"She helped me bake you cookies once," I say, recalling the memory as a tear tracks down my cheek that turns into a wet laugh. "I was twelve, definitely too old for a babysitter, and we were getting ready to move to LA because my mother had just gotten me my first role in a film. I was heartbroken. I didn't want to leave. So Suzie helped me bake your favorite cookies—"

"Chocolate chip with peanut butter cups in them."

I nod. "Yeah. They came out good."

"They did. So good in fact, Suzie ate half of them."

I smile, wiping my face and blowing out a breath. "I never knew that, but it sounds like her, so I'm not surprised." I turn away from the picture and skip over to the long counter that has the same distressed wood as the floors, and drop my hands down on it. "I love this place. It's very cool. It makes me want to get a piercing."

Brooklynn's dark eyes light up. "It does?! I can do that. What are you thinking about?"

I laugh lightly and shrug. "I don't know. My nose?" I scrunch it. "I've always sorta wanted a nose ring."

"We should go," Lenox says, and both Brooklynn and I throw him a death glare.

"Let me pierce your wife's nose. She'll look cute with it."

I put my hands on my hips. "Yeah, Lenox. I'll look cute with it."

He grunts and then walks to the back, leaving me here with Brooklynn. We hear the door to the back slam, and I assume he's taking Alice for a walk.

"Are you serious? Because I'll happily do it, but it does sting like a bitch."

"Pfft." I wave her away. "I can take it."

"Okay. Pick a stud, not a hoop, from the case over here." She points to a rotating, clear case and then heads to the back. "I'm in room one. I need to get set up, so meet me back there."

Oh shit. I'm doing this. A thrill of nerves skates through me, and I quickly pick out a small white gold diamond stud from the case, keeping it in the box and walking it back. Brooklynn is sterilizing the entire room, setting out prepackaged items on a metal rolling tray.

"Now I know how my patients feel," I quip.

"I think this will hurt less than having a baby, though."

"Epidurals work wonders, and so does hypnobirthing."

"You'll have to talk me through that. Hypnobirthing, I mean. I sorta want a natural childbirth, but the doctors at the hospital keep giving me funny looks every time I mention it. Have a seat." She points a gloved finger at the pleather bench. "Feet in the stirrups and bring your butt down to the end of the table."

"That's a good one. How did you know I was a midwife?" I ask as I sit in the center of the table facing her, my legs scissoring back and forth.

She shrugs. "I looked you up. I mean, I'd heard of you," she says as he continues to get everything ready, taking the nose ring from me. "I've even seen some of your movies. But you married a guy I would have sworn would never get married. I've been working for Lenox for four years. I likely know him better than anyone else in town, but I don't even know his middle name, if you know what I'm saying."

"It's Drexler."

She smirks without looking at me. "You have no idea how happy I am that he married you. Even if there is more going on than I care to know about."

"Isn't that always the case with Lenox? I feel like that should be his middle name instead of Drexler. More going on than I care to know about."

She laughs. "So true. Alright. I'm ready if you are."

My stomach sinks. "Um."

Her eyes meet mine. "Don't tell me you're getting cold feet."

"You're very cheeky, Brooklynn. And while I am brave and can definitely handle some pain, I'm scared I'll flinch or something when the needle comes near my face." Just then we hear the back door open and close, and I sigh in relief. "Lenox!" I call out, not even ashamed of what I'm about to do. I hear him make a disgruntled noise, and then Alice comes in quickly, followed by Lenox. His blue eyes meet mine expectantly. "Can you hold my hand? I'm a piercing virgin."

I expect some derision or annoyance to be hurled my way, but he doesn't do any of that. Instead, he quietly comes and sits beside me, taking my hand and holding it in both of his. Just like that.

Brooklynn's eyebrows bounce in surprise, but she quickly

launches into her spiel about how she's going to do this and that my eyes will likely tear, which is a natural reflex, and how I need to keep the piercing clean and blah, who cares? *Just do it already!*

She tells me to close my eyes, and I do, feeling her hands on my face, cleaning my nose as she does whatever it is she's doing. I suck in a sharp breath and hold it in, squeezing Lenox's hand when Brooklynn asks if I'm ready. A second later, I feel the pinch of the needle and the sharp sting in my nose. My eyes immediately water. It's like when you get hit in the nose, only worse because, after the fire of the needle, her hands are working my nose and twisting the stud into the newly formed hole.

"Done," she declares triumphantly.

I release my breath and blink open my eyes. "How's it look?"

She grabs a mirror and holds it up to my face. "Badass."

I beam. "Totally badass!" I tilt my head this way and that, taking in the glint of the tiny diamond. "I love it. OMG, why didn't I do this a hundred years ago? It's so freaking cute and so very me." I turn to Lenox. "Right?"

He's giving me a funny look I can't discern as his eyes track around my face.

"What? You don't like it."

"Come on, badass." He gives my hand a tug, grabs a bottle of piercing cleaner from a nearby shelf, and then drags me along.

"Wait! I didn't pay."

"It's on the house," Brooklynn calls after me. "Consider it my wedding present and my I'm so sorry you're married to him present."

"Thank you! I appreciate both," I yell out as he drags me out the back, Alice leading the way. "It was great meeting you!"

"You too," she yells just as the door slams shut.

"For the record, that was rude. You didn't even thank her for watching your dog."

Lenox opens the passenger door of a large pickup truck and helps me up into it.

"Wait? Where's your other car? The hot guy muscle car?" We drove up here in a Shelby GT 500CR. It was straight up the sexiest car I've ever been in. He had it custom-built just for him, but the truck we're climbing into, while nice and obviously very high-end and possibly electric, isn't anywhere near the same caliber of car.

"I keep it in a special garage. I can't take it out to the house. You'll see why. Plus, I never let Alice in it if I can help it. Her claws would scratch up the leather."

I can't argue with that, so I slam the door shut behind me and buckle up. Alice is in the king cab backseat, her head perched in between the two front seats. Lenox hops in and starts up the truck with a soft rumble.

My nose throbs a little, and I flip down the sunshade and pop open the mirror so I can look at it. It's red, but that's not surprising. I'm pale, and my skin reddens quickly and easily. Welcome to the wonderful world of being a redhead. We look awesome when we cry too.

"This has been the most surreal few days," I comment dryly as I close the mirror and push back up the shade.

I haven't heard from Alfie or Ezra again, but I know it's coming. It's not a matter of if, but when. Still, being here, I feel so far removed from that. Finally. I know I threw a tantrum about moving here—and for good reason, hello, Lenox fingering me in a bath-room—but I also know it was the right call. I have a virtual meeting with my father's estate attorney tomorrow as well as the CEO of the financial firm my father used.

By tomorrow, everything will be signed and done.

"It looks good on you," he says, and I glance in his direction.

"The nose ring?"

"Coming out of your prim and proper good girl shell. Doing things just for yourself and no one else simply because you want to. It's a good look on you."

Oh. I try not to blush. I genuinely do. But it happens anyway. "Thank you." It legit might be one of the nicest things he's ever said to me. "I do plenty just for myself too, you know. I became a midwife just for me. My mother would have kept me in Hollywood forever, and my father would have taught me the family business six years ago when I graduated college if I'd let him."

He shrugs as he pulls us back onto Maine Street, driving away from town. "Maybe so, but you've never looked more beautiful than you do right now."

I take it back. *That* is the nicest thing he's ever said to me. And it kills me. And rejuvenates me. And makes what's about to come next even more irresistibly dangerous than it already was.

Chapter Seventeen

Georgia

MY MIND IS RESTLESS, and my chest is fluttery as we continue to drive farther out of town. This is actually happening. I'm moving in with Lenox. I know I'll have my own room, and hopefully it won't be for too long, and I won't have to interact with him too much. But... I'm moving in with Lenox.

There isn't much out here. It's a two-lane road and a whole lotta trees, and that's it.

"I ordered clothes," I say, hearing the breathlessness in my own voice and wishing my nerves weren't so obvious. "I used your shop address for everything since I didn't know where your house was."

Lenox doesn't respond, but he does shift in his seat, which tells me he heard me.

"I thought about packing up my LA townhouse, but then realized I still need it for when I have to be there for board meetings and Monroe things. Plus, I had nothing there that would fit winters in Maine. I didn't think bikinis, T-shirts, shorts, or scrubs would cut it here."

"I have a hot tub."

I belt out a laugh. It's awkward as fuck, but mercifully he doesn't comment on it. "Does L.L. Bean make flannel bikinis?"

"You didn't order clothes from L.L. Bean."

I continue to stare straight ahead, especially as we turn onto a random, unmarked dirt road that leads straight into the fucking woods. It's like *The Blair Witch Project*. All I need is a camera and a runny nose, and I'll fit right in.

"No. I didn't. I ordered a lot of sweaters and fleece-lined leggings and cool warm boots and things like that. And a coat. A few coats, actually. As well as gloves, hats, scarfs, earmuffs—"

He reaches over and places his hand over mine for a brief second before returning both to the wheel. "Do you feel comfortable driving a truck?"

"I've never tried," I admit.

He's so calm. How is he so calm when I'm freaking out? I shouldn't be surprised. Freaking out isn't part of his emotional repertoire.

"I have a Jeep too. That might be better for you."

I'm about to ask why I can't get a normal car when the dirt road turns into no road at all, and now we're essentially driving along little more than a grass-covered path cut between the trees. I could never do this at night without hitting one. I'm positive of it. How he can tell where he's going is a mystery to me. There are no markings. We're legit driving through the forest, turning here and there.

We continue like this for another half a mile or so and then creep along to a tall, thin, metal gate with signage randomly placed along it that says, Danger, High-Voltage, and others that say, No Trespassing.

"You have an electric fence?"

He clears his throat, and a few minutes later, we crawl to a stop, facing the fence. Lenox presses a button on his phone, and the gate opens, though I'd never be able to tell how he knew where the opening was.

"Lenox." I gulp out his name.

"It's okay," he promises, though there is something new to his voice. A hesitancy almost. "I'll explain everything. It'll make sense when I do."

I shake my head because I highly doubt that. This isn't normal. Normal people don't live like this, and I'm not even speaking about weird normal people like myself. People with too much money or who live like a Kardashian or even people who live totally off the grid and farm all their food and survive on rainwater and solar power. All joking about his character and personality aside, this is *actually* Batman-caliber shit. Like… how does this even exist in real life?

We pull through the gate that immediately closes behind us and continue on through the woods, with nothing visible past the dense foliage. We amble slowly along, the truck jostling us about as it navigates through branches and the soft earth of the forest floor. Then, after a few more tense, far too silent minutes, we hit a clearing and…

I gasp. "Holy fuck!"

This is *not* what I expected. Not at all. My hand covers my mouth, and I start to shake.

"Lenox."

"I didn't want to tell you." He audibly swallows, and for the first time ever, I can see he's nervous as he grips the wheel.

I shake my head. "How did you…"

"You showed it to me. Remember? You told me all about it."

That's because I was so excited about it. Only I didn't know he was paying this close of attention. "And you built it?"

"I liked it."

I can't move. I'm hardly able to breathe. My trembling hand stays locked over my mouth as emotions I can hardly get a grip on spiral through me. "I can't believe you built it."

My sophomore year of college, I took an architecture elective. Our semester assignment was to design and build on the computer our dream home. Mine was a massive farm-style white house with a huge front porch, and that's exactly what I'm staring at. It's as if Lenox took the schematics I designed and used them exactly.

Then something occurs to me.

"Did you hack my college computer for this?"

He pulls up in front and presses another button on his phone, and some of the interior lights turn on, but then he's pulling around the side of the house and straight into the four-bay garage with an attached barn. Just beyond the house, a little more than a hundred yards off, I catch a glimpse of what I assume is Lake Lavender.

Lenox shuts off the truck, immediately closes the garage door behind us, and hops out. He never answered me, but as I climb down and then follow him inside, trailing behind Alice, who seems overjoyed to be home, I can't seem to catch my breath. It's caught high in my chest, only to tumble out in a whoosh when I step inside.

Dark wide plank hardwood floors sweep throughout the entire space. The kitchen, great room, and dining room are open to each other, and the family room is two-level with matching dark pillars above and a towering stone fireplace. The kitchen is, well, my dream kitchen since it's exactly as I designed it. Huge center island, all top-of-the-line professional-grade appliances, beautiful marble counters, and a white farm sink. Even the lighting is what I picked out.

I can see there are other rooms off the great room, including one with a slightly different door and a touchpad above the handle.

The furnishings are all beautiful and expensive-looking but also cozy and inviting. A lot of soft leather and gray and cream fabrics. Five chairs surround his dining room table, and I don't have to ask why there aren't six. There are five Central Square boys and no Suzie.

Lenox is making himself busy, bringing in the bags from the back of his truck and getting Alice food and water. "I pictured all black. More like your shop. I didn't ever imagine… this."

Silence.

I turn, ready to challenge him, only to find his eyes on me from across the room, standing over by the stairs. "Do you want to see your room? I obviously didn't have time to set anything up for you, but we can do that. We can make it anything you like."

No. I'm not sure I can take it. "How many bedrooms are here?"

"Five," he says, but I knew that answer before he even said it.

I cross the room to him and stare up into his cautious blue eyes.

He's so closed off. Shuttered up tight. "Did you hack my computer in college?"

"Yes," he says simply, and fury strikes a path through me.

"When?"

"After."

My fury morphs, taking on a new form. An anger so sharp and pervasive it infuses itself into my every cell. I want to pound on his chest and shake him, but I hold myself steady, holding firm to the few feet of distance I placed between us. "Why?"

"I can't tell you. Not yet."

Now I start to lose it. "Fuck you, Lenox! You hacked my computer and built my dream home. I'm entitled to know why."

He runs a hand through his hair and closes his eyes. "I hacked it for this. I wanted to build this."

Again, I go with, "Why?"

His eyes flash open. "What good is the answer, Georgia, when you're not yet ready to hear it?"

I shake my head and cut the distance between us by half. "Tell me," I demand. "You brought me here. You had to know I'd remember the house. You had to know I'd question you."

His blue eyes darken. "I already told you I liked it."

I shake my head. "Not good enough. Did you go through my laptop? Read anything else on there?"

"No. I may have morally gray ethics, but I never invaded your privacy. Not once. I never hacked your phone, and I never searched for your location, and I never went through your computer. This was the only thing I took when I left you."

"*Why?*" I grit through my teeth, and I don't even know if I'm asking why he left me or why he built the house or why I wasn't important enough to him to snoop around.

"Georgia," he says my name like a warning I have no intention of heeding. Only he has no intention of breaking. I see it in his eyes. The most frustrating part of this man is that I never know what he's thinking unless he directly tells me and wants me to know.

"You left me. Why take this piece of me with you?" I don't get it. As far as I knew, he cut all ties with me. He told me straight up the night he left that he'd never see me again. He meant it. Only the ghost of him was left to haunt me, and haunt me it did.

He straightens his spine and hovers over me, the heat from his body a sweltering furnace of acrimony.

"I let you go," I snap. "I didn't try to chase you, and I never planned to change your mind because I knew I'd never be someone you'd miss. So why'd you do this?" Everything about us was tragic from the start. I thought my love would be strong enough to help, to cure, and to fix. But it wasn't, and when I told him I loved him and saw his reaction, I knew no matter how much I loved him, it would never be enough to make him love me back or get him to stay.

But this? I didn't expect this.

And maybe I'm making too big of a deal about it. Maybe it is simply that he liked the design and nothing more. Only it's everything, down to the smallest detail. He could have designed a house similar to what I showed him, but he didn't. He built *my* dream house, and if I don't know why… if he doesn't tell me that I at least meant something to him back then, I might go insane.

I growl out in frustration when he still doesn't tell me, and I decide maybe he's right. Maybe I shouldn't know his answers or dig into his mind. What difference will it make? The outcome will remain the same. Only I'm still about to go insane over this, and I need distance. Now.

I plow past him, jabbing my shoulder into his arm as I do.

"Do you need me to show you which room is yours?"

"I designed the fucking house, Lenox. I know my way around." I start to storm up the stairs, only to stop when I reach the top, needing to say this now because I never got the chance, and if I don't tell him, I'll burst with it. "I didn't need you to love me back. I just needed to know I was more than a warm body to you, and when you left, you made me feel disposable. That's what hurt the most. It wasn't even that you didn't love me back. It was that I was nothing to you. Two years, and I was nothing."

"You weren't nothing, and you weren't disposable to me."

I laugh bitterly, tears stinging my eyes, and I hate him for them. I hate that even after six years apart, he can still make me cry.

"No? You sure fooled me." I flip around and stare down at him from above. "If I wasn't, then what was I to you? Just tell me that. Even if you tell me nothing else and we go back to hating each other or simply co-existing like two strangers in this house, just tell me that."

Woodenly, he stares up at me, and I watch the inner debate unfold across his face. "I wanted to build you your dream house. Even if I didn't think you'd ever get to see it."

With that, he walks off toward that room with the touchpad door, and for a few minutes, I just stand here, his words ruminating around my brain like they're trying to set up a permanent residence. *I wanted to build you your dream house. Even if I didn't think you'd ever get to see it.* Fucker was right. What good did that answer do me? All it did was poke at the scars he left behind, and I won't allow those wounds to be reopened.

Shaking that off, I look around the second floor. God, this place is massive. Far, far too big for one man. Especially a man like Lenox, who strikes me as the keeps-to-small-places type. I designed it so that the master sat in the largest room, taking up the entire space over the garage, and so I go in the opposite direction, tracking all the way down the hall to the last bedroom.

There are a lot of windows in here. The one straight ahead of me has a view into the woods, and the ones on my right comprises a wall of glass overlooking the lake. The room itself is minimal, with a king-sizde bed, two nightstands, and a long cobalt blue settee in front of the bank of windows that overlooks the lake. It's absolutely stunning, and I feel a pinch in my heart that I wish would just up and die already.

I try not to think about what he just said, and I certainly don't allow myself to analyze it. Instead, I go into the massive marble bathroom and take a very long shower. By the time I come out, my things are in my room, my laptop bag on the bed, and my suitcase in the walk-in closet. He waited till he heard the shower to do all that for me. So avoiding each other is going to be the name of our game, and it's finally one I'm down for playing with him.

I set myself up as best as I can in here, and eventually when my stomach starts to grumble, I go downstairs to find the door to what I presume to be his office shut.

Perfect.

Alice comes trotting up to me as I start to explore my way through the fridge, pantry, and cabinets and find not a whole lot. "Ugh. Men. They never have the necessary staples, do they? If we're going to be friends, you have to alert me when your master comes out of his Batcave. I realize that might be childish, and I know he's your people, but I don't care. Deal?"

She gives me a sniff and a nudge at my leg that I take as a blood oath.

"Good stuff. We can chill then." I rub the top of her head, and she nuzzles into me.

I make myself an omelet for lunch and eat it at the counter by myself, scrolling through my phone. I have a feeling this is going to be my life for the foreseeable future, and I realize I'm okay with that. I don't need company. I can do this new life and find my own path on my own.

Even without the man who says he built this house for me, all the while thinking I'd never see it.

Chapter Eighteen

Lenox

I'LL ADMIT, he's better than I gave him credit for. My eyes scan my bottom right monitor, watching as either he or someone he's hired strike commands on the dummy phone I created for them to hack while I spin the red rose between my hands. They're weeding through my email, but the only ones they'll find are shop-related ones. Purchasing orders, website updates, and customer inquiries. Yawn.

I lean back in my chair, stare at the rose in my hands, and then twist my left wrist until I see the new matching rose tattoo my wedding band will sit over after it's healed. My breath quickens every time I look at it.

You are deserving, Lenox Moore. Every bit as much as Zax was, if not more. If you love Georgia, which I suspect you do since you look at her like she's your universe, then don't let that go simply because you didn't do right by her once. Don't stand in your own way when you can have everything.

Even when this ends, she's permanent to me. I know that now. She always was.

174

She's my beauty, and I'm her beast.

The rose's petals are just starting to open, and I run my fingers over their velvety softness, wondering what she thinks about when she sees a new one in the bud vase on her nightstand every morning. So far, she hasn't called me out for sneaking into her room at random hours in the middle of the night to swap out the one from the night before with a fresh one.

It's been a week of this.

A week of nothing while feeling like everything is heightened. I have barely seen Georgia. She avoids me like the plague. We're two airplanes intentionally dodging each other's airspace. She met with the people she needed to meet with and signed all the necessary documents, and then spent the week here, hiding out, lost in thoughts she won't share.

And while she's been doing that, I've been digging into the dirty world of Alfie and Ezra Earnheart. All the while watching as they— or more likely their cronies—do their best to infiltrate my systems. Ezra has been texting Georgia relentlessly. It's been everything from apologies for the way he treated her in Vegas to asking where she is to begging for her to come back to him to threatening me if she doesn't. He's desperate, that much is clear.

Whether he's desperate for her or her money or both is unclear.

His desperation makes him dangerous, and though Georgia is safe here, I need to eliminate him as a threat.

During the day, I go to work, avoiding the few press that have bothered to come up here, and Georgia stays here, Alice keeping her company as they go on hikes, and Georgia reads by the wood fireplace in the back room that overlooks the lake. I make her breakfast and coffee and leave it for her, and when I come home, I cook dinner, which she eats either after I already have, or sits there ignoring me while working on her laptop.

She's mad, and she has every right to be.

But while she's mad, I'm in agony.

I'm tormented.

She's right here, but I can't touch her, and I don't know how to talk to her. I want to tell her. Aurelia told me I'm deserving and not to let this go, and maybe, just fucking maybe, she's right. I want to tell Georgia everything because part of me can't help but feel like this is what I've been building toward all these years apart. But is there any reality in that for us? This world that I live in… it's not meant for her.

It never was.

But… could I change that? I don't know.

So I sneak into her room like a man obsessed and bring her roses because the other day when I was passing by Naveah's flower shop, I saw these in the window and immediately thought of her. Crimson red and deep green with thorns that make me bleed for her.

I turn back to the screen and smirk. *You're only going to see what I allow you to, but now that you've entered my game, I'll have you soon enough. And then fucking destroy you and your wormy son.*

Hitting a few keys, I bounce him out and shut everything down before leaving my office. Alice is already asleep on her dog bed in my room, and I make my way upstairs in the dark, bringing the rose up to my nose and taking a deep inhale of its sweet fragrance as I go. With slow, quiet strides, I slink along the hall, listening intently for any sounds of her stirring. She doesn't stay awake for me, and she doesn't try to catch me in the act.

But she doesn't throw the roses in the trash either, so I take that as a win. She accepts my small olive branch, and as long as she continues to, I'll continue to bring her a new rose every night. Just as I reach her door, I freeze midstride, my body angling as I try to listen deeper.

A soft whimper followed by a strangled groan comes from her room, and I hear her shifting about in her bed. What the fuck? I inch closer, placing my ear to her door, and catch her whimper again, her body moving violently.

Shit. Is she having a nightmare?

I twist the knob, squinting as I enter, but my eyes quickly adjust as the full moonlight that's reflecting off the lake shines brightly into the room. Georgia is on her back, her head twisted to the side away from me. One hand is up her paper-thin white tank top, cupping her breast, and the other is shoved down her tiny purple sleep shorts as she grinds and fucks herself into it.

My mouth dries as heat and blood instantly shoot straight to my dick.

"Georgia?" I find myself saying, not even sure if she's awake since I can't see her face. But even before I know how I got here, I'm at the foot of her bed, needing to see her, to watch her, to hear her. As with every time I'm near her, everything else fades into the background and becomes nonexistent. No guilt. No common sense or reasoning.

It's only her.

"Georgia."

She starts, her eyes flashing open, wild and lust-hazy and unbridled with shock. And suddenly those eyes are on me as I'm climbing onto the end of the bed, staring down at her, and how the fuck did I get here?

I go to pull back, to force some awareness into my limbs when she says, "I can't tell if I'm still dreaming or not."

My throat thickens. "Were you dreaming about me?"

A jerky nod but now her hands have stilled, though they haven't shifted from their position.

I start to prowl back toward her, sliding my body up hers and spreading her legs wider as I go. "What was I doing? Tell me, and I'll tell you if it's still a dream or not."

I take the rose in my hand and bring it up to her exposed collarbone, dragging the soft petals along her skin and sweeping them across the swell of her breasts peeking out above the top of the cotton. She shivers, and I watch as she mentally debates this.

"Your face was between my thighs, and you were teasing me with your tongue," she finally admits in the softest of unsure whispers.

I don't hesitate before I grip the hem of her shorts and yank them down past her ankles, then toss them onto the floor behind me. I haven't been able to get the taste of her pussy out of my head since last week in Vegas, and I'm certainly not about to pass up an opportunity now. Not when she's looking at me, talking to me, telling me she was dreaming about me.

Her hand is still covering her pussy, and I lift her fingers, and slip them one by one into my mouth, and licking her arousal off each of them. I groan, practically losing my mind right here.

"Take off your top. I need to see all of you beneath me."

My pretty rose peels off her tank top, her tits swollen and heavy, and I lean down and capture one perfect nipple in my mouth, running the edge of the petals around the other. My hand slides down her stomach, my fingers swirling over her heated skin, until I reach her sweet, wet cunt.

"Oh, Georgie, you were already so close, weren't you?" I slide two fingers straight into her, meeting no resistance, feeling every inch of her slick pussy as it grips me like it already knows my fingers won't be enough to satisfy, but she wants them anyway.

I'm flirting with dangerous territory here. She woke up horny from a dirty dream, and this is the byproduct of it. She's letting me touch her. She wants to come. But she hates me, and tomorrow she may regret this.

She shivers as I pump my fingers into her, my eyes locked on hers, unable to tear myself away as I tease the rose along her tits, stomach, and neck.

This is how it used to be. I'd go a few days without her, and then I'd grow desperate, itchy, unable to stand being in my own skin. I'd need her. In any form I could get her. I'd arrive at her school hours before we were set to meet, and I'd plant myself in a position where I'd be able to observe her coming out of class or with her friends, laughing, smiling, living the beautiful, normal life she deserved.

And I'd try—I'd fucking try so hard—to make myself walk away from her. I'd tell myself that everything I was seeing was everything she deserved, but it didn't matter. I was always interminably hers. Unable to stay away. Needing her—only fucking her—like a drug.

I fall to my forearm, planting it in the bed beside her head, my face hovering over hers. "Look at me while I make you come. This is not a dream. These are my fingers fucking you. It'll be my cock after that. Look at me and nowhere else."

She shakes her head, my obstinate rose so unwilling to bloom for me when her body needs it so much.

I capture her bottom lip between my teeth, biting down on it until she whimpers and her nails scratch at my shoulders. "Eyes on me, Mrs. Moore."

I pull back, using the rose to tickle her, sweeping it all across her skin, down through the valley of her tits and lower, swirling it around her belly button, and then to her mound. The blood red of the rose is such an incredible contrast to the white porcelain of her skin and her eyes, those dazzling green eyes...

God, she truly takes my breath away.

Slipping my fingers out of her, I tickle the rose up and down her slit, mesmerized by the sight of it. She makes a soft, impatient noise, and I smirk at her, but I also want it too badly to tease her and make her wait. Dropping the rose on the bed, I situate myself between her thighs and immediately French kiss the hell out of her cunt. Her hand rips at my scalp, her back arching high in the air.

"Oh fuck!" she cries out, her eyes pinching closed as she grinds up and into my mouth, pressing her body in deeper, seeking more friction.

I smack her inner thigh and then her clit, reminding her how this works, and when those eyes fall right back on me, it's as if everything inside me is clicking back into place. I lick a dirty path from her asshole, ringing around her opening, all the way up to her clit, where I suck it into my mouth. She's so very, very wet, and I feel her pussy quiver against me.

I grab her ass in both of my hands and dig my fingers in, using the tip of my tongue to flick her clit. She moans as I trace her pussy with my tongue, licking every inch of her before sliding it deep inside her. Her taste... by God, the way this woman tastes. Like fucking mine.

"Please, Lenox," she begs. "More. Harder."

I almost die. Right here. Her sounds and the way she begs me with my name on her lips has me fucking against her mattress. I dive in like a man possessed, holding her open as wide as I can for my tongue and lips and teeth to devour her. I fuck her relentlessly, eating her in a way that lets her know I've been starving for her.

I'm going to make her come, taste it on my tongue, and then fuck her into next week.

Two fingers rim her dripping opening, and I slide them back inside her, crooking them to find the spot that will drive her to the next level. All the while my tongue plays with her clit, teasing it, flicking it, sucking on it. Georgia shamelessly grinds into me, her hand still in my hair—her favorite place to be when I do this to her —as her legs wrap themselves around me.

She's getting close, so very close, and I stare up at her across the valley of her body and find her propped up on her elbows, voyerishly staring down at me, watching me eat her. Her dark, dark eyes and her sweet sighs and moans and the way her teeth bite into her lip and her cheeks flush have me on the brink right along with her.

She's all I can taste, breathe, smell, and feel. All her. Only her.

I piston faster into her, rubbing her front wall mercilessly, and when I suck her clit back into my mouth, she comes with a loud cry, her body squirming, and her pussy clenching around my fingers. But I'm not done. I want her to come again and again. I suck on her pussy, making her whimper and thrash.

"Ah! Lenox. It's sensitive."

I lighten my intensity, but I don't pull away from eating her. Even as I'm tearing off my clothes blindly while I continue to lick and taste her. Once I'm naked, I give her one last kiss and take her legs and wrap them around my waist, rising up and staring down at her. I grab her tits and squeeze them roughly in my hands before I press them together and lick up the crease.

"Was that what you were dreaming about?"

She licks her lips and nods.

"Do you want me to stop?"

A headshake.

"Georgia, of the two of us, I'm the silent one. Tell me what's going through that beautiful head of yours."

She sighs and rubs her hands up and down her face before she sits up and touches my chest, swirling her finger along my ink and across my nipple rings. "That even though I shouldn't, I want this." Her gaze crawls up to mine. "I want you."

In a heartbeat, I grab her wrists and pin them over her head, stretching her out. My mouth attacks hers as I grind my cock against her pussy, the barbells on the underside rubbing her.

"Oh! Ah!" She arches again, crushing her tits against my chest.

She licks my lips, tasting herself on me as I rock my hips and continue to slide against her folds and clit. She's so warm and wet, and I slide so effortlessly, it's taking everything in me not to immediately slam into her.

"Fuck, Lenox. God, that feels so good. So fucking good."

I continue to hold her down, biting her breasts, licking and sucking on them all the while I grind my cock against her clit. She fights me, her arms squirming, her wrists trying to break free, but I won't allow it. I'm feral, wanting to tear her apart. Wanting to mark every inch of her skin so she knows who it belongs to.

She continues to writhe beneath me, panting and gasping, her nails scratching at my hand. "I need you inside me," she sighs.

"I want you to come again first."

I pump against her, sliding harder and faster, watching with rapt fascination as my cock rings rub her clit, and her cunt soaks me in her cum. Her thighs are trembling, her head trashing between her raised arms, and I use my free hand, the one that's been roaming over her skin, to pinch and twist her nipple. And when I do that, she detonates, coming on a wet rush all over me, and *fuuuuuck*, it feels *so* good. So good that I have no choice but to shift the angle and plunge deep inside her.

"Motherfuck!" she screams as I immediately start pounding into her while she's still coming.

The walls of her pussy are swollen and hot, and I have to grit my teeth not to come on the spot. My hand still holds her wrists, and our sweaty chests are pressed together. With my eyes locked on hers, I stare into her and fuck her.

"Come inside of me," she pants. "I want to feel you come in me."

Jesus. Her words. Her filthy fucking words spin my life around.

Because I want to come in her. I want to come in her over and over again. I want to come in her without that IUD inside her. I want to see her pregnant and smiling and happy, and I want to hold her goddamn hand as we walk down the fucking sidewalk.

This is not who I am.

But with her, it is.

I am lost to her. With her, I see a future I never imagined I could have, but now that she's here, it's all I can think about. It's all I want. This marriage is fake to her, but it's so real to me that I can't stop myself as my face falls into her neck and I nibble on her flesh and silently mouth, "I love you." Even if it changes nothing.

I stab into her, digging in deeper, using my hips to press myself against her clit with every pounding slap of our bodies. Sweat glides across my forehead and down the center of my back with how hard I'm driving into her.

I take her mouth, kissing her violently and messily but also worshipfully. I can hardly catch my breath, but I can't stop either. She's bucking against me, wild in her movements with one leg around my hip, the other bent on the bed, widened to allow me to go as deep as I can. My balls draw up, and I'm getting close. It's the feel of her, the scent of her skin, the taste of her on my lips, and the uncontained way I can't stop fucking her.

But she has to come. She has to, so I slip my fingers between our slick bodies and find her clit with my thumb.

"Hard or soft?" I ask against her lips.

"Hard. Now. I'm right there."

So I give it to her hard. I press my thumb on her clit and rub it back and forth, and within seconds, she starts to lose it. I release her hands, and they immediately wrap around my neck, her nails scratching brutally at my upper back as her face presses into my chest, and she comes harder than I think I've ever seen her come. I fuck her through it, and when I can't stand it another second, I let go and my orgasm barrels through me. I still, my back wrenching and I roar, shooting everything I have into her in hot, soul-twisting spurts.

After the last jerk of my hips, everything goes black, and I collapse, unable to catch my breath. I press her into the mattress, my body heavy and my limbs languid. Slowly consciousness creeps back in, and I roll us so she's on top of me and I'm holding her, whispering uncontained words like how beautiful she is and how perfect and how nothing feels as good as being inside her.

My fingers trail down her back, admiring the slope and curve of her body, and when I think I can manage to walk, I climb out of bed and enter her bathroom to wet a washcloth. Bringing it back to her, she reaches for it, and I shove her hand away.

"I want to do it," I tell her, and she falls back, staring up at the ceiling as I wipe up my cum that's dripping out of her. I run my fingers through it and push some of it back into her, making her emit a shaky, breathy laugh.

"Are you breeding me?"

I throw her a raised eyebrow. "Is that an option?"

"Kinky slut."

I laugh. "Cock whore."

Her eyes close, and I finish cleaning her up, and by the time I've returned from the bathroom, she's back under the covers. Only that's not going to fly. No way am I leaving her after that, so I pull back the blanket and climb in behind her.

"I didn't invite you to stay."

I wrap my arm around her belly and yank her in tightly against me. "I'm not giving you the option." I kiss her neck. "Go back to sleep, Georgie."

I get a swift jab to the flank, and I hold her closer, kissing up her neck.

"This doesn't change anything between us."

"You're wrong," I say. "It changes everything between us."

My breath stalls in my chest as the truth of that slams into me with the subtlety of a head-on collision. This wasn't just a one-timer like it was in Vegas. She's living in my house, and the notion that we'll be able to stay away from each other after that is preposterous. But more than that, I don't *want* to stay away from her.

Not anymore.

Not ever again.

You are deserving, Lenox Moore. Every bit as much as Zax wa,s if not more. If you love Georgia, which I suspect you do since you look at her like she's your universe, then don't let that go simply because you didn't do right by her once. Don't stand in your own way when you can have everything.

I swallow, lick my lips, breathe in and out, and after a quiet few minutes of coming to grips with just what this means for myself, for my life, for her, I utter, "I want it to change everything between us." Only she didn't hear me because she's already asleep. Fuck.

Chapter Nineteen

Georgia

I WAKE MUCH the same way I did after our night together in Vegas, with Lenox asleep behind me and the soft light of dawn hitting me through the window. Only now, I'm focused on three things. One, the rose on the bed beside my hand. Two, the rose that's still in the vase since he never got the chance to swap it out last night. And three, the rose tattoo on Lenox's left ring finger.

He must have done it himself this week, but when exactly, I'm not sure. I don't know what to think about it. I don't know what to think about him or the roses or any of it. He said this changes everything, but what does that even mean? Is that what I want? Do I want to go down this road again with him? Not really if I'm being honest, and yet yes, one hundred percent I do.

It's the split between my body and my mind. My body craves him, and my mind remembers all he did to my heart.

He's twisting me up, playing with things I haven't given him permission to. Things that no longer belong to him and never should have. I've isolated myself this past week, especially from him.

On Tuesday, I handled the Monroe business. I am the official majority shareholder of Monroe Securities, and all of my father's assets are now mine. But I didn't pick up my phone when my mom called or even when Zax or Grey called. The only people I've spoken to are Fallon and Aurelia, because those bitches are persistent and wouldn't allow me to shelter in place.

I wanted this week. A week of not a whole lot.

I went on hikes with Alice and explored every inch of Lenox's house, with the exception of his cave. I've read and cried and worked out a lot of what I want my next steps to be.

It's been cathartic, and I'm grateful for having that time for myself.

But today I want to go into town. I want to check out the yoga studio, the coffee shop, and maybe the library. I'm afraid to try and navigate through the fence thing and the forest on my own, so I had planned to bite the bullet and ask Lenox if I could ride with him.

But now…

You're wrong. It changes everything between us.

I pinch my eyes shut, listening to his deep, even breathing, feeling the heat and size of his body as he cocoons me. Lenox always held me like I was the most precious thing in the world to him when I slept. The comfort and tenderness were so cruelly misleading.

But… could he have changed? Could what he wants from me be different now?

Ugh. Shut up, Georgia! Don't you dare *start that shit again.*

My eyes flash open, narrowing in on the rose tattoo, and I reach over, hovering my finger above it, only to be swooped around, somehow landing on top of Lenox. Planting my hands into his chest, I push myself up until I'm straddling him and peer down, not even caring that it's bright as fuck in here and I'm completely naked and exposed to him. He cares, though. He cares a lot as I feel his cock thicken beneath my ass while his dark, smoldering eyes rake in every inch of me.

I fold my arms, partially covering my breasts. "Care to explain that?" I raise an eyebrow and pointedly zip my gaze down at his left hand that's inching up my thigh.

"I'm about to use it to make my wife come."

I shake my head, ignoring the way I get a tickly tingle in my body every time the bastard calls me his wife. "Don't play coy. You know what I'm talking about."

"Roses are beautiful, just like my wife is."

"Argh! Shut up!"

He chuckles and shoves my hands out of the way so he can cup my breasts. "Come on, Georgie, this is supposed to be our honeymoon phase."

"I don't think most wives want to kill their husbands the way I want to kill you."

He pinches my nipple, making my breath hitch. "Sure, they do. That's why they call it makeup sex."

"You're not going to tell me, are you?"

He treats me to a rare, charming smile, and my belly does a stupid cartwheel. Does he have to be so damn gorgeous? And playful right now? It's annoyingly disarming. Especially because the man is rarely, if ever, playful.

"I hate you," I mutter.

"You may think you do, baby, but your body doesn't agree." He slides me back and forth over his hard cock, over his piercings, much the way he did last night, and holy mother of kittens, does that feel so flipping good.

"I can hate you and fuck you." At least that's what I keep telling myself. "Your wonder dick has never been connected to your brain or your heart. Why should now be any different?"

"I already told you everything is different."

He grinds up into me, pumping against my pussy, practically slipping in each time, and I want him to just fuck me already. I don't want him to talk or say perfect things or look at me like this. Like I'm all he sees. Like this time, it really is different.

The weight of his eyes holds me in their possession, and the knowing grin that passes his lips simply pisses me off.

"You're not getting my pussy."

He laughs. Rubs me until my clit glides over his barbells. Then he reaches up and yanks on my hair until my face is forced down, and my lips connect with his. "The mistake you make is thinking this is your pussy when it's actually mine."

He shifts me, and with a harsh breath and a deep thrust, he plunges inside me, all the while keeping my face right with his. Daring me to deny it. To deny him. He knows I can't. Lenox Moore has always been my weakness. It's the thing I hate most about myself. It's why I've kept my distance all these years. It's most definitely why I didn't want to move in with him.

Part of me knew we'd eventually end up here.

"Don't fight it," he growls when I hold my body still. "Let me fuck you. Or better yet, you fuck me. Use me, Georgia. Make yourself come using my cock. Do it," he commands when I still don't move. "Punish me the way you want to punish me. The way I deserve for you to. Take out all your anger, pain, and aggression on me. Make me feel all that I've done to you."

"You want me to hate fuck you?"

He bites my bottom lip before he sucks it into his mouth and then slowly releases it. "Whatever it'll take to get it out of your system."

Whatever it'll take to get it out of my system? What? Hating him? My scorn?

You're wrong. It changes everything between us.

There's more to this with him. I know there is. I can practically taste it on his lips as he bites and licks at my mouth. But with him inside of me like this, with how full I am of him, it's impossible to tease it out. He wants me to punish him? To fuck all my anger, aggression, and pain out?

I roll my hips and grind my pussy against him, using his pelvic bone and the base of his cock to rub my clit. He smirks triumphantly, but I'm about to use him like he's my sex toy, and my toy is only a giver of pleasure and never a receiver of it. The nice thing about Lenox is that he's a good boy and never ever comes before I do.

He starts kissing my neck, and I pull back because his mouth on me isn't just sex. It's mind-twistingly incredible, and right now, I'm trying to hate fuck him. Only I'm not good at it because I'm moving slowly, grinding, undulating, and his hands are on my tits, rolling and pinching my nipples, squeezing them as he stares up at me in wonder. His eyes are dark and hungry, and I can see he wants to take over, to control this, but he's not. He's letting me fuck him any way I want to.

And the power in that is heady.

This is on my terms. It's all about me and not about him. And before, so much of our—whatever you want to call it—that we had was about him. He'd call or text, and I'd drop everything to be with him. We'd fuck on his terms in his way, and that was that. He never took me out for dinner, and he never spent a ton of extra time with me. It was sex and only sex to him, and I was young and stupid and in love with him.

Then he broke my heart, and I *hated* him for the woman I had allowed him to turn me into. I swore I'd never do that to myself again. Not ever, and now here I am, fucking him again. Only… this time I'm in control. I have the power between the two of us.

That's what he's telling me. That's what he's showing me.

"So good," he praises. "You ride me so good. And fuck, you are so goddamn beautiful as you do it."

I shake my head and close my eyes so I don't have to look at him and pick up my pace. I start to bounce so I can take his cock deeper while I force myself to think of him as nothing more than a vehicle to get me off.

"I'm sorry I hurt you, Georgia," he says, and I gasp, biting into my lip as a flare of emotion swells up within me. "I'm so fucking sorry. I never ever wanted to do that to you, and I was wrong, so fucking wrong for how I treated you and the things I did."

"Shut up, Lenox!" I scream, but I'm also starting to cry, and I can't stand it. His apology when he's inside of me is too much. I twist my body until I'm in a reverse cowgirl, and my back is to him and his stupid, fucktastic piercings are rubbing against my G-spot.

Only that's not good enough for him. He sits up, his chest pressing to my back, his mouth by my ear. One hand goes to my clit, rubbing it, helping me along, and his other hands around my body, cradling me to him.

"I didn't deserve you," he hums into my ear. "I knew it then. I knew it all along, but I didn't know how to give you up. I couldn't make myself walk away. I wanted you like nothing and no one else, Georgia, but I was too broken to be any good to you."

My heart clenches, stealing my breath and making my eyes burn with more tears. "Please stop. I don't want to hear it. I don't fucking want to hear it."

He kisses my neck and finally, mercifully, falls silent. He rubs my clit as I impale myself on him over and over, going as deep as I can go, rocking forward and backward, but I'm struggling. His apology is killing me, and I want to come, and I want to hate him, and I want to stay mad, but I'm struggling so hard with it that my orgasm won't come.

Lenox feels it too. A point he proves as he pushes me forward and smacks my ass before grabbing my hip and slamming me down harder on him until I moan. "That's it. Do you like that? Do you want me to make you come?"

Bastard. He knows exactly what he's doing.

"Be a good little slut and spread your legs wider for me. I want to feel all of you."

Fuck. Just fuck. He fucking knows that gets me hot. I spread my thighs wider and fall forward, planting my hands on the end of the bed.

"That's so goddamn hot. The way your ass moves as you bounce on me. How your slick cunt takes my cock. Keep going. You're not to stop until you come."

His barbells rub the front wall of my pussy, and my eyes close, losing myself in the sensation of his fingers on my clit and his cock filling me up in all the right ways. He smacks my ass once, twice, and then I finally come. Hard. So hard I nearly fall off the bed, but Lenox swoops his hand around my waist and holds me as he starts to pound into me, fucking me through it as I shake and moan.

And just when I finished, but before I allow myself to sag, I tear myself off him, spin around, and squeeze around the wet head of his cock, strangling his orgasm and not allowing him to come.

"Fucking Christ, Georgia!" he bellows, falling back on the bed and tossing his forearm over his eyes, his face pinching up in agony. He doesn't try to fight me, and he doesn't push me off. He takes it because he knows he deserves it, and worse. He's panting and wheezing and shaking, but when I think I've stopped it, I hop off the bed, grab him by his arm, and tug as hard as I can.

"Out. I need a shower, and then you're driving me into town."

He's sweating, his face is beet red, and his cock is rock hard and angry-looking. The tip is leaking like I've never seen before. But he's smiling. Somehow, he's smiling at me. Standing, he groans, ambling like a man in pain toward the door, but before he gets there, he swoops in and steals a kiss.

I shake my head, shoving him out the door and locking it behind him.

"And no making yourself come."

He laughs like I'm crazy, which maybe I am. I bite my smile. I've never considered myself a sadist, but that was liberating. And ruining. His apology…

My smile instantly slips, and a shudder racks through me. What he's doing… this game he's playing with me… it's a tempting time bomb. It's a brewing storm hellbent on destruction and utter ruination.

Then again, he didn't tell me anything I didn't already know. He wanted me. I already knew that. We were messing around for two years, and you don't continue something like that for that long unless you physically want the person. He didn't love me, and he was definitely still using me—he didn't claim otherwise—but he didn't mean to break my heart, and he didn't mean to hurt me. Fine.

I can live with that.

Or not because I'm not here for the long run.

I don't have to think too deeply about this. It's an apology for the past and nothing more.

After hopping in the shower, I wash myself quickly and then

change into leggings and a loose one-shoulder sweater. I was going to check out the yoga studio, but I think a class will have to wait for another day. With how shaky my limbs are, I doubt I could even manage child's pose right now.

By the time I come downstairs, Lenox is already there, leaning against the counter, his glasses on—I'm a wild sucker for him in those glasses—reading something on a tablet. Alice comes prancing over to greet me, nuzzling against my leg, and I crouch down to give her rubs and head snuggles.

Alice is such a love, so sweet and affectionate. So very different from her person.

"I'm ready whenever you are," I announce, going over to the table where my purse has been sitting and sorting through it, making sure I have everything.

"A box was delivered for you at the shop."

"Great!" Finally. I had an old work friend go into my townhouse and get some of the personal things I didn't bring with me when I initially flew out here. It's weird to be living somewhere else after I just recently moved. I feel so displaced without my day-to-day things. I never planned on not returning to LA. All of this happened so fast, sorta sweeping the rug out from beneath my feet. I've been living with whatever I packed two weeks ago and the stuff I bought online and had shipped.

"What do you know about your father's will?" Lenox asks as he packs up a messenger bag and starts to head for the garage door.

"Um. Not a lot. His attorney handled it all."

"Were you surprised you were named beneficiary?"

I climb up into his Jeep, closing the door behind me. Alice makes a noise but then curls down on the floor by the back seats.

"Yes. I assumed my mom would have been. His attorney was the executor and simply told us this was with the will."

"It wasn't," he says simply, though there is nothing simple about that.

I fall back in my seat, staring up at the black roof of the car. "Okay." I sigh. "I assume I'm not about to like what you're going to say."

"Georgie, there's a lot of fishy stuff with all of this that doesn't quite add up. Your father had a will originally drafted when you were born. Your mother was the sole beneficiary of everything, but you were the secondary beneficiary upon her demise. That's all pretty standard. But about eight months ago, two months before his death, your father changed his will entirely, and there are no notes as to why in his file in his attorney's system. He simply made you the sole financial beneficiary of everything from the life insurance to investments to the Monroe stock shares, with the stipulation that you must be married to inherit the Monroe stock. Your mother essentially lost billions, only getting the house and cars, which were already half in her name. Was she upset at all?"

It feels like the wind has been knocked out of me. I stare down at my hands, at the rings on my fingers, twisting them around and around. "She was upset. My father had just died, and she was wrecked over it. The two of us did little else other than cry for weeks. The will was read about two months after his death. She had been pushing my father's attorney to do it sooner, but he held her off for reasons I can't come up with. When the will was finally read, she looked shocked, but I assumed it was because she thought she would be the beneficiary. She didn't say anything about it though, and she has plenty of her own money from her acting and commercial stuff." I pause, my heart pumping out a few extra beats. "You don't know why he changed it?"

"No. And it doesn't make sense to do that randomly."

"Maybe it's because it was so close to my wedding? I mean, he did include the part about me having to be married."

"Perhaps," he finally replies as we bump along through the forest like Little Red Riding Hood. "But it still seems fishy. Your father logged in a lot of phone calls from his office phone to his attorney. No emails were exchanged. Never once did he call him on his cell phone. It was only office phone to office phone."

"I'm not understanding."

"A hacker can't gain access to a landline. The only time a landline is ever tapped is if there's a court order, and that has to go through the phone company, but since so few people have landlines anymore, there's rarely a need. Your father, who owned a cyber security company, knew this."

"Lenox, what the fuck are you saying?"

"I'm saying your father completely changed his will two months before he died. I'm saying he did everything covertly and entirely under the radar, so no one would be the wiser. But then he went and added in the stipulation that you have to be married, and that was only to inherit Monroe, not his wealth or primary assets. It's strange, Georgie. All of it."

"First, stop calling me Georgie. I can't elbow you since you're driving, and I really don't want to hit a tree right now. Second, are you suggesting I had something to do with my father's death?"

He throws me a perturbed side-eye. "Of course not. I'm saying your father had everything moved to you because he trusted you and wanted you and no one else to inherit. You had no knowledge of this. No one did as far as I can tell. But why did he do it? That's the question. No one just wakes up one day and decides to do something like that without cause."

I'm stunned silent.

"Other than me, the person who would have benefited the most is Ezra. Correct?"

He nods.

"Do you think Ezra had my father killed?"

He's silent for a moment, and eventually we hit the main road and head toward town. "I thought about that. If we assume he knew about the will change somehow or even did something to coerce it, that's a motive for killing your father. Ezra has done some very fucked financial shit over the last year. He is in deep with bookies. He sold off all of his Monroe stock, which would have been a hefty tax payment unless he plans to report a ton of losses this year. His father gave him twenty grand that he immediately used to pay off a bookie. And while I don't think Ezra is all that bright, I don't see how him blowing up your father's plane right before your wedding would help him. He would have had to have figured you'd postpone the wedding. Plus, the timing is weird. You told me your father returned early from Paris because you called him wanting to call off the wedding. By all accounts, Ezra was not in your phone, so there's no way he'd know about the early return. But is it impossible? Definitely not."

"Alright. So maybe it wasn't him, or possibly anybody. Except now I'm the majority shareholder, and instead of being married to Ezra, I'm married to you."

"Yes."

A terrifying thought hits me, sending chills racing up my spine. "If I had married Ezra, would he have killed me for my money and the shares given how financially destitute he is? And moreover, have I potentially put your life in danger?"

He shrugs. "I'm superfluous and only inherit your wealth and the company if you're dead. But yeah, a part of me is starting to think that you marrying me might have saved your life."

Chapter Twenty

Georgia

I'M silent for the rest of the ride. I have questions. Oh lord of the underworld, do I have questions. But mostly I'm not sure what to do about any of it. Or more, I'm not sure what I *can* do about any of it. It's disconcerting, to say the least, and I don't know what, if anything, I should say to my mom. She didn't know about the will change any more than I did. She wasn't even upset about the money going to me, just surprised.

Any rift between us lately has been surrounding her wanting me to marry Ezra, as that's what my father had wanted.

Speaking of...

Ezra: I miss you. I still can't believe you did this to us. All I want is you back.

I sigh. He's averaging roughly five to six texts a day. Lenox pulls out his phone, checks it, and grits his teeth, his blue eyes peering coolly over at me. I'm assuming since he's tapped into Ezra's phone, he can see that text.

"You should know he does miss you. He's a whiny bitch to his father and his friend about it."

I roll my eyes. "Oh, you mean pervy Frank?"

He tilts his head. "That's what you call Francis Caulder?"

"He stares at my tits every time he talks to me."

"I can't blame him for that, even if I now want to kill him for it. You should also know Ezra is fucking around with his assistant."

I snort. "Poor Marni. She was sweet but always very obviously in love with him. Why are you telling me this?"

"In case you were planning to go back to him."

"I'm not. He's lying to Frank to make himself look like the victim. He doesn't miss me. He misses his shot at my money. Besides, that ship sailed long before I didn't marry him. Not that being married to you has been the time of my life either, but likely better by comparison."

He studies me. "You still don't forgive me yet?"

I smile sweetly. "Nope. How are your balls? Are they blue?" My voice drops when I say that, and I make a sad face.

He grins and gives my hair a playful tug. "Nope. I had the smell and taste of your pussy all over my fingers from rubbing your clit, in addition to the mental image of you fucking me this morning. I had no problems jerking off in the shower."

"You should get used to that. You'll be doing it from now on."

He chuckles as if that's the funniest thing I've ever said and then hops out of his truck and comes around to help me down before I can do it myself. Alice jumps down after me, and he lets her in the shop's back door.

I'm fuming. More annoyed and confused and stressed now than I was five minutes ago. Men suck. "What is it about me that makes it so fucking easy and desirable for you assholes to use me without care or remorse?"

Lenox freezes, his hand that was sorting through the mail poised in midair, clutching an envelope. Slowly, he turns to face me, his eyes fierce as he takes two steps until he's directly before me. "You weren't easy to use, and I certainly never did so without care or remorse." He looks away for a moment, as if he's gathering his thoughts and figuring out the right way to say this before turning back to me. "I held nothing in my hands, Georgia. But more importantly, I wasn't deserving of anything real to fill them. I was empty inside and out. I already told you this morning that I didn't deserve you, and I knew it all along. My life was a mess, and you telling me you loved me was the wake-up call I never knew I wanted or needed. I had to go out and try and fix myself. I had to make amends for all my wrongs the only way I could. But hurting you has been one of the main regrets of my life. Up there with letting Suzie die."

I make a disgruntled noise in my throat, if for no other reason than to clear the emotion away. I have a lot to process with that, as I do with everything freaking else. But he has to know this. He has to.

"Do you know what I do for a living?"

"You're a midwife."

"Yes, Lenox Moore, I'm a midwife. That means I deliver babies and help women through their reproductive process. I have had women die on the table for no fucking reason. I have seen mothers lose babies, and babies lose mothers. And from my professional viewpoint, you have never been responsible for Suzie's death."

He gulps and then gulps again, his eyes glassing over. "How did you know she was pregnant?"

My fingers trickle over his stubble-lined jaw. "You told me."

His eyes pinch shut, and he releases a shaky breath. "Evidently, I did talk to you when I spoke to no one else."

My fingers comb back into his hair, and I grip the back of his head so he really listens to me. "Headaches are extremely common in pregnancy and can range from simple hormonal changes to dehydration to lack of protein to something scarier. Suzie was twenty-two, young and healthy, and didn't tell any medical provider about her headaches or her other symptoms. She didn't even tell Zax about them. That means they couldn't check her urine or blood for abnormalities. Yes, you knew about the headaches and a few other symptoms. But she was twenty-two, Lenox. I'm not sure as a provider I would have caught it either."

I give the strands of his hair a little shake.

"Suzie's death was not your fault. Do you hear me?"

A nod.

"Good." I reach up and plant a kiss on his cheek, then release him to head for the front door. I need to leave him. I need to be alone with my thoughts for a while, but before I can escape, he grabs my hand and joins me, leading me out the front of the store and walking us down the sidewalk together like we're an actual couple. Everyone we pass gives us a doubletake, but no one says anything.

"What are you doing?"

"Giving the paparazzi who are pretending to blend in with the townspeople something to photograph."

"Fabulous," I deadpan.

He stops and turns, and without warning, leans in and kisses my lips. And then he hugs me, holding me to him as if I'm something priceless. Something so precious to him that he has to hold me. Whether it's in gratitude for what I told him or something else, I don't care.

I needed this hug too. More than I realized.

I clear my throat and push him back. "We already did this show at the game last weekend. What more do we have to prove at this point?"

He starts to walk with me again, still holding my hand. "Since you won't text him back, I'm simply reiterating to your ex that you're mine."

I snort. "I'm not yours, Lenox, and if you want to text him back on my behalf, go for it. I won't have to deal with him until the board meeting early next month."

Lenox stops abruptly, his hand jerking me back until I practically slam into his chest. His free hand cups my face, and his eyes blaze directly into mine. "You are mine, Georgia. You've always been mine. I just have to get you to forgive me first, and then you'll know how deep this goes." He steps into me, his thumb dragging up and down my cheekbone, his eyes scorched with emotion. "Tell me how to get you to forgive me."

I realize forgiving him isn't the issue. I think I do forgive him. I think I was nearly there before, but his apology this morning and then again just now solidified it for me. It's more I'm afraid of what admitting that, especially out loud, will do to me.

His possessive side isn't new. It was actually one of my favorite things about him. I relished the way he possessed me. Hell, he even said it point-blank on the plane before we ever ended up back in bed with each other. But I'm toying with a slippery slope, and one false move could send me over the edge, falling toward a place I might not return from.

Still, with him looking at me like this, staring so deeply, so intently into my eyes, holding me this way, I find myself asking, "What happens if I forgive you?" Because I need to know his truth. I need to know if I'm the only one at risk here.

Before he can answer, my name is screamed out through the streets. "Georgia!"

Lenox groans, his forehead momentarily falling to mine, before he releases me and takes a step back.

I turn to find Brooklyn hurriedly waddling up the street with two other women, one of them also pregnant, beside her, seemingly just as excited as she is.

"You're still alive!" she yells since she's about four storefronts from us. "My husband and I were placing bets on whether or not Lenox had you stuffed in his basement yet or not."

I raise an eyebrow at her and turn back to Lenox. "You have quite the reputation here."

He leans in and kisses me. Right here on the sidewalk. Right in front of freaking Brooklyn and these two women and everyone else. Without another word, he turns and walks back toward his shop.

"Yeah, you better go, Lenox. Your dude will be here in about ten."

I head back toward the ladies. "His dude?"

Brooklynn shrugs. "His hush-hush client that I'm not allowed to discuss since I've signed an NDA. He booked four hours with Lenox. It's why he's going in today when the shop is technically closed."

Oh right. I forgot that Lenox said it's normally closed on Mondays.

"But straight facts, that kiss was hot. I had no idea Lenox was capable."

I don't say a word to Brooklynn on that and thankfully, she plows on.

"Georgia, these are two of my friends. This is Miranda," she introduces, pointing to the tall, willowy brunette on her left, "and this is Paige." She points to the pregnant blonde, who appears to be about four months, if I had to guess, but she's all belly.

"Hi! It's so nice to meet you both." I shake their hands.

"Miranda works at the library, and Paige owns the yoga studio. We were just on our way for our weekly coffee date, but then saw you, and since everyone in town is dying to meet you, I figured you might want to join us. Did you know the entire town has been trying to set Lenox up for months? He wasn't biting."

I may gasp. "You were trying to set him up? With whom?"

"Any single warm-blooded female," Paige explains.

Wow. That's some stuff right there. I cackle just picturing the town busybodies trying to play matchmaker with him. No wonder he married me without much of an argument. He must have hated that.

"That's fabulous. I wish I had seen it." The women give me strange looks, and, oh, right, I'm married to him and supposed to be in love. Oops. I clear my throat. "I was going to check out the yoga studio and the library," I say, changing the subject. "I haven't gotten a chance to explore the town yet." Because I've been hiding out for a week.

"Come have coffee with us," Paige suggests. "We'll happily show you around—"

"After you give us all the dirt on your marriage to Lenox," Miranda throws out with a teasing smile. "We still can't believe he's finally married. And to you." She blanches and doinks her forehead. "Gah, nothing I'm saying is coming out right. Sorry, I'm a bit starstruck. I've seen all of your films. My favorite is *Holiday Bright*."

I laugh. "I was like sixteen when I filmed that."

"I know!" she exclaims. "But you were so good in it, and I wanted to be your best friend. Sorta how everyone wants to be Taylor Swift's best friend."

"Yeah, I can get that," I admit. "I'd like to be best friends with her too. Or at least get sloppy seconds on some of the men she's dated."

"Right?" Paige snorts. "I'm there with you on that."

"Though you're married to Lenox now. He's a celebrity. A hot celebrity. Kind of scary and intimidating, but still hot." Miranda sighs in a self-deprecating way. "I really need to stop speaking."

"You're totally fine. I promise. But you mentioned coffee, and I'd like to get off the sidewalk if there's paparazzi lingering about."

Brooklynn gives me a funny look as we start walking. "There's no paparazzi. We scared them all off. I mean, there were several lurking about last week, but we don't fuck around in this town, especially when it comes to Lenox."

I trip over my feet. "For real? No paparazzi in town? Does Lenox know this?"

Her eyebrows bounce in surprise at my question. "Of course he knows. The last of them were run out of town on Saturday."

I wipe at the smirk on my lips. I could kill Lenox, and yet… ugh. That man is a weasel squirming his way back in.

"How's the nose ring?" Brooklynn asks.

"Good. Healing well, as far as I can tell."

"It looks like it is," she asserts, inspecting me. "Wave to my husband."

"Huh?"

She points at the hardware store. "That's my husband, Max. He owns the hardware store."

I wave to the tall man inside the store talking to a customer, though he doesn't seem to notice me. The frosty bite of the wind slaps into us, and we all huddle a bit into our coats, my boots crunching on the fallen leaves strewn about the sidewalk.

"I take it I need to get used to the cold."

"It's supposed to snow this weekend," Paige informs me with an apologetic grimace.

"Ugh," I moan. "Don't tell me that. I'm not ready for snow. It's only the second week of November."

"Sorry to be the one to tell you this, but it already snowed up here. Last month, we had a small storm. You get used to it." Miranda laughs at my appalled expression.

It's been a while since I lived in Boston. Four years, to be exact, since I graduated with my master's and then moved back to LA to be near my parents.

"You're a midwife, right? I mean, not that we haven't totally cyberstalked you, because we obviously have."

I laugh at Paige. "Yes, I'm a midwife. And you're what… sixteen weeks or so?"

"Seventeen. Good call. Brooklynn and I were wondering if you were going to be practicing locally. The nearest OB's office is at the hospital, which is about forty minutes away. It sucks. It's the one thing this town is missing. A good women's health provider."

"Yeah," Brooklynn picks up as we continue to walk to the other end of Main Street. "And since it's such a young town, there are several of us preggo women. We need you. Please tell me you can be our midwife." She holds up her hands in supplication, and I'm rendered momentarily speechless as the idea swirls through my head.

I miss practicing something fierce. This past week, I filled out all the necessary applications and forms to get licensed in Maine. It's insanely easy, and in Maine, I can work as a sole provider without physician supervision. Even though I did that, I haven't applied, or even looked for a job because I don't know how long I'm going to stay. If the paparazzi are already gone, I might not have to stay much longer.

But I never considered my own practice.

It's…

No way. Not possible. Starting a private practice means I'm staying. Lenox and I haven't even discussed a timeframe for this. I'm only here because Ezra and Alfie are looking into contesting my marriage to Lenox, and we need to make this thing look real to everyone. I never thought of Maine as anything long-term.

But now...

I clear my throat. "I have to get my license here first, and after that, I have no idea what I'll do." It's the truth. I can't tell them that my time here is limited because no one knows my marriage to Lenox is fake.

We enter the coffee shop that has a cute little bell over the door and collectively groan at the blasting heat and the smell of freshly brewed coffee and baked goods. The store is just as cute as everything else in this town seems to be. Cozy-looking chairs and mixed seating areas with a gas fireplace in the back. The walls are more of the exposed brick that Lenox has in his shop, with a giant chalkboard affixed to the wall behind the counter boasting various drinks and sandwiches.

My stomach growls accordingly.

The people in the café are definitely staring while blatantly whispering about me.

"It's because you're married to Lenox," Paige explains. "That's all. He's done so much for this town, and everyone here loves him and protects him, but he's still a total mystery to us. Like Bruce Wayne to the people of Gotham."

Clearly, they get the Batman vibes from him too. I shake my head. "I don't understand what you mean by he's done so much for the town." This seems to be a recurrent theme I'm missing.

She gives me an incredulous look, but before she can answer me, a woman with brown hair and blue eyes comes rushing from behind the counter to greet us. She hugs each of the women one by one, and then grabs my hand and starts shaking it.

"Hi! I'm Heather. This is my place. I'm so glad you're here."

"Hi, Heather. I'm so glad to be here." I hold in my laugh at her overexuberance.

"Heather, slow your buttered roll. You're going to rip her arm off," Miranda chastises.

"Right. Sorry." Heather pulls back. "I'm just so excited to meet you. Everyone in town has been talking about you. In a good way, of course. What can I get you? On the house. Any wife of Lenox's can have whatever she wants."

What is with this town and loving Lenox so much?

"Um. I'll have a cappuccino and a blueberry muffin, please."

"Coming up. I already know what they're having." She waves the other women away. "Go sit with them, and it'll be right out."

"Thank you. You sure I can't pay?"

"Your money is no good here."

I blink, too perplexed to argue, and dumbly follow the other women to a corner sitting area that's near the fireplace. Brooklynn pulls the reserved tag from the table and plops down on one of the couches.

"Like I said, this is our weekly thing, and Heather usually joins us when she can."

I take a seat but shift to face them so I can speak in a low tone without the other patrons hearing. "Can someone explain the whole Lenox is the Bruce Wayne god of this town to me?"

The women all exchange looks and lean in conspiratorially, giving me curious expressions. "You don't know?"

"Lenox and I didn't talk for a while until we reconnected." I'm getting more puzzled looks, and I feel like I have to explain, but how the fuck do I explain this? "We, uh, we were... together for a couple of years while I was in college, and then when we broke up, well, it wasn't under the best of circumstances. So I didn't talk to him for a while, and he's certainly never one to boast or brag."

The women exchange looks again, and then Heather is carrying a large tray loaded with food and drinks. She sets it down and then drops into the seat next to me. "What did I miss? Everyone is staring at Georgia like she's a lobster crawling around the floor."

That's sorta what I feel like right now. I pick up my cappuccino, which is bigger than my face, and take a sip, then lick my upper lip to make sure I don't have a froth mustache.

"She's asking why everyone in this town is so in love with Lenox," Paige informs her.

Heather laughs. "Well, Brooklynn knows him best, or should I say speaks to him the most, but despite the fact that he was a rock star in a band we were all obsessed with and obviously looks the way he looks while mastering the sexy, tall, silent type thing—"

"You realize that's her husband you're mentally ogling," Miranda quips.

Heather waves her away. "Whatever. I'm answering the woman's question." She turns back to me. "Anyway, he purchased this town six years ago, renovated the hell out of everything, and rents out the businesses essentially at cost, which is obviously so much less than market value. He earns little to no profit for himself."

Forget lobster, I'm impersonating a goldfish. "I'm sorry, what?"

They all laugh lightly. "The only buildings he doesn't own are the public and municipal ones, like the library and town hall, but he donated huge amounts of money for massive overhauls and renovations," Miranda explains. "It's all run through some dummy corporation or something, but everyone knows it's Lenox. Sorta like his house in the woods. No one actually knows where it is or how to get there, but we know he lives there."

"Um." I take another sip of my coffee, needing the caffeine more by the second. "Why would he... why would he do all that?"

They shrug in unison. "No clue," Brooklynn states. "Legit, I've asked him a hundred times, but he never answers me. It's how we can afford to own the hardware store."

"Same for me," Paige says as she picks at her breakfast sandwich and takes a big bite, chewing as she talks. "I'd never be able to own the yoga studio if I was paying premium rent."

Heather is nodding in agreement, and I can't seem to understand what's happening right now. Six years ago, is when Lenox left Boston. When he left me. But who does that? Who buys a town, shells out an untold fortune, pays to renovate everything, including businesses he doesn't own, and only charges enough rent to cover his expenses?

"It's done wonders for this town," Brooklynn tells me. "I grew up a half an hour from here, and this town wasn't much of a town. It's always been pretty run-down, but he renewed the whole thing, and in doing so, it brought families and businesses in, and that helped with the school systems. It was a snowball effect."

I'm utterly floored. I sit back against the soft leather cushion and stare out into the café.

What did he say to me today? *My life was a mess, and you loving me was the wake-up call I never knew I wanted or needed. I had to go out and try and fix it. I had to make amends for all my wrongs the only way I could. But hurting you has been one of the main regrets of my life. Up there with letting Suzie die.*

Oh, Lenox. Look at all the good you did here. Do you even see it? You certainly never take credit for it.

Because he doesn't feel he deserves any.

It makes me want to find him and kiss the hell out of him, but it also makes me want to find him and hold him. Lenox's demons run deep. His guilt along with them. Did he do all this as part of some strange atonement for sins he believed he committed? And am I now a part of that?

Chapter Twenty-One

Lenox

TATTOOING, like playing the piano, is a solitary, peaceful form of art. It's likely why I was drawn to it. There is no forced conversation. It's simply the client, who rarely wants to speak while someone is inking their skin, and you with your machine and creativity. Today I spent four hours shading the dragon on a mafia boss's back.

He's been flying in every month from Chicago for the last two months, and I think after one more scheduled visit, he'll finally be done. This was a particularly long session—normally I don't tattoo for that long.

It was four hours of absolute peace, only to now be interrupted by the redhead, who is once again never far from my thoughts. Like a siren, she walks toward me, purpose in her expression and determination in her stride.

"Lucy, you have some explaining to do," she says, doing a horrible impression of Ricky Ricardo.

I fold my arms and lean back against the bench seat I just cleaned, wanting her to keep walking to me and never stop. Considering how this morning went between us, the fact that she came to me, that she's here, that she's looking at me this way—with a hint of mischief and a touch of awe and admiration—is so much more than I ever thought I'd get from her. Eventually, if I'm lucky, I'll have a reckoning to face with her cousins, but that time hasn't come yet.

I don't ask her what I did. I can imagine she knows all the local gossip about me. Small towns are big on gossip and short on privacy, though they do, for the most part, manage to give me mine.

She stops about a foot in front of me, and for a few minutes, she silently stares up at me, examining me, searching my face as if she's never seen me before. Then, without a sound, she drops to her knees and it's as if she just punched all the air from my lungs.

"What are you doing?" I manage, which seems foolish since it's obvious, especially when she starts to work on my belt, button, and zipper, but this morning she told me I was going to be spending a lot of time with my hand, and this is a gross contradiction of that. Not that I'm complaining. Not even close.

"Giving my husband the pleasure he deserves."

My heart slams against my ribs like a jackhammer. Fuck. Motherfuck. Her calling me that just about kills me. It sure as hell makes me harder than I think I've ever been.

I comb my fingers through her hair, brushing the pretty red strands back from her face so I can see her face better. My thumb drags slowly over her bottom lip and her mouth opens, her pupils blooming into a delicious, sensual darkness. I haven't forgotten how much she used to like doing this. She told me once she loved knowing how easily she could unravel me.

If only she knew that's all she's ever done to me.

She continues to work my pants until she's slipped them down along with my boxer briefs, where they get trapped around my ankles. My cock springs free, and immediately she takes me in her hand, stroking me, rolling her thumb over the barbells, and around the hoop in my tip. My head falls back and my eyes momentarily close as pleasure so sweet I can hardly think thrums through my blood.

"I've never done this before with piercings."

My chin lowers, and I continue to stroke her face, brushing more strands back. "I'd be disappointed if you had."

She smirks, but there is a note of hesitation and uncertainty in her eyes. Perhaps a touch of fear too, since the piercings are menacing in their own right.

"Anything you do with that mouth of yours is perfect."

"Even when I tell you to fuck off and that I hate you?"

My lips twist up. "Maybe not then."

Her tongue snakes out, licking the crown and flicking at the piercing there, and my lips part to accommodate my ragged breaths. Seeing her like this for me—the desire in her eyes, and the fact that she's fucking here—is so much more. She is so much more.

Inhaling a deep breath, she opens her mouth wide and dives down, taking my cock in as far as she can go, all the while using her tongue to drag up along the underside of my dick and barbells. I clasp her hair, tugging on it as mind-twisting ecstasy shakes through me.

"Fuck, Georgia, that's so good. Look at you with your sweet lips wrapped around my cock. You look so unbelievably sexy right now, baby."

She moans, opening her mouth wider and angling her head to suck me in deeper until she gags. With a slow drag, she does it all again, paying extra attention to my piercings, playing with them, using her lips and tongue, and even a hint of teeth that give me just the right amount of pain. Her tongue swirls around the head of my cock, and on her next breath, she dives back down, gagging once more only to swallow. The way her throat rolls over the head of my dick, over the ring there, is like nothing else.

Pleasure skyrockets through me, tightening my balls and making my abs clench. The urge to start fucking her mouth is compelling, and when the hand not gripping the base of my cock slides around to the back of my thigh, urging me deeper into her mouth, I don't deny myself. I start to pump in rhythm with her sucking, watching with rapt attention as my goddess bobs on me like a champ. Her eyes are watering, running some of her mascara down her cheeks, and Christ, I could come just from that sight alone.

Her crying not from the pain I've caused her but from the pleasure.

Because I know she loves this. I can see it in the flush of her cheeks and the wild darkness of her eyes. In the way her thighs are spread on the floor and she's gently undulating as if seeking contact where she too needs it.

And because she's being so good, because she's here, I need to reward her.

"That's it. Show me how hungry you are for my cock." I groan. It's so good. "Do you want to know what I'm going to do to you after you swallow all my cum?"

She nods vigorously, humming and sending a fresh wave of vibrations straight to my balls. *Fuuuuck*, this woman and her mouth.

"I'm going to stand you up and then push you over the bench. You're going to spread your legs for me, and I'm going to peel down your leggings and eat your cunt from behind. I need to feel how wet you are. I need to smell how turned on you are. And then I need to taste you as you come for me."

Her eyes roll, and she moans, louder this time, like she's already close without even needing to be touched. And that sound with the deliriously lust-drunk glaze to her eyes and the way she's sucking me and swallowing me down, and just simply the way I fucking need her, has me coming on a loud, tangled growl. My cock continues to pump into her mouth, forcing her to take and swallow all of me. Tears pour like rivers from her eyes, but she holds my gaze as her throat rolls with every pulse of my cock. I swear, my knees are about to give out just at the sight of her.

Immediately after the last swallow, I grasp her by the back of her neck and yank her to her feet. My lips fuse to hers for a brief but impossibly deep kiss, and then I spin her around and bend her over the red leather bench. I hold her down like this for a moment, taking in the rose flush high on her cheeks, the swollen, bee-stung look of her lips, and the fiery green of her eyes.

She is intoxicating. A revelation. Her hold on me is pure witchcraft.

I'm crazed with how I want her. Past the point of obsession or madness. She is my purpose. My mission. She makes me a stronger, better man, and she does all that simply by being everything perfect and lovely that she already is.

Her hands go up on either side of her head, almost as if she's surrendering to me, though I know that will never be the case. Not with her.

I shudder out a pleased breath, and then in the next inhale, I tear down her leggings just as I told her I would. She makes a noise in the back of her throat. A noise that grows louder as I crouch behind her and take in the pretty, wet, pink sight before me. I move my thumb, gliding up and down her soft folds, loving how she trembles in anticipation for me. I blow cool air on her and catch her biting her lip.

I smack her ass in warning, one cheek and then the other, loving the quick flash of a red handprint that follows. "No stifling. I want to hear you, Georgia. Every fucking sound you make is mine to hear."

She starts to move, to push up against the bench, and I rip my belt from the loops of my pants with a loud *woosh*, band it up in my hand, and swat her ass with it. She yelps, and I do it again before running the smooth leather along her now-dripping pussy.

"You are mine to do with as I please. That includes spanking you how I want."

"Oh God," she moans as I lick the red lines on her flesh, nipping at them and dragging my teeth.

"Do you want me to spank this next?" I ask, moving the leather back and forth.

She doesn't say anything, but I can see the heat unfolding in her eyes, her inhales so quick she's practically hyperventilating. "Tell me," I command, spanking her ass again with the belt.

"Yes," she cries, and a dark thrill runs through me. She likes it rough and dirty with a hint of naughty taboo, just like I do.

I reward her by licking her clit, and then I pull back and smack her pussy with the belt, three quick strikes in a row, before I push the leather up inside her. She rips at the table, her back arching as she whimpers. I want to feed the beast inside both of us. Bring us both to the brink in the most intoxicating way.

"You're soaking my belt, baby." I push it in and out of her, fucking her with it and then I stand up, press my hard cock into her ass, and run the drenched leather across her lips. "Lick it."

Her eyes flare at the degrading command, but she does it. Her tongue sweeps out, and she licks the leather, only to lick her lips after. I rub my aching cock against her ass, so fucking turned on I can hardly stand it. My filthy woman is so perfect.

Pulling the belt back, I start spanking her with it. Alternating between her ass and her pussy. Her clit throbs, filling with blood and growing more sensitive. All the while my hand runs through her hair, and I tell her how beautiful she is, how perfect she is, how I can't stop thinking about her or wanting her.

She's moaning like crazy, grinding against the bench, helplessly trying to fuck it, desperate to come. I smack her one last time, take her hands, and pull them behind her back, then wrap the belt around her wrists and forearms to restrain her.

She gasps and moans, and once I'm positive she can't escape and the binding isn't cutting off her circulation, I crouch back down, spread her ass cheeks, and shove my tongue straight up inside her.

"Ah, Lenox!" Her pelvis bucks forward, but my hand is there to catch it, my fingers pressing into her mound and using the butt of my palm to press into her swollen clit.

"Now grind into my hand while I eat your cunt. Make yourself come on me."

She doesn't hesitate. My girl starts rolling her hips, using my hand to rub her clit on all the while my tongue fucks her pussy, my nose practically pressed into her tight asshole. I've taken her ass before, both with toys and with my cock, and I'm dying to do it again, but not now. Not when this thing between us is so precarious. Not when she might still be trying to hate me.

Her legs tremble and shake as she gets closer and closer. My hand is soaked, my face too, and God, she tastes so fucking good. I plunge two fingers straight inside her as my tongue moves back to her ass, where I start to lick and fuck her there. She cries out, bucking and jerking, her body moving faster, harder against my mouth, pumping down into my fingers, and grinding mindlessly against my palm.

"I need it," she moans, thrashing on the table, her upper body helpless with her hands bound behind her. "I need it now. I need it so bad."

"Fuck, baby, me too. Come for me, and then I'm going to fill you up."

And she does. She comes so hard, and it's so wet, and it's tearing through her body, making her scream and me grunt as my cock jerks and leaks against me. The moment her pussy stops squeezing my fingers, I make quick work of untying her wrists, massaging the skin, and bringing circulation back into her limbs. Then I rip off her sweater and bra because I need to see her and touch her skin. Her hands immediately shoot in front of her, gripping the end of the bench when she feels the head of my cock rubbing at her entrance.

I stroke myself, my head just inside her tight, hot center, and on the third stroke, I slide inside her, both of us moaning together. I hold her hips steady, and I start to fuck her at a slow, even pace. Something that will drive her wild with want, build her up patiently, and finish her with fireworks.

But hell, does she feel good. And this angle, the way she's moving…

"Georgia…" My forehead hits the center of her back, my hands gripping her hips as if I need her to keep me upright. "You feel so good." Too fucking good.

My left hand reaches up and clasps hers, our fingers latching, and my eyes snag on our tethered rings. I push up, rolling onto the balls of my feet with my thrusts, desperate to feel every inch of her pussy with my every move.

She is velvet. She is heaven. And every time I'm inside of her, it is better than the last because every time feels like a new chance to be with her. A new opportunity I wasn't or shouldn't have been afforded before.

"You're everything," I murmur reverently, though my words are splintered and incoherent. I pump into her, faster and faster, feeling the tight walls of her pussy hold me in. Her body rocks back against mine, meeting me thrust for thrust.

I shudder, licking up her spine, tasting the salt and sweat on her skin, feeling her body quiver as I grind into her, rubbing her. But it's not enough. I want more. I want deeper. So I slide out, ignoring her groan and protest, and flip her over onto her back so the length of her body is taking up the length of the table. I grasp the end of the table and then slam back inside her. Her green eyes cling to mine as I press my body weight down on her and command her body.

My mouth takes advantage, licking and sucking and nipping at her neck, nuzzling at her racing pulse while I grind into her, rubbing my hips until I find her perfect friction point. She gasps, her hands moving to my shoulders so she can hold onto me. I lift my head, anxious to see her face as her body quivers and trembles and rocks beneath mine.

"Harder," she begs, and I'm only too happy to obey. My slow push and pull now forgotten as I hike myself up onto my knees, lean forward so we're chest to chest, and begin pounding into her. Her head rolls to the side, her eyelids flutter, and her lips part.

I watch her face, enchanted by her as I piston in and out.

"Like that?"

"Mmmm…" she hums. "I'm so close. Don't stop."

Like I ever would. The way her cunt is gripping me, so warm and wet and goddamn perfect. The way she rubs herself against me with every upthrust. But I see it. The moment her orgasm starts to hit her, the way her body thrashes and her mouth falls open on a strangled scream as pleasure races through her like a drug. Her nails dig into my shoulders, almost pleading with me to pump deeper.

But when she says, "I want to feel you come inside me," and her pussy starts to convulse, squeezing my cock practically to the point of pain, I can no longer hold off. My balls draw up, and my orgasm barrels through me, cutting off my breath and robbing me of my vision. I give her two more jerky pumps, and then I'm spilling myself inside her, just as she told me she wanted.

My body sags against hers, but the table is narrow and angled, and my fucking jeans are still around my ankles, and because I'm still in a post-orgasmic haze, I start to fall off the table, only to catch myself right before I eat hardwood.

"Shit," I yell as I collapse to the floor, lying on my back, my forearm over my eyes, smiling dumbly, laughing lightly, especially when I hear Georgia's giggle from above me. I move my arm up and peek one eye open to find her leaning over the edge, staring down at me.

"We might have to work on your landing for next time. I give that a 6.0 at best."

I laugh harder, my chest feeling lighter than it has been in years.

"As long as the sex was a ten, I'll swallow my pride at the dismount."

"A ten?" She scoffs, rolling her eyes. "Definitely not. That was more like a four."

In a flash, I reach up and snatch her arm, yanking hard and forcing her to fall off the table. She comes tumbling down on top of me with a shriek, but I catch her before I hurt either of us and cradle her against me, rubbing her abused ass and wrists and kissing her forehead, cheeks, and nose. Falling more in love with her by the second while trying to figure out how I can keep her forever because this time I don't think I can give her up.

Chapter Twenty-Two

Georgia

"YOU KNOW I'm following you, right?" Alice keeps trotting along through the woods like she's been doing for the last fifteen minutes, crunching on leaves and picking up random sticks in her mouth until she finds a better one. "As in, I hope you know where we're going. These woods are no joke, and I don't want to end up on a missing person's flyer."

She gives me a small bark that tells me she's got me, and we continue on. Lenox left early this morning for the shop since it's Saturday, and I'm assuming a relatively busy day for him. I waited in my room until I heard him leave before I came downstairs and ate the warm pumpkin scone he left for me and drank the coffee he brewed for me.

It's been a strange few days since I dropped to my knees for him in his shop. I was overtaken by all that I had heard he's done for the town and the people. For what I suspect are his primary reasons for doing it. There was no way I could hold back. It took all my strength to wait those four hours until he was done with his client.

But I realized as he held me on the floor, his fingers trickling along my skin and his breathing slow and peacefully even, that I was repeating old patterns. Old patterns I swore I wouldn't. So since then, I've gone back to playing duck and weave around him other than the few times I've gone with him into town for yoga and to hang out at the library. But even then, we didn't talk much, and I get the impression Lenox doesn't know quite what to do with me or is fine with what we've done and likes us having our space in between.

In the meantime, I've hung out a bit more with Brooklynn and her friends and am starting to like them the more time I spend with them. In between that, I've been doing research into the company I now own so that when I go back to LA early next month for the board meeting, I'm ready.

Other than that, I stay mostly in my room when he's home, and when he's not, I explore the house and the woods around it. He makes sure I have food—yesterday's breakfast was bacon, egg, and cheese on an English muffin—and he's been leaving Alice home with me. I'm grateful for that because otherwise, in addition to getting lost and becoming a hiking statistic, I'd be talking to myself in an unhealthy way instead of spewing my thoughts to her in a healthy way.

I don't know what to do or what to think about him.

He surprises me at every turn.

He's taking care of me, doing sweet things just for me like the food and coffee, leaving me a hangout buddy, and putting the roses in my room. I won't even get into his tattoo. He cleared a space in his massive home gym where he hung a punching bag for me and bought me a yoga ball, some resistant bands, and a yoga mat. He's trying to make me feel at home, and I'm grateful. I'm grateful for so much with him.

But the longer I'm with him, and the more things he does just for me—things that show thought, consideration, and care—the more I'm afraid. I loved him once, and that love wasn't simple. It was twisted and complex and consuming and dangerous with where it took me and how it left me. So for now, with a litany of unanswered questions and ugly answers between us, I'm keeping my distance.

Alice barks, dropping her latest branch when she hears a snapping sound about fifteen feet from us. Thankfully, she doesn't give chase. "That better not be a bear. Or a wolf." I pause. "They have wolves in Maine, right? Oh, maybe it's a moose, though I've heard they're mean sons of bitches."

She gives another bark but then turns right, heading away from it.

"I'd see a moose, though. They're freaking huge, and if it's a wolf or a bear, just give me a heads-up so I can run… away, I guess since I have no clue at this point where the house is."

She nuzzles my leg to let me know she's got my back, and I bend down and rub the top of her head.

"I know. Besties for life. Let's head to the lake. I feel like that's a solid place I can find and weave my way back toward the house from if I have to."

And since Alice is the best dog in the history of dogs, she snatches up another wet branch from the ground and then takes a right and leads me toward what I'm hoping is the lake since I can't see it through the dense trees and multicolored leaves. I can't get enough of the changing fall colors. We don't get this in LA, and to see the fall foliage and feel the autumn chill in the air really brings out the season.

Sipping a pumpkin-spiced latte at the beach doesn't have quite the same feel.

We reach the edge of the lake, a frigid mist rising off it, and I understand its namesake. The lake is, well, lavender, or more like a gray-purple with the way the muted light settles on it. Snow is supposed to come in this afternoon, the news calling it a November nor'easter, and the air already has that static electric feel to it that comes before a big snowstorm. I drop onto the trunk of a fallen tree right along the rocky shore of the lake, my knees hiked up as I listen to the gentle sound of water lapping against the stones near my feet.

"This really is so beautiful. I can see why he lives here. I mean, I don't get the fortress of solitude and fuck off thing, but he picked a good spot."

Alice comes and sprawls out on the rocks by my feet, chewing on her stick, and I pick up a rock, trying to skip it into the lake and watch as it instead plummets into the water with a noisy plop and a loud splash. Alice has the grace not to tease me about that.

"Clearly I need to work on my nature girl side." I sigh, stretching my legs out in front of me. "So, tell me, how often does he bring home women?"

She gives me a *don't be that girl* look and she's right. But I can't help but wonder all the same. Does he bring women back to my dream house? Does he fuck them in rooms I designed? A miserable spike of jealousy surges through me, and I wonder if I'll ever not care. It's a bleak and disheartening thought, knowing that he might always own a piece of me.

On Monday, I have another coffee date with the ladies in town, and it's almost Thanksgiving, my absolute favorite holiday. But almost immediately after that, I have to fly out to LA. I haven't asked Lenox anything about what he's been doing or not doing with Ezra and Alfie. Not since we had that conversation about my father's will.

It's easy to not think about it when I'm here.

It's easy to allow myself to get lost and stay there.

Just as I pick up another rock to try and skip it across the lake, my phone rings in my jacket pocket. I pull it out and groan when I see it's my mother. At least it's not Alfie or Ezra. Alfie, I haven't heard from, but Ezra, yeah, that boy doesn't relent.

For a few rings, I debate answering, but my mother has been through enough already, and I haven't talked to her since the morning after my wedding. What Lenox told me Monday about the will being changed has sat heavily on my mind, but I'm not sure I want to tell my mother yet. At least not until I know more about what it all means. At the very least, I need to ask her for Dad's laptop.

Pulling out my AirPods, I slip one in my ear and then swipe my finger along the screen. "Hi, Mom."

"Georgia! Where on the planet Earth are you?"

I laugh. "I'm in Maine at my new husband's house." I swallow and shift on the log.

"And you're doing okay? Living in his house, being around him all the time?"

"Yes. I'm doing okay. Better than okay, actually. Lenox gives me plenty of space in his house." Speaking of... "Mom, do you remember the house I designed in college?"

She's quiet for a beat. "The dream house thing?"

"Yeah. That. He built it." I huddle into my coat, tucking my body in to protect myself against how saying that aloud feels.

"What do you mean he built it?"

I sigh. "He built the house, Mom. The house he lives in in the middle of flipping nowhere Maine is the dream house I designed in college. Every inch, every room, even some of the furniture and finishings."

"Oh."

"Oh?!"

"I need a minute with that, Georgia. I mean, you're telling me the guy who treated you like disposable trash and broke your heart built your dream house. Did you know?"

"No, and neither do Zax or Grey before you ask. Only you, Dad, and Lenox knew about that project."

"Why did he do it? Did he say?"

I slide a rock through the sandy mud with the toe of my boot. "Because he wanted to build me my dream house, even if I never saw it."

"Jesus Henrietta Christ, Georgia. What on earth does that mean?"

"I don't know," I squawk. "He apologized to me for everything. For the way he treated me, for how he left me. For all of it. I'm giving myself some distance right now because things are intense with us, though that's all me and not him. He's been... different." Great, actually.

She makes a displeased noise in her throat. "Can you please just move out of there already? He's trouble with a capital T. You're going to fall for him again, if you haven't already, because he does things that are sweet and thoughtful and endear you to him, but he's not the commitment, settling down, and starting a family type. He's going to break your heart again."

I sag and my heart goes along with it. "I know," I admit because I'm pretty sure she's right. About all of it. Including the breaking my heart again part. "It's only for a year, and I likely don't have to stay here with him nearly that long. Just until Alfie and Ezra are convinced it's the real deal and they can't argue it in a court of law."

"Well, at this point, as much as I hate to say it, after all that's happening, I don't think you have a choice but to stay married to him. At least for appearances."

"What?" I bolt upright, shocked by that since my mom has been firmly parked in Camp Ezra. "Did something else happen?"

"You don't know?"

"No. Tell me."

She makes a noise that's almost like a laugh but isn't. It's her uncomfortable *I'm not sure how to react or feel about this* laugh. "Ezra got pulled over in LA yesterday for speeding. When the cop ran his plate, she discovered he had several unpaid tickets for other traffic incidents, but get this, he also had an outstanding warrant for drugs. The officer searched his car and found drugs stashed there and arrested him."

I sputter so hard I nearly topple off the log, startling poor Alice. But holy shit. Holy freaking shit! "Are you serious? *Drugs*?"

"Yes. Drugs. Cocaine and ecstasy, to be exact."

I laugh incredulously, my hand over my mouth as I stare wide-eyed out at the water. "Is he still in jail?" Because the thought of Ezra Earnheart in a LA jail... he'll be someone's bitch within five minutes.

"No. Alfie had his attorney bail him out after he was arraigned, so he only spent a few hours in jail. Ezra evidently swears it's all bogus, that the drugs were planted, and that they have the wrong person. But he has to show up in court in a few weeks for it."

Lenox. I mean, that's what comes to mind. Did Lenox get Ezra arrested? Did he create bogus charges and have drugs planted in his car?

A thought I'm nearly positive of when my mother continues on with, "His arrest made the news, and with it, it was discovered that he has a lot of gambling debt and is in great financial trouble. His future at Monroe is now in jeopardy over all of this."

"Good thing I didn't marry him," I quip, unable to hold back my grin. Lenox told me he'd punish him greatly, and it seems he has. And while part of me does feel bad, I have no doubt Alfie's attorneys will get all the charges dropped.

"Good thing you didn't marry him," she parrots only her tone isn't as light as mine. "But the press will start with you again since you're his ex-fiancée, so even though I hate you being there with *that man*, I'm also relieved you're there since it's keeping you safe and protected." She sighs. "It's a mess. All of this is a mess."

"Mom, it really isn't. The shares are in my name, the company is staying with our family, and I didn't have to marry Ezra to make that happen." And hopefully, that means Alfie will back off once and for all. At the very least, his winning pitch to somehow get me to marry his son is over. There's nothing else either can do. They lost. Speaking of. "Mom, I need Dad's laptop. Do you have it?"

She hesitates. "Yes. Why do you need it?"

"I'd like to go over some of his business stuff," I partially lie. I mean, I would, but that's far from the main reason I need it.

"Oh." A sigh. "Yes, I'll send it to you. It should go to you anyway, and no one else."

I squint at the way she says that. "What does that mean?"

"Alfie has been asking me for it. I told him I threw it out. That if he needed to find it, he should search the LA dump. He wasn't happy about that."

"Why did you tell him that if you still have it?"

"Because I don't want Alfie to have anything that was your father's personal property. His work laptop went down with him on the plane. This is his personal laptop, and Alfie isn't family."

Hmm. There is a lot to explore with that, considering how adamant she was that I marry Ezra and play ball with Alfie.

"No," I say resolutely. "They're not family. And now they never will be. Mom, did you know Dad changed his will shortly before I was supposed to get married? He made it so that it all went to me and added the stipulation that I had to be married. Can you think of any reason why he'd do that?"

She's silent for a few minutes, so long in fact that I lift my phone from the log and check the screen to be sure she's still there. "I don't know. As far as I knew, everything was going to me, as that's how we had set it up when you were born." She's silent again and then clears her throat. "Two months before he died, he did that?"

I feel awful telling her this, but I have to know if she knows something I don't. "Yes."

"I don't know. Maybe he…" She trails off and stops that thought before redirecting. "Your father was just very serious about you marrying Ezra."

"I know, but why? Why was that more important than my happiness? He knew I didn't want to marry him."

She releases a breath. "I don't know. He didn't talk to me about it, but when you threatened to leave Ezra two months before the wedding, I know your father was under a great deal of stress about it."

Two months before the wedding. That's when I told my parents I was leaving him, and that's when my father told me I had to stay and stick it out. That's also around the time he changed the will.

"Whatever his reasons were," she continues, cutting off my thoughts, "a Monroe cannot marry a man who is arrested for drugs."

"No. Talk about bad PR." I'm smiling. So big and bright and stupidly goofy.

That is, until my mother says, "But you didn't marry Lenox to make yourself happy." And my smile slips. "You married him so you wouldn't have to marry Ezra. Now that that's all done and taken care of, you need to plan your exit strategy from him."

"My attorney recommended a year of marriage to not only make it look real for stockholders' confidence but to anyone—like Alfie and Ezra—who might try and challenge it."

"And because of that, I worry about the impact the man you married will have on your heart. A year is a long time to spend with someone who hurt you once. I know he's helping you, but just remember, what feels like acts of love in the moment can backfire on us in the next."

I freeze as something in her voice and the way she says that hits me—and hits me hard. Did my father do something to her? Were they not as happy as I always imagined them to be? Is that why he changed his will?

"Just safeguard yourself, okay?"

I'll try, are the words that immediately hit my head. Instead, I don't manage to say anything at all, and after a bit more back and forth, I say goodbye to my mom and ask Alice to lead me back home. Home. Is that what this is, and for how long now that Ezra has been neutralized? Could I start thinking about moving out of here to Boston or back to LA? Is that even what I want?

Alice and I weave our way along the lake just as snow starts to fall. It's beautiful. The way it dusts the exposed ground and sticks to the trees, the way it floats into the lake and gets lost in its icy waters. Eventually, we end up back at the house, but when I enter, shucking out of my winter gear and dropping my boots back by the back door, I find I'm not alone. Lenox is sitting at the piano all the way in the front of the house, his back to me, playing an intricate and haunting melody I've never heard before.

I didn't expect him for at least another two hours.

The entire walk back to the house, my mind swam with every-thing my mother said. Especially about what feels like acts of love, might not actually be. But in that thinking, I realized I can't be a child and avoid Lenox forever. My plan was to make dinner for him and see if I could be around him without jumping him or falling for him. He hasn't slept in my bed again since Sunday night, but he continues with the roses. Sometimes I hear him come in and pretend to be asleep. Sometimes I never hear him but wake to find a new, fresh one.

He's giving me space and not pushing me for more, but he's still… there. Watching and lurking and trying with all the thoughtful things he's doing for me. But are those acts of kindness, of trying to make me feel comfortable, or even a prolonging of his apology?

Or are they more?

My mother was right about my heart being in danger. There is no one more irresistibly dangerous to me than Lenox Moore.

I watch him for a moment, his tall, broad frame and the strong muscles in his back moving against the soft fabric of his gray Henley as he plays. How this beast of a man can pull the most achingly beautiful sound from a box of wood and strings is pure magic. Does he truly like being this alone, or has it become second nature to him? Is he hiding from the world because he doesn't feel deserving, or is his reason for that far more sinister?

I find myself padding softly over to him, my fuzzy socks slipping silently across the floor, but he doesn't react to my presence when I finally reach his side other than to scoot over to make room for me to sit. He must have heard me and Alice come in. He continues playing, his hands flying up and down the black-and-white keys, with no sheet music set before him. Whatever he's playing is either from memory or being created in the moment.

Of all the Central Square guys, he and Grey are by far the most talented, and I can't help but get lost in the way he plays. In the incredible music that fills the room, bouncing off the high surfaces and surrounding me in the beauty of its notes.

After a few minutes, I'm lulled into some sort of hypnotic state, my eyes closing and my head landing on his shoulder. He places a kiss on top of my head, and I sigh, smiling wistfully. I'm suddenly filled with such a tragic sense of misery and irony I swear my heart is about to give out on me.

Because I could do this.

I could live in Maine in my dream home on the lake in the middle of the woods. I could open a private practice in town and make it my own. I could fall asleep every night and wake up every morning with him wrapped around me. And I could happily sit on this piano bench and listen to him play anytime he does.

I could do all that forever.

But in my heart, in my head, I know this is only temporary. And

I realize I'm hurting with that because I want that picture in my head to be my reality, my future. I've always wanted that with him. And no amount of protection or distance can erase that reality.

It's Lenox. It's always been Lenox.

There is no getting over him. There is only living with the pain of never being able to truly have him. Like a chronic condition, I may be able to treat the symptoms but will never be able to eradicate the underlying disease. I revel in that truth, bleed with it, and when I've come to terms with it, I tuck it into its own space in my heart instead of allowing it to continue to bleed me dry.

"Did you get Ezra arrested?" I ask when his fingers start to slow and I'm positive I have control over my voice and emotions.

He finishes off his song and shifts on the bench, forcing me to sit upright. He peers at me and answers, "Yes," without so much as a blink of his eyes or a twitch.

"Are the drug charges fake?"

"The warrant was fake. The drug use and what they found on him is not. I didn't have anything planted."

"I never knew he was using drugs."

"Recreationally. More since you left him. I noticed it in Vegas, and it prompted me to do some more digging into that. He did also have an unpaid speeding ticket, which is what gave me the idea in the first place. I didn't set him up with anything he wasn't already guilty of."

"Okay."

He gives me a wry smirk. "Just okay? I was expecting you to ream me out when you found out what I did."

I shake my head and run my fingers through his soft, thick hair, staring at him with resigned sadness. I can say all that I want about him. I can put up a thousand walls and remind myself a thousand more times where letting him in once took me. But the truth is, hating him is ridiculous, avoiding him is futile, and building wall after wall only ends with him repeatedly knocking them down.

All without him even having to try.

"I spoke to my mother."

"And?"

"And she's sending me my dad's personal laptop. Alfie has been asking for it, and she told him she threw it out. She also doesn't know why my father changed his will, but she reminded me of how I had come to them two months before the wedding and told them I couldn't marry Ezra and that my father pressured me into staying and seeing it through. She told me he was under a great amount of stress because of it."

"I haven't found any link that ties Ezra to your father's death. The only people he's paid are bookies, and those were to settle debts. As far as I could tell, Ezra hardly ever interacted with your father directly and wouldn't have any direct way of knowing about the will change since your father was so careful with it."

That's a relief, I guess. "And Alfie?"

"I'm still working on him. He's a hacker, Georgia, and they take more care and time as their secrets are more difficult to find and unravel. Last night, when he tried to dig into your computer, I reverse-hacked him because he left it open and didn't mask himself. A stupid mistake, but now it's just a matter of time, and it will move faster than it has been. I'm in something he doesn't want anyone in, and I will discover what he's hiding."

I still can't believe all that I'm hearing. It's too much. And yet, I'm not sure I've ever felt safer than I do here with Lenox. I stare at him, at this fierce, loyal, determined man. I'm so grateful for all he's done for me. For all he's doing for me.

Still… "I wish I had never fallen in love with you. It would make my fear of doing so again so much less."

His eyes crinkle at the corners, telling me that hurt him, but it's true. It's so very, very true. Love doesn't make sense. If it did, we'd never continue to love people who hurt us or forgive them for it. There is a natural, physiological response to danger. A fight or flight response. A distress signal in your brain that activates a rush of adrenaline and sets you into motion.

You fight, or you flee.

Love doesn't trigger the same response. Not even when it's hurting us. Not even when it's dangerous and we need to fight or flee for our very survival. It supersedes common sense by making us second-guess our baser gut reactions.

Love is a weapon. Whether it's wielded by others or ourselves against us, it doesn't matter. But when it cuts just right and makes you bleed just so, there is no sweeter weapon nor more exquisite pain than love, danger be damned.

Lenox's eyes grow accusatory even as his knuckles gently graze up my cheek. "You still haven't figured it out, have you?"

I gulp at his expression. "Figured what out?"

"You were everything to me, Georgia." His voice floats over me like a whisper in the wind, but it slams into me with the force of a category-five hurricane. "I never wanted to love without you. I wanted you to love without me," he rasps, his voice almost pleading. "You think I didn't love you? I *hurt* with how I loved you. But I was already hurting too much. I had nothing to offer you. Two empty hands and a broken soul. I walked away because I had to. I let you go because I would have rather died than wrecked you along with me. And I'm tired of you not knowing it."

Chapter Twenty-Three

Lenox

I'M NOT sure Georgia is breathing right now. I know I'm sure as hell not. But after the way this week started between us and having her subsequently shut me out again, I'm done. I'm just fucking done. There are moments in our lives when holding intricate pieces of ourselves back is wise, but this isn't that time. I have spent the last six years rebuilding myself into a man who could one day go toe-to-toe with her and know beyond a shadow of a doubt that I am fucking worthy of that footing.

I had to rebuild my mind, my life, my fucking karma, and my psyche. I had to not hate my reflection. I had to not blame myself for the death of my sister and the death of my father and the man he killed. Those aren't overnight ventures. And bringing the woman who you consider to be your endgame—the love of your fucking life—along for that ride isn't something you do. Love is letting go when you need to let go and hoping that their life turns out better without you in it.

That's all I ever wanted for her.

And then she showed up at my house needing my help and now here we are, and I can't do this anymore. I can't pretend like it hasn't always been her. I can't pretend like every decision I've made since I left her six years ago hasn't been made with her at the forefront of my mind.

"You told me——"

"I know what I told you. I lied."

"Why?"

I sigh plaintively. "I blamed myself for Suzie's death. And then I didn't do anything to stop my father's downward spiral because I was too deep in my own. I watched as he killed a man and then killed himself, and I was *disappointed* that he hadn't killed me instead. I walked around with that for two years. I couldn't shake it. I didn't even try to. I earned that misery, reveled in its suffering, but you… you were light and air, and you made me want."

"Want what?" she whispers, her voice tremulous and unsure.

"*Life.* You made me want to live again, Georgia. When you told me you loved me, it was as if your words shocked me out of myself. You made me want more for the first time in two years. But I was too broken, too messed up for it, and I wasn't ready. I had treated you so poorly, and I didn't deserve your heart or your love. I had to earn it. I knew that, but I fucking wanted it so badly. So I came clean to Zax, and I left Boston. About a week later, I was in a diner in Maine, and I heard a man who owned a bunch of real estate talking with another man about how a small town was going into mass foreclosure and the townspeople didn't know what to do. So I bought the town, and I fixed it up so that the people who lived here and owned businesses could still do that without worry. Then I built your dream home because you were my fucking dream too, and even though I knew I'd never have you again, I wanted to give you that. All I wanted was to be a man who could be worthy of you. But when I left you, I wasn't him yet. Not even close, and I couldn't do that to you."

"Because you didn't feel you deserved me?"

My eyes flash. "I didn't."

"So you've spent the last six years working to become that man. For me."

"Yes," I say simply because it's true. I did it for me—all of it—because I wanted to be a better man, a better human, someone I could respect, but it was always with her in mind.

"And now?"

"Now I fucking deserve you." I cup the back of her head and press our foreheads together. "I can't breathe when I'm not near you. You have my heart, Georgia. I'm yours. I've always been yours. I will always *be* yours. You are my favorite everything, and I can't live without you anymore. But more than that, you're my wife, and I have no plans to ever let you change that."

I hold up my left hand, at the band that's there covering the rose tattoo.

"You are this rose. And you are forever."

Her eyes pinch shut, and her body trembles against mine.

I press my lips to hers, holding her so close. "Don't be afraid to fall in love with me. I swear, I'll never hurt you again." My hands glide up and down her face, touching her skin. "God, Georgia, I love you so fucking much. There is madness in how much I love you. You are all I think about, day and night. There is nothing in my life more important to me than you."

I kiss her quivering lips and wrap her up in my arms.

"Please give me another chance," I whisper in her ear. "Everything is different now, and it will never again be like how it was."

"What about Zax and Grey?"

I laugh because I can't help it. After everything I just said to her, that's what she asks? "Well, once I know you're willing to give me a second chance, I plan to tell them you're mine."

"They won't be mad. They love you."

I smile and kiss her cheek, trickling down to her neck. "They will be mad, Georgia, and they have every right to be. I didn't keep my promise. I told them I'd keep my distance and that I wouldn't touch you, and I've done both while hiding it from them. Yet another thing I promised them I wouldn't do."

"Will that change this?"

I shake my head. "No. I don't care if they're mad, and it won't stop me. I love them, and there isn't anything I wouldn't do for them... except let you go."

Georgia climbs onto my lap, and I hug her to me, moving her hair back over her shoulders so I can kiss her neck, her face, her lips. She lifts my left hand and kisses the rose I have there, then places my hand on her chest, right over her heart.

Her eyes burn into mine. "I'm giving this back to you. Don't make me regret that."

"I'll keep it safe this time. I promise."

"Don't ever stop loving me because I know now, I never stopped loving you."

"I never stopped loving you either." My lips slam down on hers in an untamed rush. I need to be closer. I need to feel her every breath, every sigh. She's mine. She's finally fucking mine. I've never experienced this before.

This... rush. This... need. This... *everything.*

My hands slide beneath her, and I stand, lifting her in my arms as I do. I push the piano bench back and walk her across the room to the couch, where I lay her down on the soft leather and cover her body with mine. Her fingers twine up into my hair as my hot breath falls across her ear, making her shiver.

"I thought about you all day," I whisper, trickling kisses along her neck up to her jaw. "I couldn't stop. I couldn't focus. I had to come home and see you. I've been in agony all week without you."

I want to give Georgia everything. All of me. I never want to disappoint her again.

I twist to snatch her lips with mine, demonstrating my impatience, my desperation for her. Her eyelids flutter as I lick the seam of her lips, nibbling lightly until she opens for me. A groan sears past my throat at the first taste of her tongue, and I press in, pushing her deeper into the couch, needing to feel her body as I kiss her mouth. Our tongues coil and massage in deep, penetrating movements, and I try to slow myself down.

Not wanting lust to overtake passion.

My body vibrates with her heat as she wraps herself around me and forces me tighter against her, grinding ever so slightly against my hard length as if she can't stop herself. My blood thrums as I devour her mouth, her kiss so intoxicating I don't know which way is up. She hums into my mouth, a sound so sweet and clear and bright that I groan in return, twisting my head so I can take her mouth deeper, anxious for more and more.

With her body pressed against mine, trapped beneath me like this, my access to her is limited. My hands have nowhere else to go other than her hair and face and they're growing impatient, restless with the need to touch and explore her as ours.

"Georgia," I whisper, reaching down and adjusting her thigh, shifting it higher up my hips so I can press myself closer against her. She moans at the hard press of me into her, and my clothes feel like they're strangling me, too tight, too restrictive. I need them off. I need hers off too.

Shifting my body to my left side, I move my hand between us, rubbing her pussy through her leggings as my mouth continues to work at a dizzying pace over hers, stealing her breath, tasting her pleasure as she whimpers into me. I pull back, catching the stunning look on her flushed face, and dive back in, flicking her tongue with mine.

My hand dives into her leggings, so grateful I don't have to waste time fumbling with a button or zipper or deal with the cumbersome task of trying to fight with stiff pants. The leggings glide effortlessly down her legs, and she kicks them and her fuzzy socks off her feet, shivering ever so slightly when her bare skin touches the cool leather. Impatient hands trickle along my arms, ripping at the back of my shirt, and I reach behind my head to pull it off.

The storm brewing outside has nothing on the storm inside her eyes as she takes in the lines of my chest and the markings of colorful ink. I lift her sweater up and over her head, casting it on the floor along with the rest of our clothes. Her hands meet my shoulders, and she pulls me back down against her, anxious for the heat of my skin against hers. My palm flattens against her inner thigh, and I trail up marveling at her smooth skin until I'm back at her blazing hot center. I slip inside her panties, gliding my fingers up and down her wet slit while thrusting my throbbing cock against her thigh.

"Lenox." She gasps as I circle her clit.

I lean down, my teeth nibbling at her jaw, watching as her eyes roll and then close. Her head falls back for a moment before she's gripping the back of my head and dragging my mouth back to hers.

"Kiss me," she rasps. "Don't stop kissing me."

I'm only too happy to oblige. Kissing her is like falling into a dream you never want to wake from. My finger dips into her pussy, bringing out the wetness and spreading it all over her clit.

"Oh, God."

I don't stop. I continue to play with her in between watching her face and kissing her lips so I can swallow her moans.

"Lenox, please."

I thrust into her hip.

"Say it again," I order, rubbing faster and faster, though I know she's desperate for my fingers to pump inside of her. I can practically feel her empty core clenching with how badly she wants that.

"Lenox, please. I need your fingers inside me. Push them inside me."

Shifting my wrist, I slip two fingers inside her, growling when I feel how fucking wet and tight and warm she is. I start to work my fingers inside her while using my thumb on her clit. Her head rolls back, and her hands shoot up, clutching onto the arm of the sofa, making her tits spill up and over the cups of her bra like a delicious invitation.

I free her nipple from her bra and suck it into my mouth, angling my head so I can watch my fingers fuck her. My mouth curves into a smile, loving how her hips rock up, fucking my hand in return. My tongue swirls around her nipple, nibbling on it, playing with it, and goddamn captivated by the wet sheen of her cunt on my fingers and the smell of her arousal. I lick my lips and then lick her tits as I increase my speed, rubbing her clit faster and harder with my thumb as I curl my fingers inside of her.

Her chest heaves as she sucks in air, her breathing ragged and out of sync the closer she gets. My long fingers fill her up again and again, pumping harder until I'm practically holding her entire pussy in my hand so I can fuck up into it. It's messy and wet, and Georgia's cries and pleas are loud, her body thrashing as she gets closer. It's the best fucking thing I've ever seen.

Between her face and her pussy, I can't stop staring at both.

And then she detonates, her orgasm exploding through her with a loud cry and a wet gush as her thighs tense and squeeze against my hand. I groan at the feel of it, rubbing my cock into her leg, crazy with the need to drive into her as I toy with her clit and fuck her pussy through her orgasm. She sags into the couch, a sweet, contented smile on her lips, and I slip my fingers out and bring them to her lips.

Her tongue comes out and her eyes open, immediately locking on mine as I slip one finger and then the other inside her mouth. With a smile, I lean down and kiss her, tasting her orgasm on her mouth and licking every place inside her that my fingers just were. Reaching down, I rub my tenting cock over the rough material of my jeans before one-handedly undoing the button and zipper and shoving them down my legs, all the while my other hand is behind her back, unclasping her bra.

I run a possessive hand down her side, feeling every curve and dip, relishing the softness of her pale skin. I swirl her nipple with my tongue, taking myself in hand and stroking a few times, dragging out the sensation, building this up again for both of us. She moans, and that sound—that fucking sound she makes—could tempt an angel to fall into sin. Her hands go to my hair as I open my mouth wider, taking in as much of her tit as I can.

Rolling on top of her, I pin her down, sliding my body between her thighs that she has willingly spread wide for me. I reach down and grab the hem of her panties and rip them away so I can grind up into her slick heat, feeling her cum coating my cock.

"Is that what I did to you?" I tease, flashing a smug smirk.

Climbing up her body, I straddle her upper thighs without lowering my weight and press her legs closer together. I continue to play with her, using the hoop in my tip to rub her clit, only to slip down and rim her entrance.

"Oh, hell. I'm burning with that." She gasps, and I breathe out a quiet laugh as a sweet little blush races up her face as if validating her words. I do it again and then once more before I wedge my cock in the tight fit of her pussy just like this. Her hands scramble up, gripping my arms and tugging me forward as she cries out at the first thrust.

My eyes close, and I savor the feeling of her, letting my head fall back for a moment as I sit here, both of us adjusting to this angle. Opening my eyes, my chin drops, and I stare down at her, holding her gaze as I slowly slide back and then thrust up. With a firm grip on her hips, I yank her body to me at the same time, demanding she feel every inch of me like this.

All the air leaves my lungs as I slide in and out of her, rubbing her G-spot with every pump, watching her as I roll my hips and fuck into her.

"Do you like that?" I can't help but ask. "Do you like getting fucked like this?"

Her hands wrap around my neck in answer, dragging my face down to hers. Our foreheads meet, and our lips layer.

"Now I do," she says. "Fuck me hard. I want every inch you can give me until I'm so full you're all I'll feel."

I shake as I plant my hands on the couch on either side of her head and roll my hips in an undulating rhythm that quickly has us both gasping.

"Ah! Lenox, God."

With my thighs on either side of hers, I've got her pinned in place, with no ability to do much other than let me drive into her the way I want. My lips claim hers, my tongue coaxing, kissing her soft and gentle even as I fuck her deep and thorough.

"Georgia," I breathe against her mouth. "Nothing ever feels as right as when I'm inside you."

She moans, holding me close, taking me as I push into her, against her, digging in and driving my thrusts so all she can feel is me. I struggle to catch my breath as her pussy grips my cock like a fist. All the while I roll in and out of her, deeper, a little harder, more intensely each and every time.

I lower myself fully until there is no room between us, my pumps growing harder and faster, deeper somehow. Her moans turn louder with it, her pleas more insistent, desperate, anxious for me to make her come. Her pussy tightens around my cock, and my head flies back, my mouth opening on a silent groan.

"Jesus, Georgia." I squeeze one tit and moan, "Oh, fuck," as my orgasm threatens.

"Lenox," she wails as I ram harder into her sweet spot. "Don't... I'm... oh, God, yes."

A growl tears past my lips as heat, almost painful with how it burns and sears through me, shooting like a blowtorch. Her body jerks and thrashes as I pick up speed, pounding into her now, fucking her through this orgasm, and then the other that quickly comes on its heels. And when she's finally lost her mind, when I can no longer hold off even as I want this to last and last for-fucking-ever, I let go, my back arching and a bellow seizing my lungs.

My forehead slips to her shoulder, and I jerk twice more into her, unable to catch my breath as stars dance behind my eyes. I collapse in a heap, staying inside her, and turn her head so I can capture the corner of her sweet lips. My chest swells as I hold her, as I continue to rock slowly and deliriously into her.

She's mine. My wife, my lover, my future, and my past. No more dancing around this, no more fighting—at least not without the good kind of making-up—and no more pretending it's not as real as it gets.

No matter what.

Chapter Twenty-Four

Lenox

GEORGIA HAS BEEN DANCING around the kitchen for the last two hours, baking what I believe to be sugar cookies, wearing one of my shirts, knee-high socks, and nothing else, all the while listening to Christmas music. The next song comes on, and Alice gives a bark.

"I know," Georgia exclaims, doing a little shimmy to the upbeat, croony voice of whoever is singing. "This is one of my favorites too."

I groan as I lift my gaze away from my laptop. I've been sitting at the breakfast bar watching her while needing to get work done. I could go to my office. I could lock myself away. But the view is just too damn good for me to even attempt to put one foot in front of the other. Over in the great room, I have the television on mute as I casually watch the football games. Asher is playing in the four o'clock game, and he already texted me this morning to tell me that he'll miss me at the game.

During football season, I do try to go to as many of his home games as I can, but between Georgia and the snow, that didn't happen this week.

Still… "Georgia, it's not even Thanksgiving yet."

She throws me a menacing glare. "Uh, next week is, and it's a blizzard outside," she states in such a way that suggests this is standard blizzard protocol.

"So? It's Maine. A blizzard isn't exactly uncommon up here. We get them through April."

Her eyebrows shoot up. "April?!"

I shrug. "Sometimes, yeah."

She shakes her head. "How am I going to deal with that?"

That gives me a moment of pause. Because while I chose Maine for several reasons, she didn't. She is a self-admitted city girl. "Would you rather move back to Boston?"

She freezes and does a swivel in her socks to fully face me. "But you live here."

I nod, watching her carefully.

She tilts her head. "I can't tell if you're asking if I want to move back to Boston without you or if you're offering to move with me back to Boston. Sometimes your short answers, silent demeanor, and stoic expressions make it difficult to glean your full meaning."

My lips twitch. "You're not living anywhere I'm not."

"Okayyy." She drags out the Y sound. "So, you're offering to move there?"

I shrug and she rolls her eyes.

"No wonder you've been single since me. If you weren't a totally hot nerd and didn't know how to fuck like a porn star, women would never bother with you."

I bark out a laugh.

"Women talk too much."

"It's so true. We do. But in answer to your question, I don't know."

"Women do that too. Give vague responses."

"Agreed."

The timer goes off on the oven, and Georgia immediately springs into action, throwing on her oven mitts and pulling out the third tray of sugar cookies. How or when we'll ever eat all of these, I have no idea. She removes them from the tray, and places them with care onto the cooling rack so she can frost them later like she did the first two batches.

Once that's done, she turns back to me. "Do I have to decide now?"

"No," I tell her. "Of course not. I just didn't want you to think we had to stay here indefinitely if it's not where your heart is. We can stay or go or do both, however or whenever you like."

She gives me a flirty smile. "You're going to make me wet again with talk like that."

"You're not warning me against anything I don't always want."

"My vagina needs a minute to recuperate after the workout you gave her this morning." Yeah, I might have pounded her a little rough while I had her blindfolded and tied to the bed.

"Don't worry, your pretty pussy is safe for a little while longer. I'm getting work done."

She laughs, seeing through me, and goes back to icing the already-cooled cookies. "Speaking of Thanksgiving, are we doing it here or going to Boston? My mom has already informed me she's going on a solo cruise, which I think is fantastic."

"Boston," I tell her, watching as Alfie tries to pull some shit with the bogus financials I gave him access to. "Probably Zax's, though it might be Asher's since he's not playing on Thanksgiving. Fallon was saying she might be on call, so she didn't want to do it at her and Grey's warehouse." Which is where we had it last year, though Fallon wasn't back in the picture yet.

"When do you want to tell Grey and Zax?"

"I was thinking somewhere between the turkey and pumpkin pie, but only after they've had the vat of expensive bourbon I plan to bring them," I answer distractedly as I hit the command then wait, watching carefully to see if Alfie notices that I just disabled his antivirus. The thing with hackers is that you can't just penetrate their systems the way you would a standard person. We have alarms and are constantly checking for things like that. Paranoia over

241

getting doxxed is real, not to mention hackers love to go up against other hackers.

I feel Georgia move in beside me, and I lean back in my chair so she can climb on my lap. "What is all that?"

I wrap my arms around her, still waiting, still watching, a silent mouse hiding in the wall, not yet ready to sneak out and go searching around for crumbs.

"That is Alfie." I point over to the window on the right of my computer. "He's trying to fuck with my banking."

Georgia gasps, and I kiss her neck reassuringly.

"It's not my real banking. I set up a completely fake computer and phone system that he believes is my real one that he's gained access to. He's been weeding through work emails and banking and other nonsense but keeps getting locked out of doing much with it, which I can tell is frustrating hm by the frequency that he returns. And this"—I point to the other window—"is Alfie's computer. I've had access to it since he 'hacked me.'" I put air quotes around that since he only hacked what I allowed him to. "But I just enacted my first command since setting up a rootkit on his computer last week. I was letting him grow comfortable in my system, but now I'm done letting him feel comfortable."

"Rootkit?"

"It basically means I have the highest privilege in his system. I can do anything I want with it."

"Will he know it's you?"

"No." I trail kisses up and down her neck. "He thinks I'm as dumb as a sack of bricks, and everything I've shown him has increased that belief. He's gotten an eyeful of my bogus searches. Everything from workouts to protein shakes to sports podcasts to tattoo groups and forums. I even threw in some basic porn."

She laughs. "Really? Porn?"

"Georgia, I think it's something like over ninety percent of males, regardless of their sexual preference or desires, search for some form of porn at least once a month."

"I believe it." She leans back against me, and I take a deep inhale of her. She smells even more like cookies than she normally does, and I can't help my body as it stirs against her.

"What will you do now that you're in his world?"

"Depends on what I find. I turned off his anti-virus, and I will do something with that, but I'd like to look around first. Discover his true demons. Alfie doesn't strike me as the sort to give up, but he also has a very public image and job he wants to protect. He's the CEO, making plenty of money, and truthfully, he wasn't going to get access to your shares or money. His sniveling, rodent of a son was ,and now that Ezra has been arrested and some of his skeletons have been brought to the light of day, Alfie needs to save face and not do anything stupid."

"Like stalk and threaten the chairwoman of the board."

"Like that."

"You mentioned the other day that they're no longer trying to have the validity of our marriage called into question, right?"

"No. Their attorney told them they have no case."

"Do you think this is all behind us? I mean, do you think they'll officially let it all go?"

"I don't know, Georgie. I'd love to tell you yes, but in my experience, men like them don't like to lose at any cost. But where their egos and pride lead their charge, it's ultimately their biggest weakness and what we can use to our advantage."

I get an elbow jab for calling her Georgie, which makes me chuckle, and then I nip at her bare shoulder that's slipped out of the side of my oversized shirt she's wearing.

"I haven't heard a peep from them since Ezra got arrested. Not one. The board meeting is the week after Thanksgiving. Maybe they're waiting for that, but I honestly can't think of anything else they can do at this point. They have no legs to stand on. It's why I married you." She pivots on my lap and gives me a cheeky smirk and wink.

"I'm not saying they're going to try to get you to marry Ezra anymore. But I don't trust that their fight is over. Alfie is poking around your stuff too."

"So you said the other day."

I hold her tighter against me, dragging her back right up against my chest. "He won't get anything we don't want him to have. I've gone through your stuff and locked it all down. He's good, but I'm a lot better. He's searching for vulnerabilities, the same way I did with Ezra, but he won't find anything he can use to discount you or me."

She sighs. "How have you not had the FBI or NSA knocking on your door?"

"Because I have nothing to prove to anyone. I'm not a hacktivist, and I don't have a master plan to overthrow the government. I don't need to hack something just to prove I can, or do it simply *because* I can. My father always told me not to hack something for pride or arrogance because that's how you get in trouble. Like our friends here."

"But what you do is still illegal."

I stiffen because we've never directly talked about this. "Yes," I hedge and clear my throat. "Does that bother you?"

I watch her face as she thinks about that, and her hand trickles along my stubbled jaw. "No. I mean, as long as you're not doing it for evil or to unnecessarily hurt people."

"I don't. Unless someone tries to fuck with someone important to me."

She smiles and rubs her nose against mine. "I love your protective side. It makes me feel safe. Like I know that no matter what, you'd never let anyone hurt me."

"I won't," I promise her, my lips grazing hers. Knowing I'll do whatever it takes to keep that promise and never break it.

⊂⊃

"WHAT IN THE Long Island Sound are we doing out here?" Georgia shrieks as icy wind along with an unpleasant pelting of snow and ice barrages us.

"We have a dog."

"Can't she poop inside?"

I laugh watching Georgia jump up and down, hopping from one foot to the next as if the snow-covered earth she's standing on is made of hot coals, and she's afraid of burning her feet through her knee-high snow boots. She's wearing about ten layers, including the biggest, puffiest coat I've ever seen. Her hat covers practically her entire head, and she has cashmere gloves under her snow mittens.

She's goddamn adorable.

"You didn't have to come out for this."

"I thought it would be fun to play in the snow."

I grin. "And now?"

"Now it's not as fun as I thought it'd be."

We're standing on my large deck, which already has about a foot of powder on it, with more to come. It's supposed to stop sometime tomorrow, and the power hasn't so much as flickered once. It's honestly not that bad. Just another storm, but Georgia isn't buying that from me. Alice, meanwhile, is loving it. She's prancing all around, jumping and diving in and out of the snowbanks.

"How are we ever going to get out of here?"

"What?" I laugh with a bemused chuckle.

"You live in the woods in an unpaved area. It's not like Mr. Snowplow Man can come through."

"Mr. Snowplow Man?" I might die a little at that.

"You know what I mean."

"I have a truck with a plow on the front of it. I've never had a problem getting out before and I've lived through some big storms." Just then my phone rings, interrupting us. I pull it out of my pocket, squinting against the ice and snow as it almost instantly covers my screen. Swiping my finger along the screen, a spike of urgency crawls over me as I answer. "Brooklynn?"

Georgia immediately stops jumping and stares at me, her brows furrowed.

"Oh, thank the elves you picked up."

"What's going on?"

"So, funny, not so funny story. My water broke about two hours ago. No big deal as I'm just hitting thirty-seven weeks, except the road to the hospital is closed because there is a major accident there, and no ambulance is available to come to get me because they're all at the accident. Apparently, it's really bad. Like a thirty-car pile-up with a lot of injuries."

Fuck.

She starts panting into the phone. "I tried calling Georgia, but she didn't pick up."

"We're outside letting Alice do her thing. Hold on." I move my phone away from my ear and set it on speaker so Georgia can hear. "Brooklynn's in labor," I tell Georgia. "Her water broke."

Her eyes pop open wider than dinner plates. "Brooklynn, what was the fluid like? Was it clear or bloody, or did it have some green stuff in it?"

"Um, first of all, ew. Second of all, it was clear."

Georgia rolls her eyes but breathes out a sigh of relief. "Good. How far apart are your contractions?"

"They were like fifteen minutes apart when this all started, but now they're closer to three minutes."

Georgia grabs my arm in alarm. "Why aren't you going to the hospital?"

"There's a massive accident," I tell her. "The road there is blocked, and all EMS crews are stuck on the scene. Welcome to Maine."

"Welcome to Maine?!" Georgia screeches incredulously. "Nu-uh. We're on our way. Lenox just informed me he has a plow. We're coming now. Whatever you do, do not push until I get there."

"Right." Brooklynn pants. "No pushing."

"Good. We'll be there soon." Georgia hits the end button on my phone and then runs into the house, skidding on the hardwood floors in her wet boots and nearly wiping out, only to save herself at the last second and race for the stairs.

What the absolute fuck? Is she actually planning to deliver Brooklynn's baby?

"Lenox, let's go!" she yells from somewhere inside.

I guess she is.

I slip my phone back into my pocket and give Alice the whistle that lets her know she needs to get her ass inside. She comes skipping in, kicking snow and sending it flying behind her. I wipe her down with the towel I keep here just as she enters the back door, but then I'm quickly closing and locking everything up and gathering my shit.

"Georgie?!"

"I'm changing and gathering up my stuff. Thank God my friend sent me this box."

I don't ask. I just grab my own first-aid kit and gather things like internet boosters and mainstream laptops because I don't know what sort of videos or internet access we'll require. That's how my brain works. Thankfully, Georgia doesn't require a YouTube tutorial on delivering babies, and within minutes she's flying down the stairs wearing scrubs with a large bag banging heavily against her side.

I snatch it from her and take her hand, leading her out to the garage and then down and around the corner toward the attached barn, where I keep things like a tractor, my motorcycles, and the large truck with the snowplow.

"How many vehicles do you own?"

"Several."

"Several," she mocks me in a deep voice. "Okay, Batman. We get it. You're super fucking cool and sexy. How do you have so much money again? Something to do with your huge brain and stock markets, was it?"

I shake my head at her as I help her up into the truck, shutting the door behind her and racing around.

"So, the first rule of delivering babies is you do not talk about delivering babies," she says as I start up the loud engine, pressing the button on the automatic garage door.

"What?" I murmur incredulously, my heart already hammering in my throat, and we're not even there yet.

"You don't. I mean, it's almost bad luck. But I'm excited. I likely shouldn't be, and I'm obviously nervous too since I've never delivered a baby outside of the hospital before and Brooklynn is on the earlier side of being full-term, but fuck do I miss this."

I throw her a side-eye as I back out into the snow, the large tires of this truck rolling over the deep bed of it, flattening it down. I close the bay door and spin the truck around, using the shifters to lower the plow and clear our way out so we can get to Brooklynn.

"If you love it and miss it that much, I will build you a clinic."

Her breath hitches. "You will?"

I laugh, but it's shaky. So are my hands. I've never been around a baby being delivered, and while I don't love people outside of my people, Brooklynn is the second closest to them.

"Baby, I'll build you a goddamn birthing center."

"I have my own money, even if there is something wildly sexy about a man willing to do anything to make his woman happy. But I don't know, you think?"

"I think."

"Yeah," she says dreamily. "Me too, actually. My clinic will be dope. We'll do all the women's health stuff."

"With Georgia O'Keeffe images on your walls?"

She sputters out a laugh. "I never put that together until now. She painted flowers that look like vaginas, and I help vaginas bloom into flowers."

"What?"

"Yeah, that didn't come out as poetic as it sounded in my head. But she is my namesake, sorta, even if I'm named after my mother's great-grandma Georgia."

Waves of white flow on either side of the truck, like the parting of the Red Sea, as I plow through the path that leads us back to the road. "Georgia, I have no clue what you're saying right now."

"Samesies. I'm just amped. It's adrenaline rambling. I wish my paperwork for my Maine license were already approved."

She falls silent after that, a little tense as the truck digs through mountains of snow in the dark, scooting through trees in ways that make her breath hitch, but she doesn't have to worry. I've done this drive so many times I could do it with my eyes closed.

Five minutes later, we hit the main road that hasn't been plowed in at least the last few hours. I curse under my breath but push us along. Brookylnn and Max's house is on the other side of town, and by the time we reach their house, I think Georgia is on the brink of her adrenaline rush.

The second the truck stops, she flies out and trudges up the front steps through the thick snowbanks that have settled there, then pounds on the door.

I grab her bag—the one she forgot in the truck in all her excitement—along with all my stuff and follow her up just as the door opens, and a harried Max greets us with the look of a man wandering through the desert only to spot an oasis when he sees Georgia. I can't imagine how scared and helpless he must feel with Brooklynn in labor and not being able to get her to the hospital.

I follow past her, clapping Max on the shoulder. "Thank you," he says and I give him a nod because he doesn't need to thank me.

Brooklynn is in their living room, her head down on the arm of the couch, her body crouched, her face twisted in visible pain. Shit. This is really happening.

Chapter Twenty-Five

Georgia

SCARED OUT OF my wits has a very new meaning in my vocabulary. Brooklynn is drenched in sweat, wearing a short, loose black dress, and bent over the side of her sofa with her forehead pressed down in the arm as she works through a contraction.

"The ambulance told us that they're forty-five minutes out," her poor husband Max tells me, his hands wringing in front of him. "I had nine-one-one on the phone for a while, and they were going to walk me through what to do, but I—"

I give him my best version of a reassuring smile, the one I give to all my patients no matter what's going on. "I've got this."

I hope. I'm honestly terrified, and I don't know if I have this because I have no monitors, nurses, or backup help should I need it. I don't even have a lot of equipment, practically none, actually. And when the baby comes, I don't have a lot for him either. I throw on my stethoscope and reach the diaphragm around to Brooklynn's chest. Her heartbeat sounds good, but I hate that I don't have a blood pressure cuff.

I just have to pray that I won't need anything beyond what I have and what I know.

Max blows out an uneven breath and collapses into a chair, his head dropping to his hands as he starts to shake. The poor guy thought he was going to have to deliver his child. I nod for Lenox to go over and comfort him, but Lenox isn't catching my drift. His eyebrows pinch, and he gives me a quick head jerk, like he wants me to spell it out for him. I give him and then Max a pointed stare and a very obvious head bob.

Lenox is still confused and truly, that's just so Lenox I can't even.

I sigh. "Comfort him, Lenox. Get him a drink or give him a pep talk or do whatever it is guys do."

"I've never in my life given anyone a pep talk."

Brooklynn releases a wrecked breath. "Why does that not surprise me?"

"I don't even know what to say to that, but I need to check Brooklynn's cervix, and I'm guessing she doesn't want an audience for that."

"I don't," Brooklynn agrees, but her expression is very serious, and she's not moving much, her position holding which tells me she's at the transition phase, which could mean she's close.

"Exactly. So please leave the birthing theater to us women, because *this* is what *we* do. Right?" I peer down at Brooklynn as I rub her back.

"Right," she grits out as another contraction starts to take hold of her. I stand her upright and drape her arms over my shoulders, letting her lean into me.

"Hum, Brooklynn," I direct. "Humming helps with the pain. Relax your facial muscles and shoulders as much as you can. Visualize a warm, bright light on your body. See it. Hum to it all the way through your contraction."

"Ah! It fucking hurts."

"I know. I know it does. But visualize that light and hum to it. That light is warm and feels good. That's it. Keep leaning on me. Bend your knees. You've got this."

I glance over at Lenox, who is paler than I've ever seen him.

"When her contraction stops, I'm going to check her. Now is the time to go."

"Right. Just." Brooklynn pants, clinging harder to me. "Be here when it's time, Max."

Max rises off the chair and comes to us. He takes her from me and cups her face in his hand so he can look directly into her eyes. "There is nowhere else I will be. I will be holding your hand or your leg or rubbing your back or whispering in your ear or whatever you need me to do. But I will be here every second of you birthing our son." He blows out a breath. "But I'm so fucking glad Georgia is here too."

Brooklynn presses her forehead to his. "Me too."

"Great. Me three. So now Lenox is going to take you out of here for a few minutes. I promise to call you back when we're done. Lenox, you're on Max."

Lenox hauls Max away from Brooklynn and drags him off to the kitchen. Now that Brooklynn's contraction has subsided, I guide her over to the chaise part of their couch, that is already wisely without the back cushions and is lined with a plastic tarp and sheets over it. I kneel down beside her, cup her jaw in my hand, and drag her dark eyes to mine like Max just did.

"Hey, babe. You hanging in there?"

She swallows, and a tear tracks down her face. "I'm scared. I didn't want to say it in front of Max, because he's already losing it, but I really, really am."

"I know. It's okay to be scared, but we'll get through this with each other's help. Got it?"

She pushes some of her sweaty hair back from her face. "Yes."

"Great. I have a doppler and some basics that my friend sent me, and I'm going to check your cervix. Okay?"

She nods, but she can't mask the overwhelming fear in her eyes or the way she's barely hanging on.

"Women have been doing this for centuries, and I'm more than trained. But what I need from you is honesty. I don't have monitors or anything else, so I'm going to have to rely on your accurate description of how you're feeling."

"I promise."

I give her a bright smile. "Alright. Let's do this. Is there anything I should know about your pregnancy?"

"It's been normal so far. Healthy."

Thank God for that. "Great." I snap on gloves and use a large dollop of Vaseline that I brought with me on her belly since I don't have ultrasonic gel. The good news is the Vaseline will also help when it's time for her to push. Taking the probe of the doppler in my hand, I smear it into the Vaseline.

Loud static fills the room as I slide it around, moving lower, lower, and then to the right, before we hear the loud *woosh, woosh* of the baby's heartbeat.

"That sound never gets old. One fifty-two. He sounds good and strong." I give her a reassuring smile, and more tears fall. "He's low though," I tell her, considering the diaphragm of the probe is a little above her pubic symphysis. "Do you remember his approximate weight on your last ultrasound?"

"Um. I think they said he was six pounds and three ounces."

"Fantastic. That will make this easier. I'm going to check you now, okay? I'm also going to use some of the Vaseline on your opening. I know this is TMI, but you're going to feel my fingers doing things down there, and I want you to know why I'm doing this. The Vaseline will help smooth the canal and make it easier for the skin of your vaginal opening to stretch. That will reduce the likelihood of tearing and make it easier for your little man to come out."

"I like the sound of all of that. Georgia Monroe, you're my hero."

I bark out a laugh. "You just Ferris Buellered me."

"I did. But ah!" She tenses up, her face pinching up, her eyes scrunching shut as she fists the sheet beneath her. "It's... a lot. A lot of pressure."

"Do you feel like you have to push?"

"I... I don't know."

"Okay. You're doing great. Hum for me." I have the doppler still on the baby because I want to make sure his heart rate doesn't go low during the contractions. "The moment the contraction is over, I'm going to check your cervix."

I continue to monitor her and the baby as best as I can through the contraction, and the moment it's over, I reach my lubed and gloved hand inside her, wishing I had sterile gloves.

I don't get far. I don't even reach her cervix because there is something blocking it.

"You're fully dilated because I've got the top of your little man's head on my fingers."

"That explains the pressure."

"It most certainly does. I don't have anything to give you for pain. We're doing this au naturel."

"Fabulous. Good thing I pierce people for a living and can handle pain. But I need to push."

"Wait for the contraction to come and start pushing. Max!" I yell, and both he and Lenox come tumbling out of the nearby kitchen as if they were waiting by the entrance. "She's ready," I tell him, and I swear, the poor guy is about to pass out. "So, this is what I need." I hold up the probe. "I would really love you to keep this on the heartbeat as much as you can. While she's contracting and pushing, it will flutter out most likely, and you might lose it the farther south he goes, but as much as we can, I want to monitor him."

Max shakes his head as if English is far from his first or even second language.

Lenox comes in and takes the probe from my hand. "I've got it."

I blink at him. Holy shit. Lenox is kneeling beside Brooklynn, pressing the probe right above her pubic bone.

"Lenox, if you look at my—"

"Brooklynn, that is the last place I ever want to look." He shifts so that his back is to the birthing field, his eyes trained only on her stomach.

"Brilliant. Now that that's sorted, Max, you have two choices. Either you're up by her head as her birthing coach or down here assisting. But I cannot have you passing out on me."

"Birthing coach," he says without missing a beat and climbs on the sofa, crouching by her head and holding her hand as he speaks in a low soft tone by her ear.

"Like this?" Lenox asks, pressing the probe in and moving it a little when he loses it for a moment. I didn't think I could ever be more in love with him than I already was, but I was wrong. Because I just fell so in love with him all over again. Harder than ever. He's a nervous wreck, same as Max, and Brooklynn, and even me, only he's even more out of his depth here since he's not the dad.

"That's perfect."

He gives me a wink. "So are you."

Oh God. My ovaries are overfiring right now, but I manage to bring myself back to the task.

Brooklynn lets out a scream of pain, her body tensing up once more. "I have to push!"

"Push, Brooklynn. Push for a long three-count and break for one and start again until the contraction subsides. That's it. Keep going. Add to it. Max, help her count. Keep her focused."

"Ah!" Brooklyn screams. "It hurts. Fuck!" But she's pushing like a champ, and when the contraction subsides, I tell her to rest. We do this three more times. Each time the baby is progressing nicely, and then on the sixth go, I manage to get my hands on his head, helping to position him as he moves and then his shoulders.

"Stop pushing," I command. "Max, I need the towel. Bring me the towel." Max rushes over with a pile of clean towels, and I pull the baby out and immediately cradle him with one. A wet, high-pitched wail hits the air and talk about a sound that never gets old.

I'm all breathless smiles as I place the baby on Brooklynn's chest so she can hold him against her and keep him warm.

"Congrats, Mom and Dad. He looks great."

Max is up by Brooklynn's head, holding her, speaking to her as they both stare in wonder at their newborn son with his dark eyes and dark hair that so closely match his mother's.

"Thank you," Brooklynn cries. "Oh God, Georgia. Thank you so much."

I suck in a shaky breath, overwhelmed. I don't usually cry during deliveries, though the magic of bringing new life into this world is never lost me, but tonight I'm crying. I'm crying hard because everything turned out okay. Against all odds, we brought this baby into the world, and he's perfect.

I deliver her placenta, putting it into a trash bag, and clamp off the umbilical cord, and when I hand Max the scissors, he passes them to Lenox. "You do it."

And I start crying all over again as Lenox, always reluctant to take center stage, cuts the cord. I go and wash up in the bathroom, taking a breath and laughing incredulously at my reflection. Holy shit. Holy fucking shit. I just did that. I just fucking did that.

There's a tap on the door, and I call out, "Come in."

Lenox opens the door and enters, standing behind me and staring at my reflection in the mirror, his blue eyes bright. His arms swing around me, and he pulls me back into his chest, kissing my temple. "Fucking amazing."

"That's how this feels."

"That's what you are," he murmurs against me. "I'm so proud of you. That was…"

"Yeah." I'm grinning like a mad woman, high in a way I've never been before. "It was."

We leave the bathroom and find Max, Brooklynn, and the baby curled up on the sofa, all snuggled in together.

"He's perfect," I tell them. "You did such an incredible job, Mom. What's his name?"

She peers up at Max and then back at me. "George isn't my favorite name for a guy."

I bark out a laugh. "Not unless he's an English king."

"How about Gabriel, using the G for Georgia, and we'll call him Gabe?"

I wipe at my face, getting choked up all over again. "I think that's beautiful. I'm honored. Truly."

"We could never repay this," she continues, glancing down at her son and then back up at me.

"You just did," I tell her. "But how about you pierce my nipples when I'm ready and we'll call it even."

Everyone breaks out into much-needed laughter just as there's a knock on the door. The ambulance has finally arrived.

———

AFTER THE AMBULANCE comes and takes Brooklynn, baby Gabriel, and Max off to the hospital, Lenox and I drive home in near silence. It's still snowing. A no-joke snow at that. The sort of snow that makes visibility nearly impossible and your headlights only flash against the white flakes that fall directly in front of them.

Lenox goes slow, both of us hungry and tired and frankly in need of a shower. I sag back against the seat, my body flayed and my mind exhausted.

"Do you know what you did tonight?"

"Hmmm?" I question, unable to lift my head to glance in his direction as he plows us home.

"You delivered a baby."

I grin. "I did. My three hundredth and thirty-second. Including graduate school and assists as an OB nurse while I was in grad school."

"Brooklynn has been working for me for four years. She doesn't press. She doesn't push. She runs my business as if it were hers while always protecting me and my need for privacy."

I twist my head on the seat and take in his profile, unsure what to say to that.

"It's rare," he continues, "to meet people in this world who have your back and unconditionally support you without it benefiting them."

"I got the biggest earful on Monday about how you're the saint of Lavender Lake. The Bruce Wayne of the town. You don't see it, but you're amazing, Lenox. You are. Whatever your reasons for all that you've done, you've done a lot of people so much good. But Brooklynn knows you without knowing everything and respects you for who you are without question. That's why *she's* so amazing."

He reaches over and takes my hand, lacing our fingers together.

"It's taken me a long time to feel worthy of anything, but with you, I feel more than worthy, I finally feel deserving."

My heart flutters like a drunk butterfly in my chest, and I squeeze his hand, getting choked up again. "You need to stop with this. All night you've been making my ovaries explode, and me subsequently want to jump you."

He chuckles, but I'm straight-up not kidding.

"Lenox Moore, you are more than deserving. You are everything. You made me fall in love with you again, and you continue to do so over and over."

He gives me a soft smile that almost seems impossible coming from such a serious, broody man. He brings our joined hands up to his lips and kisses my knuckles before releasing me so he can steer with two hands. "Seeing them tonight, watching them do that... I kept thinking that I wanted that to be us someday. I want to see you pregnant with our children because you'll be so fucking stunning like that, and I want to be there, helping to coach you through as you bring them into the world." He pauses and takes a breath. "I never... I never imagined I ever would. Children are... fantastical and emotionally needy and I'd... I'd never want to fuck them up. I'd want to be perfect for them."

Oh, Lenox. "I want to make babies with you too," I tell him. "I might want a lot of them. I don't know yet. But I already know, after watching you tonight and knowing you as I do, that you will be perfect for them."

"I'm not sure I'd teach them to hack."

"Then don't."

"I'd want to name one of them after Suzie."

My heart clenches, and I rise over the console so I can kiss his cheek. "Then we will."

"I fucking love that it's you. No one else could ever get me like this."

I drop my head on his shoulder for a minute. "I feel the same way about you." Because he does get me. Even when I'm rambling nonsense, panicking over something, or simply wanting to listen to Christmas music in November while baking sugar cookies in the middle of a blizzard, he sees me, understands me, and loves me regardless. No matter what.

This... this feeling... this man... I'm married to Lenox, and it's no longer fake. It's everything real it's supposed to be. I don't know how we got here from where we started, but none of that matters anymore. The past is no longer important. All that matters is our future and where we go from here.

"Good."

I grin. "Good." Settling back in my seat, I smear a lather of vanilla ChapStick on my lips and comb my fingers through my hair. "Tonight was a fantastic night, but I need food and a hot shower." We pull into the barn side of the garage, and Lenox shuts off the engine.

"Same," he says as the garage door slowly closes, and we climb down from the truck. My bones are weary, and my muscles ache. "Go start the shower, and I'll fix something for us."

I don't argue it, and frankly, he could roast me a squirrel from outside, and right now I wouldn't complain. Much. Thankfully, he pulls some hamburger—not squirrel—meat out of the fridge along with some pasta and gets going on a very quick meat sauce. I drag myself upstairs, stripping as I go until I reach the top step, and then I am suddenly swooped off my feet. Lenox carries me into the bathroom, setting me down on the large tub and starting the shower for both of us.

"I'll make the meat sauce when we go back down," he tells me. "I have twelve minutes before the water starts to boil."

"That's barely enough time for you to fuck me."

He grins. "I bet I can make you come twice in that time."

"Impossible."

"Not if I'm trying to knock you up."

My hands meet my hips. "I have an IUD, and I didn't say I wanted to have babies *now*."

"Practice, Georgie. We need a lot of practice before we're ready to start trying for the main event."

Chapter Twenty-Six

Lenox

HACKING IS LIKE CHESS. You're always thinking three moves ahead and anticipating your opponent's every play. It's a game of strategy and skill. But unlike chess, the stakes are higher, sometimes as high as they can go. I was right about Alfie Earnheart. His public CEO of Monroe Securities face is very different from his real one. That good guy, mild-mannered, I care about you like a second father, routine is pure facade.

Simply put, Alfie Earnheart is a monster.

A soulless, remorseless psychopath. The Joker with the manufactured social image of a nun.

It's taken me a week to feel fully confident he didn't know I was in his system, but in that week, I lost time. Georgia's mother shipped us Tyson Monroe's laptop, and I've been sorting through that. And in doing so, that led me back to Alfie's tonight, all of this spinning into a giant, convoluted web, and I need more time. A year wouldn't be long enough to sort through all this and be able to put the missing pieces together.

And there are missing pieces. Several, in fact.

Georgia and I are set to leave for Boston today for the Thanksgiving holiday. I have to talk to Zax and Grey about Georgia, and while I could have done it on the phone—on any one of the five or so calls we've had where I felt like a guilty, lying piece of shit—they deserve to hear it from me in person. I need them to look into my eyes so they know this time everything is different.

After that, Georgia will be flying to LA for her board meeting, and I'll be joining her.

Georgia is not safe anywhere near Alfie. Or Ezra.

If all goes to plan, I can make this happen fast and remove them. If not, that poses the challenge.

I've spent the last six hours combing through piles of data, text messages, and emails. I've been cross-matching that with dates and timelines from Tyson Monroe's information. I have things I have to tell Georgia. Things that will hurt her greatly, but things she has to know about all the same.

Now. I have to tell her now. I don't think this can wait any longer.

I finish reading through the last email and blow out a strained breath. My eyes are bleary, and my muscles are stiff. I swear, in all my years of hacking, I've never encountered something so dark and convoluted. Taking off my glasses, I scrub my hands up and down my face.

Fuck.

Just fuck.

Checking my watch, I see it's sometime around six, and while Georgia might kill me for waking her this early, it can't wait any longer if I'm going to try and catch a few hours of sleep before we leave. Exiting my office, I twist my spine, cracking my back as I go into the kitchen to brew some fresh coffee. Light snow is falling, piling on top of the two feet we got over the weekend that hasn't melted much.

Once the coffee is going, I jog up the steps, slowing my pace as I enter our bedroom. Georgia is fast asleep, curled up on her side, and a pang hits me. A pang of guilt for waking her, but also the same sweet ache I get every time I see her. Being with her like this still feels like something out of a dream. I stare down at my left hand, at the thick metal band that's partially obstructing my rose tattoo and wish I could do this with her all over again, only differently.

Maybe when all these threats are behind her, and our relationship is out in the open, I will.

Pulling back the undisturbed blankets on my side, I crawl in bed and wrap myself around her. She stirs and groans, but there is a smile on her lips, and my heart quakes in my chest. Life is so much harder when you're afraid to lose something, and I have already lost enough. Her included. I lost her because I gave her up, but that's not something I can ever afford to do again. Still, knowing what my world is like without having her in it makes me a determined, protective beast with this.

"It's early," she half-heartedly complains. "I don't even have to open my eyes to know that. I can feel that it's still dark out."

"It is early, but I've found some things I need to tell you, and then I need a few hours of sleep before I can drive."

"I can drive."

I smirk against her neck as I trail kisses along her skin. "Not my Shelby, you can't."

"Oh, we get to take the Shelby. Fine. You can drive your hot-guy Shelby. But I have a feeling I'm not going to like anything you're about to tell me."

"You're not." At my serious tone, she rolls over in my arms and slowly blinks her eyes open. Her hand comes up, her fingers running along what are likely bruises beneath my eyes.

"You need more than a few hours of sleep. Whatever you've been doing all night is all over your face."

I sigh and press my forehead to hers, needing to hold her closer, needing to make sure she's real and here in my arms. Needing to make sure she's safe when all she's been is in danger for the last several months.

"Do you want to see what I'm talking about, or do you just want me to tell you?"

She thinks about this for a beat. "I want you to show me."

"Then come with me. The coffee is already brewing."

"You go down and make me a cup. I have to pee and brush my teeth first."

I smile against her lips. "I love you."

"I love you too. Now let's do this because I'm anxious to get to Boston and see my people."

I climb out of bed and go back downstairs to make her a cup of coffee while she does her stuff upstairs. By the time I have it ready and am walking back toward my office, she's flying down the stairs, wearing my Rebels hoodie that goes down past her knees and those freaking knee-high socks that always seem to have her sliding around. She looks fucking adorable and I hate that her playful smile is about to fall from her face.

I hand her the coffee and take her other hand, bringing her to my office. "The password changes every thirty seconds and connects to a VPN that requires a facial ID from me on my phone plus a retinal scan on the door itself. That said, I will give you your own facial ID and access."

She shakes her head. "That's a hard pass. I get you're trying to be inclusive and all that, but the last thing I want is access to the Batcave."

I roll my eyes, but then let us into my supposed Batcave. Georgia takes it all in, from the couches on opposite walls to the small fridge to the four racks of servers in an air-conditioned vault with their own biometrics to the long, wooden desk with two keyboards in front of two homemade computers and one laptop to the six large screens stacked in columns of two across the wall.

"This is... holy fuck, Lenox, what the fuck do you do? I mean, I think I've been laboring under a massive misconception here. I didn't think hacking really meant... I thought you were kidding about how to enter this room, and then you just did that, and now there's this room that's... this is insane."

There is no way to respond to that, so I take her hand and walk her over to my chair, sit down, and position her on my lap. She sits sideways, her legs dangling over my thighs, her coffee landing on the desk as she tries to figure out what the code and windows mean on the screens.

"Georgia, I'm not really the guy who gives it to you gently, so I'm just going to tell you what I know. That doesn't mean I don't care, and that doesn't mean I'm insensitive to your thoughts and feelings on this."

"I know," she says in a breathy whisper. "It's just how your brain works. I get it, and I won't get upset or mad at you. Just tell me."

Fuck, how am I this lucky that she knows me this well and still loves me?

I plant a kiss into her hair and shift her weight to my left thigh so I can access one of my keyboards. "I accessed Alfie's system, but I held back digging in until I was positive he didn't know I was in it. I didn't want him shutting anything down or erasing stuff, and he would have if he had known. In the meantime, your mom had sent your father's laptop. In going through things on here, I found a ton of evidence of mass financial indiscretion by Alfie. It was a ton of things, from acting as a threat actor and intercepting a third-party payment, to briefly shorting stock, to presenting false and manufactured financial reports to the board that would impact the stock price. He embezzled money while also committing a ton of SEC violations, but he did a brilliant job at covering his crimes and also showing them as legitimate financial gains and losses and even created data to back it all up."

"But if you discovered this on my father's laptop, he clearly knew about it."

"Correct. Your father is who had discovered that Alfie was the third-party event actor and went from there."

Her brows scrunch. "I'm not sure what that means."

"Alfie hacked the email system of a third-party vendor company that Monroe used and sent out an invoice to Monroe acting as the company but using a bogus payment system. Basically, he intercepted what would have been a legitimate transaction and rerouted the payment to a numbered offshore account. Monroe paid it, not realizing it wasn't legitimate, and weeks later, the intercept was discovered. I'm not sure what tipped your father off that it was Alfie, but that led to your father secretly investigating Alfie for about a year as he built a case against his, at that time, CFO and best friend. Essentially, Alfie embezzled money from Monroe, acting as another company."

Georgia's eyes are wider than Rebels Field as she grapples with this. "That's... insane. I mean, it's just... wow. *Alfie* did this? I've known him my entire life. I don't know how to wrap my head around that." She pauses, thinking this through, and then her eyes flash. "But wait, if this was going on for over a year, I was with Ezra during that time."

"Yes. You were. I'll get into some of that in a moment, but what I have to tell you next is going to be very difficult for you to hear."

Her body is a marble statue. The back of her head is all that's visible to me as she stares at the screens, one by one.

"Just... fuck." She emits a rough sigh. "Just tell me."

"Your mom was having an affair with Alfie."

I squeeze her tighter as she sucks in the harshest gasp I've ever heard. "Are you fucking kidding me?"

"Just listen," I tell her. "So, per your father's documents, that's what was going on. He didn't trust Alfie, and so he was having him investigated. But, because Alfie is a hacker and your father was not, your father didn't get access to what I have access to now. He was flying blind, picking up scraps Alfie was foolish enough to leave behind while having him followed and privately investigated."

"I can't..." She shakes her head.

"You still with me?"

"Yes. Keep going."

"You sure?"

"Yes. I need to hear this. All of it."

"Okay. So what your father knew was that your mother and Alfie were having an affair. What he didn't know was that Alfie drugged your mother at a party, got her extremely high, and then had sex with her at the party in a bathroom."

She starts to shake. "That motherfucker!"

I kiss her neck, holding her as close as I can. "After that, he threatened to come out publicly about it. He had pictures that weren't the kindest, and he promised to ruin her name and her marriage if she didn't continue the affair and report back on your father's doings. She put him off as much as she could. Through this, much like his son, he became obsessed with her. At least that's what his private texts to her from his real phone show, though he denies drugging her and says it was all her, which I believe is more for proof purposes than fact."

"Jesus, fuck, Lenox." Her fingertips touch her trembling lips. "Is he… is he still… are they."

"No. As far as I can tell from their texts, she hasn't had sex with him since your father died. Alfie was threatening to tell your father and the media that the perfect Harmony Monroe had an affair with her husband's best friend if she didn't continue to sleep with him. I have more on that too. But all your father knew was that she was having an affair, and he had planned to confront her and Alfie —along with his financial indiscretions—shortly after the wedding."

She climbs off my lap and starts to pace back and forth.

"Keep going."

I spin in my chair to face her as she paces. "I believe that's why your father changed his will in secret. It also seems that Alfie believed all along that your mom was the sole beneficiary of Monroe and knew that your father was investigating him. Alfie wanted your dad gone, and Monroe and your mom as his. He gave Ezra twenty grand to hire someone to take your father out."

She pauses mid-step and glares at me as if I just told her the sun was about to explode and the world was going to be thrust into an ice age. "Twenty grand. You told me Alfie gave that to Ezra, and he paid off a bookie."

"He did. Ezra was in deep and hiding it from the world. He took the twenty grand and paid off a bookie who is also a mafia boss of sorts. Alfie and Ezra promised this bookie two hundred and fifty grand to pay off all his debts if the bookie killed your father after you and Ezra were married. Only it seems the mob boss didn't wait for reasons unknown."

She collapses onto the sofa, and I climb down off the chair and crawl to her until my hands are on her knees and I'm staring straight at her.

She looks sick, her skin void of all color, her eyes glassy and red. Her hands rake through her hair, and then she just sits here, holding her head, completely overwrought with this. "My dad was murdered."

I nod, my chest clenching painfully for her as I say, "Yes."

"By a hired gun from my fiancé and his father, my father's best friend and business partner, who was coercing my mother into an affair with him."

"Yes."

She sits up, her forearms dropping to her parted thighs I'm positioned between. "But… why did my father add in the stipulation about me needing to be married?"

I throw my hands up in frustration. "I have no clue. It doesn't make sense to me, and I feel like that's a big piece of this pie that we're missing."

"I agree with both of those. Why would he be so adamant that I marry Ezra if he was onto Alfie?"

"We also don't know why he changed his will, other than we can assume it was because he was suspicious of Alfie and no longer wanted your mother to inherit anything."

She falls back against the couch, only to stand and start pacing again as she works this out. "But it's not like he knew he was going to die."

I climb up onto the couch and watch as she paces. "I wish I could tell you more. I have a lot of unanswered questions, and much of what I just told you is from educated guesses based on data."

"It's the worst thing in the world to know that I've spent all this time with men who murdered my father. Who would have likely murdered me and my mother given the chance and timing. I very nearly married one of them. I don't even know how to reconcile this in my head. I never suspected them of something like this. Maybe it's naïve of me, but how can people be so two-faced, and you don't even know it? I guess it's true what they say. You never really know someone's true character until it's too late."

"I'm sorry, baby. I truly, truly am."

She stops pacing and faces me, visibly raging, yet with a calmness to her I didn't expect. "Do we have any proof?"

"Yes. We have a lot of proof. Enough to take both men down. Your father built up a hell of a case, and I have the paper trail leading from Alfie to Ezra a week before your father's death." I swallow and lick my lips, shifting to the edge of the couch as my eyes lock with hers. This is where it gets tricky. "I'd like to send all of this anonymously to the FBI. I sorta have a contact there that I've sent other things to before, and she'll handle it the right way. Alfie never thought anyone would ever be able to hack this. It's a burner phone he uses with Ezra, only that's exactly the same phone he used to hack my dummy system."

"The FBI," she parrots. "And they don't know it's you?"

I shake my head. "No. Nor will they ever. Alfie fucked up. I never do. But honestly, governmental agencies aren't known for their timely interventions. With that, I'd like to leak some of this to local law enforcement and media who will take it and create a public demand for something to kick it into gear."

She blusters out a breath. "And my mother's stuff? The affair?"

"I don't see any reason why that needs to become public. At least from our side. The financial stuff and the paid assassin are enough to put both Alfie and Ezra away for a very long time and keep your name out of it. Well, as much as possible. But you, as board chairwoman, will have to wade through this storm and all that comes with it. And Georgia, there will be a storm."

Chapter Twenty-Seven

Lenox

I SPEND another hour creating an encrypted document and then send everything over to Agent Smalls. She's been the head of cyber-crimes for the FBI for the last ten years, but this goes beyond his cybercrimes. This is all kinds of SEC illegalities, so the truth is, I have no idea how long it will take for them or anyone else to act.

Plus, we're heading into a holiday weekend, and that always messes things up.

So, to that point, I leaked the money trail and text message stream between Alfie and Ezra, and Ezra and the mob boss guy whose name I left out of it—because I'm not fucking stupid—to the police and *LA Times*.

Now that all the pieces are in play, we wait. But once this goes live, Alfie will know he's been hacked, and I don't know what he'll do or how he'll react.

The only good news for Georgia is that because she married me, she's safe. I've protected all of her systems, her financials, every-thing. More to that point, if she had married Ezra, who knows?

Between her own money, her father's inheritance, and the shares, she was a target, and she didn't even know it. Now there is no benefit to them hurting her because it'd all go to me, and if they hurt me, it'd all go to probate, and their chances of getting anything are minimal at best.

Still, I'm not taking any chances.

I put a tracker on Georgia's phone and in her purse. She wasn't happy about it, but she also didn't argue it too strongly either. After that, I passed out for roughly three hours, and now we're driving down to Boston, both of us quiet as we listen to music, so very different from our initial ride up here together.

"Does this FBI agent have any way to contact you?" Georgia asks as we approach the outskirts of Boston.

"No. I send my person the stuff, the FBI analyzes it and then does what it wants with the information. I don't get involved beyond that, and honestly, this is only my third time sending them stuff. The first time I had intercepted a Russian hacking organization that was targeting US federal banks, the second was a bunch of assholes who were going to target multiple hospitals' EMR with ransomware and were stupid enough to brag all over a dark web forum about how they were going to roll in it because hospitals have to pay so patients don't die."

"So you reported it?"

"More or less. I fucked with both organizations a bit first, and then I reported it."

Georgia gives me a wry look, and I shrug.

"I never claimed to be an angel or a hero, and I don't typically fight fair. So, while I did send everything to the FBI this morning because those fuckers need to go to jail several times and ways over, I've also cleared out Alfie's foreign bank accounts. The city schools of Los Angeles, New York, Chicago, Dallas, DC, and Boston will all receive large anonymous donations that will go through on December 15, so it doesn't seem too closely tied timing-wise. I've also locked both Ezra and Alfie out from making any changes or deleting anything from their systems. Other than that, I haven't done much else because, while the FBI won't care about the missing money in the accounts, I don't want it to seem as if anything was toyed with or planted by an outside party. It has to look as clean as it can."

Georgia crosses her legs and stares out the window at the looming city before us. "This is a mess. My mother was right when she said that."

"Baby, money does funny things to people, and you have a lot of it. But with all this information out there now, it's not a matter of if, but when they'll go down."

"Right. But it's the waiting that has me uneasy."

"As of right now, they don't know it's us or even that someone has done this to them."

The simple truth is, I don't know if everything I'm telling her will turn out as cleanly as I hope it will. Life doesn't always follow a plan like that.

"Try and relax."

She laughs. "Oh, you mean the way you are?"

I change lanes and take the exit that will lead us into the Seaport District, where Zax's penthouse is. "That's different. I've been fucking around with my best friends' cousin for weeks and haven't told them. And this is after I promised them I wouldn't touch her again. Or lie to them. Ever."

"Is fucking around all we've been doing?"

She can tease all she wants, but I know she hates hiding us from them. I've told her I love her. I've told her it's her and only her forever. And though I never said anything even remotely close to her like this before, hiding our relationship from her cousins, my friends, is repeating old habits, and though she's too stubborn to admit it, it bothers her. I'm doing this as much for me and my relationship with Zax and Grey as I am for my relationship with her.

My girl is a force to be reckoned with, but right now she deserves someone to fight for her instead of against her. And honestly, as much as she hates us hiding what we are, I hate it even more.

I wipe my grin away with my fingers at the playful gleam in her voice. "Well, in fairness, until the other day when I told you I loved you, yes. You were using me for my… what did you call it? My wonder dick?"

She rolls her eyes. "Pfft. It was meant to be ironic, and it certainly wasn't me using you."

"Hmmm… I seem to remember someone seducing me on our wedding night, followed by having naughty dreams about me and then dropping to her knees in my shop."

She glares balefully at me. "Interesting, since I seem to remember you biting my lip on a plane and finger-fucking me to orgasm in a public bathroom. And for the record, I never invited you into my room in the middle of the night. That was all you, Pervy McPervster."

"I bit you to abate a panic attack, and it's not my fault that you only listen to reason once you've come."

She rolls her eyes and leans over and flicks my ear with her finger. "See, I was going to help you with my oh-so-scary cousins that you're obviously rightfully terrified of, but now you're on your own."

I laugh as we pull into a spot in Zax's garage, put the Shelby in neutral, and pull up the parking brake before shutting her off. "Maybe I should make you come then in order to secure your allegiance against your oh-so-scary cousins that I'm terrified of."

"In the Shelby in a public garage?" She gasps in feigned horror.

"Whatever works. These are desperate times."

I catch her sharp intake of breath as I reach over to lift the hem of her skirt, grateful she's wearing one, when she smacks my hand away.

"Nu-uh. I don't see why I should reward you right now."

I choke on my tongue. "How about because I'm about to help put your thieving, murderous ex and his father in prison?"

She shakes her head as she leans back against the soft leather of the seat, a twinkle flashing in her eyes. "Give me more than that."

Every inch of me starts to melt as I watch her thighs part and her hand slide up. "I married you."

She smirks. "Mmm," she hums as her hand reaches her pussy

beneath the hem of her skirt where I can't see. "That is true. You have done a lot for me lately."

I feel like fucking Alice begging for a treat. "Exactly. Now lift up that skirt." I fist the steering wheel, wanting to touch every inch of her smooth, creamy skin, salivating over every glimpse she gives me as she finally starts to slide her skirt up, only she stops before she gets anywhere close to where I want her to be.

The hand under her skirt, though? That hand doesn't stop. It climbs up and up until I watch as she starts to play with her pussy, my breath held in my lungs. She's masturbating. Again. Only this time she's not including me.

"Oh," she moans when she makes contact, her neck arching and her head rolling. "Oh, that feels so good."

Fucking brat.

Her hand that I'm insanely jealous of continues to move beneath her skirt, and where my jeans had been tight before at the thought of making her come, they're brutal now. She drags her bottom lip between her teeth, all the while keeping her eyes on me.

"Lift the skirt," I tell her.

She gives me an innocent look, her cheeks flushed the most beautiful shade of rose. "Do you think that's a smart idea? I mean, we are in a garage."

"Lift the fucking skirt, Georgia. Now."

"If you're sure," she murmurs coquettishly as she uses the hand not fucking her pussy to lift her skirt up to her hips, giving me an unholy view of her thong pushed to the side and her fingers shoved deep in her cunt.

Jesus.

"Spread your thighs wider, baby. As wide as they can go."

"Like this?" she asks, all soft and delicate in a way that's one hundred percent meant to fuck with me. Her fingers plunge in and out, covered in her slickness, but then she kills me as she brings in her other hand to rub her clit.

The enclosed air in the car is stifling. Every move of her fingers and every twitch of her body completely dominated my senses. Her moans vibrate over my skin, filling the air with their sweet sound.

She's not even putting on a show. No porn-style moaning for Georgia Monroe.

Speaking of… "I want to change your last name."

She raises an intrigued eyebrow but says nothing.

"Moore. I want you to be Georgia Moore."

"And I want you to be Lenox Monroe. It has a better ring to it."

"How about you let me finish what you're doing for you?"

"I don't think that's a good idea. Not when this feels as good as it does," she breathes out, teasing me cruelly. "If only I could watch you jerk off while I was doing this. Oh!" She moans. "That would make me come so hard."

"Are you trying to make me come in my jeans?" I stare around at the leather of my car and then back between her legs. Fuck it. It's just leather. Shifting, I undo my jeans and release my cock, groaning when she licks her lips like she's hungry for it. "See what you do to me."

"Show me. I want to watch your wonder dick shoot everywhere."

A strangled laugh-groan slips past my lips as I spit on my hand and start stroking my cock in time with her fingers pumping in and out of her. Her other hand continues to rub her clit, and her eyes stay locked on my cock as I jerk him hard, fast, and furious.

Just watching her do this, I could come, but knowing she's getting off to me as well turns my blood into liquid fire.

"I keep thinking about how good it feels when you fill me up. When you pound into me. When you give me exactly what I need."

Christ. This woman will be the death of me.

"Tonight, Mrs. Moore, I'm going to tie you to our bed and tease you until you beg me to let you come."

"But what if I drop to my knees first, Mr. Monroe? What will you do to me then?"

Fuck. "Make yourself come, Georgia. Do it now and show me it on your fingers. If I'm not satisfied with what I see on them, I'm going to make you come again, and I won't be gentle."

"Yes, Mr. Monroe." Her hand picks up its pace, and mine follows, my grip tightening, sliding over each barbell, pulling myself closer to the edge right along with her. Her thighs part wider, her eyes a dark jade green, and I want to feel how her pussy clenches her fingers. I want to feel how wet she makes them when she comes.

Her whimpers and cries grow louder, my breath held tight in my lungs, and when she starts to come, I feel my balls draw up in response.

"Ah! Yes." Her hips roll and roll, fucking her body into her fingers, and that's it. I growl out a harsh breath and cum without anything to catch it all over my fucking Shelby. But God, who cares when Georgia looks this beautiful?

The moment I'm done, I lean across the front seat and kiss my wife full on the mouth, my tongue thrashing with hers, swallowing her small whimpers, and loving how her hand dives into my hair so she can hold me tighter against her.

I pull back, and she shows me her wet fingers. "How'd I do?"

"Good enough for now." I reach over and lick them clean, feeling my cock twitch at the taste of her.

"We need to get upstairs," she rasps into my mouth, and reluctantly, I agree with her.

Reaching across her, I open the glove box and pull out a pile of napkins I keep in here just in case. I use them to wipe up the mess I made, already cringing since I don't have a proper cleaner. "If this doesn't prove my love for you, I don't know what would."

Georgia rolls her eyes. "Boys and their toys. Though, admittedly, this car was hot. You know, until you came all over it." She winks at me, adjusts her clothes, and opens the door so she can slide out.

Christ. After tucking myself back in, I wad up the used napkins and then get out of the car, then toss them in the trash bin by the elevator door.

"Feeling better?' she asks with a self-satisfied smile.

I lean in and kiss her lips. "No."

The elevator door opens, and I wave her on before following, pressing the button, and entering the code for Zax's penthouse. The car shoots up, and my stomach lifts with it. I've thought about what I was going to say to them a lot. I've put myself in their shoes. But at the end of the day, I need to just lay it out there for them and hope I don't get my nose broken over it.

Or worse, lose them.

The doors part, and we step out into Zax's foyer, only to immediately hear Asher's heavy footsteps as he yells, "They're here. The newlyweds are here."

I groan. Fucking Asher.

The moment we turn the corner and spot him, he stops short, his eyes wide as he takes us both in, and starts cracking up.

"Holy shit," he exclaims. "It's actually not a joke. Look at the two of you. You're all flushed and mussed up. You're totally fucking."

Both Georgia and I freeze, blanching, but I don't have it in me to look at her and see for myself, and neither does she. Shit.

"You better hope Grey and Zax don't see you both looking like this."

"Too late," comes from Grey as he walks into the foyer to greet us, Zax right behind him. And man, are they fucking unhappy.

Chapter Twenty-Eight

Georgia

"HOW LONG THIS TIME?" Zax asks with a cold austerity that tells me he's fuming fucking mad. Lenox was right, but I don't think this is his gloating moment.

"Practically since the beginning," Lenox answers honestly, and wow, Grey and Zax did *not* like that answer. They are *pissed*.

"Fuck!" Grey hisses, dragging his hands through his hair and pacing away. "What the fuck, Lenox? You couldn't keep your dick in your pants and out of my cousin for three fucking weeks so you could help her and not make it about you?"

I sigh. Older brothers. They're like this. Overbearing and over-protective, and while I appreciate some of that—the part where I know they always have my back and would do anything for me—right now I think they've forgotten I'm a grown-ass woman.

Asher throws Lenox a sympathetic look, but Lenox is too focused on Zax and Grey to see it.

"You promised us," Zax says coolly, his dark eyes locked on Lenox. "You fucking promised us."

"I know."

Zax huffs a breath, his hands meeting his hips and his eyes dropping to the floor. "You know! That's what you say? Are you fucking kidding me with that?!" he shouts. "Because she wasn't vulnerable enough, huh? You had to go and fuck with her already fucked with head and heart?" He eviscerates Lenox with his eyes. "Or wait, are you going to tell me it's just fun and no feelings are involved?" he mocks acerbically.

"Does anyone want to hear what I have to say in this?"

"No!" Grey and Zax both yell at me without so much as a glance in my direction.

Yikes. The tension over here is thick enough you could cut it with a scalpel. And while their blatant disregard for my position in this hurts and is frankly annoying and chauvinistic, I'm not sure I should intervene since Lenox told me this was between the three of them.

I get it. They're pissed Lenox broke his promise to them. After he kept us a secret from them for two years and broke my heart.

So yeah, they're angry. And I guess they technically have a right to be.

But the truth is, Lenox and I are two people who never knew how to stop once we started. We could have made a million rules and laws, said anything we wanted, and had a million obstacles between us. But at the end of the day, we were inevitable. It was always going to turn out like this.

The only difference between now and then is that the timing is right for it to really happen. Georgia and Lenox. Two people who couldn't be more opposite from each other, and yet I'm not sure two people were ever more right together.

"Georgia, why don't you and I—"

"No," I tell Asher. "I'm not going in the other room. I'm sorry, but this is crap."

Everyone ignores me.

"It's not just fun, and there are feelings involved," Lenox answers Zax's comment from like three minutes ago, because that's how this is going right now.

"I trusted you with her," Zax snarls, and Lenox makes an aggravated noise in the back of his throat.

"No, you didn't. Neither of you did, and I understood your reasoning for that. She needed help, and I was the only one who could deliver it. But you never trusted me with her. Not for a second."

"Because you fucked her behind our backs for two years and then broke her heart!" Grey yells.

"Wait," Asher calls out, stepping forward. "What is this? I thought they were just pissed because you were screwing around with their cousin." Asher steps in front of Lenox. "When did that all happen?"

"Six years ago," Zax tells him, and Asher frowns, shaking his head in consternation, but he's looking at Lenox, really looking at him.

"Six years ago, huh? I remember you six years ago." He puts his hand on Lenox's shoulder. "I remember you the two years before that when you were evidently screwing around with Georgia behind our backs. Two years," he repeats. "That's no joke time right there. Tell me I'm wrong with that."

"You're not," Lenox answers, and Asher nods, understanding lighting his features.

Lenox swallows hard, and then we hear footsteps, several of them, and then Callan and Aurelia are there. "Katy and Mason are with Layla, Wynter, and Fallon in the other room," Callan announces with an air of annoyance in his tone. "We had them put on a movie. So how about you tell me what has you all yelling the word fuck when there are little children in the other room who were able to hear you?"

"Lenox is fucking Georgia," Grey announces. "After he promised us he wouldn't touch her."

Aurelia rolls her eyes and comes over and stands beside me. "Men," she grouses to me.

"Totally." I smirk, only to quickly wipe it away.

"Should we let them work this out or step in?"

"Work it out," I whisper back to her. "And only step in if necessary."

She nods in agreement.

"Again?" Callan murmurs, and everyone sort of freezes and then looks at him in surprise including Lenox. "What? I knew about it."

"How did you know and I didn't?" Asher challenges.

Callan rubs the back of his neck, his blue eyes flickering around to each one of us. "Because I was there. We were all drowning in our shit, but Asher, you were in college in Alabama trying to get your football career going. Grey, you were working on music in LA and made your first solo album. Zax, you couldn't handle looking at Lenox without losing your shit about Suzie, but I was there. I was in medical school and living in an apartment not far from Lenox's place in Cambridge, and I'd go there to study because I was fucking worried he was going to kill himself one day. But then he started going out, and when he'd come home, he was different. Calmer. Less restless and self-destructive. He was in his head less. I saw Georgia's name in a text once on his phone and put it together. I figured she was helping him when no one else could and in ways no one else could, so I didn't say anything because I was afraid it would stop."

"I saw it too," Zax admits, his expression anguished. "I did. I didn't know it was Georgia, but when you told me it had been going on for two years…" He trails off and heaves a heavy breath. "It's why I couldn't bring myself to hate you or let you go. Georgia gave you something we couldn't, but I couldn't handle you hurting her for it."

"I couldn't handle that either," Lenox promises, moving over and standing before Zax and glancing over at Grey. "I loved her. When I loved nothing in this world except for my dead sister and you guys, I loved her. I've loved her since. I've loved her always. She and I just didn't get there until very recently because she hated me for the majority of the time we've been married. There was nothing to tell you, not really, until now. This isn't how I wanted you to find out. I had a plan for it."

"Yeah, that's sorta my bad," Asher apologizes, and Callan grabs him by the shoulder.

"Come on, brother. Let's let them figure this out. No one is bleeding, and no one needs to be held back. Am I right with that? Will it stay that way?" Callan asks Zax and a still-emotional Grey. Both nod.

"And miss the show?" Asher pouts.

My lips bounce, and Aurelia pats Asher on the back. "I'll give you the highlights reel after."

"Thanks, doll, but I'll need more than highlights. I'll want the play-by-play." He gives me a conspiratorial wink, and Aurelia shoves him in the direction of the media room. But Asher, as always, has managed to lighten the mood, which was obviously his intent.

"You love her?" Grey asks, standing before Lenox, searching his face. "This isn't just sex?"

Lenox shakes his head and holds out his hand to me. When I take it, I feel his trembling, and then his eyes meet mine, and one by one, he slips my wedding band off first, followed by my engagement ring. My breath catches and my eyebrows knot together, and I frown when Lenox hands Zax Suzie's ring back.

"What are you doing?" Zax questions.

"This isn't her ring," Lenox states simply. "When we were kids, you asked me if you could date Suzie. You promised me you'd never hurt her and that you'd always be good to her. I didn't give you the same respect with Georgia because I wasn't in a position to make that same level of promise. But I am now. My plan was that I was going to ask you both for your permission to be her husband. Then all this happened, and now…"

He trails off and turns back to me, his blue eyes all over me.

"I love you," he says slowly. "I'm completely in love with you, Georgia Monroe. I don't just want you, I need you. Every day, I need you more and more. So I don't want you to wear Suzie's ring. I want you to wear mine."

He lowers himself down onto one knee, and mine just about give out.

Reaching into his pocket, he pulls out a ring, no box, and slides it right onto my finger. "We're already married, but now I'm asking if you'll be my wife."

Oh hell. My chest clenches, and tears instantly burn my eyes.

"Yours and no one else's," I whisper, my voice cracking at the end as a tear slips out and tracks down my cheek. He smiles softly and slips my ruby band back on my finger, nestling it against my new diamond ring. He stands, his hands sliding up to cup my cheeks, his thumbs wiping away my tears, and then he kisses me.

Right here in front of his cousins and Aurelia.

No more hiding. No more sneaking around. No more trying to hate what is impossible not to love.

The moment he pulls away, Zax and Grey grab him and haul him in for giant hugs. They're whispering stuff to him that I can't hear, but whatever it is has Lenox smiling and laughing.

Aurelia snatches my hand and jerks it in her direction. "That's a hell of a ring."

I gaze down at the large emerald-cut diamond with tapered baguette side stones. Simple. Beautiful. Classic. "It's perfect."

"Yeah. It really is. Your husband did good."

I laugh. My husband. "It feels so strange now after how this all began."

"We should throw a party. An actual party this time. Give you a proper wedding. I bet Asher would get ordained for it and remarry you. You know him."

I glance over at Lenox, who is watching us, and tilt my head. "What do you think?"

"You want Asher to marry you?" Grey asks incredulously.

"It can't be you or Zax. You're family. It's not exactly Callan's thing, but it totally is Asher's."

"I'll do it!" Asher calls out from down the hall and comes sprinting back toward us. "I told them I had to go to the bathroom, and the fools didn't challenge me or think I'd sneak back over to listen. It's like they don't know me at all. Anyway, yes, I'll marry you. Mason can be your ring bearer, and Katy your flower girl. Let's do it. Let's fucking do it!"

"Did you take something?" I ask, and he shakes his head.

"No, I'm just amped. I want to ask Wynter to marry me, but she'd tell me it's too soon, which it likely is, but whatever. This is the next best thing. Let's do it Friday since I have to leave Saturday for Dallas for a game on Sunday."

Lenox's lips twitch with amusement, and he threads our hands, his eyes all over me as if the decision is mine.

"Sure," I say, loving the idea more and more. "Let's do it."

"Yay!" Aurelia jumps up and down and pulls out her phone and starts texting. A second later, Wynter, Fallon, and Layla all come running in. I'm swarmed in hugs and congratulations and oohs and aahs over my ring. Zax and Grey are all smiles, happy that this didn't end in tears and heartbreak and broken noses all over their faces.

I'm getting married. And though my dad or even my mom won't be there, I already know it's going to be the wedding of my dreams since I'm marrying the man of them.

After that, we finally leave the foyer and gather in the great room, Boston Harbor and the skyline beyond the large windows. Lenox has me on his lap as he silently listens to everyone chattering around him, his fingers toying with the rings on my hand.

We told everyone about Alfie and Ezra, though Zax already seemed to know most of it. As far as I'm concerned, they're on borrowed time, and with them both being clueless and across the country, I'm not going to overthink now. Not today, at least.

That time will come.

"We should go shopping tomorrow," Fallon says. "I'd love a fun dress for this."

"Same," Layla agrees. "And not that I'm inviting myself to be, because I realize we don't know each other all that well yet, and while I'd be honored to be a bridesmaid, please do not make us all wear the same thing."

I laugh. "What? You don't all want to wear pastel pink?"

"No," all the women say at once.

"Wear whatever you want, and obviously you're all my brides-maids because that's how this works. I bought a dress when we were in Vegas. It's the one I got married in there, but it's up in Maine."

"Pfsht." Aurelia waves that away. "That dress doesn't count, and you definitely can't re-wear it for this. Talk about bad luck. We'll all go to my studio tomorrow, and I'll get you set up in a gorgeous gown."

"A gown?" I scrunch my nose. "You don't think that's a bit too much for this, for just us, for just here?"

"No," all the women cry once again in unison making us all crack up.

"Fine. I'll wear a gown. With a lot of sparkly crystals on it, because that's what I want." I twist on Lenox's lap so I can see his face. "You can't wear a tux."

His eyes glitter. "No?"

I shake my head. "No. Definitely not. You're not a tux guy."

"What should I wear then?"

I press my lips to his. "Surprise me."

Just then a notification sounds on Lenox's phone, and he shifts me around on his lap so he can dig into his pocket to pull it out. His eyebrows bounce, and a grin curls up the corner of his lips.

"What?" I ask. "What is it?"

"It seems the LAPD are moving fast for once." He flips his phone around so I can read his screen.

"What is that?" I ask because it's sort of difficult to tell.

"That's the inside of the LAPD's computer systems. They have a warrant for Alfie and Ezra Earnheart on charges of conspiracy to commit murder and aiding and abetting murder. Once the FBI gets wind that they've been arrested for this, it'll all come together."

"And you, Georgia, will be thrust back into the media spotlight," Callan says.

"Yes," Lenox agrees. "Only this time, she won't be in it alone."

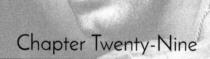

Chapter Twenty-Nine

Georgia

LET it never be said that my husband isn't a freaking genius. The LAPD detective that Lenox anonymously leaked the texts between Alfie and Ezra to is the same detective who originally told Alfie that my father's plane was missing. The detective noted in his report that Alfie's reaction was suspicious and that further investigation was warranted.

Evidently, Alfie wasn't shocked or sad or scared that my father's plane had gone missing. He wasn't despondent the way my mother and I were.

He was angry.

Most likely angry because it fucked up his timetable by happening sooner than he wanted, but angry all the same. After pieces of my father's plane were discovered, Alfie was questioned—we all were—by the FBI, and that notation in a random file by the LAPD was overlooked or forgotten or possibly never seen. At that time, Alfie was appropriately devastated, and nothing else came of any of it.

But when these new files landed in the detective's inbox, he remembered Alfie, he remembered his notation, and he was quick to act on the information that was presented to him. He also got in touch with the FBI, and things quickly snowballed from there—clearly everyone wanted this done before the holiday tomorrow.

Alfie was officially arrested by a joint task force early this afternoon at his home. He tried to make a run for it but was quickly apprehended and every device in his home was confiscated. Lenox pulled himself completely out of Alfie's and Ezra's systems, and there will be no trace that he was ever in them. Alfie is sitting on suicide watch in a federal jail cell awaiting arraignment, which we're told with the holiday might not happen until Friday at the earliest.

Thankfully, they didn't arrest him in the office, but I've been on the phone with the board, playing shocked and heartbroken while working with them as we prepare a statement that our PR people will release at eight this evening.

It's a mess.

But a good mess in a way because now Alfie is in jail, Ezra will likely follow any second, and we've got a clean slate at Monroe Securities. The board can hire a new CEO and a new COO, and we can rebuild the company into the premier cybersecurity force in the industry, led by honorable men and women instead of blood-thirsty, money-hungry fucktwats who don't deserve any designation beyond that.

I told Lenox I'd love for him to be our new CEO, and he laughed. Loudly. I took that as his firm no.

Who cares? I'm standing in an Aurelia—Lia Sage since that's her designer and model name—gown as she pins fabric and points to where she's going to add a million sparkles just for me. A Cinderella dress so I can feel like a princess as I marry my anti-Prince Charming.

I love her. Have I mentioned that? She is my people. So are Fallon, Layla, and Wynter, who hung out with me all day here and drank champagne and pilfered through the Monroe and Lia Sage design closets and picked out what they wanted to wear to my wedding.

A wedding I am, for once, beyond excited for.

"Do you ever take that earpiece out of your ear?" Aurelia gripes at me. "I've been saying your name for like five minutes."

"Sorry." I wince. "I'm still listening in on the board meeting. They won't stop."

"That's good though," Fallon comments as she moves to sit sideways on the hair and makeup chair, her legs now kicked sideways over the arm. "It shows they care. My parents are all about boards, and they don't give two fucks. Theirs are all about appearances."

"How much champagne have you had?" Layla snorts.

Fallon holds up her glass, spilling some on the cement floor in the process. "I think this is my third glass."

"You're officially cut off," Wynter tells her, only to start cackling as she twirls around and around in her own makeup chair since this is where the dress platform is located in Aurelia's design studio. "But this is my fourth, so maybe I'm cut off too."

"You're all cut off."

Fallon snorts at Layla. "Oh please. You're a twenty-three-year-old Fritz. You know exactly what we're talking about, and I'd bet you could drink us all under the table."

"I'm also twenty-three," Aurelia points out.

"Christ, you're young. Why do you not seem that young?"

Aurelia lifts her eyes to mine. "Because I've been living my best life on my own since I was sixteen, so my age is in dog years."

"Same," all the women say in unison, and I realize I'm not the only one here who has an extraordinary and strange life. Not to mention the men we're all with. They're a lot in their own right.

"Ugh. Hold on." I unmute the call. "Yes, Charles. I agree with that point. But I think the statement is solid, and more is just unnecessary. Short, sweet, to the point." I mute the call again. "I miss delivering babies."

"Soon enough. You know, we could open our own practice. One where we serve emergent orthopedic pregnant women."

All of us turn to Layla.

"It sounded better in my head," she mumbles. "Pretend I didn't say that. Clearly, champagne goes straight to my head."

"Okay, you're done," Aurelia tells me. "I'll finish this up Friday morning, and it'll be perfect for that evening. Eeep!" she squeals, her exuberance overtaking her features. "I'm so excited. Lenox! You're marrying Lenox."

"You got engaged first. Like over a year ago," Fallon quips dryly at Aurelia. "Don't you think it's time you and Zax tie the knot?"

Aurelia stands and undoes the gown in the back and helps me out of it. It's a lot of dress for not a lot of wedding, but who cares?

"Um, did we not just establish that I'm only twenty-three?"

"I thought we just established you're like a hundred and two in dog years," I remind her.

"Technically, a hundred and sixty-one since each dog year is seven of ours. But I only count that when it's convenient for me."

"Crap." I unmute. "Sounds great. Thanks, everyone. We'll reconvene after the statement goes live. Go enjoy your evenings. The hard part is over." I hit end on the call. Finally.

I step out of the gown and then throw back on my bra, leggings, and cropped sweater I wore here. Sitting down, I slip back into my Louboutin Vidura Spike booties.

"You need something super sexy for under that," Layla throws out. "I mean, you've got great tits and all, but it's your wedding. You need lingerie."

"I wore sexy stuff the night we actually got married, but you're right. I almost need to one-up that."

"There's a French boutique lingerie store around the corner from here," Aurelia notes. "I bet they'd have the perfect thing."

"Oh! Let's go look. I need to get some sexy things too," Wynter squeaks, only to sigh. "This is why I don't drink." She stands on shaky legs. "Come on. Let's go do this, and then I'm going to Uber home to Asher, who will feed me and put me to bed."

An hour later, I have a bag filled with naughty delights—including a few toys they had for purchase in the store—when my phone rings. I slip one AirPod into my ear and answer. "Hey. I'm heading home now."

"Why are you still downtown?" Lenox's voice comes through my ear.

"I'm walking to the car now. We just finished shopping. Why? What's up?" His voice sounds funny.

"The LAPD and the FBI haven't found Ezra. He wasn't in his house or anywhere in LA. I've been searching for him for the last two hours, and I've tracked him to LAX yesterday, where he used a fake passport to get on a plane to Boston."

Ice runs through my veins, and I quickly search the street around me. It's dark, though it's only a little after five, but I don't see anyone beyond the usual rush hour crew of people trying to get out of work before the holiday tomorrow.

"Where is he?"

"I don't know," he barks into my ear, agitated in a way Lenox rarely, if ever is. It makes my heart rate and blood pressure spike. "Every device I have on him shows him at his LA home. He's dumped everything. He got on a hotel shuttle at Logan Airport when he arrived but never registered at the hotel or any as far as I can tell using his real name or the alias he flew under. But he's here, Georgia, and why would he be here if not for you?"

"I don't know."

I shake my head as I open the driver-side door of Lenox's black BMW XM. He keeps this car in his garage in Cambridge, which feels like a waste, but right now, I'm grateful for it instead of having to order an Uber and wait for it. Only the moment I slip inside and buckle up, I freeze.

"Ezra," I say in a low voice.

"What?" Lenox growls in my ear. "Why are you saying his name like that?"

"How did you know I was here?" Ezra asks, sitting up in the back seat from where he was hiding. He can't hear Lenox since Lenox is speaking directly into my ear, but Lenox can sure as hell hear him since the microphone on my AirPod is picking up his voice.

"Fuck! Fuck! He's there? He's in the car with you? Fuck. Get out of there."

"I smelled your cologne," I respond, speaking only to Ezra. My hands tremble as I slowly move one to the handle on the door and the other to the seat belt latch.

"I wouldn't try that, honey." Then I hear a strange click and spin to see Ezra is pointing a gun at me. I flip back around, breathing heavily.

Fuck is right. "A gun, Ezra? You have a gun? Why are you doing this?"

"Can he hear me, Georgia?" Lenox asks.

"No," I respond to Lenox and quickly continue. "No, this isn't you, Ezra. What are you doing?"

"The only thing I can do," Ezra claims. "Now start driving and take me to your asshole husband's house."

"No," I say sharply. "You'll kill him."

"Do it, Georgia," Lenox snaps. "Do everything he says and bring him here. I'm recording him, and I'll be ready for him."

I shake my head. Ezra has a gun, and I know he'll hurt Lenox.

He presses the barrel of the gun painfully into the side of my head, and tears spill from my eyes. "Now!" Ezra yells, and a sob slips out.

I slam my fist into the steering wheel, furious that I just showed him how scared I am. Enraged that he's doing this. And terrified beyond my wits that he'll kill Lenox and me.

I press the ignition button and put the car in drive, forcing myself to take calming breaths. To remember my years of martial arts training that taught us that the worst thing we can do in a crisis is panic.

"Talk to him, Georgia. Get him to talk to you. Get all the information you can. It's okay, baby. I'm here with you, I'm tracking you now, and he doesn't know that. We have the upper hand with this, and I won't let him hurt you."

But can you make that same promise for yourself?

Another tear tracks down my cheek, and I hastily wipe it away. I pull into Boston rush hour traffic, inching up the city street to head toward the Harvard Bridge that will lead me into Cambridge.

"I need you to lower the gun, Ezra. I'm driving in Boston, and that's tricky for me on a good day. You aiming a gun at my head is making it impossible to focus on anything else."

I hear him shift in the back seat, but with as dark as it is outside, the only times I can see him are through glimpses in the rearview mirror when the streetlights hit him just right. Still, it's not difficult to tell that his eyes are dark and wild with chaos.

"There. But it's not far, so don't make me use it. Yet."

"How did you get in the car? Hell, how did you even know I was driving it?"

"I was watching you this morning at *his* house, and I saw you get into this car. You never lock the car because you always keep the key in your purse. It's a chronic problem you have. We had a fight about it once. Remember?"

Shit. He's right. I never locked the car. I made it all too easy for him. Fucking stupid.

I shake my head. "Why are you doing this?"

"I wanted to talk to you away from him," he says as I turn onto Mass Avenue. "I need to convince you to be reasonable with this. I fucking love you, and I know you love me. I fucked up, okay? I know I did, but we were so good together and you just... how could you just end it with me like that, Georgia?"

Christ. Is he kidding with that?

"You changed," I voice instead of saying that I didn't love him, and he made me feel trapped.

"I can change back. I'll be anything you need me to be. Just be mine."

I grip the wheel as I get onto the bridge. Even with the traffic, I'll be back at Lenox's place in less than fifteen minutes.

"You killed my father. You and your father paid a man to kill him. Why?"

Ezra makes a deranged noise, and I hear him shift again. "My father is a fool. He always told me I was stupid, careless, and not good enough, but now he's the one in prison, and I'm free."

"Ezra, tell me what you did to my father," I demand, needing him to tell me everything. Needing all the pieces of this puzzle to finally come together.

"My father is in love with your mother. He wanted your father gone. I knew that. My father asked me to plant bugs inside your father's office to spy on him, and I did. Except I heard your father talking to his attorney on the phone. He knew my father and your mother were having an affair. Did you know that?"

I'm not sure how to respond since that's not public knowledge, so all I say is, "No."

"Well, they were. Your father's attorney told him to change the beneficiary of his assets before doing anything about it so that your mother couldn't get them in a divorce if everything was going to you. He knew she'd never take anything that was set to go to you. You had been slipping away from me. I knew it. I could feel it. And I couldn't let that happen."

I shake my head, not understanding, as I change lanes. "What does that mean? What did you do?"

"I acted. I confronted your father, and I blackmailed him into adding me into the will, stating that you had to be married to me in order to inherit, and in exchange, if he kept me on and named me COO after my father was gone, then I wouldn't say anything to my father about what your father was planning to do."

"You had my father killed, and the will didn't stipulate you directly. Only that I had to be married."

"Your father double-crossed me. He found the bugs and removed them, so I never knew any of that until it was too late. Matis was supposed to kill your father while we were on our honeymoon. Unfortunately, your father was in France, and since Matis is French, he took the opportunity to use one of his local guys there, and it was done too soon."

"You speak about this as if it's not everything. As if something like that is forgivable."

"You would have never found out!" he bellows, the sound practically rattling the windows. "You would have inherited the money and the shares, and we would have been married. We would have had everything, and then you went and married him! Now it's all falling apart, and I can't let that happen. Not again."

"I won't let you hurt Lenox," I say, my voice even as I mentally devise a plan.

Lenox has been silently listening, but I can hear his harsh breathing through my ear, so I know he's still there.

"If both of you play ball, I won't have to. Judging by his array of cars, he has money. A lot of it. And so do you. I want it. Fifteen million dollars to an offshore account, and I won't hurt him. But you and I are flying out of here tonight, Georgia. On your cousin's plane."

I laugh, and it isn't a kind laugh either. "I'm not going anywhere with you. You're fucking crazy. Not to mention a remorseless murderer."

"Business is business, Georgia. I'm not different in that from anyone else out there. And you *will* fucking come with me, or I will kill Lenox and your cousins. Don't think I don't still have connections that can do that. That's my deal to you, and since I know you couldn't live with the guilt of having their deaths on your conscience, you'll do it."

He has to be high if he thinks I'm going to let any of this fly. Or maybe he is, and he's freaking delusional about this.

"Tell him, okay," Lenox whispers in my ear. "Tell him you'll do anything he wants."

I make a displeased noise at that and grit out, "Fine, Ezra. You're right. I can't let you hurt my people. I'll do what you want."

I catch him out of the corner of my eye as he sits back in the center seat, seemingly mollified by that. Only I have no intention of doing this the easy way, and I already know Lenox isn't going to like that.

Chapter Thirty

Georgia

NERVES SKITTER OVER MY SKIN, making the hairs on my arms stand up and my pulse thrum like a jackrabbit. I make a right and sigh out, almost as if I'm bored with all of this. "We're close. What's your plan when we get there?" Obviously, I'm asking both men, but I want to know what Lenox wants me to do.

It's not every day you have your ex in the backseat of your car pointing a gun at you. It's honestly the most awesome of coincidences and timing that I have my AirPod in my ear with my husband on the line, and my hair covers it completely from view. One can only hope that will save the day—or night in this case—and that Batman will once again thwart the enemy.

But why does a woman always have to rely on a hero to save her?

"I'm calling the police now. I didn't want to risk them showing up just as you did or being here when you arrived and having Ezra freak out and react. I'm waiting on the side of my garage. I want you to keep him outside, Georgia. I don't want him in the house.

294

He'll be easier to disarm and take down if he's outside. I'll surprise him from behind."

Lenox says this at the exact same time Ezra says, "We're going to go inside and have a nice chat with your fake husband before you and I take off for the airport."

I laugh. It's strangled and not based in any form of humor. "Why would you say he's fake?" That's actually the least of my curiosities. Does he think this will actually be a chat where Lenox is like, *sure, cool, here's some money and you can take my wife, no problem. Oh, and the Monroe jet? Of course, let me just get Zax on the line,, and he'll clear that for you Jiffy Pop.*

Gun or no gun, that's not how this will go down.

"Because you can't love him!" Ezra screams. Not just shouts but *screams*, making me jolt in my seat, and his flip from somewhat calm to that is jarring and has me sitting up a little straighter in my seat and checking the rearview for where that gun is pointed. I can't see it, which I'll take to mean it's not pointed at my head currently.

Ezra is unhinged and unpredictable, and more than just having a gun, him in this state is what makes him so dangerous. He wants me as much as he wants the money. He's made that much clear. Otherwise, he'd just cut me loose, take the money, and run. If he's jealous of Lenox, if he believes for a second that I truly love him, he'll kill him. In fact, knowing Ezra as I do, that's exactly what he's going to do anyway.

Lenox is a paper trail. An uncertainty. A potential challenge for him.

A point that will be proven when Lenox naturally tries to protect me. It'll be his instinct because that's Lenox for you, and he won't know all the ways it will drive Ezra past the point of his current madness. It will undoubtedly set Ezra off, and he'll kill Lenox, and then… then I don't know. Perhaps he'll kidnap me, or the cops will show up in the nick of time, but it'll be too late for Lenox.

Of that, I'm positive.

Either way, I have to do something before either man gets to each other.

Determination swarms through my blood like a pack of killer

bees all banding together in a blood-thirsty tribe. My adrenaline has found a new purpose, and instead of making me jittery and panicked, it's making me sharp and purposeful.

I pull into Lenox's driveway, all the way to the two-car detached garage in the back, all the while scanning for my guy without seeing him. He hides well, though that shouldn't shock me. He always has.

Clicking the button for the garage door, I slow my breathing as I pull in and shut off the car.

"Now what?" I ask Ezra, afraid to act without instruction.

"Now get out and stay beside me."

"I don't want anyone to get hurt," I tell him, my voice smooth even as I gracefully pull the earbud, from my ear, essentially ending my call with Lenox. I set it down on my seat where Ezra can't see since it's nothing but darkness in the car right now.

"Then you better follow my instructions."

"But how do I know you won't hurt me? Say I go away with you, what assurance do I have that you won't kill me the way you killed my father?"

"I'd never hurt you, Georgia," he growls adamantly, fiercely. "I love you."

"Okay then. I'll do what you say. If you promise me that." I bat my eyelashes like a sweet little thing to him in the rearview, not even sure if he can see the gesture, but he can hear it in my voice.

Unbuckling my seat belt, I open the door with a soft click. I don't know where Lenox is, and right now, with me ending the call, I've turned us blind. Still, I don't want Lenox to come charging, and if he doesn't know what's going on, it might make him hold back for a few extra seconds.

The moment I shut the door, Ezra's hand is on my forearm. The other hand with the gun is raised but not aimed at me, and I take that lapse in judgment and run with it. I twist in front of him and kick at his left hand. The spikes lining the edge of my boots stab into his skin, and never in my life have I been more grateful for the weird design genius of these boots that are lined in spikes. Ezra howls in pain, releasing me and clutching his now-bleeding wrist, and with that, the gun immediately drops from his hand, clanking on the cement floor of the garage.

In my next motion, I grab him by the back of the head and slam his face downward just as I raise my knee until the two connect. I both hear and feel the crunch of his nose breaking, but before I can continue, Lenox is there, dragging him back by his hair and walking him out of the garage.

"What are you doing?!" Lenox snaps, fury lacing his every feature. "Are you out of your fucking mind?"

"He was going to kill you! No two ways about it," I yell, miffed because I just disarmed a man and I get no credit for it. "Men do not get to always play the hero. Sometimes, women are better at it."

Annoyed, I go for the gun, only Ezra isn't having that. Whatever he's on, he's not feeling any pain as he jabs his elbow back at Lenox, hitting him straight in the gut and ripping his head away from Lenox's grasp, a collection of hair going along with it in the process.

He does a Superman dive at me, knocking me down onto my back on the driveway and stealing the air from my lungs. He rolls me once, all the while struggling to take the gun from my hands. My arm flies, knocking him in the side of the head with the gun just as Lenox picks him up like a rag doll and body slams him straight onto the driveway.

Ezra oomphs and gasps out a loud cough before he starts thrashing and yelling a thousand obscenities as he tries to squirm free, but to no avail. Lenox is a lot bigger and stronger and has Ezra's arms pinned by the press of his knees as he sits on his chest with his full weight.

"Cut the shit or I'll have her pistol whip you again, asshole. If you think I can fuck you up, you haven't met my wife yet."

I snicker.

"It's not funny," Lenox barks at me, clearly still angry I attacked first, but his lips are twitching now too. "Stop laughing. I'm seriously fucking mad at you, Georgia Moore."

"I'm not laughing, Lenox Monroe." Except I am. I start to cackle like a hyena. Not my best look, but I don't even care right now. Why that's funny in this situation, I don't know. Maybe it's the adrenaline rush making me high, but I can't stop it.

"Dammit, Georgia!" Ezra yells. "Get him off me."

"Right. Of course. I'll be sure to do that, Ezra. You just lie there for a minute and wait for me to act." I roll my eyes at him as I flip the safety on the gun and walk to the edge of the garage and set it down because I hear sirens, and the last thing I want is to be holding a gun when the police show up.

"I'm bleeding! Look what you did to my nose and wrist."

"I know." I glance down and hold out my foot, twisting it this way and that. "How cool are these boots? Be thankful I didn't kick you in the nuts with them. Or ram this heel that is also no joke up your ass."

He bucks and jerks and starts yelling at Lenox. "Let me go, you fucking asshole. I'll sue you. I'll sue you for everything you're worth."

"I believe you just tried to kidnap and blackmail that out of us," I deadpan.

The moment Ezra catches the sirens, he starts to lose it. He's spouting a thousand threats and promises, and Lenox just stares down at him as if he's trash and doesn't care. He presses in deeper, making Ezra bark and snarl like a wild beast, but it's futile.

The police show up, literally a dozen of them swarming with guns drawn, and we're raising our hands—except for Ezra since his are pinned—and then it all begins. Lenox stands up, and the police handcuff Ezra. The gun is confiscated, and I explain how I had it in my hands.

Ezra is whisked off in an ambulance with some scary-looking dudes in black, and Lenox and I are just sort of here, standing around, waiting for them to decide what they want to do with us next.

"Do you think it's done?" I ask him, wrapping my arms around his waist and burying my head in his chest. He smells good. He smells like home.

His lips press into the top of my head as he holds me tight. "I think some of this is about to begin, but I do believe the threat of danger is behind us."

I press my chin into his sternum and peer up at him through my lashes. "I love you."

He stares down into my eyes, his expression serious. "I was going crazy. I couldn't handle him being there with you and not being able to get to you or stop him." He cups my jaw. "I can't lose you, Georgie. Not now. Not ever. It's more than just this life for us. I'll need you always."

He bends down and kisses me, his lips melding fully to mine in a fierce possession I'll never grow tired of. I'll always need him too.

"Mr. and Mrs. Moore?" A police officer calls our attention, and reluctantly we break apart, but not before I catch Lenox's cocky smirk at the officer calling me Mrs. Moore. "If you're ready, we'd like to take you in now."

Lenox and I are brought down to the Cambridge police station and then separated.

I'm placed in a five-by-four room with a table and two chairs on either side, just like how they do it in *Law & Order*. I'm waiting to be interrogated. I'm waiting for them to press me for details I don't know and have them play good-cop-bad-cop with me.

Except, unfortunately, none of that happens. A female detective with a kind smile and warm honey eyes comes in and takes my statement. She asks me questions in a gentle, understanding tone and records everything.

When that's done, she asks me to kindly wait a bit longer, and I'll be able to leave.

"Where is Ezra?"

"He was brought to the hospital to have his wrist cleaned up and stitched, and he'll be arrested by the FBI, who is currently with him."

Wow. I sag in relief. They can't hurt me. They can't hurt my people.

After that, she leaves, and it feels like hours that I'm stuck here alone when the door finally opens and Asher—freaking Asher!—walks in.

"What the hell are you doing here?"

"Springing you from this joint. Cal is with Lenox, and Zax and Grey are speaking with the detectives handling everything."

I raise an eyebrow. "They just let you in?"

He grins smugly. "What? Don't look so shocked. I own this town, woman. We all do." He pounds his chest like a caveman, and I huff.

"You killed my fantasy," I tell him as I stand and fold my arms. "I was hoping they were going to change their minds and send someone else in for the hard press, and I'd give them the strong woman front and watch them fold like a crepe."

"Next time, babe. Next time. Take it from a man who has been arrested a time or two. It's never as cute, cuddly, or cool as it looks on TV. You'll always need a Lenox to make it disappear. Now come on."

"How is this legal?"

"Welcome to Boston."

Epilogue

Georgia

"WHY ARE YOU SO QUIET?" I ask Lenox on a half-yawn, my head tilted back against the seat, my large, black sunglasses over my closed eyes. I'm flipping exhausted. We both are. It was a long goddamn flight from LA, and we made the dumb decision to take it by redeye, and now we're driving back to Lenox's place in Maine.

Well, I guess it's my place too now.

"I'm always quiet."

I roll my head in his direction, even if my eyes are closed. Yes, Lenox is always quiet. But there is Lenox quiet, and then there is quiet, even for Lenox. He's the latter. His flat tone isn't fooling me. But truthfully, I'm too tired to press him. I just want to get home and sleep until next week.

It's been a whirlwind few weeks.

The moment we stepped out of the police precinct after our friends came and sprang us, the press ate us alive. Zax—always the forward thinker—was ready with a no fucking around security detail, and Lenox and I were whisked back to Zax's, where we spent the night in the luxury and security of his penthouse. Since then, it's been one thing after another.

Thanksgiving happened, and we didn't allow the events of the previous evening to overshadow our joy. It wasn't difficult. Not with our people, our family, by our side. The following day, we had our wedding—our real wedding. Only this time, I had no tears. I was all smiles and laughs and pure joy.

It was the wedding I had always wanted. My dream wedding in my dream dress. The only thing that would have made it better was if my parents had been there. I wish I could talk to my dad. I wish I could have let him know all that I know about what was going on with Alfie and Ezra. I also wish he knew my mom never wanted to cheat on him, because when I spoke to her on the phone, she burst into tears.

Alfie was a monster.

The things he did to her, the things he said to her, were nothing short of abusive and I can't imagine all she endured with that. But enough of that.

After the wedding, Lenox scooped me up—literally—and had Ashley drive us across town to a swanky hotel, where we spent the following few nights locked away from the world. No press. No outside noise.

Just us.

And a lot of room service.

In short, it was a perfect honeymoon escape that I never wanted to end. It was certainly far more favorable than flying out to LA and dealing with the nightmare that was waiting for me there.

I spent five solid days dealing with the board. We made press statements and started running positive PR campaigns. We did blast interviews, searching for a CEO and COO who could lead us forward and bring us into a positive light. The press was camped outside my LA townhouse. It was the worst sort of déjà vu.

I went and visited Alfie, who had been in solitary after he was caught attempting to bribe some guards to help him escape. I told him all about Ezra. About how his son had tried to play him with my father's will. How we have audio of him confessing everything, including Alfie's misdeeds, and that the FBI seems to have quite the cybercrimes case against him.

I also made it clear that I was going to make sure that neither of them would ever take a free breath again. And when he asked me how I had managed to get the upper hand on him, I simply smirked and walked out.

The FBI has my statements, as well as the audio from Ezra's attempted kidnapping of me. The federal prosecutor for the case has already informed me I'll likely have to testify, which is fine. I'll do whatever I have to do with this.

Thankfully there is nothing connecting Lenox to any of this. No one will ever know he's the one who brought Alfie and Ezra down. He's simply my hot, muscled, tattooing husband.

Speaking of…

"I've been thinking about the tattoo I want," I murmur sleepily, even though the urge to smile is overwhelming.

"Oh?" is his only reply, though there is no masking the surprised curiosity in his voice.

"I was thinking about getting a rose on my ring finger. We can be twinsies. Though obviously, I'd want someone skilled doing mine, unlike the guy who did yours."

He makes a noise at my barb, that's something close to a mocking chuckle. "A rose? Like mine?"

"Like yours. Only maybe black? You are a rather dark fellow, after all. Oh, but maybe with some gold and blue accents."

I can hear the smile in his voice as he says, "You know, if you tattoo a rose like that on you, we're forever."

"I assumed that was part of the deal when I said till death do us part."

"I'm just saying, a contract can be broken. Tattoos are permanent."

I make a sardonic noise. "They can do all kinds of brilliant things with lasers now, so don't get too cocky there, hero. But it warms my heart to know you're already thinking about how break-able our wedding vows are."

"Your rose isn't going anywhere. As I said, we're forever and permanent." He clears his throat and then tacks on, almost apologetically, "The fingers hurt."

I balk at that, sitting up and finally opening my eyes so I can glare at my husband. "Are you saying I'm not woman enough to handle it? I birthed a baby in a blizzard, fought—and beat—a man with a gun, and I'm married to you." I poke his shoulder. "I think something like a little finger tattoo is child's play after all that."

His lips bounce, but he turns to give me a brief, taunting look. "Very bold words there, Mrs. Moore."

"I'm aware, Mr. Monroe."

"You're planning on using numbing cream, aren't you?"

My smile finally slips. "One hundred percent."

He reaches over and takes my hand. "Can we do it now?"

I think on that for a moment, because while I am badass and all tough chic who can take on the world in my heels and red lipstick, the thought of a fucking needle piercing my skin a thousand times scares the ever-loving shit out of me. And I am woman enough to admit that to myself. But I made it through the nose piercing without even a whimper, and that bitch hurt. Only this time, he won't be able to hold my hand if he's the one inking it.

What the fuck. It'll be cool.

"Do I need to call in a prescription or do you carry such creams in your shop?"

He brings my hand to his lips and kisses my fingers knuckle by knuckle, holding at my ring finger. "We'll stop and get you some first."

"Then I'm in. Let's tat me up. Maybe after I'll have you tattoo 'kiss this', one word on each ass cheek."

"Except we both know I will, so it's not exactly the fuck you, you hope it will be."

Probably true. I do like it when Lenox kisses my ass. And does other things to it. "Fine. I'll start with the rose, and we'll go from there."

He continues to drive us into Maine, bringing us closer to Lavender Lake. I must eventually doze off because suddenly the BMW SUV that freaking Ezra planted his slimy ass in the back of comes to a stop. Evidently, once December hits, Lenox leaves the Shelby in his heated garage in Cambridge for the winter. Boo.

"We're here," he whispers, leaning over and kissing me awake. Raising my sunglasses up to the top of my head, I thread my fingers into his hair and hold him close, kissing him soundly.

"Do I have to move? It's warm in the car and so very cold out there."

He smiles against my lips. "You wanted a tattoo. We have to get you magic cream first."

All my bravado crumbles like potato chips. "We could go home first. I could sleep, and you could sleep since I know you didn't get a lot on the plane and you must be so tired, and you could ink me in my dreams."

He licks a trail up my neck and places an open-mouth kiss on my jaw that makes me shudder. Damn him. "Oh, Georgie, you're braver than that."

Am I though? Am I really?

I give him a skeptical glare. "How much pain are we talking about?"

He grins like the Cheshire Cat, his freaking blue eyes sparkling like sexy, rare gems. "I'll make it hurt so good."

"You can't give me an orgasm while you're inking me. My hand will need all your expert focus, and I'm assuming staying still is of the utmost importance, so that eliminates me riding you while you do it."

He nips my bottom lip. "I'll let you sit on my face after. And then ride me if that's what you want."

"You better," I grumble, shoving him back and climbing out of the car, only to immediately huddle into my winter coat.

Freaking Maine in December.

He parked on the street, two storefronts down from the shop, all the way at the end of the strip. I spin on him. "Why didn't you park in the back?"

He takes my hand and walks me onto the sidewalk, so I don't get hit by an oncoming car. "They're doing some construction back there," he tells me, but there is a glint in his eyes that I can't quite place. A glint that grows as he walks us toward the vacant building on the end, pulls out a random key, and inserts it into a lock.

"What are we doing here? I doubt I can get lidocaine cream in an empty building."

"We're having a quickie first. All that talk about you on my face and my dick made me hard. What's the point of owning all these buildings if I can't take advantage?"

While part of me is eager to agree, there is another part of me that—"What the fuck?!"

Lenox continues to hold my hand, giving it a firm yank when I stop moving and forcing me deeper into the space.

He licks his lips and turns back to me. "I was thinking this made sense as a waiting room and possible triage space if you need it." He pans a hand around an open space where there are couches and comfy chairs and a front desk area filled with monitors and computers, separated from the sitting area by a large half wall. "There are eight patient rooms in the back, as well as a space for phlebotomy, an ultrasound room, and a room for prenatal nonstress tests. I was told bathrooms in OB-GYN offices are essential, so I had them install two over there"—he points toward the lab area—"and three more in the back patient area, including one for staff only."

"Lenox…" My voice dies as my hand covers my mouth as I take in everything around me. He walks us back to the patient area, showing me one of the exam rooms completely outfitted with everything I'd ever need.

"It's a big office, so if you wanted to hire staff or other providers, you can. There is also massive space in the back of the building for what I think could potentially be a birthing center, but there are a lot of laws with that, and I didn't have time to navigate them before getting this front space ready. I figured you'd want to come up with the name for your clinic and put on the decorative finishing touches, so I didn't do that."

I can't breathe. I. Can't. Fucking. Breathe.

"You built me a clinic," I croak as the first of the tears start.

He turns, and a smile erupts across his face as he reaches over and wipes a few away. "It's just the start of one. You're the one who's going to build it."

I stare around the massive space, walking from room to room, taking in all the equipment he purchased, the layout of each room, to the way it's fucking painted in a soothing pale blue-gray. I even have a big, beautiful office just for me.

He did this.

He did all of this.

For me.

So I can have everything while living here with him in Maine.

"I'm doing this," I say, almost bewildered, past the point of comprehension. "I'm really doing this. I'm living in Maine and setting up my own clinic."

He turns to me, taking both my hands in his, staring intently into my eyes. "If that's what you want, it's all yours. If it's not, then I'll lease it out to someone else or sell the properties and we'll go somewhere else. Whatever you want, Georgia, I want you to have."

This man. This fucking man.

How do men like him exist when we're taught from a fundamental age that they don't? He broke my heart in the worst of ways, but no one could have rebuilt it as perfectly as he did. He made me stronger by breaking it, but now I'm invincible with his heart beating beside mine.

"It's what I want. And I want the birthing center. And I want to hire on staff. And I want it. I want it all. With you."

He cups my face in his hands. "It's yours, Georgia. I'm in the process of having it moved to your name on the property. This is your start, and you can take it as far as your imagination and aspirations go."

"EEEEEP!" I squeal at the top of my lungs, jumping up into Lenox's arms and kissing him like a woman who couldn't possibly be any more in love with her husband. "Okay," I say, pulling back from him. "Thank you. I love it. I love you."

"I love you."

"Good. Because now it's tattoo time. Ink me, baby, because we're forever. Till death do us part."

THE END.

Not done with Lenox and Georgia yet? Scan the QR code below for more of their HEA.

Keep reading for an excerpt of Irresistibly Broken.

Irresistibly Broken

Zaxton

The headline was all anyone cared about. It was all that was repeated over and over and over again ad nauseam across every news network, entertainment magazine, and blog. "Suzie Moore, manager of the hugely successful pop band, Central Square, and girlfriend of Zaxton Monroe, found dead in the shower."

The headline was followed by mass speculation because even though there were some leaks and a few statements here and there, no one knew what actually happened except for us. And even then, I'm the only one who knows the truth. A secret I will take to my grave. A fucking heartbreak that has turned me into the delightful motherfucker I am today.

Especially today.

Eight years ago, I lost the love of my life.

And it doesn't seem to get any easier with the passing of time. Maybe it's because I lost more than just her that day. I lost a piece of myself I haven't been able to retrieve.

My phone vibrates on the seat beside me, but I don't bother checking it. It's either one of the guys, my brother, or work. None of which I want to deal with right now. I should have stayed home today. I shouldn't have gotten out of bed this morning, but today we have a photo shoot for a few pieces in the new women's fall line, and I have to be in it, and who gives a shit?

Bed and whiskey for breakfast were a much better option.

My driver, Ashley, sits quietly and patiently up front, staring straight ahead and allowing me this moment. He knows. He's been with me long enough to know I'll get out when I'm ready and I'm just not there yet.

Will I ever get past this? Will the hurt ever dissipate?

"What happens if I call in sick?" I mumble under my breath and notice Ashley stirring up front. I'm not asking him, but I wouldn't mind if he answered me all the same. He's the closest thing I have to a fatherlike figure in my life even though I pay him to be here because my actual father is a world-class piece of shit. He's the reason I'm the CEO of Monroe Fashion instead of him.

"May I suggest, if you talked about that day, it might help to unburden your soul."

"One has to have a soul for it to be unburdened."

He breathes out a mournful sigh in a way that tells me he's not amused.

"Talking about it won't unburden me. It will only burden others." The truth shall not set me free. It shall ruin someone who is already suffering more than he should.

"You know——"

"I know. And thank you. If I ever do want to talk about it, you might hear more than you ever wanted."

He chuckles at my wry tone just as a flash of whitish-blond whisks past my window, snapping me out of my miserable thoughts. Inadvertently, I follow the trail it makes, transfixed by the unique color and wavelike flow as it bounces and plays in the summer sunshine and breeze. That is until it drops from my view in a sudden swish and swoop along with the body it's attached to. Then there's the scream.

"Shit."

Snatching my phone, I fly out of the car and race up the three cement steps to the first landing where a woman is yelling and fighting with a man trying to snatch her purse. Gripping the leather handle, he gives a solid yank, managing the upper hand with the purse while simultaneously shoving her to the ground. Hard.

Without thinking twice, I collide with him, the full force of my size and weight knocking him back. The purse slips from his hand, skidding on the steps, but before he can catch himself from falling or right his body and flee, I grab him by the shirt and haul him up. Feet dangling from the ground, I get a better look at him.

"Jesus," I hiss in dismay. "What the hell are you doing snatching purses at your age?"

The kid, who can't be any older than seventeen, sneers at me, all punk-ass bravado despite the fact that I have him dangling like a proverbial worm on a hook. "Fuck you, man. The fuck you care what I do? You don't know me."

I set him down, but I don't release my hold on his shirt. "You think stealing from women makes you tough? Makes you a man? Do you know what being tough is?" I get right up in his face. "Tough is being a man even when the odds are stacked against you. It's doing the right thing when the wrong thing is easier. Grow up. Get out of your shit and do better. Now go before I call the cops."

I shove him away but make sure he sees me staring after him. For a second, he falters, his gaze snapping down at the woman who is still on the ground, then back up at me before he runs off.

I turn, taking in the now-seated woman swearing under her breath and staring incredulously at a high heel clutched angrily in her fist. The long, narrow heel of the shoe hangs limply from the black stiletto, having snapped.

"You're not supposed to do this," she bemoans. "Not today! Your job is to carry me from point A to point B without snapping like a twig. Don't you know what this means for me? Now look." Her hands fly about her body. "I'm a bloody mess. Literally." She threateningly shakes the shoe. "I'm gonna tell Marie you did this to us, and she won't be pleased. Not at all."

Marie? I take a better look at the shoes. Marie Marcato. Exclusive and expensive. But clearly, she's speaking in jest and ire because no one knows or speaks to Marie directly. Not even me and I've been trying for longer than I care to admit. Still, I can't understand how she's more upset about her heel snapping than she is about the fact that she was almost *mugged*.

My shadow looms over her, blocking the blinding summer sun. "What were you thinking fighting with him? He could have been armed or seriously hurt you. Are you okay?" The cuts on her knees are dripping blood down her shins and onto the concrete steps, but she's more focused on her broken shoe.

Alarmingly bright cornflower-blue eyes snap up and glue themselves to my face. And the moment they register me, they grow round as dinner plates, her plump pink lips parting. "Shit," she breathes harshly.

"Now you're catching up. That's what I said when I saw you were struggling with him. Are. You. Okay?" I repeat, my annoyance dripping through into my tone now that she's staring at me like, well, like everyone else does. Starstruck, awed, and terrified. "Do you not know how to answer questions or is English along with common sense a difficulty for you?"

She scowls at my sharp, curt words. "Did you honestly just ask that? Do you have any sense of how insanely rude and condescending that is after what just happened?"

My lips bounce, attempting to curl up into a smirk, but I beat it instantly away. "Whatever gets you to speak."

She blinks away from me, staring down at her knees that are bleeding and oozing everywhere. "He shoved me, and my shoe broke," she shoots back. "Obviously, I'm not having the best of mornings."

"Obviously," I deadpan, mocking her snarky, sardonic tone. "And now you're hurt. For the third time, are you okay?"

"Um. I don't know," she admits with a shaky breath. "I'm pissed. And hurt. And annoyed. At so many, *many* things right now."

"Can I help you up?"

"You might be the last person on earth I should ever ask for or accept help from."

Okay. I'm not sure what to do with that. "Do you work here?"

"Probably not for much longer. I'm a design intern. First day." Regret immediately strikes her features, and she frowns, shaking her head violently. "I seriously wish I hadn't just told you that."

I chuckle and with the sound of my laughter at what she inaccurately assumes is at her expense, she scathingly glares back up at me with those arresting eyes. Then there is her hair and those sexy lips and those entrancing pinpoint freckles on the bridge of an adorably petite nose and across the upslope of her perfect high cheekbones and shit.

I can't stop looking at her.

Though I know I've seen her face before, I'm struggling to place where exactly. Even so, my stupid cock stirs in my pants. Not the most opportune time for that, given her vantage point of me from the ground.

Slowly, she starts to stand, albeit awkwardly because she can't roll onto her knees to help herself up and the pencil skirt she's wearing is restrictive around her thighs.

"That's not a good idea," I tell her. "You're bleeding. Your shoe is broken. Not to mention, you just admitted you're not sure if you're okay."

"I'm fine." She hisses out a shocked breath as her knee scrapes the ground. "I can't exactly live here and besides, I don't want to be late on my first day."

"I'm sure they'll understand when they see you."

She rolls onto her side, attempting to use her elbows, and this is just ridiculous.

"I don't know what that move is, but you're only going to hurt yourself more," I admonish. "Was your purse really worth this? Here, take my hand."

"No, thanks." She shoves my proffered hand away, her pride getting the better of her.

Or maybe it's because you're being a dick to her after she was just attacked. I push that thought away.

"Do you know who I am?" I ask coolly, annoyed she's brushing me off when I helped her with the mugger and am offering to help her again.

She strikes me with a look. "You mean other than the jerk standing over me, making fun of me? Yes, I know who you are."

"Then I'm shocked you're still speaking to me like this." She's an intern. That means she works for me whether directly or not. So her talking back to me like this?

"Me too. Must be all the blood loss and adrenaline making me loopy. I take it no one talks back or insults you?"

"Not if they have any sort of natural self-preservation instincts, which I think we already established you don't."

"Wow," she mocks. "You're a real prince amongst mortals, there, *Zaxton*." She snorts. "What kind of name is Zaxton anyway? Paxton, Jaxson, Saxton even, but I've never heard of a Zaxton."

My eyes narrow into menacing slits. I can be terrifying when motivated. "A none of your business, *intern*, name. Speaking of names…" I raise my eyebrow expectantly at her.

"Nuh-uh. I'll be fired for sure if you know who I am."

I have no idea what that means, but I don't care enough right now to fish for more answers. I can't stand watching her flounder about another second whether she wants my help or not. Bending down, I loop my arm around her hips, pulling the majority of her weight up to spare her knees. I do my best to ignore the way her body feels against mine. And how good she smells. Perfume, shampoo, body wash, or her natural fragrance—whatever it is, if I could bottle it up and sell it, I'd be richer than I already am.

Once she's upright, albeit a bit wobbly, I take a step back, releasing her as fast as I can without her falling back to the ground.

"Thank you," she murmurs. "And thank you for saving my purse. Maybe I shouldn't have tried to fight him for it, but I've had enough of people taking from me and walking all over me to let it happen with some kid." Turning away from me, she starts hobbling one-heeled up the steps, anxious to get inside and away from me. Is she for real?

"You're dripping blood everywhere," I call after her, hating how quick she was to dismiss me. Hating how I want her eyes back on mine. "Will you stop? You can barely walk like this."

She emits an exasperated sigh because she knows I'm right.

Blood is running all down her legs and across her heelless foot and even into the other remaining good shoe.

I'm fed up with this game.

"I don't remember asking for your—ah!" She belts out a half-scream as her legs are swooped out from beneath her and I lift her body into my arms. "What are you doing?"

"Carrying you in. You're bleeding all over my steps and were just attacked. I have to make sure you're okay."

I hold her tightly against me while I carry her bride-style up the steps. She's tall and thin, but with perfect fucking curves in all the right places. Her hair kicks up in my face as I adjust her, assaulting me with her delicious scent. I pull her in closer, liking the way she feels against me a little too much. What is that fragrance? A goddamn summer afternoon in the country with wind, wildflowers, and sun? It's killing me not to bury my nose in her silky hair and breathe it in deeper.

"I can walk," she protests, completely oblivious to what she's doing to me.

"I beg to differ. Stop squirming."

"I'd stop squirming if you put me down."

"We're almost there. Now stop. Squirming." My hand on her thigh clenches in warning, and she gives up the protest.

"I'm trying not to get your suit sleeve covered in my blood."

"Appreciated, but I'm going to be changing suits in a few minutes anyway."

She laughs bitterly at that. "That your standard practice, Mr. Monroe? Just how many wardrobe changes a day do you have?"

My head tilts down. My eyes, dark and hooded, lock with hers. I smirk at how brazen she is with me. "You've got quite the mouth on you for an intern speaking to her boss on her first day."

She shrugs against me, trying to keep her face hidden since people are absolutely staring at us. I can't exactly blame them either. Of the many, many things I'm known for, carrying damsels in distress up the steps and into my building isn't one of them.

The door opens, a blast of frigid air making her shiver when it hits the blood on her skin. I press her tighter. "You all right there?"

"I'm fine. Totally great. I mean, considering it's my first day and I was nearly mugged, the heel of my shoe snapped, and I'm bleeding like a bad bitch out of hell. Oh, and I'm swearing at my boss, who just so happens to be you of all people." She claps a hand over her mouth, murmuring, "Sorry," through her fingers. "I just." A heavy sigh. "I didn't want to see you like this. I didn't think I'd ever have to see you at all. That's what he said and then you swoop in to save the day and I... I'm done talking now."

I'm not sure I understand anything she's saying. My confusion must be evident because she gnaws on her lip and shakes her head, indicating to me she's not going to clarify.

"Mr. Monroe, what happened?" The lobby security guard walks briskly by our side as I carry her over to a bank of seats along the wall between the elevators and floor-to-ceiling windows.

"She got hurt outside on the steps. Do we have a first aid kit down here, George?"

"Of course, sir. I'll go fetch it right away."

George scurries off just as I place her upright on the cushioned leather. Then I'm kneeling before her, tugging my white silk hand-kerchief from my breast pocket and pressing it against the cut that's bleeding the most.

I know it has to burn. Her chin wobbles and she sucks in a sharp breath as her pretty blue eyes glass over.

"You know his name." It's a half whisper as she stares down at her knees, refusing to meet my eyes.

"Yes. I know his name." My tone is terse. "I know his wife's name as well as his children's names. He's been working here since I was a kid and he's a good man."

Her head bobs up and down. "Didn't mean for that to come out as judgmental as it sounded." She tilts her head. "Or maybe I did. Sorry." She touches the sleeve of my suit coat. "My blood is on you."

My eyes stay locked on her pretty face. "Should that bother me?"

"Doesn't it?"

Does it? It feels like it should be gross, yet it's erotic in some strange way.

"No."

She peeks up at me through her long lashes, a coy smile curving up her lips, and the air leaves my lungs like someone just drove a knife right through my chest. She's easily the most stunning heart-breaker I've ever encountered.

"Does everyone hop to do your bidding the second you snap your fingers?" she asks, ignoring everything but my sour attitude while dropping her broken shoe to the floor and checking her watch. She's late or getting there. So am I, for that matter, but I don't care all that much right now.

I like her attitude. I like that she fought back even though it cost her her shoe and knees. I like her snapping at me and calling me out on my shit while asking me bold questions no one ever has the balls to ask.

"Yes," I answer flatly, still crouched before her, unable to so much as shift away from her.

"You're quite the intimidating man."

I grunt in dismay at her cheeky tone and mockingly flirty expression.

"No, I mean it," she insists. "You are. I bet you can feel it every time you touch me."

My eyebrows bounce in surprise and my grip on her calf tightens while my other still presses in on her wound. I intimidate her, but she's not afraid of me.

"What exactly does my touch do to you?" Thumbs on both hands brush back and forth along her skin and goose bumps erupt in their wake, her pupils expanding ever so slightly.

Fuck.

That's what my touch does to her. I'm not the only one feeling this. I shouldn't be reacting to her—she is an intern, and this is *not* what I do—but it's as if my brain and body are on disconnect. Because I recognize her elegantly radiant face. I never catalog a woman's features anymore. Not beyond the scope of professionalism and necessity of business.

But I know her face from somewhere.

"Repulses me," she whispers, still half-smiling at me.

"Is that so?" My thumbs brush again, dragging a longer trail on her skin, and her breath skitters in a sharp hiccup. I smirk arrogantly. "Are you always this much of a brat to people who help you?"

"I think it's just with you. You seem to have a strange effect on me."

"What if I like having this effect on you?" Not words I should be saying to her, but again, I want to see how she reacts to me if for no other reason than my own perverse need.

Mercifully and before this can go any further, George returns, proudly carrying the first aid kit. "Sir, you're needed upstairs."

"Tell them—"

"I can take it from here," she interrupts, snatching the kit out of George's hand. Swinging her legs out of my grip, she places them up on the seat and pops open the white top of the large box, effectively dismissing me.

I stand, pocketing the blood-soaked handkerchief when I should throw it away.

"Thank you for your help," she tells me, forcing a weak smile that doesn't reach her eyes. "I'm sorry if I was short or even insubordinate with you. It's obviously already been a day for me and hopefully, you can pretend I was nothing but respectful and polite."

I scowl, annoyed with everything. Her. Me. The way I want to clean her wounds and bandage her up. How I want more time with her when I shouldn't.

Without another word, I'm gone. The tap of my perfect, nonbroken shoes on the marble floors echoes through the lobby that is progressively growing more and more crowded as the official start of the day approaches. The elevator is already there waiting, but before I step on, I glance back in her direction.

Our eyes lock for the briefest of seconds, my pulse jumps, and then I'm on the elevator alone. No one else dares to step on while I'm in here. I press the button for the top floor and curse under my breath as the doors close. What the fuck did I just do with that girl and why do I want to do it all over again?

I scrub my hands up my face. I never should have gotten out of bed this morning.

Want to find out what happens next with Zax and Aurelia? Scan the code to find out.

End of Book Note

Thank you lovely reader for taking the time to read Lenox's and Georgia's story. I hope you enjoyed it. They were particularly fun and challenging to write. It was not easy getting in Lenox's head. He doesn't like to share or talk too much and that was a bit challenging at times for me. But I just loved the way he loved Georgia and I knew he had the best story to tell.

I am SO sad this is the end of this series as I've fallen so hard for these characters. But don't worry, there is more to come from this Boston world in my next series and we will definitely see more of these characters.

I want to thank my beta team Danielle, Patricia, and Kelly for their help with this story. They had to listen to my insanity over it more than once. Also to my amazing street team who help push my books out to the world. And most importantly, I want to thank my incredible husband who helped me with a lot of the technical elements that Lenox came with and three irresistible girls who I love more than anything.

I can't wait to give you more characters to fall in love with. Thank you again or reading my stories!

Much love!
Julie (J. Saman)

Milton Keynes UK
Ingram Content Group UK Ltd.
UKHW011126080124
435661UK00006B/586